BEYOND THE GREAT RIVER

BY ZOE SAADIA

Beyond the Great River
The Foreigner
Troubled Waters
The Warpath
Echoes of the Past

Two Rivers
Across the Great Sparkling Water
The Great Law of Peace
The Peacekeeper

At Road's End
The Young Jaguar
The Jaguar Warrior
The Warrior's Way

The Highlander
Crossing Worlds
The Emperor's Second Wife
Currents of War
The Fall of the Empire
The Sword
The Triple Alliance

Obsidian Puma
Field of Fire
Heart of the Battle
Warrior Beast
Morning Star
Valley of Shadows

BEYOND THE GREAT RIVER

People of the Longhouse, Book 1

ZOE SAADIA

For more information about this book, the author and her work, please visit www.zoesaadia.com

ISBN: **1539650685**
ISBN-13: **978-1539650683**

AUTHOR'S NOTE

The Great League of the Iroquois, the People of the Longhouse, was created somewhere around the 12th or maybe 14th century, a remarkable league of five nations that inhabited the upstate New York and southern regions of Canada near Lake Ontario and beyond it. Governed by the most remarkable constitution, a very intricate set of a hundred or more laws that did not change for centuries to come, this confederacy had a great impact on the entire Eastern Woodlands areas, its influence reaching far and wide, sometimes through trade, often through warfare.

Before the Great League was created, the Iroquois' immediate vicinity was troubled by ferocious warfare according to all versions of the Great Peacemaker's story; the prophet and the messenger of the Great Spirits, who had managed to make the brother-nations live in peace with each other. The mutual warfare stopped there, but the young men still needed to wield their weapons, while the borders of the newly created confederacy needed to be guarded.

And so it might have come to the first encounters between the Iroquois and their eastern neighbors, the River People, or Mohicans as we came to know them later on. Different in their ways and customs, the Mohican People spread around the valleys of the Hudson River, the River Whose Waters Are Never Still as they called it, living in simpler settlements, not as large or fortified as their prominent neighbors to the west.

It is said that the years, and maybe even centuries, of warfare with the Great League, reshaped the way the Mohican People lived into habits more similar to the Iroquois than their original brothers, the other Algonquin nations of the east. If nothing else, it made the Mohicans build strongly fortified, permanent settlements, and later on, to organize into an alliance of related nations with no mutual government, probably for the purpose of defense mainly.

However, at the time this novel is set in, all those changes had yet to take place, with the east and west only beginning to be aware of each other.

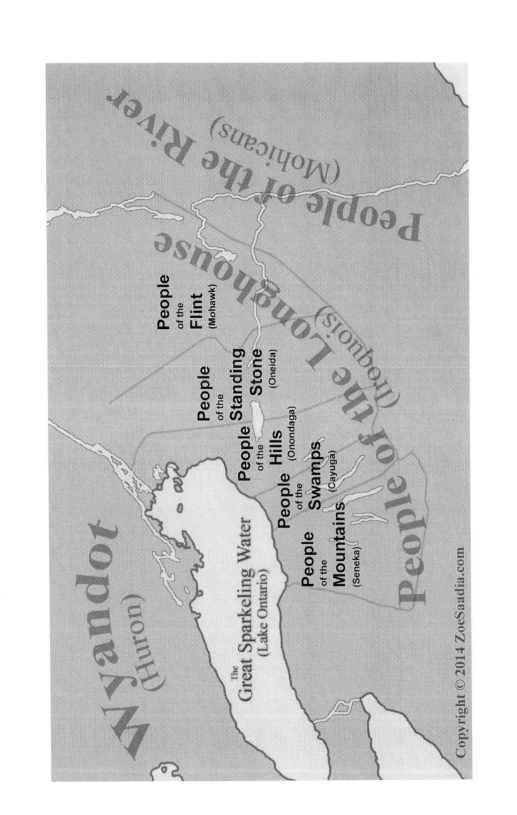

People of the River
(Mohicans)

People of the Longhouse (Iroquois)

People of the Flint
(Mohawk)

People of the Standing Stone
(Oneida)

People of the Hills
(Onondaga)

People of the Swamps
(Cayuga)

People of the Mountains
(Seneka)

Wyandot
(Huron)

The
Great Sparkeling Water
(Lake Ontario)

CHAPTER 1

Crouching in the thickest of the bushes adorning the hillside, concealed in her favorite spot behind the protruding rock, Kentika held her breath. The invaders, at least twenty of them, but maybe more—she was too terrified to count properly—concentrated on the shallow beach, dragging their canoes up, gesturing silently, making obvious efforts to keep quiet.

Warriors, most clearly! She fought the urge to close her eyes. A few heartbeats earlier, she had tried it, and it didn't help. The terrible vision did not go away. The foreigners were still there, carrying their canoes into the woods now, working in perfect silence, displaying no intention of stopping, or better yet, of disappearing into thin air.

Fascinated against her will, she watched their backs and the way their muscles bulged as they struggled with the heavy boats, their skin glistening with sweat. The decorated patches of hair upon the tops of their heads and napes swayed with the breeze, promising no good. Warriors, seasoned warriors. Brutal, evil, unhuman. The worst of their kind. Anyone coming from the lands of the setting sun was as evil as Malsum Spirit, or maybe even worse.

Afraid to move a limb, she glanced back, into the cool dimness of the swaying forest. To ease her way along the small, twisting path that sloped down the hill seemed like a good possibility, offering safety. It would just be a matter of timing and her ability to run fast, halting for no reason, not even to catch her breath. Not an impossible feat. She was renowned for her speed, and for her stamina. She could outrun quite a few boys of her age, now young men, all of them, not eager to answer her challenges, not anymore. More often than not, they were scowling now, frowning direfully at her when she dared suggest such things. Just like the elderly women of her clan—and the entire village—did. It was good for a girl to be strong and resilient, high-spirited to a certain point, was the verdict of the people, but it was not good when it made her act like a boy, preferring physical actions and contests to activities appropriate for girls, while boasting her successes.

"She would have made a good warrior, that wild thing," she had overheard one of the renowned hunters, a prominent man of their village, saying, making his companions laugh. "Pity her brother inherited none of that spirit. The leader of our clan must be sick with disappointment. To think of all this strength and fire wasted on a girl." The man snorted again, his satisfaction with this state of matters concealed only thinly by the pretended innocence of the remark. "That weakling, the chief's son, will never inherit his father's position."

The remark that had left her breathless with rage, huddling behind the corner of one of the houses, shivering with cold. It had been the second Awakening Moon back then, but the frost persisted, reluctant to leave. Such a harsh winter! And a lean one. With hunters not overly successful, the food supplies ran low, forcing people to eat less, making them hungry and irritable. Even the clouds of wandering pigeons that were supposed to invade their hills like they did at the end of each Frozen Season seemed to delay, in no hurry, deterred by the unusual cold. And yet that was not what had made Kentika's blood boil with anger only those few moons earlier, before the benevolent warmth and the harvest time came. Not even when another man had spoken, remarking on her lack of beauty, claiming that her fire might have been an attractive thing had she possessed any of the regular female charm, even a little bit of it. She knew she wasn't pretty, and she didn't care. But her brother was no weakling. He was not! True, he might not have been as strong as many of the young men, not as fast and agile as she was herself even, but it was only because he was not attracted to this sort of activity, never interested in any of the favorite children's games when younger.

Fascinated with the storytelling of old men, with prayers and tobacco offerings, with the mystery of healing and herbs, Migisso could go absolutely still, following the paths of his inner thoughts. He did not fit his spectacular name, The Eagle, and he did not fit the expectation of their powerful father, the leader of their village, the elected Warriors' Chief of the Bear Clan. And yet, a weakling Migisso was not!

Coming back from her reverie, she concentrated on the opposite bank and the ominous presence of its uninvited guests, as those seemed to be more at ease now, talking in low voices, exchanging curt sentences. She tried to listen. The wind was blowing in her direction, and with a little effort, she thought she might be able to pick up the general gist.

A smile was dawning, to be suppressed quickly. She could understand their foul-sounding tongue, not very well, but she could. Neewe, the captive who had stayed in their village so many summers ago, had been a nice woman, interesting to hang around and try to communicate with.

Shutting her eyes, she strained her ears, but the current of the river was stronger, overcoming the other sounds, even those of the forest behind her. It was just one of many streams, a small thing compared to the Great Waters That Are Never Still. And yet the spirits that lived here did not favor her wish to hear.

Never mind, she thought, watching one of the men straightening up, shielding his eyes while surveying the hill, *her hill*. Her heart missed a bit. It was as though he was peering at her. Oh, Benevolent Spirits! She fought the urge to jump to her feet and just run, crashing through the bushes, pell-mell, in a headlong flight. Of course, it was not a wise thing to do, but she would have done it if she could, if her limbs would follow the commands of her panicked mind, if they hadn't froze, together with her heart.

Like a rabbit facing a snake, she found herself staring instead, her eyesight good enough to decipher his features, to see that he was young and striking, his shoulders broad, his chest well developed, padded with muscles under the coat of now-smeared paint, a tattooed pattern depicting a form of what looked like a wolf, or some other predator, peering menacingly from one side of his well-defined face, sure of itself. His head was shaved in the terrible fashion of the enemy, leaving the skin of his skull exposed beside the lone patch on top of it. This patch flowed down arrogantly, in a long braid decorated with feathers. The depiction of the bloodthirsty enemy.

Unable to move, she watched him frowning, scanning the river once again. Was he sensing her gaze? She knew he was. Oh, all the great and small spirits!

She shut her eyes again, not daring to address the deities, to bother them with her personal petty requests, but just thinking about them, about Glooskap, the child of light, the twin spirit who had created everything good that existed in the world. He would understand the urgency of her and her people's need, and he would help.

The wind was strengthening. She could feel its chilly touch upon her skin. The spirits were urging her to be strong.

Okwaho stretched tiredly, exhausted but reluctant to show any of it. Since sunrise, he had been rowing hard, navigating the long, heavy canoe he had been entrusted with among a multitude of underwater rocks and obstacles until his head buzzed and his vision blurred. It was as though the entire world was nothing but the water spitting between the sleek, threatening rocks, sometimes more viciously, sometimes less so. No sky, no forest, nor people. Just gushing current.

Fighting the urge to collapse onto the invitingly smooth surface of the small beach they had dragged their canoes onto, he straightened up, paying attention to his surroundings and not the quiet chatter of his peers. Father, the War Chief of the Onondaga nation, one of the most prominent leaders in the confederation of the Longhouse People and the greatest man alive, said to never succumb to the urge of resting after journeying into the enemy's land.

First you look around, the man always said. *You trust your eyes, and you trust your senses. Feel the air, the sky, and the forest. Look them over, and let them talk to you, tell you their story. It is surprising how much one can learn if one allows his senses the opportunity to listen—all of his senses and not only his ears.*

Oh, how wise Father was, how strong and powerful, and respected. The War Chief of the Onondaga People, the man required to attend the meetings of the Great Council when the fifty representatives of the Five Nations met to talk matters of peace and war and disagreements, Father was there to make sure everything proceeded as it should. Such was his duty. The representatives were the ones to talk and deliberate, to solve the problems in a peaceful way or to decide to war on someone, but the war chiefs were the ones entrusted with watching the procedures, with making sure all was done correctly and in the best interest of their nation. That important was Father!

However, there was more to it. Among five war chiefs who sat in the Great Council, one appointed by each nation, Father yielded more influence than his four other peers. Was it because he represented the Onondagas, whose lands spread in the middle of the confederation, and who held much responsibility by hosting the Great Council's meetings, represented more heavily than their neighbors? Maybe. Yet Okwaho had his doubts. The other nations were as powerful, as proud and strong. There was no inequality in the Great Union of the Longhouse People, no matter the amount of representatives. Father never tired of repeating *that*.

Shaking his head to get rid of irrelevant thoughts, he concentrated on the unfamiliar shore and the narrow river, and the towering hill. There was something about it, something wrong. What?

He strained his eyes, then looked away and concentrated on his inner senses. The thick foliage of the distant forest moved lazily, swaying with the wind. Nothing untoward, and yet he knew it was watching them with hostility and suspicion.

Well, of course it would. They had not come here to trade or pay a peaceful visit. Not to this distance east. People who inhabited these valleys and forests were bad, wild, hostile, their tongues impossible to understand, their ways corrupt and evil.

One could not speak with such people, could not sit and share a pipe. Even Father agreed on that, and Father was always the one to advocate bringing more nations into the Great Union, letting them take a seat under the Great Tree of Peace and share its shade and the wonders of its all-encompassing set of laws.

The Onondaga War Chief was a man of great influence, and yet, in this, he got nowhere. Longhouse People did not want the outsiders sharing in their affairs. Neither did the foreigners from across the Great Lake, the notorious Crooked Tongues, nor anyone else for that matter. Okwaho might have been young and not as bright as his older sibling, a promising man and a future leader beyond doubt, but he knew as well as anyone else that the other peoples inhabiting the Turtle Island, all four corners of it, were just not good enough. It was as simple as that. They were not worthy of sharing in the exclusivity of the Great Union along with the five original nations, who had greeted the Great Peacemaker and had been privileged to listen to him in person. Like Father did!

Again, he shivered at the very thought. To think of Father not only following the Messenger of the Great Spirits, helping to spread the word, but actually conversing with this legendary person, working with him, helping to create the Great Confederation, was dazzling, amazing and frightening at the same time. Oh, how lucky he was to have such a man for his father.

Again, he shook the immaterial musings off. The towering hill, what was wrong with it? His eyes scanned the steep incline. The bushes were swaying again, with the wind getting stronger. Was someone hiding there, watching? The spirits, or a wandering local?

His stomach squeezed with anticipation. He had never seen these strange people from the east, not even one of them. It had not been long since the People of the Flint, the Keepers of the Eastern Door in the Great Confederacy, among whom he lived now, began venturing so far eastward, reaching that mighty river that was larger and stronger than their own Great River was.

"What? What do you see there?" The sharp voice of Kayeri, their group's temporary leader, took his attention away, interfering with his concentration on what his senses were telling him.

"I'm not sure."

"What did you think it was?"

Okwaho shifted uneasily. "I saw nothing." He glanced at the hillside again, trying to penetrate the thick foliage with his gaze, to make it reveal its secrets. It was scared of him now, he knew, scared and wary, and full of hatred. He clenched his teeth. Stupid gut feeling. "I think someone may be hiding there, on the other side. Watching us."

The leader's eyes bored into him for another heartbeat, before clouding, sinking in thought. The warriors next to them paused. They had all learned to trust his instincts. The realization that would have pleased him, but for the unsettling churning in his stomach. He aspired to be a scout, a man who could read the earth so well everyone would ask for his help and guidance, and yet these recent near-visions were not something easy to come to terms with.

"Two of our men went scouting the surroundings," said Ronkwe, one of the older warriors, an owner of scars and tattoos aplenty. Nothing like Father's pattern of scars, but still impressive. "Should we send someone to scan the other side?"

The leader frowned, then shook his head. "We won't be splitting more than necessary. Not in these woods. We are already separated enough as it is."

The others nodded, remembering the main part of their forces, more than forty warriors that had paddled off ahead of their reinforcements, eager to investigate another stream, to see what people or settlements inhabited these woods. Pleased with having so many warriors at his disposal this time, Tsitenha, the main leader of their entire force, felt it wise to split, leaving Kayeri in charge of the remaining men, twenty five in all.

"Hide the boats for now. Conceal them in the grove. When our scouts come back, we will decide if we sail or proceed on foot." The man scanned the hillside once again. "This hill is not forested densely enough. Not a place to hunt. It will tell us nothing. No need to bother with it. No local would wander there, not at this busy harvest moon."

They turned back to their boats, but Okwaho's heart was still fluttering, beating unevenly, the sensation of those wary eyes making his skin crawl. He felt it watching him, him in particular. What spirits inhabited these mysterious lands of the rising sun?

"I want to go and scout that hill." He heard the words coming out of his own mouth, just as surprised at them as they all were. "It might be important. If there is a local watching us, he could give us good information if captured."

"I said we are not scanning these woods." There was a cutting edge to their leader's voice now, his displeasure open. "Get busy with the boats, warrior."

He bit his lips, choking the words of argument back. A warrior of his age was not to argue with his leaders, however promising and sought after he might have been. He had vowed never to make any trouble, venturing none of his opinions unless asked for, not until after he had been made a leader. His recent experience was more than enough. Stubborn hotheads, however fierce and skillful and generally talented, were a nuisance, excluded from some raiding parties, not invited to join every War Dance. Some warriors' leaders had good memories, too good to make the argument seem like a worthwhile idea.

Grabbing the side of the smaller boat, a light canoe made out of bark and not the heavier vessel dug out of a solid log, fit to carry more than two people, he lifted it with a swing, trying to make it look like an easy work.

A last glance at the towering hill made his stomach squeeze again. The presence was still there, still watching. He could feel its hate-filled gaze burning his back as he headed off the shore and toward the nearest trees, displaying as little discomfort as he could, the sleek, unpolished wood cutting into his shoulders.

CHAPTER 2

The last of the evening sun washed the poles of the palisade as it towered ahead, a friendly presence, promising safety. It pleased her, despite her mounting worry. Only the best of runners would have covered the distance from that faraway grove, reaching the village before Father Sun descended into the other world, to rest and gather his strength for the next day. Only the fastest, and those who had the stamina to go on and on, without pausing to catch their breath. Not many could do this. Not in their village, although there was this boy from Skootuck, that large settlement to the east, where the leaders of the clans were meeting from time to time…

She shook her head to get rid of trivial thoughts, gasping for breath, charging through the opening in the fence. Many people were out and about, men, women, elders and children. Some of the hunters had come back from the hills by now, after snaring doves, or shooting beavers and moose, plentiful during this season. More irrelevant thoughts. She rushed on, oblivious of the stares.

"Kentika!"

The stern voice of her Great Aunt, the prominent woman of their clan, made her heart lurch, although it had been doing anything but beating evenly before.

"Not now, Honorable Aunt." She didn't slow her step. "I need to find Father."

"You what?" The elderly woman's voice vibrated with irritation.

"That girl!" said someone with a chuckle. "She will be the end of us."

Their voices dissipated behind her back as she rounded the corner of the nearest building, then another. The council people. She needed to reach them at once. If not Father, then someone else of importance would be of help, and they would know what to do.

"Kentika, wait!" This time it was Namaas, a round-faced girl from her clan, their houses situated on the same slope, side by side, creating a corridor with the towering bark walls. "Wait."

"I can't," she gasped. "I need to find Father."

"What happened?"

As she was truly exhausted by now, Namaas caught up with her easily, falling into her step, anxious to keep up. "Where have you been?"

"Out there." She rounded another corner, relieved to see the square serving for special ceremonies spreading ahead. The end of the incline.

"I know you were out there. Both Honorable Aunts were so angry with you!" Gasping for breath in her turn, Namaas stumbled, grabbing Kentika's arm to stabilize herself. "It is a harvest moon, sister. What were you thinking?"

Forced to slow her step, secretly glad for the respite and the chance to catch her breath before she would have to face important people, Kentika shook the persistent grip off.

"They are always angry with me. What's new about that?"

"Well, they were angrier than usual." The girl narrowed her eyes, regaining her confidence now that they weren't moving at a neck-breaking speed. "We were working hard harvesting the fields, just to let you know. It is our duty. Strolling around the woods is not."

"I was not strolling. I just wanted—" She stopped herself, enraged. There would be enough time to sound excuses when facing her mother and her aunts, and others of her clan elders. She didn't owe an explanation now, not to this buzzing mosquito. "It is not of your interest what I was doing, Namaas. Mind your own business."

"It is everyone's business when one is not ready to do her

duties. It is…" The girl's voice trailed off, as she took a step back, quailing under Kentika's glare. "You can't just do whatever you like," she finished in a small voice.

Kentika's own breath hissed, drawn in loudly through her nose, as her lips were pressed too tight to allow its passage.

"It is not your place to tell me what to do, Namaas. Go away before I make you go."

"What are you doing here, girls?" The voice of the Turtle Clan's leading man startled them both, making them turn around in panic, their hearts pounding. "Have you done with your chores for today? I doubt the women of your clans would confirm that claim." He eyed them through his narrowing eyes, sternly but not unkindly. "Off with you two." There was finality to the dismissing wave of his hand.

"Has Father come back from Skootuck?" She blurted it out without thinking, the silly quarrel with her childhood playmate forgotten. What preyed on her mind, the terrible presence upon the shores of the Long Creek, loomed ominously, pushing the other considerations away.

A freezing gaze was her answer. "Go back to your family and your chores, girl." There was no amused kindness in the man's tone anymore.

She pressed her palms tight. "I need to tell you something. Something important."

The chilliness in the man's gaze increased, reflecting the worst of the Freezing Moons.

"Please, it's important!"

"Talk to your mother, girl. She will let us know if what you wish to tell us is of importance." The words lingered, weighing upon the darkening air like heavy stones.

She fought the urge to take a step back, Namaas' footsteps dying away, leaving her all alone.

"I saw… there, on the Long Creek banks… I saw…" She licked her lips, gathering the remnants of her courage. "There are enemy warriors there, many warriors. A large party. Twenty, maybe more. They were camping on the banks of the Long Creek. On our side." The widening eyes of her converser made the wild pounding of her heart subdue. "I saw them. They were taking a rest. Their canoes were out of the water."

"Where exactly?" This came out as quite a bark, making her heart lurch again.

"Where the Sacred Trail ends. Up on the Black Hill."

She watched the man's strong jaw jutting, his eyes turning darker.

"When did you see them?"

"When Father Sun was about halfway toward his resting place."

One eyebrow climbed up, then dropped back without a remark. They all knew she was a runner, one more inappropriate thing she was good at.

"Come with me."

Her stomach churning, she followed, trying to think what to say if asked what she had been doing there, so far away from home and at a time as pressing as near-harvest moon. There was no passable explanation to that, no ready-made lies she was never good at coming up with, not like some other girls. Both her younger cousins were experts on preparing excuses, fluttering their eyelashes while opening their eyes wide, getting away with anything they did wrong, quite a few transgressions. Living in the same house with those two, sharing the cozy space along with the fireplace, she had had her chances to learn their technique well. But not to implement it. Her crimes were too great to get away with pretended innocence, and she was not good at telling false stories.

The men squatting around the central fire stared at her stonily, their faces unreadable. She listened to the words of the leader who had brought her in, her mind not registering what he said, only his tone, the clipped, short phrases, with no flowery addresses, not this time. This was not the occasion to make a speech. Father would have acted the same, she reflected. Why wasn't he back yet?

"Tell us what you saw."

The silence prevailed, disturbingly heavy. She counted five men, three elders of the village and two leading hunters of the

Wolf Clan, squatting comfortably, but tense, highly attentive now. It was their duty to keep the village safe and functioning when the chief and the leaders of the other two clans were absent.

"Well, girl?" It came from a Wolf Clan man, softly, not unkindly.

"I saw warriors, foreign warriors."

"How did you know they were foreign warriors?" This time it was one of the elders, Paqua, the man of her own clan, his voice cold, holding an accusation.

"They were dressed like foreigners. Their paint. Their hair." She remembered the warrior who had scanned the hill, the way he stood there, striking and arrogant, his braid falling down his back, the shaved sides of his scalp oiled and glistening, a terrible vision.

"What does a girl like you know about foreigners and their ways of painting or braiding their hair?" The man's irritation was strange, jarring in its openness. What did it matter how she came by that knowledge?

"I know how our warriors paint their faces or braid their hair." This time, she stood the accusing gaze, angered rather than frightened. "These men did not look like our warriors. And they spoke the tongue of the setting sun lands. I couldn't hear them clearly, but the wind was coming my way, and I know they were talking in that strange way the western enemy speaks."

"You said you were on the Sacred Trail."

"Yes, I was."

"How could you possibly hear them from such a distance?" There was a victorious spark to the squinted, clouded eyes. Was the man trying to prove her wrong?

She took a deep breath. "I said the wind was blowing my way. Some words almost reached my ears."

Almost? asked the lifted eyebrows of her interrogator.

The Wolf Clan's man raised his hand. "Tell us more. How long did you watch them, and what were they doing in the meanwhile?"

She wanted to thank the man there and then, his kind eyes giving her courage.

"I watched them for some time. They took their canoes out of the water, and they were very tense, but then they began feeling more at ease."

"How would you know that?" Paqua's voice again tore her out of her painfully gained self-assurance.

She clenched her teeth tight. "They were not speaking at first, but gesturing. Then, after their canoes were out, they began conversing. Not yelling, but still talking. They didn't do it before."

"She is quite an observant little thing," muttered someone, nodding appreciatively. "Good work, girl. What else? What were they doing when you left?"

She tried to remember. "They were mixing things in jars or pots."

"What things?"

"I don't know. It looked like food."

"With no fires?"

"No."

They exchanged troubled glances.

"How many canoes?"

"Maybe ten."

More frowning.

"There might be no more than twenty of them," muttered the Wolf Clan's man. "Why would so little people head for our village? It doesn't make much sense."

Their nods had a stony quality to them, their eyes returning to her.

"Anything else?"

She tried to organize her thoughts. "I … I think not. I think I told it all to you now." The urge to escape the oppressive semidarkness, the suspicion in their gazes, welled.

"Good, good." One of the elders who had said nothing so far got to his feet. "You did right by coming back as fast as you could, daughter of the Bear Clan's Chief. You acted with courage worthy of your glorious father."

Not all of their gazes reflected these words; still, they warmed her inner being.

"You may go."

As she turned around, relieved, she heard them letting out a heavy sigh.

"We shall send an urgent word to our leaders in Skootuck," Paqua was saying. "They should be apprised of the trouble. And so should the hunters we still have out there."

"It may be of convenience that they are at Skootuck now," the Bear Clan's elder said, his voice ringing stonily, but with a lightly elated tone to it now, as though the man had managed to get away with a small mischief of his own. "A good opportunity to ask for their active help. This way, we might be joining the proposed union more readily, given proof of their brotherly love and protection."

The footsteps were very clear, imprinted in the muddy ground, twisted, uneven, obviously hurried. No warrior's footsteps, and not even those of a man. A boy on soft-soled moccasins, or more likely a woman, had been running very fast, careless of their step. That same frightened local he had sensed when the sun was still relatively high?

"We can't follow it," said Akweks, kneeling beside the place when the runner must have slipped, but then, evidently, managed to catch his balance. "We have to go back and tell the leader."

Okwaho scowled. To turn back just as it began getting interesting?

"I say we follow it, at least for a little while. Until the dusk sets. Maybe she wasn't running far. Maybe it'll bring us to her destination."

"Why are you so sure it's her and not him?" Ronkwe, the third man, the oldest among the three of them, a seasoned warrior and a closemouthed person, glowered. "This print is small enough to belong to a young boy. A lone woman would not wander about in this way. Why would she? With the harvest and all. And anyway, we are to report back. You may have managed to convince our leader to let you inspect this hill, but he was clear about our mission. We are to look around, then come back. No independent trips along the enemy countryside."

"But we did find something, a trail of prints. If we leave it, it might not be here in the morning. Not so clear and obvious like now, for sure." He moderated his tone, not happy with the addition of this man to their expedition, but trying to conceal it. If it were only him and Akweks… "Why don't we follow it, at least for a while? Father Sun is not about to leave our world, not yet."

"To follow it? Have you lost the last of your thinking ability?" The man seemed to be hanging on to his temper with difficulty, his voice having a hissing sound to it. "We are in the deepest of the enemy's land, young man. In case you didn't notice. Or didn't you know you are not to stroll about, enjoying a quiet evening?"

"I know where we are, and why we are here." Against his will, Okwaho glared at the man, his hand fighting the urge to sneak toward his sheath and the knife it held. It was not appropriate to pick an argument with the older warrior, who was clearly here to ensure he and Akweks didn't make a mess out of the mission he had managed to talk their leader into. Still, he wouldn't be patronized in this way. "I didn't suggest a stroll. The leader wanted us to check this side of the creek and see if it's as abandoned as it looked in the beginning. Well, we did as we were told; we scanned this hill and found those footprints. To run back now, without checking them, would be foolish of us. Foolish and cowardly."

The man's gaze sparkled dangerously. "Watch your tongue, warrior. Be careful of what you say."

He didn't take a step back, although he wanted to, the eyes of his rival glowing darkly, promising no good.

"We can split up," said Akweks hurriedly. "One of us will go to report, and the others will follow the trail and see where it leads."

More heavy silence.

"He can go and report, while we are going on." Ronkwe's eyes were the only things to move, indicating Okwaho.

He pressed his lips tight. "Why me?"

"Because that's what I think is the best, young buck." The older man seemed to regain his composure, but not his peace of mind, his eyes glimmering with an open challenge. "We were told to check the hill, then come back. You can't argue with your elders and betters. You are nothing but a young warrior, no matter how powerful your father is."

The effort to hang on to his temper was growing more difficult. "My father has nothing to do with it. I talked to our leader, and he wanted me to check these woods. And I was right—I was! We *have* been watched. So now I want to return with more information than just silly footprints in the mud, the footprints that will be difficult to see tomorrow morning, should we decide to find out where they lead."

He remembered the effort of gathering the courage to approach the leader again while they were busy devouring their meal, ground into flour maize mixed with water and sweetened with a generous amount of maple syrup. A delicious thing, but not when eaten for days on end, as they had since entering the enemy's lands, not daring to make fire in order to prepare something else. It would spoil the surprise, although the settlement they were heading for still lay far away, almost two more dawns of sail, a reportedly large village, an important one. To take it, or just to raid it and get the most out of it, should give them a great victory. The main part of their forces must already be there, having sailed on more than two dawns ago.

Well, he didn't even start this conversation. Their leader was the one to start questioning him about that hillside, and why he thought they had been watched. Upon reflection, the experienced warrior said, it might be wise to check more of their surroundings, to make sure the enemy was not cherishing the idea of surprising them in their turn. There were no villages around that they knew of, not to the south of that creek. And yet …

So it was not as though he, Okwaho, had insisted, not on the mission itself. He did make an effort to persuade the man to trust him and Akweks to do the scouting, yes, but it was not difficult, not truly. Both he and his friend were already renowned for their skills in reading the earth. But why did they have to be saddled with the arrogant Ronkwe who thought the world of himself and his ten summers of experience as a warrior? As though there were not plenty such men, most of them reaching leading positions, most but not the annoying piece of quarrelsome meat.

"There may be not enough light to follow them all the way," Akweks' hesitant voice brought him back from his reverie. "But we can check the other side of this hill safely. I think it would be a sensible thing to do."

The older warrior's eyes were as narrow as two slits. "I'm going back to report to our leader. You two do whatever you like. Get yourselves killed or captured, if you want to. I won't be grieving, especially not over you." The glance shot at Okwaho was dark, disclosing the depth of the man's enmity. It made him shiver. It was not right to talk in this way, not while in the heart of the enemy's land. Such a clearly expressed wish could bring the attention of the evil spirits, the minions of the Left-Handed Twin himself.

"What an annoying piece of rotten meat this man is," muttered Akweks as the sound of their companion's footsteps dissolved in the afternoon breeze. "I can't believe he said what he said."

"He hates me because I'm not one of you, not fully. The filthy rat!" Desperate to cover that earlier twinge of anxiety, the words still resounding in his head, refusing to disappear, Okwaho kicked at entanglements of roots. "He wants to fight it out. One day, it will happen."

"But you *are* one of us," protested Akweks, loyal as always. "Your father was a Flint People's man before he was adopted into Onondaga nation. You are one of us, by blood, if not by the clan you belong to."

"That's not enough for the rotten skunk."

Clenching his teeth, Okwaho pushed the familiar frustration away. He had gone to live with the Flint People a few moons earlier, with the formal consent of his father and the approval of everyone who was involved: his mother, his oldest brother, the leading people of his clan and the rest of their town, which was a large, important settlement, second only to powerful Onondaga Town.

It was a good decision that everyone approved, among the Onondagas and among the Flint People, as well. Little Falls, the largest town of his hosts, never forgot that it was in their settlement that Father grew up, it was there where he had brought the Messenger of the Great Spirits to deliver the word of the Great Law of Peace. This made Little Falls the most important settlement among the Flint People, and among the entire confederacy of the Five Nations as well.

Unfortunately, situated in the middle of the Flint People's lands, Little Falls saw little action. There was not enough warfare anywhere these days. Since the Great Peacemaker, the Five Nations lived in peace among themselves, warring only with the Crooked Tongues from across the Great Lake, but halfheartedly so. Father still hadn't given up on the idea of drawing the fierce old-time enemy into the Great Union, ridiculous as it might sound, and no matter what many people thought about it, Father wielded too much influence to dismiss his words, any of his words, lightly. Thus, the lack of warfare, even against the traditional enemy from across the Great Lake, left young, ambitious warriors like Okwaho with the necessity to look elsewhere. So he had gone to live with his father's former people.

Situated on the outskirts of the metaphorical longhouse of the Five Nations, the People of the Flint bore the responsibility of keeping the eastern side of the confederacy safe from an encroaching enemy, any enemy. Not that anyone dared to encroach on the powerful union. The Keepers of the Eastern Door they were called, the title and responsibility his father's former people took seriously, seriously enough to carry the war into the possible enemy's territory. Once upon a time, they had paid no attention to the hills and the valleys beyond the end of their Great River; they were too busy warring against their immediate neighbors, other People of the Longhouse. But when the Great Peacemaker put a stop to that, the bored warriors and the careful elders, politicians every one of them, began looking elsewhere. And this is why, after some time spent in Little Falls, enjoying the warmth and hospitality of his father's former home, Okwaho moved eastward, to the frontier town situated upon yet another set of roaring falls, Cohoes Falls, or the Place of the Fallen Canoe. There he had lived for the last two moons, waiting for his first raid, participating in the daily life, enjoying himself, accepted and appreciated for the most part. But not by everyone. There were some who looked on him with suspicion. Annoying lowlifes like Ronkwe, the arrogant good-for-nothing pieces of rotten meat!

"Forget him," he said, putting his attention back to the footprints. "Let us find where these are leading. This will make the stupid rat look like the coward he truly is."

"Yes, let us do that!" Readily, Akweks sprang onto his feet, beaming now, always delightfully light, the best of company.

Silently, they slid deeper into the woods, following the invisible trail that twisted tortuously, nothing but a deer track. She knew her way around, that woman.

"Why did you claim it was a woman, and not a young boy?" whispered Akweks, echoing Okwaho's thoughts. "Ronkwe must be right about that. No woman would be running around alone, so far away from home."

"Boys are not supposed to run around alone, either. They should be moving in groups, like women." He knew he was not being reasonable about it, but the feeling was strong. He *knew* it was a woman.

"They are not supposed to, true, but don't you remember your childhood? Didn't you run away many times, doing what you were not supposed to do?" His friend's eyes sparkled with mischief. "I recall more than a few adventures of that kind from my days. And something is telling me you were even worse."

Okwaho bent to examine the faint trail of prints anew. They were engraved deeply, widely, in the confident manner of a person who could run fast, sure-footed and self-assured. Not a womanly way, indeed. And his friend was right. A wandering boy was a likelier possibility. A possibility that also meant more danger. Going by the way he had run, the little skunk had probably reached his settlement by now, alerting people. Not good.

"Maybe there is a village somewhere up there, a village our leaders were not aware of."

Akweks' face crinkled, relating his open doubt. "Tsitenha, our true leader, knows these woods. He has been raiding these lands for some time."

Okwaho made a face. "Who knows?" Shrugging, he peered at the footsteps again. "Let us follow these until Father Sun nears the tops of these trees. It'll give us enough light to come back in case we ran into nothing." He straightened up resolutely. "Her village might not be that far away. It could not be."

Her again! Oh, but why did he keep thinking it was a woman?

CHAPTER 3

When others watched his father, listening to the rolling, well-trained voice of the renowned leader, Migisso watched the crowds, curious about their various expressions, fascinated by them. There was nothing new about the people of his own settlement, a village of little importance, but this crowd of foreigners caught his imagination, made him concentrate on the world that was not the safe haven of his inner sanctuary.

He didn't leave his village often, but this time, Father took him along, overlooking the usual drawbacks, indifferent to his son's shortcomings, to all the weaknesses and flaws, too many to count. When, more than twenty summers ago, the yet-to-be head of their clan and the chief of the entire settlement had been blessed with a son, he did not expect his progeny to turn into such a glaring disappointment. A child may not grow up as expected, may become unruly or timid, not as wise as hoped for, or maybe not as forceful, not a natural leader, although some of the leading qualities could be acquired.

Yet, what was one to do with a boy whose mind was always wandering, roaming the vastness of the different worlds, uninterested in the happenings right under his nose, whether regular boyish temptations or, later on, the affairs of his settlement and his people. Not strong, not especially witty, not outstanding in any other way. Not anything. A disappointment.

Shrugging, Migisso glanced at the orating leader, then returned his gaze to the listening people. There were times when he tried to please his father, tried to be of use, to practice with weapons and fishing gear, to learn hunting secrets. He was not completely useless with any of those, but his interest was just not there. Something that Father sensed, growing angry and impatient, losing his painfully gained fortitude. He was not a patient man, the leader of their clan and their village. He had tried hard to control his temper, to be impartial and tolerant, to behave as a worthy leader should. Yet, just like the hunting and warring for his son, the patience did not come naturally to him, something his family could attest to, had they wished to do so. Which they didn't. They did not wish their master harm. He was not a bad man. To behave normally and pretend all was well seemed like the best of courses. Mother was too busy with her duties, working day and night, struggling to keep up with her high status of the chief's wife, while Migisso and his sister did their best to behave inappropriately, each in his or her way; he by displaying neither talent nor interest to lead or be involved, she by displaying too much of both, glaringly wrong gifts in a girl.

"When our forefathers came to the beautiful valleys of the River Whose Waters Are Never Still, they knew they had found a new homeland." The open challenge in his father's voice penetrated the fence of his inner world, dragging him back into the impressively large council house, stuffed with mats and decorations aplenty. What riches! The council house of their village was nothing but a few hastily constructed bark walls and a fireplace. "The lands of our ancestors forgotten, we made the plentiful valleys of the mighty river our home, our only home. It is here where Father Sun blessed us and smiled upon us, showing his satisfaction. It is here where our forefathers were allowed to stay and build their villages." The man's gaze encircled his audience, open, imploring. "We are brothers, we who came here from the west. We are a family. We should never forget that."

The speech was coming along well, if the grave nods and the creased foreheads were to serve as an indication. Migisso suppressed a shrug. They knew what Father wanted, and those who did not, were sure to understand now. A cooperation, a union. The man had been struggling to make it happen for some time now, not always listened to, not always supported or understood, not even by his own fellow villagers.

Was it really that necessary to cooperate with the neighbors they barely knew, to establish some sort of a procedure? Migisso was not so sure about that, and neither were the others. The towns and villages of River People, those who came here some generations ago, were scattered throughout bountiful valleys and along the Great River, not warring, true, but not keeping close contact aside from occasional trading. Why would they? Every settlement made its own living, and there was more than enough of that. Why would they wish to seek each other's advice, or give such if asked?

"We do live as a family, brother." The impressively tall man, the head of this town's most important clan, nodded calmly, his face a blank mask. "As our clans are scattered among the villages and towns, so our settlements are spread along these lands. It is the right way of living, the way of our ancestors. Why would you wish to change that?"

"We need to keep closer ties, like the family we are. We need to protect each other."

For a heartbeat, the leaders kept quiet, staring at the fire, each in their own thoughts. Remembering the raids, Migisso imagined, his own stomach constricting at the mere thought. When he had been a child, their village had been attacked once, torn from its tranquility with the blood-curdling war cries and the flames, followed by the screams of the frightened people. On the same occasion, the enemy had managed to get in, wreaking death. Not always by a direct killing—at least in that the enemy resembled their own people, not seeking to kill women and children and old men, not even the young ones, but eager to plunder the village's food supplies and other possessions. Such attacks always seemed to be timed with the harvest. In spring or summer only the hunters out in the woods were required to keep a watch against small raiding parties, those who enjoyed harassing and reminding them of their existence, a relatively rare occurrence, but not of late. Lately, the enemy came more and more often, fearsome warriors, terrible beasts with no hearts, no souls, no feelings. He shuddered again.

"Our villages and towns are living in peace with each other, exchanging goods and well wishes. These were the ways of our fathers, indeed, but it is not enough these days. The western beast has grown more aggressive, seeking to hurt, seeking to destroy. They have grown larger and bolder. The captives from their lands report strange happenings. These people have changed since the messenger of their evil spirits came to their lands. They have grown stronger and fiercer. We cannot contain them separately anymore. We need to unite."

The other man's eyes narrowed. "Does your village have captives of the enemy?"

He remembered that woman who had died only a few winters ago. A good-looking, vigorous captive, who went about sounding her mind more often than not, even when she had barely spoken their tongue. A fierce person, and a fascinating one. She was liked in the village, well enough not to suffer too much ridicule or harassment, even though no one forgave her countryfolk any of their crimes. Still, a likable person, she turned surprisingly adaptable, prone to laughter and argument, especially with men, sounding her mind in an unwomanly fashion, turning to respectable women of the clans when in need of council, instead. Imagine that!

No wonder Kentika, his wild, boyish sister, only a girl back then, took a passionate liking to the foreigner, spending as much time in her vicinity as possible, despite Father's frowning. She had managed to learn some of the enemy's tongue, and she ran around boasting, speaking entire foul-sounding phrases, her strange too-widely-spaced eyes glowing with happiness. Another unusual person, more alien than the foreign woman in some aspects.

He suppressed a smile. Kentika would enjoy hearing his report on this spectacular town, sprawling on a towering hill, about its wonders and its people and the speeches their father was making, impressive, fair-sounding speeches that had gotten them nowhere so far. She was always curious about Father's ideas, always fascinated, trying to be involved. Was it the foreign woman's influence? Sometimes he wondered about that, although it was apparent even before that woman's arrival that this wild thing called his sister should have been born a man.

Instead of him, maybe, yes. He knew what some people thought or whispered. He was a disappointment whichever way he looked upon it. Suppressing a shrug, he forced his concentration back to Father's words.

"Our settlement hosted a woman who was captured close to ten summers ago, in a raid that humbled the enemy's spirit." There was no expression on Father's face, not a flicker of the pride he must have felt. "She died a few spans of seasons later. In the winter of illness."

More thoughtful nods.

"So tell us, brother." The town's leading man narrowed his eyes, his forehead knitted with creases. "How do you see it? In what way should our people be striving to work together, to protect each other, as you so eloquently put it?"

Holding his breath, Migisso watched his father's frown deepening. They weren't hostile, the people of Skootuck, but neither were they friendly and open. If anything, the way their leaders' were talking was arrogant, unbearably patronizing.

"We need to unite against the raids of the enemy," he heard Father saying, his voice unperturbed, but his lips pressed into a thin line. "Whenever there is an attack on a village or town, the others would have to come to this settlement's aid."

"To receive word of an attack, then gather warriors and reach the place in trouble takes more time than a raid would take, brother." This time, it was a burly man at the edge of the squatting half circle who spoke. "You talk about an enterprise that takes days. An enemy does not take more than one dawn to attack a settlement."

"If the settlement is holding on, resisting the attack, it might take longer than a day or two for the enemy to get inside."

The smile upon the burly man's lips was gentle to the point of offensive. "When has it ever happened that a village like yours, or even some larger towns, managed to fight off an attack, while keeping the enemy busy around its fence? If you have heard of such an occurrence, brother, do tell us, because I have most certainly not."

Frightened, Migisso watched the vein pulsating on Father's forehead, knowing the signs. The leader of their village was losing his patience fast.

"It might happen. If our warriors are brave, our fences are strong, and our people are prepared, it will happen."

"But they are not, are they? Your fence cannot stop the enemy, and your people are not always prepared, even if your warriors are brave enough and fearless, as our warriors are." The shrug of the squatting man was all innocence. "How are we to help, brother? How are we to aid you and the other small settlements scattered too close to the enemy from beyond our River Whose Waters Are Never Still?"

The silence that prevailed was so heavy one could feel it hovering, making the air sticky, more difficult to breathe. The glares of the guests and the hosts had a scorching quality to them, burning each other.

"Wait outside," said one of the leading men curtly, gesturing to the warriors and the others who crowded both entrances of the building.

Pressed by the curious townsfolk and its visitors, Migisso found it difficult to clear his way out, relieved to be outside, in the fresh breeze and the pleasant sun of the afternoon. In this time of the late summer moons, it was still too hot to wear a shirt and leggings, although ambitious young men of Skootuck sported them regardless.

He shrugged. An ambitious person he was not, nor a person envied or admired. A state of affairs that suited him, but not his father or other prominent people of their village. Yet, in the large foreign town barely anyone knew him or cared for his shortcomings, so it was a pleasure to stroll along the muddied alleys that the bark houses, scattered in disarray, created.

"We are to leave at once." Achtohu was out of breath, having evidently run around for some time. "You are coming, too."

"Why?" He eyed the young man with a measure of wariness, never comfortable around that particular crowd. Some young warriors were nothing but a nuisance.

"Your father says so. He is to stay here for another day with a handful of our men. Something to do with our guests, snotty squirrels that they are." The narrowed eyes flashed. "He wants to makes them listen? Or did he despair already? Were you there in the council house?"

Migisso just nodded.

"What went on there?"

"The usual speeches." He shrugged. "Father spoke well. Some of the leaders in there were attentive to his words." Another shrug. "Others were not. The chief of their Porcupine Clan argued."

"The leading bastard of Skootuck? We should have expected that!" Achtohu kicked at the stone, then moderated his tone, glancing at the people around. There were so many of them. How did they manage to live together, tucked in that impressive double row of palisade, protected, with not a care in the world?

"There were those who did listen. Our leader spoke well."

"Your father always does. But his words are not always falling on attentive ears." The young man picked a stone, then threw it away. "Well, come with me. We are sailing now."

"Now? So close to nightfall?" Puzzled, Migisso glanced at the sun, which was tilting toward the western hills, clearly visible over the nearest houses and the distant silhouette of the fence.

"Yes. We will camp out there. Reach home before the next nightfall." The young man's eyes sparkled with impatience. "Come."

A group of girls swept by, their decorated skirts swirling, their laughter infectious. Trying to avoid their scrutinizing gazes, he averted his eyes, still puzzled over the sudden change of plans. Why would they go back in a hurry and without their elders, after arriving only this morning? Had it something to do with the negotiations, with his father's farfetched ideas?

"Who stays to escort our elders back?"

"The warriors. A handful of the real ones. More than half of twenty, enough to keep our elders safe." Achtohu's eyes followed the colorful group, his frown fading away. "Nice sights they have here."

"Maybe it has something to do with the hunting. Maybe they

realized that most of our people are needed out there, storing meat and fish."

"Maybe," said his companion absently, eyes still wandering, lingering on one of the girls, holding her gaze. "Or maybe they just don't like so many of us around, reminding them that we are not some poor, distant cousins, but people just like they are."

CHAPTER 4

"Are you certain this is the shore?"

The old hunter knelt again, this time in the shallow water, scooping some of it with his palm, studying the wet sand, letting it run between his fingers.

"Yes, I'm sure."

She hated the way her stomach churned, with a mixture of anger and fear, wishing for the safety of her people that the enemy would be anywhere but here, hoping they would still be around for her annoyingly doubting companions to see them and know that she had been right to give them her warning. No one believed her, not fully. At this point, she began doubting her own observations as well.

"I was up there, on the Sacred Hill," she added, her anger giving her courage. "I saw them most clearly. I'm certain of what I saw."

"You must have an eagle's eyesight, girl," said one of the older hunters, his lips twisting unpleasantly. "It's a long way to be able to see all you described. Their faces, their paint, the way they had done their hair... Even their words! Are you sure your spirit was not wandering, entering the dream worlds?"

"Or they might have been a hunting party," added another man not unkindly, obviously trying to be helpful, but not helping at all. "Maybe she saw some of our people, or the villagers of the Long Creek."

"I know what I saw!"

She prevented herself from stomping her foot at the last moment, remembering her company. Her companions were not girls of her age to grow angry with and throw insults. They were respectable men of the village, the hunters that came back home expecting a happy welcome, receiving nothing but an agitated commotion and spells of fear from their womenfolk. And now, instead of a day of rest, they were trailing along the western woods after her, not pleased or grateful. Their side-glances told her so.

She pressed her lips stubbornly.

"I know what I saw. They were warriors, enemy warriors. I could hear them speaking, not enough to try to understand their words, but still. They were not speaking our tongues. They were armed like warriors, not hunters, and they were careful to keep quiet and to make no fire."

"Did you watch them until nightfall?"

She returned their gazes. "No."

"Then how do you know they didn't make fire?"

"They stopped to eat, before dragging their boats behind the trees. They would have made a fire to cook some meat if they were hunters." It came out muffled, seeping through her clenched teeth.

"What did they eat?"

"Something out of jars."

"Meat?" Schikan, one of the younger hunters eyed her with an open friendliness, his eyes dancing. A companion of her brother for quite a long time, he was the one to teach her all the unwomanly things for which she received frowns, from shooting a bow to running the right way, not like silly girls did.

"No, it must have been some sort of dough. They used spoons."

"It still proves nothing." The older hunters were not about to be pacified, set against the demand to spend their day verifying the strange claims of a strange girl. A silly attempt of a useless female to get attention, was their mutual verdict. One could not mistake *that* expression.

"This shore certainly shows signs of someone being here recently," said another man, coming from behind the bend of the river. "If they were warriors, they covered their tracks well. Still, one can see that it was not abandoned, not recently." The man frowned. "The lower bank down there shows that a long boat was dragged out of the water. Not a light hunters' canoe, but a heavy dug-out. It was picked up quickly, as there is no trail, but it might have been a long boat."

They looked around, perturbed, and again, she felt the peculiar wave running down her spine, a wild excitement mixed with an acute fear. What if they were attacked?

The trees guarding the shoreline moved slightly, rustling a warning. Had they sent the same warning to the enemy who had stood here only yesterday, busy and unafraid? That warrior with the tattoo of a wolf and a terrible hairdo. Had he sensed the same uneasiness? Somehow, she knew he had. He had been watching her side of the hill most intently. Though unable to see his expression or what his eyes held, she had known he was perturbed and on guard, maybe even aware of her watching him.

Catching her breath, she peered into the semidarkness behind the trees. There must be some evidence there, something that would make her people believe her.

"I think we can look around some more." Schikan's voice rang with sincerity, deferring to the older members of their party, but not about to give up. "There is no harm in doing at least that, since we came so far."

Their foreboding expressions reflected the frown of the opaque sky. Such a cloudy day.

"I can take you to the place I was hiding yesterday," she said in desperation. "You'll see that I'm not exaggerating, that it was possible to see clearly…" The heaviness of their gazes made her voice trail off.

"I will check this grove." She was sorry Schikan's eagerness to help made him dive into the darkness of the trees, leaving her to face the rest of them alone. It was daunting to battle their prejudice.

"I'll go with you," said one of the men, shrugging as though tired of being upset with the uselessness of it all. "The young man is right. If we are here anyway…" With a light wave of a hand, he disappeared behind the muddy embankment.

"We all should join young Schikan," said the older of the hunters grimly, the unofficial leader of their expedition. "See if there is any evidence we missed scanning this shore at first."

"There is none, and there will be none." The glance the speaking man shot at Kentika was dark with disdain.

She summoned the remnants of her anger. "You will find evidence, and plenty of it," she said, meeting the glare with enough fire in her own. "I'm not lying, and I'm not mistaking what I saw. Our settlement better be prepared for the coming of the enemy. They are roaming our woods, and have been for a full day now. They are here."

The glances they shot at the river and the trees were perturbed, openly unsettled. She regretted saying the last words. They scared her as much as they scared them. It sounded like a prophecy.

"Stop talking nonsense, girl!" Paqua was the man of their own clan, as dignified as Father and almost as influential. Almost. He was a friendly rival, Father used to joke. Well, he looked anything but friendly now. "Your words will bring us trouble, if you keep talking this way. Do not tempt the spirits that are guarding our woods." Another of the squashing glances. "Just keep quiet. Sit here until we are finished looking for your non-existent evidence. Enough that you dragged us all here with no reason. Do not make more of a nuisance out of yourself, girl."

"I am not—" Their stony gazes stopped her words, making the lump in her throat grow. She was never listened to, never taken seriously, never! But this time, it was so very important. "Please, you must believe me! You—"

The man who had gone to inspect the next bend appeared almost at the same time that Schikan burst from behind the trees, both breathless with agitation, waving frantically. The boats, their hand gestures said. Her body went limp with relief. They had found the boats!

The enemy might have covered his tracks, leaving no evidence of them lingering among the rocks and the muddy forest ground, but their boats were not something they could make disappear, to reappear later, at their convenience. However well hidden between moss-covered rocks, camouflaged by plenty of branches and rotten logs, the vessels were there, a clear evidence, an unbreakable testimony, one large, heavy dugout, with many lighter canoes, decorated to this or that degree, painted, proclaiming the enemy's might and ferociousness.

Holding her breath, Kentika watched the men dragging the vessels out, in a frenzy now, their silly remarks forgotten, their demand that she wait on the shore as well. Of course she did not stay.

Her heart pounding wildly, chest swelling with both satisfaction and fear, she rushed after them, hot on their heels. No more poison-dripping reproaches and dark glances. She had been proved right. The boats confirmed her story.

However, they did more than this. They told them how serious the situation was, how threatening. The well-hidden vessels professed one thing. The enemy was out there, planning the attack on their village. There was no other likely destination, unless the invaders were prepared to walk for days. Which, of course, made no sense whatsoever.

"What are we going to do with those?" she asked Schikan quietly, catching the other side of the heavy vessel he was lifting with a visible effort, remembering the warrior with the wolf tattoo tossing the bark canoe upon his shoulder as though it were a branch of a tree.

He looked at her briefly, his eyes twinkling, assessing her, clearly debating whether to remark on her volunteering help as though she were another man, or to just accept it. But for the heaviness and the uncomfortable slickness of the boat's side, she would have stared back.

"We'll take what we can sail, and burn the rest, I presume." Pausing briefly, he wiped the sweat off his brow. "Or maybe hide what we can't sail in another place. Those vessels are good."

"What will they do when they come back and don't find them?" She tried to pay no attention to the nauseating fluttering in her stomach. "I mean, won't they grow even angrier, more dangerous than before?"

His face darkened. "By the time they come back to retrieve their boats, our fields may be burned and our people killed or captured. They are warriors on the raid, sister, not traveling foreigners." Grimacing, he shifted his grip, trying to take the most of the canoe's weight. "So to answer your question, no, they won't get any more dangerous than they are now."

But for the heaviness of their cargo and the necessity to watch her step, she would have shut her eyes, terrified by his words.

"They won't manage to get to the village, will they?" It came out hoarsely, more of a whisper.

The boat shifted as though he attempted to shrug. "We'll do everything to prevent that. Thanks to you, we were forewarned." Another kind glance over their cargo. "You did good, dancing girl. You did right by bringing your timely warning, and then battling their lack of trust."

Despite her mounting worry and her anger at the earlier sneering of the others, she chuckled, the old nickname he had given her once upon a time making her smile. Everyone called her that now—Kentika, the dancing one—although she was a terrible dancer, worse than anyone in the village. The toddling baby girls barely able to walk on their own could dance better than she could. Good for them. She had no wish to dance. None of those who paced gracefully enough to be allowed to perform at the rituals, and all those who could sway beautifully when everyone was allowed to join the ceremonial circle, could climb, run, or shoot a bow better than her, and these were the things that mattered, not the silly dancing.

Yet, they called her Kentika now, the dancing girl, because, once upon a time, this same Schikan, still a funny boy full of jokes, said she could never stand still, always dancing with impatience. She had seen probably eight or ten summers back then, and they were out there beside the fence, and he was about to show her how to fit an arrow into a small bow he had made especially for her behind her father's back, but his friends, other youths, came along, and he stopped to talk to them, and as much as she tried to wait patiently, her feet were moving on their own, making her pace back and forth and hop all around, tapping out the sounds of her barely-contained excitement, until someone laughed and said: "What is this dance all about?" And ever since, they had called her that, dancing girl.

"Why did they have to argue and ridicule instead of just believing me?" she asked him, her brief amusement gone. "I didn't lie, and I wasn't mistaken. They see the proof of it now. I proved myself right. But I know they will refuse to listen to me again, next time I say something. Why don't they ever listen?"

The boat was slippery, and she propped her shoulder against its rough surface to aid her straining arms. He seemed to appreciate her help, although it made him bend a little in order to be even with her, as he was taller, but not by much.

"It was something no one wanted to believe." He would have shrugged, but for their heavy burden. "This is a sort of a trouble no one wishes to hear about. They did not assume you were mistaken. They *hoped* you were." A fleeting smile flashed. "It was not something against you personally. Not this time."

She glanced at him from above the muddied splinter-covered bark, then returned to concentrating on her step. "And the other times?"

His sigh was loud enough to rustle in the morning heat. "You know the answer to that, little one. You are not so little anymore."

Her stomach tightened anew. "No, I don't know the answer to that. All I know is that no one ever wishes to listen to me, to tell me things of importance, to take me seriously." His silence was annoying, carrying a message. She felt like dropping their cargo, or pushing it onto him. "I know I'm just a girl, and it is not my place to talk about wars and agreements, or to shoot a bow. Or to search the woods, and run, and bring news. But... but I'm no good at anything else, and..." The struggle to keep her voice from breaking was turning difficult, and she clenched her teeth, swallowing hard, determined to say it. "Like now, you see, it was useful, me being out there. I spotted the enemy. It was useful; it may give us time to prepare. Why weren't they grateful instead of growing angry and impatient?" She swallowed another lump that was forming rapidly in her throat. "I could do it more often, you see? I'm good at reading the earth. I know our woods so well. Why can't I do this?"

Back at the shore, the sun burst upon them, shining unrestrained, yet the breeze of the open ground was most welcome.

"They won't let you do this," he said quietly, easing the boat off her shoulder, making it slide smoothly onto the glittering pebbles of the shore. "You can't battle them on this. They have broken stronger spirits, Kentika. And you are a girl. You can do nothing but learn to fit in now that you are not a child anymore." There was sadness in his eyes as they brushed past her, turning away quickly, refusing to meet her gaze. "This is the only way for you, to accept your lot and to do the things you are supposed to do." His mirthless chuckle was more of a snort, barely audible because he was turning away, to head back into the woods and the rest of the enemy boats. "And yes, to hold your tongue more often than you do. They would appreciate that."

Before he disappeared behind the rustling trees, she could hear him muttering, "They don't know you the way I do, the way your brother does. I wish they did."

CHAPTER 5

He saw the ascending people first, before the others did. Nothing but a faraway, blurry spot, moving imperceptibly, climbing the hill, to disappear into the rustling greenery.

He would have missed it altogether had it not been for some inkling, something that made him turn away from the village they were watching and, for the thousandth time, to try to see the river beyond the hill; the hill they had climbed twice by now, once on the evening before, when he had managed to convince Akweks to follow the footprints all the way, and the second time in the predawn grayness, when he was required to lead them all here.

Pleased with their findings, Kayeri, their temporary leader, did not scold him for taking the initiative by following the trail. Whatever Ronkwe might have said was evidently not enough to make Okwaho look bad. Instead, he was made to recount all that they had seen—what kind of village was it? How large? Did they see the fields?—and then, nodding thoughtfully, the man decided that this place was worthy of investigation.

With the major part of their force sailing on earlier, negotiating the dangerous waters of that huge foreign river, only a day or so of traveling from here, heading for a prearranged destination, and them being a mere reinforcement, it was difficult to fight the temptation. What was to stop them from storming a small but well-hidden village that Okwaho's senses and insistence revealed? Depending on the defense means of this place and its fields and their condition, it might be a great opportunity. They all knew of Kayeri's ambition. The large boats they had brought were kept empty for a reason. It was more difficult to negotiate frequent rapids in such a long, cumbersome vessel, but the extra space it offered was valuable, purported to serve the raiders on their way back, to carry the fruits of their daring enterprise.

Weapons and pretty trinkets were a welcome addition, but true spoils, true purpose, were baskets of maize, squash, and beans, jars of sunflower oil, stocks of rare trading items like white and purple seashells or pottery. Captives were welcomed too, of course, but in this aspect, the warfare had changed since the Five Nations stopped warring on each other. Once upon a time, the captives had been the main purpose, either for adoption or for the spectacular ceremony of their execution. Among the apparent brother-nations, it was a natural thing. Yet now, warring against true strangers, the adoption custom turned a bit questionable. Too many foreigners did not understand the subtlety and the wonders of the Longhouse People's culture. They didn't know how to live, or how to die properly for that matter, neither adoptees nor captured warriors destined to leave their earthly world in an honorable manner, in pain and dignity, gaining much respect and adoration. No, civilized the foreigners were not.

Straining his eyes, Okwaho watched the suspected hill for a few more heartbeats, then returned his gaze toward the ugly fence. One pitiful row of sharpened beams, tied together, not too closely fitted. What sort of fortification was that?

He remembered the intricate corridor the double row of palisade created in his people's towns, everywhere he had happened to live, his native High Springs of the Onondagas, or Little Falls of the Flint People, or the last town of Cohoes Falls, where their current expedition came from. No enemy could surprise his people, and even if someone had managed, an outright assault on the towns' walls would see the invaders fighting for every step in the tortuous labyrinth, jammed between high stakes, getting slaughtered by the furious defenders.

He eyed the fence in front of him once again. What were those people hoping to achieve with that thing, besides keeping the forest creatures out? Probably nothing, although they did not venture to the fields this morning. There was not much activity to be spotted outside as it was. Were they afraid, preparing? Most probably. Forewarned by the owner of the footsteps, they must have been ready to put up their best defense now.

Damn silly to be spotted by a wandering local in such a way. But then, if not for that, they would not have discovered the village at all. How ironic. The warning of a scout was what put these people in jeopardy in the first place.

He suppressed a twinge of anxiety. Was it wise to try to storm this village with their relatively small force? Some of the veteran warriors weren't so sure, but Kayeri insisted. The man claimed that a small settlement was nothing twenty experienced, hardened warriors could not deal with. You trap the locals in the fields first thing in the morning, get over the unprotected fence, take their food supplies and some captives, and go away. The village was too good an opportunity to miss. So here they were, spread too thinly around the fence, hardened veterans some of them, yes, but still a small force, vulnerable to all sorts of surprises.

Returning his gaze to the hill, he calculated the possible path of the enemy who might have been climbing it now, heading for the village. How many people? Hunters or warriors? If they followed the same trail that had brought them here at night, they might be visible again not long from now.

He gestured at the warrior who was crouching next to him, bored.

"I'm going to talk to the leader."

His companion narrowed his eyes. "What's amiss?"

"Nothing. I just think we should scan some more of these surroundings."

Raised eyebrows and a shrug were his answer. He began easing away. Irritating or not, they had all learned to trust his sudden impulses.

The bulk of their warriors concentrated above the village, in a grove that concealed their presence but gave a generous view of their prey, allowing the sight of two ridiculously short houses and the edge of what looked like tobacco plots.

The sun shone brightly, unrestrained. Rustling in the nearby fields with no familiar conical mounds, the breeze brought a welcome relief in the heat, yet no women were down there to

enjoy the friendly weather. The high stalks of maize swayed
forsaken, deserted, the cobs heavy, weighing the stems down,
begging to be picked.

"They know we are sniffing around," muttered Kayeri,
greeting Okwaho with a barely perceptible nod. His eyes didn't
move from the farthest edge of the fence. "Circumvent it once
again."

The short order sent two of the warriors hurrying off.

"Prepare the fire arrows." Another curt motion made a few
more warriors who were crouching nearby, listening avidly,
scamper off. "Bring the oil and the cloths here. We'll be preparing
them as we go. No point in trying to conceal our presence
anymore."

Taking the light motion of the head as permission to speak,
Okwaho crawled toward the edge, careful not to disturb a leaf or a
branch. From that vantage point, the village looked better, not too
large, but not too small either, with the roof of the nearest
dwelling covered in bark, in the familiar longhouse's fashion, yet
so different, *so short*. As though a section of the building was cut
off. Strange.

"What do you wish to report?" The questioning gaze brushed
past Okwaho, making him concentrate.

"I saw people coming up the hill, from the direction we came
from. They must have been sniffing around the river. I think they
are heading here."

The man tensed. "Where did you see them?"

Okwaho took a deep breath. "They were still far, only
beginning to ascend." The narrowing eyes made him
uncomfortable. "I saw the movement, for a brief moment. But
those were people, a group of people. I'm sure of it."

The eyes studying him narrowed to a slit. "The same hunch as
with the footprints?"

"No. I just saw …" He felt like cursing himself for not keeping
quiet, staying in the place he was assigned to watch. "I saw them
moving. I was watching the trail we came from. Where we are
staying, it is easy to see the entire hill. There was a spark, a certain
spark of sunlight. It came from something polished, someone's

weapon, maybe. Or another people-made tool. Then I saw it moving. They might have been crossing some clearing. They disappeared, but if they are following our trail, they will be visible again, in a short while." He swallowed. "We are only twenty people. If they surprise us …"

A freezing gaze stopped his words in midair. "Did I ask for your advice, warrior?"

He fought the urge to drop his gaze. "No."

"Then offer none." The coldness dispersed, but the cloud was still there, shadowing the piercing eyes. "Take five men and go down there. Follow our trail. See what this is all about." A curt nod addressed the nearest warrior. "Help him get organized." The pursed lips pressed tighter. "Take Akweks and Ronkwe again. If it comes to the fight, Ronkwe takes the lead. Is that understood?" The gaze grew stonier. "No more arguing with people who are your elders and betters. Our leader might have trusted you, but until we reunite with our main forces, you are answerable to me, and I will tolerate no arguments."

Still in a state of semi-confusion, Okwaho stared at the wide nape that was turned on him already, then crawled away, welcoming the opportunity to get back to his feet under the protective coverage of the grove. Even the earth of the enemy was unfriendly, covered with too many branches and spikes, the multitude of pinecones taking a pleasure at tearing at his skin, as did the sharp gravel.

The questioning gaze of one of the warriors made him angry.

"I'm to take five men in order to scan the woods and the trail we came from."

"And leave us with less than twenty people to attack this place?" It came out icily, openly hostile, yet Okwaho could not help but see the merit of this question. They were painfully not enough, open to all sorts of surprises, with his spontaneously organized scouting mission serving no apparent purpose, other than splitting their already meager forces.

"Yes," he said firmly, not averting his gaze. "That's what our leader wants me to do."

Their gazes locked, and for another heartbeat, the silence

prevailed, heavy, uncomfortable silence. Then the man shrugged, pressing his lips tight.

"Well, go on, young leader. Choose your following." The eyes filled with more ice. "Make sure I'm not among them."

It was difficult to turn around and head off, saying nothing. For a brief moment, he thought he wouldn't manage.

"Something is wrong!"

Startled by his own exclamation, Migisso straightened up, forgetting the canoe he was dragging up the sandy shore. Which made the man who was holding the other end of it curse.

"What?" he cried out impatiently. The others, two more pairs of warriors, hesitated as well.

Migisso paid them no attention, concentrating on the smell. It was very light, nearly imperceptible, lingering in the heat of the high noon, reaching out, retreating before he could get a grip on it.

"What do you feel?" Achtohu shook his head, irritated by the flies as much as by the unwarranted delay.

"I don't know, but something is not right." In a desperate attempt to catch the troublesome scent again, Migisso almost shut his eyes, turning his head, his nostrils quivering.

They said nothing, exchanging glances, their eyebrows raised high, of that he was sure. No one made the mistake of trusting him. He concentrated on his senses, willing the breeze to come back, to let him explore the suspected odor. Was a fire raging somewhere?

"We want to reach home before Father Sun goes back to the other world," muttered someone, and the others smirked.

"Yes, Man of Senses. Let us go on. You can explore the dream worlds when we reach home. Plenty of time to do that, then, brother."

They were right. He bent to recapture the side of the boat he carried, when the smell wafted in again, this time unmistakable.

"Can't you feel it? There is a fire, somewhere up there." He glanced in the direction they were heading, the top of their home hill towering ahead, offering safety. Or maybe not. "A big fire."

They followed his pointing hand with their eyes, their gazes skeptical.

"I smell nothing," said his canoe partner.

"And even if there was something," contributed Achtohu, shifting his hold on his boat, "what is wrong with the smell of a fire? Our hunters and fishermen are all over the place these days, smoking meat and fish. There is a lot of fire all around."

A new gust of wind brought more of the same.

"This is different. This is no campfire. This one is big." He tried to listen to his inner voices, but with their contemptuous gazes and their crowding, it was difficult, impossible to summon the right concentration. "Something is wrong," he repeated, shrugging, resuming his walk, their glances and barely hidden grins not bothering him, having been a part of his life since he could remember.

"Maybe they have been having a celebration back home," mused someone, his laughter light and derisive, rolling down the trail that led toward the well-hidden construction they had stored their boats in. "Maybe your highly sensitive nose has been smelling a huge bonfire to broil some deliciously fresh buck or doe. Maybe we better hurry."

"He said it's no good. How can a freshly broiled doe be no good? Even our prophet of doom would not say that."

More laughter. He paid them no attention. It had been a while since anyone took him seriously, except at the ceremonies or if someone got hurt and there was no healer around.

Father allowed him to practice the secrets of the healing, learning from the medicine men or any of his helpers, but only a little. This was not his destiny, Father had said once, growing angry at the mere mention of the subject, when Migisso dared to ask. Actually, it was not him who had asked, but his sister, bringing what preyed on their minds up in that dauntless, careless fashion of hers. The fierce little thing wasn't good at keeping her thoughts to herself. She knew he was good with herbs, that he loved them, understanding their usefulness, intuitively knowing what plant should be squeezed for its juices and what should be boiled to become an ointment or brew. Not having been allowed to study, he had come to this knowledge all by himself, finding it impossible to resist the urge to experiment with the new plants he discovered on his frequent, if lonely, wanderings. It was stronger than him, the urge to escape the town as much as the urge to explore the earth and its wonders. Back in the old days, only Kentika knew. A wild thunderbolt of bursting energy, his sister provided a rich practicing field with her endless scratches and bruises, even a dislocated limb from time to time. She wished to conceal her inappropriate running around as much as he wished to conceal his frowned-upon healing interest. They had served each other well.

The thought of her warmed his spirit, taking his thoughts away from the possible danger. She would love to hear all about that large, haughty town Father was trying to bring to their side. He could picture her strange too-widely-set eyes growing to enormous proportions, sparkling with excitement, refusing to believe that so many houses and people could be amassed in one place, surrounded by a high palisade and a long line of tobacco plots. Not to mention the ceremonial grounds. Such a wide space, with that huge maple tree in the middle of it. She would listen breathlessly, then start cutting him off with too many questions, following that pattern of thought that had become her own. People often thought her silly, when she hopped from subject to subject, with no visible logic to it. But he knew that was not true. She was smart and thoughtful. Just not very organized, too easily excited, that's all.

Again, the odor of the burning wood reached his nostrils, now more prominent, marring the crispy air. Not peaceful, not belonging, not like a campfire.

"Don't you smell it?"

This time, they halted more readily.

"Maybe," muttered Achtohu, his frown deep. "There is something strange in the air, yes. Some odor."

"Smoke."

Frantically, they scanned their limited view. There was

nothing, and yet the brightness of the sky was not as crisp, not as clear as it should have been.

"Something is wrong."

This time, they peered at him with no sneering accompanying their expressions, their frowns deep, eyes troubled.

"What do you feel?"

"I'm not sure—"

A curt gesture of one of the older men's hand interrupted his words, cutting them in midair.

"Keep quiet!" It was a command.

If their breaths were not held before, they surely stopped breathing now, not daring to move a muscle.

Shivering, Migisso listened to the sounds that interrupted the quietness of the woods, a careful creaking of an occasional branch, the strange way everything seemed to go still. Then the terrible scream tore the momentary silence, unhuman in its intensity, the depth of its suffering.

Sweat ran down his back, making his shirt cling to his body in the most annoying of manners. What was happening up there, in their woods? He wasn't sure he wanted to know.

"Follow me!" The whisper of the older warrior barely moved the stillness of the air. "Make no sound, and do as I say."

Somehow, it reassured them all. He could see it in the surrounding faces, his tightening stomach reflecting their expressions. An enemy might be somewhere around, doing terrible things, but the advantage of surprise was on their side.

CHAPTER 6

It was easy to follow the trail without walking it, as the trees were not so dense, with the ground being relatively flat, dry, not slippery. The perfect season.

His senses tuned, ears pricked, feet careful to disturb no leaf, Okwaho led the way, having walked this land more than one time since the previous afternoon.

Not perfectly local, he thought, amused, but not a total stranger either. That inkling about the watching villager was the best thing that happened to him so far. He had been right in taking the risk of looking ridiculous in case it was nothing. It hadn't been, and since then, their leader trusted him, his feelings, and the logic of his conclusions.

And so, here he was now, leading a group of warriors on a scouting mission, a young man who had barely seen twenty summers. Not bad, even for the son of his father; although, of course, there was no way to eclipse Father, in that more than in anything. The Onondaga War Chief was as young as Okwaho now was when he came into his exalted position, some said. Maybe even younger. Certainly, Father had been their people's leader for more summers than he, Okwaho, or even his elder brother had seen.

His ears picked up the sound of trickling water, and he gestured for his companions to halt. The trail would be forking by the narrow brook, he remembered, where the climb turned steeper. Anyone coming up that trail would be exposed at this point, their attention on the hardening conditions. According to his calculations, the people he had spotted earlier would reach this crossroad soon. He had been afraid they would pass it before his party reached the right spot, but so far, those fears had not come true. Unless those they searched for were heading some other way he didn't know about, or the movement he had seen was not a group of people at all, his conclusion too hasty, reflecting what he wanted to happen rather than the real thing. He disregarded the tightening in his stomach.

"We'll wait here," he breathed, gesturing rather than actually speaking.

The warrior next to him shrugged, his eyes narrow, heavily lidded, unreadable. Another one displeased with being led by a younger man. Okwaho's stomach heaved again. *Oh, Mighty Spirits, let my instincts be true again. Don't let it be that I dragged these men out here for nothing.*

He crept closer to the exposed ground. Nothing.

The wind tore at the treetops angrily. Should he go on, following the trail until they reached the river? Try to find more footsteps? Oh, Benevolent Spirits, why was it taking the stupid locals so long to arrive?

Another quick calculation, but it didn't help. All he had seen was a movement, a brief glimpse upon the exposed side of the hill. It could have been anything, really. Why had he decided it was people? Because of some silly spark? Weapons were not the only thing that sparkled in the light. Many things could do that. If polished, or just thoroughly wet …

"Nothing?"

Akweks' whisper cut the panicked turn his thoughts were taking, welcome and irritating at the same time.

"They'll come." He was surprised with the firmness of this statement, with how his own whisper related conviction he didn't feel.

"What if they are not heading this way?"

"Where would they be going if not back to their village?" More of an effort to banish the rising tide of misgivings.

"Hunting, harvesting, gathering things." Akweks crouched beside him, troubled. "Going to some other village they may have around here, even though it would be a strange arrangement."

The ice was piling up in his insides, but before he could burst out protesting that no people would be building villages so close to one another—why would they bother instead of living together in one settlement?—there was a sound, a muffled something brought by the increased wind, something that jerked his attention away from his friend's words and the trail they were watching. The rustling of the trees and the buzzing of insects made it difficult to pick out the other sound, yet his senses told him there was a presence out there, a presence that wasn't there before. The people they were waiting for?

His companions tensed as well, following his gaze. There was no need for a special ability to hear the occasionally cracking branches, the muffled footsteps of people who tread the earth carefully, but not soundlessly, not on a warpath or a hunt.

Silently, he slipped back in between the trees, motioning them to follow. This time, no one argued. Concentrating on his inner world, the way Father had taught him, he didn't try to see through the thick brown and green, listening instead, probing with his senses, taking in the howling wind, the rustling bushes, the natural sounds as opposed to the less natural ones.

There.

One of the older warriors motioned with his head just as Okwaho's ears picked out the muffled creak of a broken branch. His nerves as tense as an overstretched bowstring, he readied his body, relying on his instincts as much as on his mind's decisions when the time came. But for a bit of knowledge of these woods! To have a better idea where these people were coming from and why.

More careful footsteps. They were nearing, heading straight here. The trail! They were trying to reach the trail, he realized. Good! Maybe they were the locals he had spotted before.

He strained his eyes, trying to see through the greenish thickness, the club grasped tightly in his sweaty palm. Why was he sweating? Was it that hot?

The footsteps died away. The cracking of the branches stopped. He felt his heart coming to a halt. One heartbeat, then another. When it resumed its movement, it was fluttering in his chest, filling his mouth with a bitter taste. The forest was still, listening, waiting, just like they did.

Then, with a clarity of mind he didn't know he possessed, he knew that they had to charge, to charge now, surprising the enemy that refused to be surprised otherwise. The trap didn't work, but they could still make the best out of the situation by attacking first. The approaching group could not be numerous, judging by the little noise their previous progress made.

Bettering his grip on the club, he looked around, meeting Akweks' questioning gaze.

"Come."

He didn't say it aloud but motioned with his head. The others stared at him, but he disregarded their frowns, gesturing with his free hand again, turning away and bursting toward the next creaking sound, not completely sure he was not running out there all alone.

The bushes tried to block his way, but he jumped over them, not attempting to keep quiet, not anymore. The club was alive in his hands, wishing to fly, to pounce or to rotate in a half circle, to do its work.

The first man he saw gaped, taken aback, his hair tied simply in hunters' fashion, his eyes wide. He held a harpoon, a spear-like stick used for fishing, not a bad weapon, far-reaching and light, maneuverable; yet, he had no chance to as much as wield it before Okwaho's club crashed against the side of his head, filling the small clearing with a revoltingly wet thud.

His heart pounding insanely, he froze for a moment, watching the man toppling over, collapsing like a cut-down tree. One moment staring in bewilderment, the other nothing but a mess of dancing limbs, an unsettling sight.

A familiar hiss jerked him away from his observation, making him duck, throwing his body aside. Losing his balance, he would have fallen, but for the unexpected support of an old tree, its bark rough and bumpy against his grip, hurting but in a friendly manner, not letting him fall.

The heavy footsteps behind his back urged him to release his temporary support, sending him ducking again, darting aside.

The weighty tip of a club smashed against the old tree, exploding with a thud.

Splinters and pieces of bark showered the ground, as he struggled to turn around in time to meet the next onslaught, to stop it before it had the chance to crack his head open and cause his legs and arms to twitch in the most disgusting of ways. The sun was in his eyes, and he couldn't see how many people he was facing, nor where his comrades were. *Was he fighting all alone here?*

His club blocked the next blow in a satisfying manner, but his arms trembled, holding on barely, giving way. His rival pressed on. He was a strongly-built man, much older than himself, clearly a warrior with great experience, his face glittering with sweat, oily hair collected on the top in an elaborate braid. His eyes were large, and they sparkled victoriously, but before Okwaho's arms gave way, he kicked at his rival's unprotected legs, slipping down the trunk he was pressed against, rolling away from the remnants of the blow.

Again, the sound of the club brushing against the crumbling bark startled him. Those strikes were too powerful, too well directed. Leaping to his feet, he took a good look at the clearing for the first time, a mess of colorful garments, swinging clubs, and flashing knives. So he was not alone here after all. The realization reassured him, and he pounced on his limping rival, elated, glad that he had enough presence of mind to direct his kick well, right into the man's knee.

His own assault was met by a club, blocked firmly; still, it pleased him that he was the one to attack now. It gave him strength, cleared his mind, let it analyze the situation. The man was not as agile as before, so if made to chase his prey around the clearing, he might lose his guard.

A strategy that should have worked but for someone's spear interrupting the plan. As Okwaho faked fear, easing away carefully, preparing to dart, the sturdy shaft brushed past his side, nearly pushing him off his feet again, leaving a burning sensation under his right arm. It almost impaled his rival, and had the man not been so quick himself in darting away, waving his hands to keep his balance, it would have done so.

He calculated fast. To reach the spear was possible but pointless. He had his club, the weapon of his preference anyway. Yet to disregard the long-ranged weapon was to invite trouble, to allow the lowlife who had thrown it the chance of picking it up again.

The man with the club was about to regain his balance, and he hesitated no more. One leap placed him next to his rival, his own club coming down fast, unstoppable now. He knew it would reach its target; this time it was a sure thing.

Another revolting thud and he was standing victorious, his heart fluttering in his chest, pounding in his ears, deafening. His rival was gasping for air, twisting upon the ground, gurgling sounds pouring out of his mouth, along with a trickle of blood.

Okwaho straightened up to deliver the final blow. *Oh, Mighty Spirits, please see to this worthy man; please make his Sky Journey smooth and pleasant.*

In the clearing, the battle still raged, the hunters numerous, angry, unafraid. Yet, their numbers were evening out, with more of the locals dotting the dank, moss-covered earth, twisting or lying still. There must have been at least ten hunters they had encountered, surprised but not unready, not helpless. Were these the people he had seen from the top of the hill? Such a large group?

There was no time to ponder these questions. Seeing two of his fellow warriors pitted against a group of spearmen, he darted their way, his club high and ready, the war cry vibrating upon his lips. Startled, the attackers turned, some jumping away, out of instinct probably. It gave his companions a much-needed opening, a heartbeat of respite.

While the spearmen attacked, waving their weapons as though they were clubs, he ducked, avoiding the touch of the razor-sharp flint, his club adorned by a vicious spike too, better and sturdier but not as far reaching, demanding a closer combat.

He saw Akweks escaping the thrust of a javelin, leaping away, to bury his knife in another man's side, twisting it viciously, for the maximum effect.

Ducking another onslaught, he felt the club slipping and didn't dare to take his eyes off the attacking men in order to regain possession of his weapon. Gaze clinging to the darting spears, trying to anticipate their movements, his hands tore at his sheath, desperate to get hold of the knife.

From the corner of his eye, he saw one of their warriors wavering, letting out a strange sound, the tip of an arrowhead peeking from his throat, placed in a perfect symmetry, as though belonging there, glittering darkly. In the next heartbeat, the man was upon the ground, his face buried in the slippery mud.

An observation that cost Okwaho a cut upon his upper arm, the spear thrusting forward, determined to impale him. As his body twisted, getting out of the deadly flint's reach, he slipped on the muddy ground, and didn't try to regain his balance this time, but rolled away, his free hand snatching up a stone, fingers tightening around uneven edges.

There was no time to take good aim. Leaping back to his feet, he hurled his newly acquired missile while still in the process of getting up, seeing the enemy rushing forward, eager to finish his victim off.

The stone met his attacker halfway, crushing into the flushed face with a resounding bang. It was a funny sight, the way the man flopped his hands in the air, as though in a dance, his spear flying sideways, followed by its owner before the next heartbeat was over.

Already back on his feet, Okwaho felt like falling again, this time in a wild fit of laughter. It was too funny, the sight of the dancing man, now upon the ground, twisting like a snake, gurgling through the bloody mess of a mouth. He tried to make the laughter stop, the wild pounding of his heart filling his ears, making it all even funnier. Oh, Mighty Spirits!

A scream beside his ear helped, taking his attention away and back to the battle. Akweks was staggering by his side, one hand flailing in the air, the other trying to reach behind his back, where a feathered shaft was fluttering, sticking out of the massive thigh, the colorful feathers trembling with the frantic movements, not belonging.

Plunging ahead, he caught his friend, struggling to keep him upright while not falling himself, finding it difficult to hold on against the limpness and the additional weight.

"Hold on!"

Trying to see the enemy who might be attacking them from behind, he twisted, desperate to locate his club, then noticed the silence. Not a dead silence that always preceded some terrible happenings, but a relative calm of an aftermath. The battle was over.

His eyes scanned the clearing, taking in the terrible sights and the smells that should be familiar by now, but were not. That scent of fresh earth and the forest mixed with the revolting odor of blood and discharges, the terrible stench that came from the inside of human bodies and everything it released with its life forces trickling away with no warning or preparation. Oh, how he hated that smell! And the sights it always accompanied, broken limbs and smashed heads filling the world, leaving nothing outside of it, no hope of escape.

He swallowed hard, then forced his mind back to his friend, who was leaning heavily against him, calmer now, not fighting to reach the arrow any longer.

"You'll be well," he muttered, struggling to better his grip on the wide shoulders. "We'll get you over there, where you can sit. Then we will take care of this annoying thing in your leg."

He could feel Akweks nodding stiffly, bereft of words.

"Over there." To Okwaho's imminent relief, one of the older warriors took hold of the young man's other arm, taking some of his weight away. "Sit him there, where there is more light."

A curt nod indicated the edge of the clearing. Okwaho said nothing, struggling with his burden. Ronkwe, the third warrior, he noticed, was kneeling beside their fallen comrade, muttering a prayer.

"Let me see if we can extract it now, or if it would be better to take him back as he is." The man wiped the sweat off his brow, smearing a mixture of mud and dried blood upon it as he did so. The cut on his right arm was still bleeding, and so was the narrow gash on the swollen side of his jaw.

"Lie still." That was directed at Akweks, who was twisting his head in an attempt to see the wound from behind, his face a pasty gray mask, his lips an invisible, twisted line, pressed too tightly to part.

Okwaho's heart squeezed.

"It's nothing. Just a stupid wound." Squatting next to his friend, he peeked at the glittering flint sticking out of the bleeding mess, then took his eyes off as quickly. It didn't look good, that wound, not when they were so far away from home and with no healer around, just the collective knowledge of their fellow warriors, their experience good, but not as good as that of a medicine man. "We'll get it out in no time."

The naked agony in his friend's eyes made him shiver. That and the flicker of fear, too obvious to miss. Akweks was always so brave, so full of jokes.

"How does it look from behind?" The croaking voice was difficult to recognize.

"I ... We'll take care of it. In a short while." He glanced at the man who was busy cutting off one of Akweks' leggings, working around the feathered shaft. "How will you…"

"What do you think?" Grimly, the man muttered something that sounded like a curse. "We pull the point off, break it, then pull the shaft out of the back of his leg, where it entered. Think this is the best of ways to deal with it."

Perturbed, Okwaho watched Ronkwe, who now towered above them, having finished seeing their fallen comrade off.

"We can't stay here. We need to leave fast. We need to reach our people."

He glanced at the greenish foliage that separated them from the trail they were watching earlier, desperate to penetrate its deceptive calmness, to hear anything, an indication. It was not all peaceful out there. He would have bet his most prized of possessions on it, a necklace of bear claws Father had given him for safekeeping when he had left home. Oh, yes, he could have bet even that priceless thing against the claim that the people they came to catch were coming here, heading up the trail, where he had planned to waylay them earlier. His hand sought the softness of the leather bag that contained the necklace, tied firmly to his knife's sheath. The feel of it gave him confidence.

"Take their weapons in the meanwhile." Narrowing his eyes, the man inspected the protruding flint once again, its glow dulled by the bloodied mess, clinging to it, looking terrible, obscene. Sighing, he glanced up. "We are as safe here as we can be. The filthy enemy is dead."

"There are more out there. The people I saw. The people we were looking for before."

"They are all here."

He tried not to avert his gaze, to pay no attention to the disdain and the accusation, both written clearly across his companions' faces.

"No, these are different people. Not the ones we were looking for."

Their stony expressions hardened. "How do you know that?"

He took a deep breath. "The people I saw were going the other way. And they were a smaller group, not as numerous as this one."

More heavy silence.

"They could have split earlier." Shrugging, the first man reached for the wound. "Could have changed their way, too. Followed another trail." As the rough fingers fastened around the slippery flint, digging into the raw flesh to get a better grip, Akweks' suppressed groans filled the air. "You have no knowledge of this forest to arrive at the conclusions you keep coming to. I wonder why our leader chose to listen to you in the first place."

He felt his own sweat breaking out anew, the sight of his friend's pasty features and the barely concealed terror in his eyes mixing with the familiar frustration. They were determined not to listen! He would have spent his time better collecting the fallen enemies' weapons, indeed. Yet, the anguished eyes clung to him, pleading, the grip of the young man's fingers on his own arm threatening to crush his bones.

"I'll be pulling it out now," said the man, addressing the wounded, his tone not unkind. "You two hold him still."

The fingers clenched harder, making his palm go numb. He

tried to get ahold of Akweks' shoulders without releasing his arm.

"Ready?"

He couldn't even nod, watching Ronkwe taking hold of the youth's legs, both of them, the healthy and the hurt one. As though the wounded could do something, give worthwhile resistance, with his damaged leg?

To take his thoughts off his mounting worry and the bloody mess of Akweks' thigh, he scanned the clearing once again. Was he mistaken? Had it truly been just a large group of hunters he had spotted earlier, returning to the village, by separate routes, maybe?

He found himself wishing that was the case, even if it cost him his reputation as a good scout. Was he to return back home disgraced, to leave the Flint People's lands, to never become as good a warrior and leader as Father?

The stab of longing was sudden and piercing. What were they doing back home now? Not in Cohoes Falls, but back in High Springs, in his true home. Like anywhere else along the Longhouse People's lands, the women would be busy gathering crops now, of course; the first, deliciously crisp Green Corn, so tasty and sweet one could gorge on its cobs for days on end, seeking no other treats.

He could feel his friend's agony, seeping through the stretched limbs, the body under his grip arching, making him struggle not to let it go. Wounded and exhausted, Akweks was still spectacularly strong, all energy and muscle. They had grown friendly from the very beginning, on Okwaho's first evening in Cohoes Falls, when Akweks had challenged the newcomer to a spear-throwing contest, amusedly derisive, throwing friendly insults, wagering his spectacularly decorated javelin against quite a few of Okwaho's possessions. His spear was not of the same quality to even the bet.

He suppressed a grin, remembering how desperately he wanted to win, or at least not to shame himself with some especially bad throw, the Flint People's hoop smaller than he was used to at home, more difficult to fit one's spear through as it was sent to roll around too forcefully, too fast. Oh, how he had feared to shame himself by missing all of the throws.

The muffled snap brought him back to the present, to the foreign forest and the agony of his friend.

"Turn him over."

For a brief moment, he just stared, watching the older man as he studied the vicious-looking arrowhead, its polished spark muted under the bloody coverage.

"It came off quite easily." The man shrugged, then threw the precious piece of flint away. "Their arrows are worthless."

Not that worthless, thought Okwaho, supporting Akweks' limp body, trying to turn his friend over as gently as he could.

"It is going to be over soon," he muttered, crouching beside the wounded, desperate to will the stark, twisted features into a calmness he did not feel himself. "Just one more time. It is almost out now."

But he knew it was not, that the most painful treatment was yet ahead. Fiddling with the loosely tied arrowhead was nothing like the actual pulling out of the rough, sturdy shaft. His friend was in for a real test of endurance.

"Hold him tight now!"

He wanted to turn his eyes away but could not, his gaze glued to the stern, bloodied palm taking hold of the ragged shaft just below the colored feathers, tightening its grip, preparing to pull. A heartbeat of hesitation, then Akweks' body shuddered, going rigid as his bubbling scream pierced the air. Muffled by the moss-covered earth in which the youth's face was buried, it still rolled over the clearing, spreading between the trees, startling them all.

"For all the good and bad spirits' sake, keep him quiet!" hissed the man, pressing the struggling patient with his own weight, hands covered with fresh blood, face smeared, hair sprinkled with crimson. "I can't pull it out with all this thrashing about."

Sweat rolled into his eyes, threatening to obscure his vision. Letting the other man handle the struggle, Okwaho took hold of his friend's head, his own trembling hands seeking, running along the sweat-and-mud-covered face, pressing against the gaping mouth, trying to hold the screams in.

As though in a dream, he flattened his limbs against the wet earth, terribly uncomfortable, pressing with desperation, not sure he was not strangling his ward for good, his lips muttering, whispering stupid encouragements, the taste in his mouth revolting, nauseating, making him wish to vomit.

"Help me bandage him." The voice broke into the mindless tide of panic, welcome this time. "Get up and help. Stop lying there like a dead carcass."

Akweks' head was lolling limply in his grip now, quiet for a change. He took a deep breath, then listened. Was his friend still alive? He wasn't sure, and the wild pounding of his own heart didn't help, interfering with his ability to hear.

"Is he still with us?"

He got to his feet with an effort, doubting his capability of keeping an upright position. His legs felt jittery, with no regular firmness to them.

"Cut this thing." A muddied part of Akweks' legging was hurled at him. "Make a few broad strips. They will do for now."

He saw Ronkwe going around, inspecting the scattered bodies, collecting their weapons.

"It needs to be washed."

He stared into the reddish mess of his friend's leg, the swollen flesh, the seeping blood. Seeping, not pulsating. One good thing. It could have been gushing out in a vicious flow, like that other time, with that warrior whose leg was almost severed, cut so deeply that his spirit had hurried to leave too, along with the palpitating flow.

"It will be washed when we are back with our people. For someone who's urged us to leave right away, you are suddenly in no hurry at all, young man."

The returned anger helped. It made the trembling and this strange uncertainty of the limbs disappear.

"For someone who didn't want to listen, you are suddenly all anxious to go," he retorted, not caring for the consequence of his rude response, not this time. Older warriors were not in the habit of taking such talk kindly, but there was a limit to his ability to take the continued goading and the barely veiled accusations.

The eyes of his converser positively glowed. "Watch your

tongue, warrior," he growled. "Do not speak to me again in this way."

It cost him an effort not to drop his gaze, but he did not back away, not this time. Enough was enough.

"We better start moving." Ronkwe's voice broke the tension. "We have a long way to go yet, carrying one wounded and one dead."

"One wounded and one dead! What a useful mission it was," muttered the man, getting to his feet, his eyes dark with anger. "That will teach our leader not to trust young cubs and their stupid observations."

This time, he found it next to impossible not to pounce on his offender, hitting the man hard for the unfounded accusation. Killing him maybe, yes. How dared he? But for Akweks beginning to stir, he would have done the unspeakable, paying with his life maybe; with his honor and good name, for sure. Instead, he found himself rushing toward his friend's side, the grayish pastiness of the stark face and the wildness of the wandering gaze making him forget all the rest.

"I'm taking him down to the river, to make him drink and wash his wounds." He didn't bother to look at them, adjusting one of his arms around Akweks' shoulder, to make the pulling up easier. "You can go back in the meanwhile."

"Still giving orders, you brilliant scout?" Ronkwe's jeering did not make him mad this time, not like before. He was too busy struggling with the impressive weight of his friend's body. "Try not to lose your way when you are heading back."

I hope you lose yours, he thought, swaying but adjusting. The youth was reeling badly, murmuring, his mind clearly still wandering. But for a little bit of help.

He tried to make it look like an easy feat, their derisive gazes burning his back. It was not the wisest thing to do now, to go the opposite way, descending the rest of that hill in order to reach the shore they had left at night, battered, exhausted, and in the heart of the enemy's lands, who were surely aware of their presence by now. Had their people begun attacking already? The distant clamor and the faint odor of smoke told him all he needed to know. And they should have been there, helping to overcome the fence. Not wandering all over the enemy forest. And yet …

Akweks' wound looked bad, the dirty mess at the back of his leg, where the arrow had come out, alarming. It needed a thorough wash at the very least, something their current position at the top of the hill did not offer. There must be a spring up there, of course, maybe more than one, otherwise there would be no fortified settlement there. But to look for such a thing would be impossible now, with the battle evidently developing, keeping everyone busy, the attackers and the defenders, unacceptable to wander a hostile, unfamiliar forest under such circumstances. Back at the river, the wash would be quick and timely, before the bloodied mess could begin rotting for good.

He shivered. The death of rotting wounds was a terrible thing, just terrible. He had heard many stories, and once, when his brother had broken his arm, falling out of a tree and tearing quite a lot of flesh along the way, the damaged limb had actually begun swelling after a day, smelling terribly, the most revolting odor he had ever sensed. He, Okwaho, had been very small back then, barely three, maybe four summers old, but this was something he hadn't ever forgotten. The swollenness of the wound and its smell; and Mother's open fear. She who had always known what to do and how, always sure of herself and opinionated, even with Father sometimes, suddenly scared beyond reason, with all the commotion and running around, healers brought from all over, a messenger sent to Father, who had been at the far west back then, attending an important meeting with the war leaders of the Mountain People, something not to be interrupted by private family matters, but she sent for him all the same; she who had never lost her strength, her confidence before.

He shivered again, then forced his attention back to his present predicament. His brother's wound had healed in the end, leaving only an ugly scar to remember this incident by, where one of the more courageous healers from the False Faces Society had cut the rotting flesh away. But since then, Mother had been hysterical about washing wounds, any wounds, every bleeding scratch. Her endless lecturing on the subject made them roll their eyes, but none of their silly childhood cuts got swollen or painful again, ever.

He bettered his grip on Akweks' torso.

"We'll get you to the river, wash your wounds," he muttered, trying to reassure, whether his friend or himself he didn't know. "Then back to our people, to get that attack on. Take the village, with all its goods, and speed back home. No more rowing against the current, eh?"

Akweks grunted something inaudible, panting, his hobbling terrible, not helping a bit. He could hear the river speeding not far away. A short walk down the path, really. He remembered the way too well by now, having walked this trail three times since discovering it on the last evening. Was it only a day before that they landed upon that sandy shore, with him sensing the local, persuading Akweks to follow the trail of footsteps?

The shouts exploded behind his back, blood-curdling yells that could not be mistaken. War cries! Coming from the clearing they had just left, they left little to wonder about. The locals he had spotted earlier!

Darting to his right, he dragged his groaning friend into the thickest of the bushes, heedless of the wounded's ability, or inability, to walk anymore. There was no time for that. The sound of the surging river was close, offering protection, a possibility of escape. It was still there, reachable, even if not by the trail. But for his companion's previous agility!

Long branches flogged their limbs, catching their clothes, as though trying to hinder their progress. But of course. This forest did not want them here.

"Come on!"

Akweks was practically lying on him, moaning, barely conscious. The sloping ground didn't help. It made him struggle against the incline in addition to the hostile foliage and the limp body he was dragging along.

He felt like giving up, or at least pausing for a heartbeat or two. Just to catch his breath really, to clear his vision. It was full of blurry brown and green, and the wild pounding of his heart made his ears deaf, his throat hurt, his chest about to explode.

The ground turned slippery, and he was barely able to grab a thick branch with his free hand, stopping his fall while still clutching Akweks, not letting him go, however tempting the possibility was.

Blinking, he tried to clear his vision, the gushing of the river assaulting his ears. Had they reached it already? It didn't seem like a possibility. It was too soon.

The view of the treetops swaying in the distance jumped on him, making the halt look like a good thing. They were on the edge of a cliff, the river not far below, but not close enough either, rushing with gusto, inviting no silly ideas. To jump in was a possibility, yes, but not an advisable course of action with unknown waters and a half-conscious wounded hanging on him.

Hurriedly, he scanned the current, recognizing the place they had passed before the landing on the previous day, before hiding their boats in the grove. If he could reach those, they might have a better chance. He could take care of Akweks' wounds, then leave him with the boats, while rushing uphill, to get help. Had Ronkwe and his companion managed to reach their people? But for all the war cries, he might have been hopeful.

He listened intently. The worst of the yells had died away, but he could still hear much noise, people shouting and branches cracking. So close yet!

He leaned Akweks against the tree, wrapping his friend's arm around it. "Hold on to it for a while!"

The youth murmured something, but did cling to his new support, to Okwaho's immense relief. His mind must have been already back in their world.

At the edge of the cliff, he knelt carefully, inspecting the rocky wall. It had footholds, not very wide, but satisfactory. One could climb at least half of it down, until the jump would not look like such a bad thing. But for Akweks' wounded leg! He wanted to curse aloud. No, his friend would not manage even a step of such descent.

The noise was receding, enabling his ears to pick out more sounds. A branch cracked not very far away, then another. His heart went still, then, before he knew it, he was on his feet, rushing toward the sagging figure, tearing him off his rickety support, dragging him along toward the edge.

"Jump, we jump," he breathed out, not trying to make sense of his own actions anymore, following his inner voices instead, feeling better at doing so, as always. "Don't mind your leg, it will be better off in the water, anyway. Just hold on until I get to you. Just do it."

He could feel Akweks' hesitation, and his fear.

"You can do it—"

The familiar hiss cut short anything he might have thought to add, causing his body to twist out of instinct, losing his balance, making his jump bad.

Flailing his hands, he whirled in the air, feeling stupid, spinning around, unable to project his body in the right way, to direct it into the deepest of the water, parting the gushing surface with his legs or hands. Instead, it hit him with vicious firmness, resonating through his limbs, taking his breath away. The eerie silence enveloped him, and then it turned peacefully dark.

CHAPTER 7

The fire arrow swished in the air, brushing past one of the tilted roofs, to slide behind it and disappear into the smoke-filled haze surrounding this part of the fence. A new outburst of commotion followed, with people running around, some quite purposelessly, waving their hands and screaming, or carrying buckets of water.

Clenching one such in her sweaty palms, Kentika paused for a moment, trying to catch her breath, the air stinging, hurting, clinging to the sides of her throat, making them stick to each other, causing her to heave and cough. But for a gulp of a fresh air! Her mouth was so dry, even without the accursed cough that took the last of the blissful wetness away. She fought the urge to dip her face into the bucket she carried.

Resuming her run, she headed toward the smoke-covered part of the fence and the melee surrounding it.

"Bring earth, sand, all sand you can gather!" bellowed a man on the top of a short ladder. It was wavering, making him clutch onto a blackened tip of the fence's pole. "Stop pushing."

Someone's container went flying, splashing the water it held. People gasped, and a few hands shot out, catching the woman who dropped it as she wavered, seemingly about to follow suit.

"Oh, Mighty Glooskap!"

The crowd wavered as another fire-arrow swished, adding to the tongues of flame that were licking the fence.

"Water! Water!" yelled someone. "Bring more water."

Coming out of her trance, Kentika rushed forward, clutching her heavy cargo with both hands, her mind in a jumble. So much fire! And more kept coming. Those lethal arrows! As if it were not enough that the regular ones had taken their toll already, killing a few and injuring more. But now these were bringing fire, spreading so much destruction, so much fear and desperation. How could one put the fire out if more kept coming?

"Here!"

Someone snatched her bucket, relieving her in time to see anther harbinger of fire sticking into the roof of one of the nearby houses, dripping destruction. In the new gust of wind and a momentarily clearing smoke, she saw it was wrapped in something, a sort of a cloth, glittering wet in the flames and the last of the sun.

"Bring more." The bucket was stuck back in her hands, along with a light push into her upper back. "Go, girl, go. Don't stand here and just stare."

"Yes, yes."

Choking on a cough, she rushed back, up the incline and toward the shallow spring that ran through the village, now barely visible in the billowing smoke. The fires were not that bad, not yet, but the wind made the smoke spread everywhere, adding to the panic and the confusion.

Elderly women were orchestrating here, filling offered containers and doling them out, as though distributing food on a day of a ceremony.

"Kentika, come here!" Mother's voice held the usual note of reprimand, so typical when it came to her name being uttered. "Stop running all over."

"I'm not ... not running all over," she gasped, out of breath again. But for the damn smoke. "I'm bringing the buckets to the fire fighters."

A pair of wrinkled hands snatched her empty cargo. "Stay here and help to fill those," said an elderly woman, the oldest member of their clan. "This is what women and girls do." The bucket was full again, pulled up deftly, splashing not a drop. "Let the men do the running and fighting, whether fire or enemy. It is their duty."

"But..."

A furious gaze stopped her words of protest.

"Go bring more kettles and pots. Search through the houses on the other side of the village."

The run down the incline was easier, with less smoke filling this part of the enclosure. She gulped the fresh air greedily, drawing long breaths, as much as the swollen insides of her nose would take. People huddled near the undamaged houses and inside them, children, the sickly and truly elderly, with a few exceptions of young girls, too terrified to be of use.

"What are you doing here?" flared Kentika, spotting the familiar willowy figure of Namaas in the semidarkness of the house she broke into.

"I am ... I'm keeping these people safe."

A few frightened children huddled next to an elderly woman, with another younger one curled on a mat, hugging her huge belly, swollen with child. Kentika gave Namaas a blazing look.

"You cowardly fox. Get that pot from up there and come with me!"

Indifferent to the sobs of her frightened cousin, she searched through the cupboards adjacent to the bark walls. A set of baskets tucked one into another made her smile.

"We'll fill them with earth or gravel. They need it up there too, as much as the water." One more murderous glance directed at the crying girl. "Come!"

On the other side, the smoke was heavier now, billowing thickly, making their eyes water long before approaching the swirling gray. Two houses next to the fence burned fiercely, beyond salvation, although the blackened poles of the palisade were still in place, glowing like embers of the campfire but holding on.

Around the burning houses, people dashed madly, trying to prevent the fire from pouncing onto the next dwellings or back toward the fence. The fire arrows were nowhere in sight, but the regular ones poured in, not densely but firmly, coming down from the sky, like lethal rain of razor-sharp flint.

"Oh, all the big and small spirits!" Namaas' moaning reached her, along with the girl's panted breath, irritating, making Kentika wish to push the disgusting weak-gutted fox away. She was scared as it was, without her silly cousin there to remind her.

Turning violently, she thrust her set of baskets into the girl's trembling hands. "Fill those with earth, all of them." Her voice was taking a shrill note, but she didn't care, her growing anger helping to push away the splashes of latent fear. "Give me that stupid pot, and do as you are told." Her snatching the larger vessel made her cousin waver and almost fall. "Stop clinging to it, and stop being useless. Fill your baskets, bring them to the fire fighters over there, then take them back and fill them again. Be useful!"

"Where are you going?" whimpered Namaas.

She barely managed to avoid the girl's persistent grip, as her cousin tried to grab her arm.

"I'm going to fill that thing with water." The temptation to push the silly fox truly violently, to make her fall, welled, but she fought it, knowing that it was not a decent thing to do. She was as frightened, or maybe more. She was such a coward, no better than this quivering mess of tears. "Go away and be of use, Namaas. Or I'll hit you, I swear I'll do it. I don't care if you tell on me or not."

Back by the spring it was more orderly, either because the elderly women managed to make it all work, like they always did, or because this part of the village was not under attack. No arrows fell from the sky, and no fire threatened to demolish dwellings, to kill people in horrible of ways.

Still, the smell of stale blood and scorched flesh was strong here, and upon reaching the elevated ground, she saw that a part of it was covered with blankets, stuffed with the wounded and those who treated them. So many! She felt the panic coming back, laced with such strong nausea that she felt like choking.

"Come here and help with the wounded!" commanded one of the women, waving at her.

"I ... I have to bring water ... water to the fires." Her feeble muttering was not audible enough even for her own ears.

"Come here, girl. Hurry up. Put your pottery somewhere, for all the forest spirits' sake!"

Still clutching her heavy vessel, she stumbled nearer, the sight of the man groaning on the ground, his face glittering pinkish red, peeling off, with something dripping out of an empty socket where his eye should have been, making her need to vomit grow.

"Hold those for me." A pile of wet clothes were thrust into her hands. "Get rid of the stupid jar!"

The man upon the ground was gurgling, thrashing his limbs. He would break her jar, she reflected, concentrating on this immediate task, finding it safer to think of nothing else. She had to put it somewhere away, out of the wounded man's reach.

"You are not trying to make Kentika help with the wounded, are you?" Her great aunt's voice broke into the hubbub, welcomed if in nothing else than in its familiarity. "Leave her be, sister. Our warrior girl can't be trusted with treating people. She'll do more damage than good." The old woman turned to her, face caked with mud, sprinkled with blood, furrowed with lines of worry but still amused, if only a little. "Go, little niece. Go fight the enemy. Or at least, fight the fire. Fill that jar of yours with water and be gone."

Unable to say a word, Kentika just nodded, clutching her vessel with all her might. Sweat rolled into her eyes, making her blink. The first woman was trying to make the man lie still, but he was struggling, evidently in great pain. Oh, Mighty Glooskap!

"I'll tell Namaas ... tell her to come here and help." It was difficult to recognize her own voice, so low and broken it sounded.

The great aunt nodded sadly. "Yes, do that," she muttered, turning around and heading toward the rest of the wounded. "And any other girls you see."

Back by the smoking fence, people were pushing more frantically, fighting the billowing tongues of flame that were consuming the nearest houses and the tobacco plots, raging unrestrained, eager to spread on to the next buildings.

"Bring it over there!"

A wave of someone's muddied hand indicated the orange tongues that were licking the storage bin, in too close a proximity to the next round house, the gusts of wind showering it with glittering embers. Slipping on the soggy ground, Kentika rushed on, trying to pay no attention to the waves of heat. It was hurtful, the way it scorched her face. She would have covered it with her arms, but for her heavy burden.

"Here, give me that."

Gratefully, she allowed large hands to snatch her cargo, blinking against the waves of heat. People were pressing from all around, rushing and pushing, panic-stricken, so many of them. Some stomped at the flames upon the tobacco plots with their feet, some tried to strangle them with the blankets. The arrows still flew, though not densely and wrapped in no burning cloths now. At least that!

Some men mounted ladders and were shooting back, and just as she shielded her eyes, one ladder came crashing down, with the shooter atop of it waving his hands wildly, his bow flying in an arch.

Jumping away from the path of the falling beams, more out of an instinct than as a thoughtful reaction, Kentika watched the other people scampering, even the two men who were supposed to hold it in place. When it hit the ground, trapping the warrior underneath it, but only temporarily, as the ladder was light, made of thinner beams, she rushed to collect the arrows that slipped out of the shooter's quiver, scattering all over, about to get trampled on. In the commotion, many would have been ruined, and just as they needed each one of the precious weapons.

"Get the ladder off him!"

The shooting man was struggling to push it off, his face bleeding, one leg turned under him, in an unnatural manner. His panting breath added to the frantic cries all around. She concentrated on her spoils.

The polished shafts felt good in her hands, sturdy, dangerous, reassuring. Better than the improvised arrows Schikan made for her small bow from time to time, just sharpened sticks usually, sometimes with a piece of flint glued to it, but not always. It was enough to shoot an occasional rabbit. She needed no more than that anyway, he would claim, laughing against her pleas to receive one real arrow.

Without thinking, she picked up the bow, another precious item lying momentarily unattended, in danger of being stomped on. Some men were dragging the ladder up, pushing it back against the fence but paying it no attention, too busy with the spreading fire. Others came to pick up the injured man.

Like in a dream, she eyed the ladder, a rickety, unsteady structure, with no one to support it, to hold it in place. Still, leaning against the poles of the fence, it offered a possibility.

She fastened her hold on the bow. Long and heavy, unlike her half toy of a weapon, it made her feel better, protected, not as helplessly afraid as before. To climb the rungs of the ladder was easy. It didn't even sway.

The wind tore at her hair, as the protection of the fence disappeared, giving her the view of the familiar outside, the clearing of the open space next to the poles and the swaying trees not very far away from it, down the incline, now dotted with the enemy. This same war paint she had seen only a day before, on the people down the river, toiling with boat; boats that were hidden anew now, tucked safely behind another shore, where the filthy invaders would not find them easily.

Involuntarily, her eyes strayed, seeking the tall figure and the wolf tattooed on a prominent cheek. Of course, it was not possible to see, with the enemy darting between the trees, shooting upwards, then disappearing again. To make the arrows rain upon the settlement, she knew, having been taught all about this sort of shooting. Schikan enjoyed rambling about the secrets of warfare. It made him feel important, she knew, not grudging him any of it but enjoying herself as much. Explaining things to her made him feel like a seasoned warrior with wisdom and experience of many moons.

Between the trees, her eyes picked out two warriors, crouching above what looked like a large jar, dipping their hands into it. Tucking the treasured arrows into the hem of her skirt, having no quiver to put them onto and out of her way, she brought the bow up. It was so heavy! She tried to force her arms into stillness, to make the trembling abate. It was difficult enough to adjust the first arrow, without her hands dancing as though in some strange sort of a ritual. It made her ashamed.

The men between the trees were still there, still kneeling above their jar, holding arrows of their own, wrapping them in dripping cloths. Making fire missiles, she realized, her heart lurching with fright. So this is how they caused the flames to burn, not to die while the arrow was still flying. How devious!

She pulled the bowstring, willing her hands to stop their dancing. It was so terribly tight. Was she strong enough to make the arrow fly at all?

Almost shutting her eyes, she disregarded the hiss of another missile that brushed past the man upon the nearby ladder, making him waver. She needed every grain of her power now, dedicating all of it to the effort of pulling the bowstring.

Her arm on fire, wrist hurting, heart pounding, she felt the sturdy shaft slipping between her pressed fingers, firmer now, rubbing hurtfully against her skin, less rickety than before. When the polished flint touched them, it was almost steady, pointing at the kneeling men, not dancing anymore.

Seeing with surprising clarity, she watched her target for another heartbeat, then let it go.

Oh, Benevolent Spirits, but it was a relief! Her pulling arm felt it first, before the rest of her stretched muscles relaxed. She let it fall, leaning the hand with the bow against the top of the ladder, groping for the next arrow. The warriors between the trees were on their feet, shooting angrily, their jar nowhere to be seen. Her disappointment welled.

"Get down!" yelled the man on the other ladder, himself crouching behind the blackened poles, as much as his unsteady perch allowed him.

She ducked, which made her own ladder jerk. But it let the arrow aimed at her go over her head, to slip against the shattered beams, harmless. The men she had tried to shoot were not aiming at the sky. They were shooting at her! The realization made her lurch as another arrow came, then another. They were true shooters, not needing countless time to reach for the next missile. How did they do this?

Peeking out again, she saw other warriors joining them, waving their hands, cursing most certainly. Her hand pulled the next arrow, acting as though of its own accord. It adjusted more readily, although now, she was crouching in the most uncomfortable of positions, pressed against the splintered top of the pole, leaning on it, not daring to rise again. Not until she was ready to shoot.

The man on the next ladder shot again, then lost his balance and went tumbling down as three arrows at once came after him. Her breath caught, she didn't follow his fall with her eyes, but leaped up instead, barely aiming, releasing her next arrow halfway, having no time to pull it properly.

It was a bad shot. She saw her missile falling down, as harmless as a small bird. Cursing her own cowardice, she did not take cover as her instincts urged her to do, but pulled the next arrow up, seeing a broad man, a spectacular painted warrior, turning in her direction. The long bow clutched in his hand looked light, easy to manage. He brought it up with no visible effort at all.

Struggling with her own weapons that were slipping, twisting in a cumbersome way, refusing to behave, she watched the man's other hand pulling at the string, looking like a porcupine, displaying more arrows clutched between his bent fingers.

Fascinated, she saw him releasing the first as her ladder wavered, shaking her off her rickety perch like a deer would in order to get rid of an annoying fly. The rough surface of the fence hit her limbs as she half-fell, half-slid over it, landing with a thud, splashing the water-soaked mud.

Feet rushed past her, many feet. She noticed the decorations on their moccasins, some muddied, partly torn. Blinking, she tried to make sense out of what happened.

"Are you all right, girl?" Hands grabbed her shoulders, hauling her to her feet.

"Yes, yes." She shook her head in order to clear her thoughts. "The ladder fell."

"Well, no one was holding it for you. You leaped up there telling no one." The squinted eyes examined her anew, worried but amused as well. She recognized the man, a hunter from the Wolf Clan, whose cluster of houses was spread on the other side of the village, one of Schikan's friends and companions. "Quite a warrior you are." His hands turned her over, pushing her lightly in the direction of the fire and away from the fence. "Good shooting, but now go, help the women and the wounded."

"It was no good shooting." Resisting his push, she studied the muddied mess of her dress, her legs bruised and hurting. "I missed, missed both times. Didn't hit anyone."

"You spilled their oil!" The man laughed. "There will be no more fire arrows, not until they bring more, if they have any." Picking up her bow, he rubbed the mud off the wooden shaft. "How did you manage to pull the string all the way? This is a hunters' bow, a serious thing." Another gaze full of amused appreciation and he rushed off in the direction of the fire, to join the fire fighters, she presumed.

Trying not to limp, she followed, her knee hurting with every step, refusing to calm down. Did she twist it? She leaned to inspect the grazed skin once again. Migisso would know what to do. He would know right away if it was damaged or just bruised badly. If only he had been here. And Father!

The thought hit her, making her limbs go numb with fear. What if they were on their way back now, about to run into those fierce warriors out there? *Oh, Mighty Glooskap, don't let it happen!*

Unless they were coming back in force, bringing visiting warriors from Skootuck, maybe. Such things never happened — why would the haughty Skootuck people wish to visit an insignificant village? — but there could always be a first time. Father went there to talk of an alliance, didn't he? He never shared his plans, not with her, and yet she knew. A few overheard conversations, then a questioning of Migisso, and here she was, apprised of Fathers intentions, supporting his ideas, finding them good, useful. Unlike some other people, her doubting brother included. Father never sought reassurance from anyone, let alone from her, and yet if he had, she would have told him that she believed in what he planned.

Oh, but for the possibility of his return with many warriors, and now, before nightfall. Or at least with tomorrow's dawn. To surprise the dirty enemy, to catch them between two fighting forces, to finish them all off. If only there was a way of sending them word.

Her breath caught, and she stared at the shimmering smoky air, seeing nothing, not even coughing anymore. The boats! The enemies' boats they had taken and hidden not far away. If a messenger could sail a light, speedy canoe, like the one she and Schikan had carried together, one could reach Skootuck in a day or so. And then another day to hurry back, and here they would be, maybe in time to save the village. Their people were fighting so bravely. Surely they could hold on for another two days, dousing fires and repelling the worst of the attempts on the fence.

Frantically, she turned around, forgetting her knee, paying the pain no attention. It was receding anyway. Her mind registered this development but barely, too busy with the swelling excitement. She needed to find Schikan. He would listen, if no one else did.

Or maybe…

Her excitement welled. Maybe she could just sneak out on her own. There were so many holes in the fence, so many cracks to slip through. She, of all people, knew all about it.

This, and the shortest way to reach the river. There was no need to take the usual path. Why, she could be sailing before Father Sun's descended into the other world for his night rest, tired of watching the enemy harming the people of his choosing. Oh, she could reach the shore and the boats way before that happened, being firmly on her way, to arrive at Skootuck after high noon, the current being in her favor most of the way.

A group of hunters rushed past her, their bows out and ready, about to climb the ladders, she presumed. Letting them pass, she glanced at the commotion around the burning houses and the blackened tobacco plots, remembering that with Schikan's friend taking her newly acquired bow, she would need to fetch hers as she went. To run out in the countryside full of wandering enemy with no weapon to defend herself was ridiculous.

Shrugging, she slipped away, along the blackened poles of the fence and toward the relative quietness of the remote part of the village.

CHAPTER 8

The darkness dispersed slowly, painfully. As he emerged from its suffocating depths, he felt it closing in on him again, enveloping, trying to pull him back.

For a heartbeat, he stayed there, on the brink, undecided. The oblivion was smothering but tempting. No pain there. The other side offered no such comfort.

Hesitantly, his senses reached out, tasting the water-drenched reality. There was trickling, much of it, everywhere it seemed. It made noise, and it touched him too, splashing very near, licking his limbs, trickling under his nape, caressing it, but in an unpleasant way. It was as though he were a rotten log, a broken canoe, a dead body floating on its own, tossed about, played with by the river, or the mysterious spirits' inhabiting this land.

In panic, he lurched upwards, but the pain exploded in a spectacular show, spreading with many colors, pretty, but offering nothing besides the suffocating darkness again. He retched and retched until his throat convulsed, its muscles going numb from the sharpness of the pain, but the waves kept rolling over his tormented chest, bringing up more of the revolting substance.

Grateful for the hands that pushed him over, he wished they would offer support. It was easier to vomit lying on his stomach, but the necessity to keep his head up, not to let it drop straight into the foul-smelling pool, sapped the last of his strength. It was inconsiderate of whoever was there to do nothing but watch.

"Feeling better?"

The familiar voice made him wish to look up, to seek the owner of it. Still, he didn't find it possible to lift his head any higher, exhausted by the struggle to keep it where it was, in the air and out of the water, his stomach propped on a hard surface, trying not to slip from it, its sharp edges jutting against his skin.

"Okwaho!" the voice repeated again and again, the worry in it obvious. "Okwaho, come on. Stop choking. Drink some water."

The hand grabbed his arm, pulling him, ruining his painfully acquired balance. Though not much strength was applied, it still made him lose his rickety support, rolling down and into the splashing water. The panic was back, mindless, all-encompassing. *He was going to drown!*

Thrashing with his limbs, it took him a while to realize that the water was shallow and calm, the sprinkles marring his vision nothing but the fruit of his own panic.

"Calm down, for all the good and bad spirits' sake!"

The blurry forms of the rocks and the green undergrowth kept swaying before his eyes, making his stomach turn again. This time he knew it was Akweks, the familiar broad face swimming into his view. Pale to the point of frightening, bleeding and bruised badly, the sight of it still reassured him beyond reason. They weren't dead, neither of them.

"Where are we?" he croaked, nauseated by the mere attempt to move his lips. It brought the cough back, the pitiful attempts of his tormented throat to bring out more of the disgusting phlegm. The effort had him doubling with pain.

"Stop talking and drink something. You look terrible. Scary. Like a bad spirit."

If he had any strength left, he would have elbowed his friend before commenting on how bad he looked himself. As it was, he merely accepted the offered drink that was disappearing quickly, trickling out of the cupped palms.

"What happened?"

"We jumped into the stupid river." Akweks was sitting awkwardly, leaning against the nearest rock, his injured leg out of the water, the other washed by the light current. The shore was near, just a rocky strip of land, slightly familiar.

"We did?" He tried to remember. There was a grove, yes, and

the other warriors, and Akweks had been hit. Yes, with an arrow through his leg.

He narrowed his eyes, struggling against the fog, the nausea overwhelming, the clubs hammering inside his skull, determined to shatter it. His hand was heavy as he brought it up, and it shook, the touch of his skin warm and sticky against the trembling of his palm, unpleasantly numb.

"Yes, we did." Grimacing, Akweks leaned forward, pointing vaguely. "But you did it in a lousy way. Nearly cracked your head open."

He touched the sticky numbness again. "It feels cracked."

"It's not. Well, not badly." The youth reclined again, his face awash with sweat, glimmering in the last of the daylight. "When you went down, I thought you did crack it open, went on your Sky Journey. But when I dragged you out, you were gulping air, making stupid noises. So it looked like a good idea to take you along."

"Didn't they try to shoot at us?" Pushing with both hands, he tried to regain an upright position, disregarding the dizziness and the pain that was spreading everywhere. Was he hurt in more places than just the annoying head?

"Don't know. Maybe. By the time we managed to surface, we weren't anywhere around that accursed cliff."

The nausea was receding, and it made his head clear. "You saved my life. I will never forget."

Akweks' generous lips twisted into a crooked sort of a grin. "Don't fret about it. You saved my life before, dragging me to that cliff and over it. I just paid you back."

"Oh, please!" Narrowing his eyes, Okwaho glanced at the darkening trees, the cliff towering above their small inlet, unfriendly, ominous, promising no good. "Where are we?"

"Don't you recognize it?"

He blinked to clear his vision, taking in the narrow strip of the rocky land and the trees towering too close to the water line, its peculiar outline.

"Our boats." Akweks jerked his head, indicating the woods. "Up there."

"Oh, the boats!"

Now the familiarity made sense. So they weren't lost. He let out a breath of relief, then scanned the shore anew. It was darkening rapidly, yet they still could have made their way back to their people. It was a fair possibility. With Akweks limping, yes, but with his, Okwaho's, support…

He blinked forcefully, to make the worst of the headache retreat. How badly was his head cracked? A new inspection produced more of the pulsating stickiness somewhere above his ear. Not as numb as before. Painful, but bearably so. A bit higher, around his temple, and he might have been done for, he thought, shivering, aware of another pain throbbing behind his shoulder. A careful tilting of his head had him staring into a blurry, angrily red spot. Was his back cut too? He remembered the push. Oh, yes, he did not jump off that cliff of his own accord. So it must have been an arrow. Curse them all into the underworld of the Evil Twin!

"We'll sneak back under the cover of the darkness," he said, pleased with his success of maintaining his balance. Swaying and propped with his hands, he was upright and looking as though about to keep it that way.

"Not sure about that." Akweks was struggling too, trying to move his injured leg, using both hands in order to lift it, his face breaking out in a new bout of sweat. "You go… I wait here. Can't go… not yet."

With all the swimming and struggling, his leg looked worse than before, an angry mess of torn crimson tissue, dripping water, and oozing blood, glistening in a bad way.

Okwaho tore his eyes off the unsettling vision. "We'll go together. We'll manage."

Leaving the slippery support, he plodded in the shallow water, grabbing his friend's shoulder, maybe offering help, maybe seeking to support himself, he didn't know.

"Come, we'll get into the woods first. Out of this water and away from wandering eyes."

Taking most of Akweks' weight again, he suppressed a groan, his nausea returning, the throbbing in his head and his shoulder taking away his ability to concentrate. It was difficult not to slip on the glittering pebbles, without the need to watch every slippery step, holding onto another unsteady body. He clenched his teeth tight.

The light was still strong, but it wouldn't be long before it began dimming. Relieved to stand on a steadier ground, Okwaho looked up, studying the bushes. They did not look familiar. And so was the lay of the land. The rocks were not as protruding, and the trees not as close to the waterline at the shore they had hidden their boats at. For some reason, he felt something close to relief. No watchful eyes in this place, no palpable fear or hatred. The woods stared indifferently, not moved by the hobbling intruders.

"Stay here till I check the surroundings."

It was good to be free of Akweks' weight again. He straightened his shoulders, watching his friend slipping along the nearest rock, leaning heavily against its slippery surface.

"The boats can't be too far from here." Wiping the sweat off his brow, Okwaho looked back at the river. "I'll know better when I wander up there, behind the curve."

"They have to be somewhere around," groaned Akweks, his face grayish, lips pressed into a colorless line. "I was sure this was the place."

"Well, it's not, you brilliant scout." Okwaho forced a taunting smile. Anything to keep the panic from rising. "That's a completely different shore. But if our boats are not too far away, then we are better off. I'll get you supplies, something to bite at, and a blanket to keep off the cold. Then you will stay here until I come back. If not," he shrugged, wincing with pain from his wounded shoulder. "If not, then we'll go back together."

The thought of the twisted trail that they followed for a considerable part of the night only a day ago, walking briskly and happily, full of high spirits, filled his insides with ice. How were they to climb it now, battered, wounded, and exhausted?

"Wait here."

Scooping more water, he sprinkled it onto his face, to make the dizziness go away, then straightened up. The narrow strip of sand stretching behind their rocks glittered peacefully in the last of the light, smooth and undisturbed. Yet, something was wrong there, too. He narrowed his eyes, willing the nausea away. Oh, but he needed his senses sharp to survive the upcoming night.

The shoreline curved, then straightened again. It should not be such a long walk, and but for the pain in his back and the clubs pounding inside his skull, he would have been rushing on, unafraid. There were clearly no people around this part of the river, with all the warfare concentrated up there, judging by the clouds of smoke. Had they burned that settlement? The thought made him uncomfortable for a moment. It took much work and many days, or even moons, to build a longhouse. But then, he remembered the ugly, mutilated constructions he managed to look over this very morning, while watching the village from a nearby hill. These villagers did not even live like normal people.

A darker gap in the trees caught his eye, as he leaned against a rock, exhausted. A trail seemed to be starting there, a natural thing, but for the fresh cavities that led to it. Not many and sparsely spread, they glared at him, unmistakable. People had been walking this shore, not very long ago. Maybe half a day, maybe less. And they were careful to conceal their trail.

Perturbed, he knelt to study one of the cavities. Yes, a footprint. The blurry form of a moccasin belonging to a man, a young man, a warrior surely. Or maybe a hunter. Both options boding no good. He thought about Akweks curled behind the curve of the river, wounded, suffering, in no condition to fight back, a perfect captive. And he himself, exhausted, wounded too, even if not as badly. Oh, Mighty Spirits!

All ears now, he neared the trees, spotting more prints as he went. Just a few more, but still footprints. Different looking, this time. Lighter and smaller. The same prints he had followed a day before?

He shivered, then forced himself to drop down in order to study them, even though the clubs inside his skull were busy redoubling their efforts, threatening to make it explode. If he sat, he might have no strength to get up again.

He narrowed his eyes, willing the prints to tell a different story, to show no likeness to the yesterday's local. Same length, same width, but it might just belong to a person of similar size. A boy or a woman, wandering out here? Why would they do that? And through the morning prior to the attack, too, when they must have already known about the warriors, thanks to the same nosy local.

Why would she go out again? And why did he keep thinking of her as a woman? The moccasin prints indicated nothing, not even something peculiar that would help him tell if it was the same person or not.

Catching the trunk of the nearest tree for support, he forced himself back onto his feet, hurrying toward the darkness of the grove now, hoping against hope to find nothing there, no prints and no people, and most importantly, no essential items belonging to his people. It was certainly not the shore they had hidden their boats on.

Under the cover of the thick foliage, the dusk was deep, blocking the last of the light, trying to hinder his progress. It was difficult enough to follow the invisible path, with only an occasional print, without the woods working against him. He muttered a silent prayer, asking for forgiveness at his intrusion, begging the local spirits to pay him no attention, as he would be leaving soon enough.

No sound penetrated the thickening darkness, but he knew he was being watched by the ancient giants and their wards, all the creatures that inhabited this haven. Safe in these foreign woods he was not.

Fighting against the rising wave of the bad feeling, he stopped and listened, then pushed on. It was obvious that the clearing was near, and when he came upon it, he wasn't surprised, neither by its existence nor by the boats scattered all over it. The intruders didn't even bother to hide them. They took the vessels and dropped them at the nearest available place. What lowlifes!

He tried to breathe evenly, to make the panic go away. *What now?*

The longest vessel was sitting on its side, as though thrown out of the river by a rapid current. He inspected its insides, but as expected, the jars of ground maize, some tools, and the additional weaponry stored in it were gone. Filthy thieves!

He tried to think what to do. To take the boats, hiding them in yet another place seemed like a good solution. At least the lighter ones. He was in no condition to drag the two longest vessels. Then, he would have to run back, as fast as he could. Kayeri should know that their canoes had been discovered, had been tampered with. Who knew what else the devious locals had done already?

The inspection of the rest of the vessels brought the same results. Why did he bother with it? The answer presented itself readily, shamefully open. Was he trying to delay the inevitable journey back? And what to do with Akweks?

With the descending darkness, the wind increased, rustling in the bushes, yet suddenly, his skin prickled, and his instincts urged him to crouch behind the nearest boat, his ears pricked. No branches cracked, yet he knew someone was coming, progressing carefully, by stealth. A human or an animal, it didn't matter.

His hand strayed, desperate to locate the club, knowing it was gone, swallowed by the treacherous river. Gripping the hilt of his knife tightly, he felt the pouch that held Father's necklace, still there, secured safely. It calmed the wild pounding of his heart, if only a little.

A new gust of wind brought a measure of moisture in it. From the river, possibly, but he checked the sky. Was it going to rain?

A figure appeared between the trees that shielded the view of the shore. Just a silhouette, progressing hurriedly. He cursed his lack of appropriate weaponry again. But for the long, decorated bow and quiver of arrows, each having its special feathering, colored in gray, commemorating his personal guiding spirit. His left hand slipped, searching the ground. A stone or a log, anything that could be thrown would do.

The figure paused, as though trying to reach with its senses too, still shielded by the trees, unsure of itself. When it headed out, its back was turned to him, and he seized on his chance, pouncing in one desperate leap, pushing the boat away with his feet as they slipped against its craggy surface, welcoming the advantage its elevated position gave.

He saw the intruder turning, responding with swiftness by

bringing her bow up. Reacting fast, he lurched sideways, but didn't lose his balance, the sharpened stick that she loosened swishing beside his face, scratching his ear, leaving a stinging sensation. In the next heartbeat, he was upon the shooter, colliding with her in such force that they both went down tumbling.

His senses screaming for a kill, he pinned his victim to the ground with his entire weight, his eyes taking in the wide, terrified face belonging to a young girl, her eyes huge and round with terror, mouth gaping, the gentle skin of the throat convulsing under the pressure of his knife.

Bewildered, he froze, trying to understand. Her eyes seemed as though about to pop from their sockets, but as he moved his blade away, they focused, flickering with resolution.

His nerves stretched to their limits, he backed away slowly, desperate to control the trembling of his limbs. Who was this girl? What did she want in this place?

Her bow jutted against his thigh, and as he eased away, he looked at it, remembering that she had shot at him with this thing. Before any more memories and conclusions surfaced, her hands flew up, fingers claws, darting for his eyes, just as her freed leg folded, smashing into his groin, taking his breath away with the suddenness and the viciousness of her thrust.

Fighting the pain, he shut his eyes against her assaulting nails, trying to keep out of her reach, while desperate to capture her wriggling body again, to render her wildly flailing limbs harmless. She was like a mad creature, like a fish plucked out of the river, thrashing about with no consideration to a reasonable way of behavior, beating at him with anything she could.

"Stop it," he groaned. "Just stop it!"

But her left hand managed to get ahold of his face, and the pain that tore at his skin, running down his cheek, informed him that her nails were as dangerous as a flint knife and worse.

Blind with rage, he tore her hand off his face, feeling the other one breaking free, pouncing at him. Yet, his fist was faster, and as it smashed into the general direction of her head, he felt her body going blissfully limp.

Afraid to lower his guard, he stayed thus for another heartbeat, then another, listening to the forest. Could it be that she wandered these woods all alone?

His face burned, and his vision refused to focus. Did she manage to hurt his eyes after all? Not to mention his lower body that still screamed with pain, his groin on fire. The damn wild fox!

He blinked forcefully, then moved away, tearing the bow from her lifeless hands, just in case. As his vision focused, he inspected her, then, satisfied, felt out his own injuries. His cheek stung, the warm abrasion starting directly under his eye. The rotten piece of meat! Just a little bit higher and he would have been left with no ability to see.

Getting up with an effort, he examined the bow, then broke it in two and threw the splinters away. A silly toy, not much larger or more complicated than the bows young boys used to practice with, shooting rabbits and small game. The damn girl, what was she thinking? Why did she attack him like that?

He watched her, uncomfortable, as she sprawled there helplessly, in a ridiculous manner, her limbs spread wide, the dress askew, indecently so, face twisted, mouth opened, trickling blood. Not a pretty vision.

What do you do with her now? he asked himself.

The answer presented itself readily. You dump her in the river, possibly slitting her throat beforehand. She could not be left here, to wake up beside their stolen boats, not such a warlike, fierce thing. She would be sure to rush and get help from wherever she had come. The attacked village up there? Maybe, or maybe some other settlement. There was no telling how those people lived, how they spread around these forests.

He bent to cover her legs, then hesitated again. Her eyes were partly opened, showing only the whites. The sharpness of her cheekbone was blurring on one side, swelling into shapelessness. His blow must have been vicious enough. Damn the stupid wild fox into the underworld of the Evil Left-Handed Twin. He could not just slash her throat or drag her into the river. Or could he?

She shuddered, and he took a step back, readying his knife. Her limbs twitched, and a light moan escaped her lips as she blinked, tossed her head, then went back into her wandering state, displaying once again the frightening whites of her eyes.

This time, he cursed aloud.

CHAPTER 9

She listened to the voices, afraid to breathe, or even open her eyes for that matter. They were talking quietly, in whispers, relatively calm, clearly unaware that she was now awake.

Earlier, when she came back to her senses, her panic almost got the better of her. Yet, something prevented her from screaming or trying to spring to her feet, something cold but firm, like a supporting hand on her shoulder, calming, encouraging, but in a distant manner. So she stayed where she was, lying upon a revoltingly muddy surface, with a multitude of small stones jutting against her cramped limbs, her head pounding, face on fire.

The monotonous hum of the water told her she was still near the river, on some lower shore and not a high bank. It should have calmed her, but didn't. Instead, it frayed her nerves. The foreigners' voices that accompanied it took the magic of the murmuring river away.

Uncomfortable and cold, she didn't dare to move, to disclose her state of awareness. They seemed to pay her no attention, talking urgently, in whispers. Only two men, according to what her ears told her, and not as sure of themselves as on the day before, when she had spied on them and their companions, who were now busy shooting fire arrows over her village's walls. Filthy lowlifes! The returning wave of anger helped. It made her forget her fear, lessened the desperate pounding of her heart, enabled her to listen.

"It doesn't make sense," repeated one of the men, his voice low, trembling. *Was he afraid?*

"Stop saying that and let me think." The other one was firm, if low and strained. *The voice of her captor, the man with the wolf tattoo, the one she had watched on the day before, scared of him even back then, when an entire hillside separated them, when he didn't know about her existence at all.*

The fear was back, gripping her insides; the memory of his powerful leap when he lunged at her, paying no attention to the pointed bow, nor to the arrow that flew at him, disregarding those, his entire being dedicated to the purpose of capturing, harming. A true beast, out of the worst of the stories. A Malsum, a bad wolf spirit, the evil twin of the good Glooskap. There was no wonder he managed to make her lose her senses so quickly. It was a wonder she was still alive. Or was she?

She moved her feet lightly, then her hands. They were not tied, and it was a good thing. Maybe she could manage to sneak away, somehow. Just to get to the river. They would never be able to track her there.

"But how did they get there? How?" insisted the first voice, rising a little. "Are you sure it was not the same shore?"

"No, it wasn't." The owner of the tattoo nearly growled now, his teeth evidently clenched, making his words come out muted. As though she had no difficulties understanding their foul-sounding tongue as it was. "I'm not blind. I can recognize a shore when I see one."

"How did they get there?" repeated the troubled man, forgetting to talk quietly again.

"The filthy locals found them." The growling was deepening, making Kentika shiver. He had a wolf tattoo for a reason, that much was obvious. Would he tear her to pieces when he found out that she was still alive? Oh, Benevolent Glooskap!

"What locals? They are all up there, fighting."

"Well, obviously not all of them." The sound of a hurled stone made her nearly jump, her eyes tearing open of their own volition, needing to see the danger, to face it, the trembling of her limbs impossible to control.

It was deep into the evening, she discovered, and the wind tore at the treetops, making them sway in an unfriendly manner. The sky peeked through the gaps it created, dark gray, free of clouds.

"There were prints there. I'm sure there were," went on the angry voice, uninterrupted. "I should have stayed and checked for those before the light faded. But for the filthy fox!"

Another hurled stone tore the ensuing silence, accompanied by a muttered curse. It bounced off some other rocky surface, and her eyes shot in that direction, regardless of her will, taking in the view of the forest line, and the muddy clearing ragged with cliffs, limiting this treeless patch of land all the way to the river behind her.

They were squatting next to one of the rocks, two dark forms, rigid and tense, one of them half turned to her, his features drawn and pale, smeared with mud as he sat there awkwardly, leaning against the uneven surface, most of his lower limbs coated with dried blood.

To her endless relief, he seemed to be paying attention to little else but his companion, whose wide, bruised back was facing her, splattered with a generous amount of old blood as well. Thank all the good spirits for that. He didn't see her!

Easing away as carefully as her reeling head and trembling limbs allowed, she tried to slip backwards, to reach some sort of a cover while attracting none of their attention. They seemed to be immersed in their own troubled dilemmas, wondering about something that was missing, too busy to guard her, although the wolf man did bother to bring her here. Why? Why didn't he killed her and been done with it?

She felt her arms slipping, struggling not to lose the support of the muddy ground. She needed to get away from this man, and fast.

"Why did you drag that stupid thing here?" The wounded man's voice piqued again, echoing her thoughts. "Why didn't you throw her into the river?"

"Would you shut up?" The words of the wolf man slashed viciously, shaking the thickening darkness. "Why scream at the top of your voice, eh? Why not shut up and let me think?"

Her palm felt the solidness of a rotten log, and it reassured her, brought her back from the brink of panic his voice had encouraged. Not a satisfactory means of hiding, it still gave her some sense of protection, making the trembling subside. The river was very near, its murmuring calming, offering safety. If only they kept busy for a few more heartbeats.

A futile hope. The gaze of the wounded man met hers as she slipped behind the log, desperate to flatten her limbs, to make herself invisible. His eyes widened, and if she thought his frown was deep before, it was nothing compared to the scowl that twisted his fine-looking features now.

"She is getting away," he breathed, but his companion needed no warning. In the next heartbeat, he was beside her, having not bothered to straighten up as it seemed, let alone run or leap. Did he just fly through the air?

His grip on her upper arm was firm, stony, impossible to break. Still, she fought it. To squirm on the slippery bank was easier than in the closeness of the woods. He had a difficult time maintaining his own balance while struggling to pull her to her feet. Letting him take most of her weight, careless of the fall that was probable to ensue, she kicked at his shin, and his muffled groan was music to her ears.

As the world swayed, and the wet ground met them both, his grasp on her arm slipped, and she half-scrambled, half-rolled away, charging toward the safety the murmuring of the river promised, blind with panic. The slick, moss-covered rocks hit her limbs as she stumbled through them, using her hands and feet to keep moving, the only sounds reaching her the deafening thundering of her heart pumping in her ears, urging her to rush on.

Another slide down the slippery stones and the water enveloped her, cold but refreshing, taking her into its embrace, pushing the mindless fright away. Surprised, she didn't have time to gulp enough air, but the fright was receding. She could swim like a fish; and hold her breath, too, for longer than many boys she used to compete against.

Her confidence restored, she kicked for the surface, intending to dive back right away, but the motion didn't help. The darkness and the thickness of her surroundings remained the same, with its distant humming and distorted sounds.

Another kick, this time desperate, and she realized, through the returning wave of panic, that something held her back, clutching onto her dress, but not in a painful way. The rocks; it was caught between the rocks!

This time, the dread swept back, overwhelming in its intensity, as she pulled, flapping her arms in a frenzy, gulping the muddy water, oblivious of reason. Her efforts were helped by a hand yanking on her arm, dragging her up, fighting the grip of the river. Still, the water was all around, closing on her, stinging her nostrils and eyes, claiming her life forces for itself, so dark it was like an underworld of the evil spirit wolf Malsum. Speaking of wolves!

When the darkness of the night was back, she had no strength left to do anything but curl up on the slippery stones, trying to breathe the cool crispness of the air in between the wild retching. It was bad enough that she hurt all over, but the inability to breathe properly, and just as she needed it the most, was terrible, draining her of the last of her life forces.

"What a wild thing," he was muttering, standing very close, keeping his guard. Did he think she had any strength left to try to run away again? But for the complete lack of it, she might have glared at him. He was so stupid!

When the struggle for breath lessened and she could hear the wind and the constant hum of night insects, instead of a blurry buzz in her ears, he hauled her back onto her feet with as little consideration as before, not picking her up but supporting while navigating their way back onto the shore. Too disoriented to resist, this time she let him lead, welcoming the strength his body radiated, as her own trembled too badly, from cold now as much as from the entire experience.

The wind tore at them cruelly, and the fact that it seemed to do nothing to add to his discomfort confirmed the worst of her fears. He was a bad spirit and not a human at all. Still, his body radiated warmth, and their walk took her away from the merciless darkness of the swirling current. The river at night was not the friendly being she had come to know and trust.

The wounded man made a face, but said nothing, moving a little to make a space for them both under the cozy protection of his cliff. It was darker here but warmer too, with nothing but a light breeze penetrating the towering rocks.

"Pity we can't make a fire," he said, giving them both a skeptical look. In the silvery light of the broken moon, it was easy to see the teasing glint of his eyes, the only thing alive in the grayish pastiness of his face.

"We can, and we will," said the wolf man firmly, although his teeth were clattering. So maybe he was also cold. The realization reassured her somehow, as she huddled under the protruding stone, hugging her legs, keeping as far away from her captors as possible. Every little distance helped. As long as they didn't try to talk to her, or touch her, she knew she could keep her returning panic under some sort of control.

"The fire will draw attention." The wounded man sounded agitated again.

"We'll keep it small, and as smokeless as possible." The wolf man did not attempt to sit down, although now his exhaustion was showing, expressed in sagging shoulders and the way he went about picking dry branches, in a listless sort of a way, untypical to what she had learned about him so far. "We can't do without a fire at all. We'll freeze, and who knows what will come out of these woods to feast on us." A glance shot at the dark mass of trees made the other man tense so visibly, she shuddered too, almost afraid to look but peering at the silent giants nevertheless. They were swaying lightly, rustling in an unfriendly manner. But of course they were. Why would their woods welcome the intruders?

"You wanted to go back."

"Yes, of course. But later. First, we make sure you and the filthy fox are well settled." His gaze leaped to her, bringing her fear back redoubled. There was a question in his eyes, a firm, unwavering suspicion, a cold calculation. He wanted something from her. Oh, great and small spirits!

"You don't mean to make me stay here and guard your precious spoil?" protested his wounded companion, his eyebrows meeting each other across his wide forehead, the amused sparkle gone. "That wild thing? Unless you tie her with a rope we don't have, I won't be able to chase her all over the way you do. Even if I wanted to." The amusement was back. "You are in no position to take captives, you lusty warrior. Not yet. Wait till you hear from our people."

"I don't want her!" The wolf man's voice piqued the way his companion's had before, when they were discussing their troublesome situation. He took his eyes away, then went toward a nearby pile of branches. "You are so annoying sometimes, Akweks. Stupid and annoying." His voice trailed off as his form began fading into the night. "Wish you would not talk so much."

The wounded man just chuckled, then busied himself with trying to organize the meager pile of firewood that was in his arms' reach without the need to get up. From close up, she could see that it was his left upper leg that troubled him the most, his thigh a mess of glaring tissue and seeping blood. Not a wound to get stuck on a foreign shore with, she decided, relieved. When the other one left, she would be free to run away. Good!

"What are you staring at, girl?" he said, making her heart jump in fright. He didn't look up, busy checking a flat, round stone, but his voice was still amused. "I wish you could speak our people's tongue and not some foreign blabbering. Maybe you would have helped us, eh?"

The stone was laid carefully near the pile, as he began searching again. For another one, she realized. Were they going to make fire by rubbing pebbles? It would take them half a night to get a spark, stupid foreigners that they were. But then, of course, with no good flint pieces or a stick and a bow to make the process easier, what choice did they have?

"I wish you would look more passable, too," he went on, dreamily. "What did he find in you, the stupid buck in heat that he is? You aren't pretty by any means."

She clenched her palms tight, but the temptation was too big to resist. "Not as ugly as you and your stupid people are."

It came out well, the best phrasing she could get out of their strange, twisted tongue. He dropped the stone and was staring at

her as though she had just sprouted another head. It made a funny
sight. His eyes turned as round as two wooden plates, and his
mouth was so gaping she was afraid a mosquito would fly in.

She laughed mercilessly and didn't care how loud it came out.
"Ugly and stupid, yes. More stupid." She tried to remember
words of cursing, something, but nothing came to mind. Neewa
hadn't cursed. She'd had such a pleasantly measured way about
her, so delightfully interesting to talk to, or rather to listen.
"Disgusting people, yes, that's what you are." He was still staring
at her, bereft of words, and she forgot the attempt to talk correctly.
"What stare for, eh?"

"It can't be," he murmured in the end, blinking painfully.
"How can you talk our tongue?"

"My people smart. Yours stupid. That's how," she said, so very
pleased with herself.

Then her sense of well-being evaporated at once, as the
silhouette of the wolf man materialized out of the darkness, his
arms loaded with branches.

Sensing the tension, he stopped dead in his tracks.

"What?" The short word pierced the air like a flint arrowhead.
His eyes brushed past her, then rested on his friend, piercing.
"What happened?"

"Your filthy fox…" The hesitant arm of the wounded came up
as the man cleared his throat. "She can speak."

"What?"

The annoying wolf man kept repeating himself, making her
wish to tell him some of the things she told his companion while
he was gone. But for the crawling of her flesh, she might have
tried. She had nothing to lose, really, and their knowledge of her
command of their tongue changed nothing. And yet, she kept
silent, wishing to disappear into the surface of the cliff she was
huddling against.

"I just told you, she speaks our tongue."

"She does?" His eyes leaped back to her, making the battle
against her fear more desperate. "You do?"

She pressed her lips and said nothing, busy trying to stand the
intensity of his gaze. Another heartbeat of staring and his brow

darkened as though his earlier scowl was not enough.

"You do understand me, that's obvious." His shrug related a fair measure of disdain, as he went to dump his armload of logs onto the ground.

"Get busy working with the stones," he tossed toward his friend, pulling smaller branches out of the pile, arranging them quickly and surprisingly prettily, as though building a tiny tent. Dumfounded, she watched him working, her mind blank, clear of thoughts.

"You," he looked up sharply, "don't make any more trouble. I don't want to hurt you, but I will if you keep making trouble."

She licked her lips. "What want from me?" It came out strangely, unnaturally high. She cleared her throat. "What want?"

He picked up a flat stone and began rubbing it against another. "I want to know who took our boats."

Her breath caught, she watched his hands moving rhythmically, stroking the stones, his palms large and weathered, full of fresh scratches and cuts. The silence prevailed, a strange, indifferent silence. It was as though they all waited for something to happen.

"Why would she know something like that?" asked the wounded, his own attempts with the stones not looking promising, lacking in the determination his companion seemed to have in abundance. "She is just a girl."

"She knows." The wolf man doubled his efforts, as the rare sparks his stones produced did nothing to the meager pile of dry grass that the wind was trying to scatter, causing him to stop every few heartbeats in order to rearrange his treasure. "She was running around there for a reason, armed with a bow, ready to shoot at people. Weren't you, warrior girl?"

Grateful that he was too busy to look at her, Kentika fought the urge to bring her palms to her cheeks, which were suddenly burning despite the cold.

"What were you doing there?" This time, he looked up, causing her stomach to tighten in a painful way.

"Nothing." She swallowed, but it didn't help. Her voice was just too high, shrill in an ugly, or maybe funny, sort of a way.

"Nothing, eh?" His laughter wasn't a pretty sound either, lacking in true mirth. "After I'm done with this fire, you will have to tell me what I want to know. Then I'll take you back to your village, *unharmed*." There could be no mistake at the hardening of his voice. "I want nothing else from you, and there is no need to make it all ugly." His hands never stopped, striking the stones in an even, somehow calming way. She watched them, fascinated. "You are from up there, aren't you?"

The thought of her village hit her, the desperate fighting that she had managed to forget while dealing with her own mounting troubles. Oh, Mighty Glooskap, were they still shooting up there, dousing the fires, lining the walls with their bows clutched tightly? Now, at night? It didn't seem like a likely possibility, but with the fierce foreigners, one never knew.

"Where is my bow?" It came out hoarsely, as opposed to her previous squeaking way of speaking.

He frowned at the scattering pile, then shifted slightly, his back toward the river, trying to block the wind.

"Back there." The light motion of his head indicated the curve of the river. "I broke it. It was a lousy bow."

Gasping, she stared at him, forgetting her fear. "It was a good bow," she said, quiet as a breath in the end. "You... you bad, really bad people, person. Lowlife, bad spirit. Like Malsum, bad wolf spirit." The tears were near, tears of anger and frustration, tears of rage. He broke her bow! How dared he? "You terrible bad. I hope you die badly—"

"Stop yelling!" He glared at her, not amused anymore. "You shot at me. In a lousy way, like a child would, but you did. So what did you want me to do?" He shrugged, then went back to his attempts to make fire. Unsuccessful attempts. He was lousy at doing that. She wished the wind would come in force, scattering them all. *Killing them.* "Anyway, it was a child's bow, to shoot at rabbits, not people. You should have tried a real one. That is, if you managed to pull a string of a real weapon."

That was too much. "I manage. I shot real bow, I did. Killed one warrior, your people." There was no harm in embellishing the truth. He had no way of proving otherwise, and she had shot a real bow, difficult as it was. She had made the jar of their people topple and break, stopping the fire arrows. "I shot a real bow. It was easy, not difficult at all."

He glanced at her with open doubt, before returning to his stones. "Well, you should have come after me with that real bow of yours." His grin was sudden, startling in its lightness. "You came after me with a toy. What did you expect me to do?"

The other youth leaned forward, forgetting his efforts to get a spark. "She shot at you, and you broke her bow? How stupid is that!"

"What?"

"We could use a weapon, couldn't we?"

"A toy bow? Oh, please!" But there was a defensive note to his voice now, and she felt something close to satisfaction. He had acted stupidly. Even his friend thought so.

"As weaponless as we are now, I could use a bow, even the one meant to shoot at rabbits." The wounded's gaze was merciless in its suggestiveness. "Or to make that fire without rubbing my hands to nothing. Any bow would help us with that."

The wolf man just grunted.

"It was a toy bow," he insisted. "It was of no use."

She wished she had a real bow at hand, or maybe a knife. Her anger kept gathering, pushing her fear away. It was a good feeling. She watched the grass whispering, turning dark in some places, yet every time a spark would catch, the wind would strangle the tiny flame, despite his attempts to cup it with his palms. The wind was always faster. Of course, it was.

"Can't make fire with no bow," she said. "Rub stones, pebbles is stupid."

"Not as stupid as it is to run around the woods with a toy, shooting at people, and just as your village is about to be taken," he retorted. "That is a real stupidity."

But this time, she was prepared. "Better run woods, enemy woods, with no bow at all, eh? Then break one, one that you do get. Real stupidity, yes. Oh, yes, real stupidity."

The way he looked at her made her afraid again, but the open laughter of his friend was encouraging for some strange, unexplained reason.

"Stop talking. You understand nothing, and we have no time for this." His stones struck each other so forcefully it was a wonder no pieces flew off instead of sparks, which now stopped coming as well. "And you, Akweks, if you don't stop laughing, I'll leave you here with no fire. And with that wild thing to keep you company, to try and kill you maybe, eh? She is well capable of doing something like that."

"Oh, but she did get you there, brother." The sprawling youth almost doubled in a paroxysm of laughter. "She is right, you know?" Receiving another direful scowl for an answer, he made an obvious attempt to calm down, still trembling with mirth. "It's just too funny to watch you two bickering, like my sisters when forced to sort maize together."

Both grinding stones went flying, bouncing off the nearby cliff. "Would you shut up!"

The outcry made Kentika go rigid with fear. Oh, this man was a bad spirit all right, still a mere youth or not. She could feel his rage seeping through the darkness, spreading in the coolness of the night air, filling it with poison.

"It isn't funny, this entire thing." He was making a visible effort to calm down, his voice low but still trembling, still vibrating with rage. "You are wounded badly enough to be stuck here, and what do you do? You laugh about it. Well, it isn't funny." His drawn breath tore the silence. "Our scouting mission failed, and we are stuck here with the others dead. While our people are also stuck up there, and only local spirits know what possible surprises are heading their way." He kicked at the pile of logs, sending some of them scattering. "Our boats are found. Do you realize that? The locals weren't surprised. They were prepared, and something is telling me we are the ones who are in for a surprise." Suddenly, he whirled around, facing her, making her heart lurch again. "Your people knew we were approaching, didn't they?"

But for the solid stone behind her, she would have tried to back away, to put as much distance between herself and the power of his menacing presence as possible.

"They had taken the boats and they got ready?" One long, forceful step and he was towering above her. "How did they know?"

She pressed deeper into the uneven surface, clenching her arms tighter around her bent legs.

"Why do you think she would know any of it?" The other youth's voice held no more mirth, ringing as eerily in the wind-stricken darkness.

"Because she does." His voice calmed all of sudden, as he knelt beside her, making no attempt to touch her. At least that. "Tell me what I ask you, and I will let you go. I will not harm you, I promise. Even when we take your village, I will make sure you are not harmed." His eyes narrowed. In such close proximity, it was easy to see what they held, anger, yes, frustration, most certainly, but there was something else in there too, something reasonable that made her taut nerves relax, if only a little. "There is no point in keeping secrets now. Our warriors are up there, and they will know about the boats the moment I reach them. If you tell me now, it will change nothing." He took a deep breath. "Yes, it will help us, but we will be successful anyway, so there is no need to anger us now. Tell me where the rest of the boats are, and I will let you go."

The urge to trust him welled, but she fought it fiercely, not about to be deceived. If her telling him the whereabouts of the boats did not matter, then why was he so anxious to hear about it anyway, before he went looking for his people?

"I don't know boats, your boats. I know nothing about it."

His jaw tightened. "Yes, you do. If you didn't know, you would have told me that before."

"I could tell nothing. You were yelling a lot. You didn't let talk."

His gaze turned piercing. "What were you doing out there now?"

"Nothing." Oh, Mighty Glooskap, she did sound silly, didn't she? His narrowing eyes told her that. "Nothing to do with the boats, that is. And the other things, the attack and all that." As always, under stress she talked better, more eloquently, in her tongue or in a foreign one. The realization pleased her, ridiculous as it was. "I no lie. No boats."

He drew in a deep breath. "For your sake, I hope you are not lying." Pressing his lips, he got to his feet, as nimble as before, his tiredness gone, or not as evident. "I can't let you go, not yet, not before I get to our people. You two will have to stay here until I come back. Hopefully, before dawn." His gaze returned to her, as reassuring as before, direful scowl or not. "I will not return alone, but don't be afraid. I will make sure you are left unharmed."

"You realize that I won't be able to chase her the moment she decides not to wait for your return." The other youth's voice held a measure of urgency now, reminding her of the moment when she came back to her senses and was listening to them before trying to get away.

The wolf man's gaze turned thoughtful, even if as piercing as before. "You won't get far, running around these woods at night."

Neither will you, she thought, but this time she had enough presence of mind to hold her tongue. He was leaving, letting her off without telling him a thing. He was such a lousy interrogator!

"My promise not to harm you when your village is taken holds if you stay here until I come back for him."

"You will not take my village." She didn't regret saying that. His arrogant self-assurance was just too much. "We fight, fight your people off. Half day, shoot them. Take..." She hesitated, searching for a proper word. "Take fire off, not let the houses burn."

The intensity of his gaze grew. "You were there?"

"Yes." But the doubts were gnawing again. Was she telling too much?

"How did you get out?"

"Oh." Frantically, she tried to think. "Yes, mistake. People not notice..."

Even in the darkness, she could see his eyebrows climbing quite high. "People not noticing, maybe. But warriors?" He shrugged, shifting his weight from one foot to the other. "Wish I had the time, or means, to make you tell it all. As it is, I'll have to trust your good sense."

He was kneeling beside his friend now, talking in whispers. Still an impressive form, even in the darkness, battered and tired. How would one get stuck in the woods, nearly weaponless and with a wounded friend, so far away from his warriors' forces, and still look every bit the forceful, imposingly dangerous presence she remembered from the previous afternoon, while observing him from a safe distance—had it happened only yesterday?—as lethal and unrelenting as the animal spirit tattooed on his cheek. And yet, he was nothing but an annoying youth, incapable of dealing with matters that required more than just fighting, clearly caught beyond his experience and abilities. Some interrogator!

"If you do something treacherous or silly, you will pay for that dearly. I'll see to that." His parting words sent a shiver down her spine, as she watched him disappearing down the steep bank.

CHAPTER 10

Migisso fought his uneasiness down, desperate to show none of his fear.

"You just keep an eye on them," whispered Achtohu. "Make sure they are going nowhere. Don't shoot unless you see them about to leave. Or to attack you." He hated the wink that accompanied the last of the youth's words. "We'll be back shortly."

Clutching his bow in his sweaty palms, Migisso just nodded, beyond words. He only hoped his helplessness didn't show.

The enemy warriors, only two of them, crouched lazily, bending over a pile of arrows, checking their flint tips, fastening those that, probably, felt loose. Not as wary or on guard as one would expect the warriors attacking a village to be, but then, no attack was mounted on this part of the grove, near the farthest side of the fence.

It seemed to be quiet on the other side as well now, although the ground leading toward this part of the village showed evidence of the earlier attempt to storm the settlement, the invaders' efforts obvious, manifested in patches of blackened palisade and the heavy stench of the burned wood and goods lingering in the air, refusing to disperse, permeating one's breath, a solid testimony.

Still, from what Migisso's companions managed to gather, sneaking around, careful to keep their presence a secret, a surprise, the invaders were attacking in a ridiculously small force, maybe barely twenty men. An encouraging discovery.

The moon was bright, too bright, painting the surrounding

woods in unfriendly colors. He wanted to wave a fly away but dared not. If these warriors saw him, he would be dead in a matter of heartbeats. He could shoot fairly well, but the warriors were no hunted deer. He had learned all about it earlier today, back in the clearing. With the enemy, one has no time to take aim, to analyze the situation. It was run and shoot, then tear the next arrow out of your quiver and shoot again, all in a matter of mere heartbeats. No time to think, unless you thought very fast. And he was famous for just the opposite.

He shivered, remembering that clearing, and the bodies spread upon it, the ground muddy with blood and discharges and smell, such a stench. The enemy were few, only two warriors, wounded and battered, and yet they swung their clubs and ducked arrows with not a flicker of hesitation, charging forward, set on the killing. If not for the fast reaction of their men, who shot arrow after arrow, with the practiced skill of warriors and not only hunters, it might have developed into a battle. As it was, the enemy was dead before having an opportunity to engage.

Before he, Migisso, had an opportunity to shoot his first arrow. How shameful. He was left to check the other bodies, to find out if those were their people who had been killed, while the rest of the men rushed to chase the remnants of that scouting party. It was evident that some of the enemy got away after the first battle, before their arrival. The uneven blood-stained path trailing off the clearing let them know that.

He shook his head, then concentrated on his current observation. Why was he left alone to keep an eye on these warriors? What were his companions planning as a means of surprise? They were fairly few, eight men in all. They could not face twice as many hardened, evidently veteran fighters. Unless aided from within. Is that what they wanted to do, to try to contact their people from behind the fence, to time an attack?

The grove to his left beckoned. He remembered the elevated side behind the ceremonial grounds, where a thick maple tree was spreading its branches, giving its blissful shade. Aside from the early spring dances celebrating the wonderful gift of maple sap, this corner of the village was usually neglected, used by the children for play.

And yet, if one was to sneak behind the giant of a tree, to slip between its branches and the fence, one could find the loose pole and a gap wide enough to squeeze through. Kentika was proud of her discovery, swearing him to secrecy before showing him her favorite way out. Not that she wasn't allowed to go in and out as she pleased. It's just that, evidently, his wild sister needed to sneak away more often than that. For a girl of her age, much chores needed to be completed before her free time would come. Also, he suspected, she liked the thrill of unauthorized sneaking away rather than just going out. To walk through the entrance like any other person would be boring, mundane, not challenging or offering a sense of adventure.

Was she well in there now? Unharmed? He fought the tightening in his stomach. What did she do while under attack?

It was so strangely quiet. The warriors crouching next to the fence were talking in whispers, and he wished he could understand what they said. Should he just leave now? Sneak away and go look for his companions? If they wanted to connect with the people inside, they may welcome the knowledge of yet another place to slip in, in case they didn't know about it already.

A cracking branch behind his back made him nearly jump, as the men he was watching straightened up abruptly, leaping to their feet together, like one person.

His heart stopped. The sounds receded, disappeared. Like in a dream, he watched one of them pouncing forward, his club long and heavy, its tip rounded, huge, polished to perfection.

The footsteps behind his back were frantic, rife with panic. From the corner of his eye, he saw a silhouette darting aside, slipping on the uneven ground. Another two emerged from behind the trees, yet before they could do anything, one of the invaders was upon them, with the first of the newcomers still on the ground, rolling away from the crushing touch of the heavy weapon, making it bounce off the moss-covered stone his body was resting against just a heartbeat earlier.

Not pausing, the clubman attacked again, this time more successfully, the sound of the hard wood colliding with live flesh making a dull, revoltingly wet sound, almost tangible in the deepening dusk. The gasp of the victim echoed, followed by a strangled scream. As if in a dream, Migisso saw the man he had shared a canoe with upon this last journey writhing in the grass, beyond the ability to scream.

Breathless, he watched the victorious enemy turning to face Achtohu, whose club was swung high, looking weightless in the young man's hands. In a heartbeat, the enemy warrior was upon the ground too, twitching beside his victim.

Something made Migisso look up, as the other enemy warrior broke into an urgent run. And then, the bow was alive in his hands, not rough or slick, but perfectly fitting, the arrow already there, firm, unwavering. It was easy to take a quick aim, to release the bowstring. It felt natural, like on a hunt.

Outside himself, he heard his arrow hissing, watched it making its way in the air, strangely slow, reaching the bare, glistening, sweat-covered back, entering it smoothly, as though belonging there. The man stumbled, flailing his hands in a funny way before going sprawling into the bushes. It was over in a matter of heartbeats.

Blinking, he watched the others rushing on, turning the shot man over, checking him briefly.

"Good work." The patting arm upon his back made him jump, his heart tumbling down his stomach. Achtohu's round face beamed at him. "This one might have spoiled our surprise."

"Yes, he might." Migisso cleared his throat, pleased to hear his own voice steady, matter-of-fact, calm. His heart was pounding unevenly, threatening to explode inside his chest. "Did you contact our people in there?"

"No." The young man shrugged, unconcerned. "There is no way to do that. There are too many warriors congregating around the entrance and some other places that may offer an easy climb." Another shrug. "It doesn't matter. We'll surprise them, anyway. They are less than twenty, a truly small force. Not that much more than us."

"We are only seven now."

Scowling eyebrows were his answer. "Like I said, we are less, but not that much less."

"A cooperation of our people in there might be of a great help, might make our mission easier, possible to achieve."

"And how would you proceed delivering them our invitation to join?" The openly mocking tone made Migisso angry.

"In a smart way, obviously. Not while storming the entrance against all odds, or while going around, complaining." He stood the direful glare. More than a few now, as the others joined them as they talked. "There are ways to sneak inside and come out undetected."

"Do you know of one such?"

"Yes, I do. Maybe." The impatience of their gazes made him lose a little of the confidence he had gained. "Over there, behind those bushes. There are loose poles there. There is a gap. It leads to the ceremonial grounds."

They stared at him as though he spoke a different tongue.

"Over there?"

He shifted his grip on the bow, his palms again clammy with sweat. "Yes."

They exchanged glances. "Show us."

As he turned toward the indicated trees, he blessed his wild sister again for showing him plenty of such openings. Oh, she would be surprised to see him returning this way.

Holding his breath, Okwaho watched the shadows darting between the bushes and alongside the dark mass of the fence.

Crouching in the most uncomfortable of positions, half-standing and half-squatting, the way he was caught when seeing them first, he tried to calm the thumping of his heart. It was thundering too loudly, threatening to give his presence away. It interfered with his ability to think, too. He needed to consider it all lucidly, to analyze the situation. Instead, the thoughts rushed about his aching head, pounding it mercilessly, like clubs, hurting it.

Enough that the pain still pulsated behind his ear, which was all swollen and caked with dried blood from the blow it had received when he dropped into the river, pushed by the accursed arrow; enough that the cut that the damn arrow left on his shoulder was still hurting; enough that he was so tired that he could barely see, with only his inner powers pushing him on, with Akweks still down there, wounded and weakened, waiting for him to reach their people and come back with reinforcements, attended by none other than some wild enemy fox that could not be trusted, not even a little bit. All these aside, to run into more of the filthy enemy, who were obviously planning something nasty under the cover of the night, was just too much. Why weren't his people alert, keeping an eye on their prey, or better yet, killing the wandering rats one by one? Where were they? Taking a nap under the fence of the attacked settlement, sleeping snugly, as though in the vicinity of their own town?

He narrowed his eyes, desperate to see better. The moon was generous, and if before, while climbing the hill, keeping close to the path but avoiding taking it just in case, he wished the benevolent night spirit would disappear behind a thick cluster of clouds, now he thanked the shiny deity for illuminating the enemy so well. Their silhouettes were like a drawing on a rock, so very clear, darting in and out, busy like ants. What were they up to?

He shifted carefully, unable to keep his weight on one leg anymore. What to do? To stay and see what this nightly activity was all about seemed to be the most sensible thing. And yet, he needed to reach his people, and fast. Akweks could not be left out there, wounded and alone, with the enemy girl knowing all about their situation, probably running back to her village as fast as she could. He should have found something to tie her with. His silly threats and promises were surely not enough when dealing with such a fierce fox.

Where did she come from? he wondered, watching a cluster of silhouettes sneaking out of the grove this time, hesitating, their heads turned back, staring into the darkness of the fence. And for what purpose? Why would a girl run all over the countryside while her village was being attacked by the enemy? It made no sense, and yet, there she was, sniffing around their stolen boats, trying to shoot him, fighting like a mountain lioness, heedless of danger. Not pretty, not womanly, speaking like a man, with no restraint and no shyness, and yet, still nothing but a girl. Vulnerable, unprotected. It still felt wrong, the fact that he had to hit her back there near the boats. He should have found some other way to render her harmless. No woman deserved such treatment, however armed and aggressive and desperate to harm.

The shadows near the bushes were talking in whispers, disturbing none of the night's tranquility. He tried to listen, knowing that he would not understand one single word, wishing for the girl's ability to speak both of their tongues. How had the wild thing come to learn their words, and so coherently at that? Was she a captive who had been adopted when a young child? Or had she a captured Longhouse person for a parent, mother or father? It might have explained…

The silhouettes whispered for a few more heartbeats, then fell silent. Almost against his will, he listened to the night taking over again, the murmuring of the wind, the buzzing of mosquitoes, the cracking branches in the distance. Their people's footsteps? He hoped they were.

The moment the shadows disappeared, dissolving into the night, he hesitated no more. It might have been wise to try and follow them, but he was not up to this task. He was too spent, too tired to move in absolute silence while scouting such unfamiliar terrain, and his people needed to be told too many things, the enemy's nightly enterprise included. Although the boats and Akweks were the first priority. The very first one. Had the girl run away already? Had she reached her people and told them what she knew?

He eyed the dark mass of the fence. Had she used the same invisible opening he witnessed others using? That might explain her ability to sneak away undetected by his own people. The fighting clearly went on everywhere but here. Such a canny fox. He should have made her talk, no matter what it took.

Treading carefully upon the moss-covered ground, he slipped

away, heading in the direction opposite to the scheming locals. His people must have been congregating near the other side, the one facing the opening in the fence and all sorts of flammable targets, houses and such. Even though spending his afternoon elsewhere, he knew that many fire arrows had been used, many wooden objects put to fire. The heavy stench enveloping the entire top of the hill told him that, the peculiar odor of oil that was not usually present in forest fires.

The intensifying smell let him know that he wasn't far from his destination. As did the growing noises, voices and rustling. His people didn't bother to conceal their presence. But of course. What could the pitiful village do but fortify their walls and try to do their best against the invader? And yet…

He frowned. And yet, some determined, fast-moving locals were sneaking from the unwatched side of the settlement, behaving as though they knew exactly what they were doing. Who knew what devilment they had planned? Nothing good, that much was obvious. But whatever it was, Kayeri, their temporary leader, should not have succumbed to the temptation of feeling safe and secure. They were barely twenty people, now that his scouting group was lost or wounded and of no use.

He shivered. Would he be blamed for this failure? He was the one to suggest checking the terrain and the movement he had observed. Wasn't he the one expected to return with the people he had been entrusted with, unharmed?

The desperation was back, mixed with a now-familiar sense of angered frustration. From the moment he had sensed that local watching them, from the moment he insisted on checking the footprints, it had all gone wrong, so terribly wrong. Had he kept his observations to himself, none of these things would have happened. They would have sailed on, to the larger settlement they intended to raid in the first place, their warriors' force united and not split. Akweks would not have been wounded, and the other three would not have been killed. He himself would have been in better shape now. Oh, it was his fault, curse them all into the underworld of the Evil Twin.

Clenching his teeth against the red wave of rage, he trod on, toward the voices, and now a faint flickering as well. Oh, but his people were sure of themselves, to light a fire, and in such an open manner. He fought his uneasiness down. The leader of their expedition was a hardened warrior. He surely knew what he has been doing, putting Kayeri in charge of this particular raid.

"It's me, Okwaho," he called as soon as he was within hearing distance. There was no need to tempt his fellow warriors into a night shooting. Good illumination or not, it would be easy to mistake him for a scout, or maybe just a wandering local.

As though answering his misgivings, a shadow darted from behind the trees.

"It's me," he repeated. "Don't attack."

The man came closer, followed by another. In the silvery light, he recognized them easily. "Where is the leader?"

Two pairs of eyes still peered at him, as though he were a ghost, an uninvited spirit of the local woods.

"You are alive?" The question lingered, filling the darkness.

"Yes, of course. Why wouldn't I be?"

They shrugged in unison, their frowns deep. "And the others?"

"Akweks is alive too, but wounded. I left him by the river. I need help to carry him back here."

"How badly?"

"Not too badly, but he can't walk."

"Come." A curt gesture invited him to follow.

As though he needed their permission to approach their temporary leader, he thought, seething, the clubs pounding inside his skull redoubling their efforts. Oh, but he needed to sit down, even for just a little while.

The strip of clear land was narrow and dark, barely lit by a small fire, hosting less than ten people around it. The others must have been wandering, reflected Okwaho, following his guide, fighting the urge to bypass him, if for no other reason than to make a point.

Their stares made him uncomfortable.

"Where have you been all this time?" Kayeri looked him up and down, not bothering to get up or invite his unexpected guest to squat beside the fire.

"Down there by the river." Taking a deep breath, Okwaho tried to suppress his uneasiness, the open hostility unsettling, setting his nerves on edge. He had done nothing wrong. Had he?

"Tell me what happened."

He swallowed hard. "We were surprised by a group of hunters. A large group, about ten men in all." Another deep breath seemed like a necessity. Nothing shameful about it. Or was there? "We killed them all, but Akweks was wounded. He got an arrow in his leg. Ronkwe took it out, but the wound needed to be washed. So I took him down the trail, in order to reach the river." He swallowed again. "Ronkwe said they would come back here in the meanwhile to get help. And… Well, then more enemy came. I don't know how many. They shot at us, and we fell off the cliff, me and Akweks. And it took time…" He heard his own voice trailing off, and it served to discourage him even further. "We were in no shape to rush back here—"

"Quite a story." Kayeri cut him off with no additional thought, paying no attention to his own rudeness. "However, now that you are here, we are sure to succeed." The raised eyebrows and thin half-grin bestowed on Okwaho related barely concealed contempt. "You see, while you were jumping cliffs, we've been busy fighting our way into this village. The locals seem to be a high-spirited people, but tomorrow, when the sun is at its highest, we will be loading our boats with the best of their food and ware."

In the dim light of the fire, the man's face looked as though chiseled out of stone, calm, thoughtful, unperturbed. Confident. Okwaho fought the need to take a deep breath.

"The boats…" He hesitated; clearing his throat helped but only a little. His voice rang strangely, higher than usual. "They were taken. They are not at the shore we left them at."

"What?"

The astounded gaze leaped at him, puzzled and full of accusation once again. It was as though the man suspected him of taking a part in the theft of their vessels.

"They are at another shore. Not far away from where we left them. But not all of them."

"How did they get there?"

"I don't know. I think the locals took them."

"They could not. They were busy fighting." The burning eyes did not leave his face, piercing. "There was no time for them to run around the river, looking for our boats."

"Well, the boats are not where we left them." He pressed his lips tight, refusing to drop his gaze. The man had no right to get angry with him over the stolen boats. He wasn't the one to lose them. He was the one to find them.

The frown of his interrogator deepened. "How did you locate them?"

"We searched the shores." There was no harm in embellishing the truth, he decided, still seething over the mounting misunderstanding. Who knew if they happened on that shore by mistake or not, washed out by the current, with him being unconscious and more useless out of the two of them?

"All the boats are there? Nothing is missing?"

"No. I already told you that some of the canoes are missing." Again, he hid his uneasiness. How many boats were missing? He didn't even know. He should have counted and checked, and maybe he would have, but for the girl's sudden appearance. The damn fox.

"Is Akweks guarding them now?"

"Well, yes, but…" He paused again, trying to clear his thoughts in order to formulate the best answer. "He is in no condition to fight. And he can't walk. I came to get help." His throat was so dry, he felt its sides sticking to each other, hampering his ability to talk coherently. "I need someone to come with me, to help bring Akweks here."

"Now? At night?" The pointy eyebrows climbed high, showing even more disdain. "You are not thinking clearly, warrior. Akweks will stay where he is, guarding our boats until we come back, ready to leave. Now," a hand came up, cutting off anything Okwaho might have said in a protest, "go and rest. Later, make yourself useful. I expect you to distinguish yourself in tomorrow's battle. No more disappearing at just the right time, no more being conveniently away."

"I did not—"

A dismissive wave of a hand stopped his words once again. "You were not in the battle today. That is all that matters. Do not disappoint us tomorrow."

The interview was clearly over. Okwaho tried to contain the trembling. His entire body shook with rage. How dared this man? How dared he accuse him of trying to avoid the battle, or even worse? Oh, Mighty Spirits, but he would show the arrogant piece of excrement. He would show him what he, Okwaho, was worth, and he would rub this man's ugly face in it, and wipe away all remnants of the haughtiness. He could feel his teeth almost screeching, so tightly they were clenched against each other. Then he remembered.

"There is enemy activity on the other side of this village."

Again, the piercing gaze; again, the open accusation. "What are you talking about?"

"I saw them on my way here. They were sneaking in and out of the bushes that seemed to be adjacent to the poles of their fence."

The mounting anger helped. He straightened his gaze and did not let it drop before the direful frown that made the leader's eyes narrow into slits.

"How many?"

"About ten. Maybe more. It was difficult to count them in the darkness and the way they came in and out."

"Ohonte, Raeks, Onyare." The leader was on his feet, waving at the nearest warriors. "Bring the others." The gaze shot at Okwaho held much suspicion, but no more disdain. "Take us there!"

CHAPTER 11

The sounds of people fighting were familiar by now; still, as it pounced on her from the darkness, she froze, unable to breath, her fear sudden and paralyzing, making her heart stop, only to resume its beating with a mad rush.

It was bad enough before, falling into the enemy's hands, with the wolf man being so rude and fierce, impossible to shoot down or to best in any other way, seeing through her and her lies, cursing, angry with her and his wounded friend, promising unreasonable things. He truly believed they would be able to take her village, pillaging it and burning it to the ground.

But oh no, they won't, she had promised herself, relaxing as soon as he was gone, heading back up the hill. The other youth was no match for her, all pale and exhausted, unable to walk, his leg in bad shape, propped against the cliff, lying listlessly, of no use to him. Still, she remained where she was for some time, wishing her captor to gain a respectable distance before heading for the same destination he did, but by a better way of shortcuts the stupid invaders would not know about.

"You won't stay here, will you?" The wounded sounded calm, not accusing, slumbering where he was, evidently in pain.

She just shrugged.

"Your people will be in no condition to send warriors down here with you." He shifted, trying to gain a better position, but the attempt left him breathless, with no more color to his face than that of a dead person. Even in the silvery moonlight, it was easy to see how badly he suffered. "Your tale about us… down here… won't make any difference."

"I no care," she said, trying to gather the remnants of her previous anger. Somehow, with no other man around, she felt none of it. "I go home. Maybe sleep, eh? And eat. And feel..." she searched for an appropriate word. "Feel good, soft, good mats, no hard earth and no cold. And no wound. Good night, not like yours."

He rolled his eyes, curiously not angered either. The wolf youth would be cursing by now, she knew, saying sharp things back at her. She thought about him making his way up in the darkness, nimble and forceful, like a real wolf. But he wasn't that good, not if he had gotten himself entangled in this mess, stuck with a wounded friend that far away from his fellow warriors, himself quite battered on top of it. Maybe he'd fall and break his neck on his way through the dark woods. If only there could be such a good turn!

"Yes, I could use a soft mat now, and some fire and food, yes," mused the wounded youth, paying no attention to her barbs. "And a healer, too."

His face twisted and lost its relatively tranquil expression. Following his troubled gaze, she fought the temptation to come closer in order to examine his wound.

"My brother good, good at healing," she related instead, for what reason she didn't know. "He would have known, known what ointments. He loves healing."

"Maybe you bring him here?" His eyes returned to her, amused, but only partly. "Make him inspect my wound. Healers should be above our squabbles, eh? They help anyone in trouble."

"Anyone but the enemy," she said firmly, not sure if he was talking nonsense to pass the time. "Your fire arrows cause damage, much. And they kill people, too. I saw, many. I was to help, help with wounded, but I went out, shoot at your people." The mere memory made her chest tighten, the screams of the hurt villagers and the terrible smell some of them had. And the burning houses and patches of earth. "Your people beasts. They terrible, they no people at all. They evil spirit that Malsum bring here, but he will not, not win. He never does."

"Who is Malsum?" There was no more amusement in his voice,

and his frown was deep as he eyed her through his narrowed eyes.

"Malsum the Wolf is evil, evil spirit. He is twin of Glooskap, but Glooskap is good. He is the light and the…" Another frantic search for words. Why couldn't they speak normal peoples' tongue? "He made all good, plants and animals and people. But Malsum, Malsum made bad plants, bad things, bad animals and people. People like you. People like your friend. No wonder… it is no wonder he has wolf tattoo. He is messenger, you see. Messenger of bad spirit."

His smile was fleeting, sudden in its warmth. "Okwaho is a wolf, yes. His name means that, and he is a wolf, for sure. His guiding spirit is that magnificent animal." He frowned. "But wolves are good, local girl. They aren't bad like your people think they are. They are courageous and strong and loyal. They are great hunters. Your people are silly to badmouth such magnificent creatures."

He licked his lips and fell silent, obviously tortured with thirst. Shrugging, she looked around, eyeing the dark silhouettes of the logs and other smaller objects that were strewn about, looking for something hollow enough to carry water in.

"We do not… do not think wolves bad," she said, getting to her feet. "Only Malsum, Wolf the Younger. He is bad. Not courageous, not loyal." A quick search through the firewood her captor had brought earlier produced a good enough piece of bark. "Like your friend, he is bad. Like your people. But yes, other wolves are good, many of them, but not all." Picking her find up, she shrugged again. "I bring you water, then I go."

He was gazing at her, as though mesmerized. "You are kind," she heard him saying as she turned to go. "I didn't expect…"

And now, clinging to the nearest tree, trying to catch her breath, with the sounds of fighting coming from the only place she needed to reach, *the safety*, she wondered briefly if this youth was still well, still alive. The woods were no place to spend one's night at, especially with no fire, no company, barely any weapons, wounded and alone. And enemy or not, he seemed to be a nice, thoughtful sort of a person. It would not be right for him to just die out there all alone.

Shutting her eyes, she listened to the muffled sounds, refocusing her thoughts on her current predicament. What was going on up there, near her favorite hole in the fence? Were people fighting there? But why would they? When she had slipped out earlier, well before dusk, the mutual shooting had almost been over, with no burning arrows trying to set the fence and the houses on fire. The attackers and the defenders were ready to retire for the night, as was the custom. Even she knew that no fighting was done in the darkness. Father told enough stories of battles to learn that. And yet, here it was, well after darkness, and there were obviously some people trying to harm each other out there, with no light and no direction. Why would they do that?

She hesitated, then went on silently, familiar with the woods to the point of not needing her eyes to guide her at all. The silence prevailed, deep, ethereal. No gust of wind disturbed the stillness, no stirring of an animal, nor the screech of a night bird. The world went dead as unexpectedly as it had come to life before.

Against her will, she froze, afraid to make a move, the wide trunk of a giant tree providing her with sense of security, even if a false one.

"Are there any more of them out there?" The footsteps broke the darkness even before the voices did, making her almost jump out of her skin. They rasped on the other side of her tree as it seemed, the enemy words difficult to understand, unlike the youth's down there by the river. "Filthy pieces of rotten meat."

"Where are the others?" The second voice seemed to be more in control, not bursting with rage. "Were any of our people hurt?"

"I don't know. I got cut on the arm, but not badly." The first man seemed to be regaining his calmness as well. "Where is the leader? And where is the young scout? He saw them, so he would know how many of them might be out there."

More rustling accompanied their words as they began fading into the darkness again, heading in the direction they came from. Kentika let out a held breath. Yet, before she could decide what to do, whether it was safe to try and sneak toward her destination now, more breaking branches erupted. Panted breaths filled the dark air, followed by urgent whispering, then shouts. Something swished; a thud of a fallen body came. A muffled groan followed it, then another.

Pressing against her tree, she did not dare to breathe, understanding too well. People were fighting in impossibly close proximity. Her people and the enemy. Who was winning? She tried to suppress the choking wave of panic.

More silhouettes darted around, slipping like shadows, dark, ominous spirits. She bit her lips wildly, but the cry still erupted as something clashed against someone with a revoltingly wet sound, and one of the forms came crashing against her tree, making it nearly shake.

The shriek of the man was awful. It washed over her, making her insides shrink. In panic, she leaped backwards, only to collide with a warrior, who cursed and stumbled, before shoving her away with his elbow. Stumbling in her turn, she waved her hands in order to keep her balance, then calmed down all at once, recognizing the words. The man who pushed her away was not speaking like the enemy.

Her thoughts clearing at once, she backed away, knowing at once who it was. Schikan! Oh, how could she not recognize him, even though in the darkness and in the middle of a battle, of all things.

The brief moment of confidence didn't last, as a dark form of a club tore the air and the silhouette of her friend uttered a funny sound before collapsing like a cut-down tree. The club owner swung his weapon again, victorious, but another hiss interrupted his movement, and he ducked, then straightened up, reassured, concentrating once again on his victim, who was trying to get up, moving clumsily, ridiculously slow.

It was a nightmare!

In disbelief, she watched Schikan struggling on the ground, his panted breath tearing the darkness, while the enemy hurried to bring his club high again. To deliver the final blow, she realized. *He was going to kill him!*

"No!"

Her feet brought her forward, acting of their own accord. One moment she was pressing against the tree, not safe anymore but still out of lethal weapons' range; the other, she was colliding against the man with a club, grabbing his arm, clinging to it desperately, making it slow its descent.

The smell struck her nostrils, sweat mixed with the sharp odor of blood. He was struggling to shake her off, both his arms clenching the club, unable to just push her away, or to strike her down.

Her grip was slipping, his sweaty skin difficult to cling to. In desperation, she kicked and felt more than heard the enemy groaning, then doubling his efforts to push her away. His kick was more hurtful, and as she squirmed out of his knee's reach, her grip on his arm loosened, and the muddy ground met her with a soft thud.

It was a nightmare. Terrified, she tried to make her mind work, her limbs paralyzed with fear, refusing to move, the terror too great, the expectation of the deadly blow the only thought permeating her mind, the vivid pictures of splattering blood, *her blood*, bursting out along with other smelly things.

The world seemed to slow down, withdraw, the sounds and the scents, coming from far away. It was as though she was under the water again. A familiar feeling. When did it happen?

Someone's elbow, or maybe it was a leg, hit her painfully, and she rolled away out of instinct, clenching her teeth to stifle a cry. Beside her, people were wriggling upon the ground. Their rasping breaths reached her, irritating rather than frightening. The sounds were back. And the awareness.

Blinking, she stared at the dark forms, one pinning down another, the enemy winning again. It was impossible to see clearly, but she knew she was right.

It was easier to grab the man's arm now, to fall upon his back, easier to make the progress of the knife stop; a child's play really, compared to the necessity to battle the strength of a standing man. In another heartbeat, the body underneath her tensed, then shuddered, Schikan's knife making a quick work out of it, she surmised.

Fighting the urge to just roll away, she put the remnants of her strength into the attempt to push the now-limp body away from Schikan, struggling with both hands, using her shoulder to reinforce the effort. It left her gasping for breath, powerless for a moment, this entire night too much. Her body was shaking, her hands and knees, and she knew that if she fell she would vomit and vomit and maybe even faint, because the earth was just too revolting, reeking and warm with terrible things.

Schikan was panting, struggling to get to his feet, unbearably clumsy.

"We need t-to go, go away… from here. Go home." She hated the way her words came out, vibrating, difficult to understand.

"Yes, yes." His voice was steady but hoarse, strident. Full of pain, she realized.

"You're wounded?"

"Yes."

He was on his knees by now, swaying, one hand propped against the ground, supporting, the other useless, pressed against the dark form of his body. It didn't seem as though he could make it any farther in his struggle to get up. The realization helped to lessen the trembling.

"I'll help you up." Pleased that the attempt to get to her feet came easier than expected, she leaned closer, careful to approach his unwounded side. "Just grab my arm. Or something."

He was heavy, clumsy, impossible to pull up. Near tears, she struggled on, until another dark form pounced on them, so very close her heart jumped.

"What is going on?"

Limp with relief, she recognized the voice easily. "Schikan… he is… he is wounded." Again, her voice trembled in the most annoying of ways, causing her to clench her teeth tight.

The man was already pulling Schikan on. "Can you walk?"

"Yes." It seemed that Schikan was able to say only that and nothing else, his voice too hoarse to recognize even, trembling with pain.

The man hesitated. "Take him back there, toward that grove. There is an opening in the fence. Right behind—"

"I know where it is."

Another pause, and even though she could not see in the darkness, she knew he was scrutinizing her with his gaze, puzzled. "Well, then, go. There should be no enemies there, although those lowlifes seem to be popping out of nowhere." His voice dropped as more noises came from the direction of the woods. "Go now."

Schikan's rasping breathing tore the silence as they staggered on, barely making any progress. He was swaying, leaning on her so heavily that she had to fight for every step, certain they would never reach as much as the fence itself, let alone the opening in it. The moment he made them both fall it would be over.

"It's not long now, not long at all," she panted, not daring to shift her grip or change their position, her shoulder numb from the pressure of his weight.

"How… how long?" His groan seemed to belong to someone else. She could feel his body stiff with pain, barely reacting.

"Not long now, truly. They'll help us, help us there."

The moonlight poured over them more generously now, the darkness not as thick as back in the grove. She squinted, trying to recognize the landmarks. Oh, yes, the tree with a split trunk. It swayed not far away, inviting, promising safety.

She breathed with relief, but the good feeling did not last. The cracking of branches and the noises of fighting, familiar by now, erupted from behind the same cluster of trees. What was the enemy doing so near the opening in the fence? The thought that never occurred to her before suddenly grew, gaining power. *How did they know?*

"We need to hurry," she breathed, and felt him reacting, trying to straighten up, unsuccessfully so. He could barely walk the way they progressed before.

The figure that pounced from behind the trees looked familiar, reaching the clear ground in one forceful leap. In an obvious hurry to cross the open space, the man almost bumped into them, halting abruptly, the spear in his hands balanced and ready, the polished flint tip glittering darkly, promising no good. It stared at them, ready to launch, but all she could do was to stare at the owner of the lethal weapon, recognizing the wide cheekbones, the strong jaw, the bruises, and above all, the dark form of the tattoo. The wolf man!

He was gaping at her too, his eyes widening in perfect proportion to his deepening frown. It was a ridiculous combination. She wanted to laugh, in a hysterical way.

"You again," he breathed. "What in the name—"

His eyes left her face, leaping to her companion, narrowing rapidly. There was nothing funny about his expression anymore.

"Please!"

The short word surprised her as much as it probably surprised him and maybe Schikan too, who seemed to be straining to stand more upright now. It was strange, out of place, but as it came out, she knew she must give it a try.

"Please. He wound, wounded. You no kill wounded man."

A new outburst of shouts and breaking branches came from behind the same cluster of trees. He turned away abruptly, balancing the spear.

"Go," he tossed out curtly, without looking back. "Go away, fast."

CHAPTER 12

The short plank fashioned to his satisfaction, Migisso eased his shoulders, eyeing his work, pleased. It was wide enough to hold his friend's broken arm in place, to allow it to heal properly, but not to hinder his movement more than necessary, not like some cruder splints did. There would be no trouble moving around with such a thing, even to work to some extent. That is, when Schikan regained the ability to do any of those things. Which would not be happening too soon, not with the addition of broken ribs. And if they didn't manage to harm the enemy as much as they hoped they did, neither Schikan, nor other wounded, would enjoy proper rest or healing.

He shivered, then put his attention back to his friend's lifeless form. Even in the fading moonlight, it wasn't difficult to see how pale and drawn he was, how his usually fit body sagged listlessly, jerked with every breath, drifting between their world and the other one, the realm of dreams and spirits. After the ministrations of the old healer, it was no wonder the young man was left with no power to even stay around.

The medicine man was busy treating another wounded, a man with a gaping gash on his thigh, his eyes shut tightly, his teeth making a mess out of his lower lip, obviously stiff with pain as the water was poured into the wound. Involuntarily, Migisso leaned closer, studying the gash.

"It needs to be closed," he muttered, not realizing he was speaking aloud.

"Yes, it does." The old man nodded, as immersed and oblivious of his own words. "Such a gap should not stay open. It'll rot." He shook his head resolutely. "Bring me more water, and my larger bag. It's lying around, somewhere." A kinder look measured Migisso, taking in his cargo. "After that, go and fix that plank to your friend's arm. He will be well. He is a strong young man, and your sister was a gift from the spirits who sent her to him."

He could do nothing but nod this time, the mention of his sister making his stomach clench. Oh, how worried he had been earlier, when among the hectic preparations to surprise the enemy with the unexpected reinforcements the town received, he had found a moment to rush home, to make sure his family was unharmed. They would need reassurance, he knew, but only upon entering the dim, cluttered space did he find out how badly they needed it.

Surrounded by aunts and cousins, his mother related to him that not only he and Father were the cause of her worry, but that Kentika was also gone, nowhere to be found. He tried to make sense out of it, to come up with all sorts of possible explanations. She might have been busy out there, helping. The fires were taken care of by now, and the wounded, but still much work needed to be done. Yet, not at night, one of his aunts pointed out. Everyone was accounted for, everyone but Kentika.

Worried, he went back to the men he came here with, as the organization of the night sortie was more important, the frantic collecting of all available weaponry, the coordination of the projected action. There must be a good explanation for her absence at home. The wild thing always tried to be in the thick of events, if allowed, which she usually wasn't, yet, in the current state of affairs, no one was there to admonish and reprimand. She would be somewhere there around the town. There was no other explanation.

And yet, the fear kept nagging, especially when he heard about her exploits through the afternoon attack. Help douse the fire and treat the wounded? No, it was not her way of doing things. To stand on the top of the ladder, shooting someone's bow was just the deed his sister was up to. The men who had told him about it laughed briefly, openly amused, even appreciative. Yet, no one had seen her later through the evening. It was as though she had just disappeared, dissolved into the thin air.

Making his way through the maze of groaning darkness, he concentrated on his step, trying not to slip or tread on someone. There were too many wounded, too many villagers with burns and cuts, too many warriors brought in now through the night. The surprise nighttime attack hadn't worked for some reason. It must have helped to make the enemy suffer, to reduce their force, not very impressive to begin with, but it did not catch the invaders unprepared. Why? How had they known?

"Where is Schikan?" Kentika's voice startled him as he searched between the blankets and the people stretched upon them, those who awaited treatment or who could not be carried to their homes due to the seriousness of their wounds. The bag with the healer's tools was not easy to locate. "How is he?"

"I don't know." He refused to look up, too angry to talk to her civilly as yet. Not that in the darkness she would have seen much of his expression.

The silence prevailed. "Where is he? Has he been treated already?"

"The healer took care of his wounds, yes. But I've yet to put his arm in a splint." Another heartbeat of heavy silence. "Have you gone home already?"

"Yes, I have." Still crouching upon the ground, all he could see were her feet, one tip of the moccasin tapping impatiently, the torn decorations jumping up and down, splattered with dried mud. The fringes of her dress seemed to be in no better condition. "I have nothing to do there, and they can't make me stay." She hesitated again. "Not with what is going on all around."

His hands locating the desired bag at long last, he got up, tired beyond reason. "And you know all about what is going on here, and out there, too." It came out as an open accusation.

"Yes, of course!" she retorted, ready to give measure for measure, as was always her custom. "I was of use. I did good things. I saved Schikan's life. Don't I get even a simple gratitude for it?" Her lips pressed into a thin line. "He is your friend, and he would have died out there if not for my help. But all you care about is appropriate behavior."

He felt like turning and running away, or maybe striking her, the unreasonableness of her accusation cutting like the sharpest arrowhead.

"You shouldn't have been out there in the first place. You could have been killed. Or taken captive. Would you have liked that? To be captured by the filthy enemy? Is that what you want? Because if yes, then go out there again, by all means."

Her hissing breath tore the darkness, but she said nothing for a moment, atypical to her. Kentika always had something to answer back, especially when admonished.

He drew a deep breath. "Mother was worried sick. And yes, I was too." A shrug proved a tiring business. "And Father, if he heard about it—"

"Father will not hear about it, unless you are eager to go and tell him. And in this case, you will get your share of his rage as well." She stomped her foot angrily. "I don't need you scolding me. I got enough chiding and dire promises of punishment already." Her foot came down again, scattering pieces of dried mud. "Maybe I shouldn't have gone out this time, but I did helpful things. My arrow broke the oil jar the enemy used to make fire arrows. And if not for the invaders on the river shore, I would have been nearing Skootuck by now, bringing them our request of help." Another angrily drawn breath shook the darkness. "And I did save Schikan's life—I did! And you didn't thank me even for this."

He eyed her helplessly, fighting the budding sense of guilt and remorse. "I worried about you," he said finally, knowing that the anger was gone, for good, as it always was. It was impossible to stay angry with her for more than a few heartbeats. "You could have been hurt. It's not like your usual sneaking out. It's more dangerous. You could have been captured or killed."

"But I wasn't." Her anger was cooling as rapidly, he could feel that. They were always too close not to read each other's moods. "And, anyway, I worried about you too. How did you manage to come back out of nowhere, and in such a surprising fashion?"

I could have asked you the same, he thought, remembering her stumbling in through the missing pole of the fence, almost carrying Schikan, who was barely conscious, in bad shape. She was, of course, tall, relatively broad-shouldered, inappropriately strong, fitter than some young men even; still, Schikan was a broad-shouldered warrior, not a girl or a child to carry around.

"How did you find him there in the darkness?"

Her uneasiness was back. "I was on my way here."

As though that explained it. He tried to stare her down, an easier feat now as the sky above was turning gray. The darkness grew less oppressive, and he could see the old healer glancing up, waving impatiently.

"They need my help. Go and sit with Schikan, if you can't stay at home. Bring him water. Make him drink as much he can. I'll come to fix his arm shortly."

A group of men swept past them, their faces gray with fatigue. "Come along. We are off to seek our wounded and dead out there."

His hesitation drew direful frowns from more than one person. He tucked the bag into her hands. "Give it to the Honorable Healer." Before hurrying to catch up with the others, he bestowed upon her a meaningful look. "No more sneaking out, Sister. Promise!"

This time, she nodded readily. Reassured, he hurried after the men.

"Be careful out there," Paqua, clearly the leader of the group was saying. "The enemy seems to retreat back to where they camped before, but we can't be sure. Some may still be wandering around." The older man's narrowing eyes almost disappeared in the depth of his frown. "They have to lick their wounds, surely. I hope they were hurt more badly than we were. They are bad spirits, but the night fighting is not their strong suit."

"Any more than it is ours," muttered someone.

The older leader gave them a stern look. "We did well. Even if not achieving the surprise and the victory, we did throw the enemy out of balance. They must have lost enough warriors to render the renewal of the attack on the morrow impossible." Another meaningful gaze. "We did well."

"What will we do now?" asked another young warrior, a man

who had come with them from Skootuck, less than a dawn ago. Had only half a day passed? Absently, he wondered about Achtohu and his whereabouts.

"The three of you will go and search for our people who might need help." A shrug. "The others will come with me. If we organize enough men and weapons, we will give the enemy another surprise."

"Without the oil, the fire arrows will not work."

"I know that!" Grimly, Kayeri kicked at the still-glimmering embers of the night's fire, sending some of them scattering.

The sparks the kick generated might have looked pretty, reflected Okwaho, but for the strengthening light. Father Sun was up and about, climbing up his usual path, oblivious to the petty dilemmas of the people roaming the earth.

Absently, he watched it, trying not to blink, somehow certain that if he didn't, everything would be well. He was dead tired, but no rest was anywhere in sight. It was not enough that their leader, now permanently irritable, wished to go on attacking the village he had failed to storm on the day before, having not enough warriors this time and not even enough weaponry to do that, but his request to bring Akweks back was denied again, as angrily as before. It was as though the man was irritated at everything he, Okwaho, said or did.

Nothing new, and yet, this time, he needed to get help. Or at least to go back there himself, to see that Akweks was weathering the night. A weaponless man, wounded and alone in the woods was exposed to enough danger even without the damn girl, the filthy fox who, of course, did not even let his footsteps die away before bolting back to her village, despite all his threats and promises. Had she told her fellow villagers about Akweks already? Surely she had, even though these people were now busy with other things, like the necessity to throw all their efforts into the attempt to banish the invaders. Should he have killed her while he had a chance?

He shrugged. Probably. But having run into her in the middle of this strange night battle, he was startled, disoriented enough as it was, taken by surprise. It was not something he had expected, so he didn't do what was right, namely kill her and the warrior she was carrying and be done with it. Letting her go just like that was the stupidest of his recent decisions.

He frowned again and put his thoughts back on his current predicament.

"They lost many men in their night prowling," Kayeri was saying. "They will be in no position to put up a fight today."

The others shifted uneasily and said nothing, twelve warriors in all, many wounded to this or that degree, bruised, scratched and dirty, gray with fatigue. Not a glorious force to storm a camp of women, let alone a fortified settlement full of fierce, enterprising locals, who had already shown they were no weaklings, no easy victory; who had reportedly fought like beasts on the day before, defending their home, not letting even fire arrows dampen their spirits.

Why, judging by that girl alone, his personal encounter with the representative of the locals, those people were strong and determined, not easily intimidated, neither by threats nor by deeds. Harmed by the night warfare or not, how was one to know the amount of men capable of fighting who might be huddling inside, preparing something dirty like that nighttime assault.

"We will wait until Father Sun climbs a little higher, then we attack." Kayeri was talking rapidly, as though in a hurry. Was he trying to convince himself as well? "A simple assault on their fence will be enough. They are in no position to defend it properly, not today. If nothing else, they are tired and spent."

"And so are we." He said it without thinking, still deep in thought.

Feeling the stares, his head cleared all at once, but it was too late to take the accursed words back.

The hardened warrior's eyes narrowed. "Maybe you are too tired, but the rest of us have better stamina by far."

"I didn't mean it that way." He heard his own voice dying

away, trailing off without consideration to his will, their stares the
only thing tangible. It served to anger him, and the anger gave
him his strength back. They were not being wise or reasonable,
none of them, following that stupid, arrogant man with not a
word of protest. "This attack, it's not a wise thing to do. We are
too few, too battered from the unexpected night fighting, to make
the best out of it. We won't succeed."

He remembered Father, his broad, dignified face, the intricate
pattern of scars upon it, the kind, confident smile, the vitality
behind the luminous eyes. The man had a calm, pleasant voice
and a measured way of speaking, the way of a person used to
talking to the crowds, accustomed to being listened to.

*If you decide to charge, to just attack blindly with no preparation and
no thinking beforehand*, the man had said when on the relevant
subject, *make sure to put it all into the first concentrated effort. Your
first assault will indicate the outcome of such a fight. Actually, your first
blow might very well decide the entire outcome, so put it all in that
initial attack. Do not have qualms or hesitations. But if it doesn't work,
walk away if possible. Do not insist on fighting a hopeless battle.*

He had been talking about personal fights when he said those
things, Okwaho remembered, when he was a mere boy, coming
home with a bloodied nose and tears of frustration in his eyes,
tears he tried to conceal at any price, afraid they would be
mistaken for a sign of weakness. What if Father thought less about
him because of that? But the man didn't laugh; neither had he
grown angry nor scolding. He took his son out, instead, to go to
the spring and wash his face. And have a talk. Oh, how good it
felt to talk to Father on the relatively rare occasions he was home
and not busy with this or that gathering or council.

Well, Father had talked about personal fights back then; yet
somehow, now, he felt this advice was good for their current
situation. They had attacked that village without preparation,
with too small of a force. They might have surprised it, might
have caught it unprepared. Yet, they had failed on that account.
The rival did not waver. It stood firmly, and it won by not giving
in. So all they could do now was leave with what was left. To
charge again was stupid, a fruitless attempt. The village was not

that important.

"Do you presume to teach me, to tell me what to do?" Kayeri was staring at him, narrow-eyed, his face taking a somewhat livid coloring.

He withstood the burning gaze. "I do not presume to tell you what to do, but I do believe we all are entitled to sound our minds." It came out well, but his voice was trembling, again from tension and rage, not from fear, yet he was afraid they might interpret it in the wrong way. "We cannot just storm a fortified settlement without enough men and not enough preparation to persist with the fight." He clenched his fists tight, because they were shaking too, even if not in a visible way. "I believe we should return to our boats, join the rest of our forces, then detour through here on our way back, if you feel it's important. When we are better prepared."

He felt their gazes boring into him, somehow less stony or disapproving than before. They were listening. Surprised, he glanced at the nearest man, and hence missed the movement, startled when Kayeri's body nearly pushed him off his feet, pressed closely, not taller but broader, intimidating.

Fighting the immediate panicked reaction, Okwaho forced himself into stillness, ready to block a blow that might come. Or maybe a thrust of a knife. This man had a reputation, he knew, having spent more than a moon at Cohoes Falls, enough to learn of its prominent people and the tales of their deeds. Particularly about this one.

The silence was heavy, encompassing. It lasted for a heartbeat, then another, then some more. Many heartbeats, or maybe just a few. He could not tell, as his heart was pounding too wildly to count the beats.

"Don't push your luck, you cheeky cub," the man hissed finally. "One more word of your unwelcome advice, and you may get hurt. I came here to kill the enemy, but you are tempting me to teach you a much-needed lesson, a lesson about respecting your elders and betters. They obviously neglected teaching that back in your Onondaga lands." The man's breath was hot upon his face, revolting. It made his skin prickle, his danger signals up, screaming a frantic warning. "Well, it is not the time to do that now, but you better get out of my sight. Go away, go back to the boats. Take the smallest canoe and sail home. I do not want you among my warriors anymore. We do not need cowards. Nor do we need spoiled brats who think too highly of themselves. You are nothing but a cheeky cub who has yet to see a real battle, but who presumes to tell hardened warriors what to do. Well, you won't be listened to. Not here. If you manage to reach our lands, our town, sail on, back to the Onondagas, back to where you came from. They must be softened by too many summers of no wars, enough to let young cubs think they can tell hardened warriors what to do."

He knew he should step away, to back off while he had a chance. He could not. His entire body turned into stone, his muscles so tense he could not feel his limbs anymore, his whole being dedicated to only one purpose: to keep calm, not to let his mounting fury get the better of him and make him do stupid things. He wasn't here to kill his countryfolk, either. And yet, he was not here to take insults, to let the arrogant piece of rotten meat intimidate, or even beat him, into obedience.

"Honorable Leader." The voice of one of the warriors broke the venomous silence. "Let us not talk in such a manner. We are at the foreign hills, about to fight the enemy. Let us proceed with our plans."

Another heartbeat of deadly staring, and the tension began dropping slowly. The air became easier to breath. Still, he didn't dare to relax, not with the dangerous man being so close, spoiling for a fight.

"Yes," murmured the others. "Let us fight the enemy, not our own people."

The tall man moved away as suddenly as he had pounced before. Okwaho dared to breathe again.

"Start organizing yourselves," he heard the man saying in a stiff, strident voice. "You," the wide back was the only thing that faced him now, "go back to the boats and wait for us there. You are not among my warriors' forces anymore, and I will let the leader of our expedition know about this incident."

CHAPTER 13

Pacing back and forth alongside the high poles of the front entrance didn't help. None other than the regular morning sounds reached her ears, no matter how hard she tried to listen. She had bitten her lips into a mess, then went on biting remnants of her fingernails off, and still nothing changed. It was as though both the invaders and the defenders had disappeared, went away, leaving the village for good, never to return. Where were they, her brother and the others?

She stopped for a moment, then shut her eyes to hear better. There was distant murmuring. It interrupted the rustling and the chirping of birds, but barely so. Somewhere out there, people were wandering around. The invaders?

No fire arrows pounced from behind the fence, so if the sounds she heard were the enemies, they were just roaming out there, preparing some new devilment. Unless stopped, surprised like at night, thrown out of balance. Where were they, Migisso and the rest?

It had been some time since they had left, then come back—well Migisso did—then left again. Her worry overwhelming, she tried to be of help, delivering the old healer's bag as she had been told, then some other requested tools, running around, bringing water to the wounded. *Doing nothing of importance.*

When the dawn finally broke, everyone who had been treated was taken to their homes, or helped to walk there, but there were still enough people who waited for the medicine man to ease their pain, their relatives suffering as much, trying to be patient, powerless to help.

Even Schikan's mother, a very sick, nearly blind woman, insisted on staying, replacing Kentika by his side, not especially friendly once she had realized who had been taking care of her son. As though it mattered. Kentika pressed her lips tight and went away, seething. So they were not about to thank her or to trust her any more than before. So what? She knew what she had done, and Schikan knew, and he would go on appreciating her even more than before when he was finally able to come back from the lands of the dreams. What did it matter what others thought?

When the graying sky turned blindingly bright, she had made her way toward the blackened ruins of the houses near the troublesome part of the fence, unable to stand the tension. Many people were crowding the space, anxious, perturbed, the question in their eyes unmistakable. Were the invaders still out there, preparing more fire arrows? Did Migisso and the others manage to surprise them again? However, her head buzzed with additional questions. What about the wounded youth by the river? Was he still alive? And his companion with the wolf tattoo and fearsome disposition?

She tried to push them out of her head. Surprisingly decent or not, her and her people were their enemies, and they were the invaders. If they died, it was for the best. They should never have sailed here, wishing her people harm.

"Here you are!" Namaas' round face jumped into her view, welcome this time.

Embarrassed by her own pattern of thoughts, Kentika shook her head. "What?"

"Where have you been?" The girl's face was pale and gaunt, but flushed, full of excitement.

"Why?" She still stared, finding it difficult to make her head work. Had this empty-headed thing been looking for her since last night, too? As though Mother's and Migisso's indignation were not enough.

"Schikan, he was asking for you. He is back among the living."

Kentika gasped. "Oh, is he… is he well?"

The girl grimaced importantly, enjoying herself. "Of course

not. He is wounded. In great pain. Would you expect him to be well with all those broken ribs of his?"

The dark look Kentika bestowed on her converser made Namaas stop her silly blabbering. "Where is he?"

"In our house. Mother made them bring him there, so she could make ointments for him, and take care of his mother, too. She isn't well, and their house half burned, anyway." The girl's face darkened, as her eyes wandered toward the blackened patches of earth and the still-smoking ruins. "Our men will show them!"

"Unless they don't manage." Turning around so sharply her matted braid jumped, Kentika ground her teeth. "They should have done something by now. Why don't they just attack the enemy or something?"

"Maybe they did. Maybe they attacked them already. Maybe they killed them all. There are no flaming arrows flying all around like yesterday, sister, if you didn't notice."

"I did notice the lack of arrows and fires!" She gave the annoying thing a look that made the girl back away. "But maybe it's you who is dreaming and walking at the same time, *sister*. No one has attacked anyone. On such a clear morning, we would hear the noise their fighting would make. The enemy is still out there. We all heard them, roaming around the place they camped before. If you bothered to spend your time out here instead of running around, relating gossip, you would have known all that." The quivering lips of her companion made her yet angrier. "Oh, don't do that! I'm off—"

The commotion exploded all at once, the cacophony of shouts and noises and blood-curdling cries, coming from behind the fence, happening seemingly next to it. As her eyes leaped toward the blackened poles and her heart jumped before tumbling down her chest, to slip all the way into her stomach, she felt the people around her going still. It was as though an invisible wave, a breath from a nasty creature of the underworld, came and made everyone freeze. Even the breeze stopped, even the chirping of the birds. The burned-out space near the fence turned into an island of terrified silence, while out there, the terrible noise peaked, and the sounds of running feet, falling objects, groans, and gasping could be heard intermingling with the war cries and shouts.

Her feet took her forward, acting as if on their own, without consideration to her numbed mind. All around, people were coming back to life.

"They are fighting!" someone gasped.

It triggered an exaggerated reaction. Everyone broke into a mindless run, rushing back and forth, carrying things.

"Ladders, bring ladders!" screamed several voices.

"Water, water is more important! The fire arrows..."

Grabbing the rickety structure of wooden planks that was lying helplessly upon the ground where it must have been thrown the moment the previous day's battle against the fire was over, Kentika dragged it toward the nearest cluster of poles, oblivious to the way it scratched her limbs. Panting, she struggled to lift it into an upright position, putting all her strength into the attempt, near tears at her lack of success. The accursed thing was more cumbersome than heavy, the ropes tying the rungs loosened, about to fall apart with her harassing it.

"Here!" Someone's hands pushed the ladder up helpfully. "Hold it firm."

The man leaped up the rickety bars, and for a moment, she did as she was told, leaning on the trembling structure with her whole body, her mind still numb, the splash of resentment going away, but not entirely. She had dragged this thing for herself to climb, not for some other pushy person. The bedlam from the outside grew.

"What do you see?" she cried out, unable to keep still. If not for the ladder being so unstable, she might have tried to climb it alongside the man.

He was pulling himself up, propping his upper body against the top of the poles.

"What is happening?" she cried out again, trembling with impatience. Other voices joined her questioning, as many people surrounded their ladder now. And the neighboring ones.

"Bring bows," shouted the man from the nearest observation point. "Hurry."

A frantic movement ensued. Kentika stubbornly stayed where she was, pressing her lips together tightly. If they were not about to let her be of real help, she would not be the one rushing to bring things.

"And stones to hurl," suggested someone. The man was clutching the base of the ladder tight, and only now she realized how helpful it was. She might have been strong for a girl of her age, but the heavy structure was truly too cumbersome to dominate.

"Do you know what is happening out there?" she asked, knowing he wouldn't know anything about it, but desperate enough and in a need to talk.

"They are fighting, that what is happening." The man gave her a look that she must have bestowed on Namaas earlier, but something in her face probably caught his attention as he smiled fleetingly before turning to watch their fellow villager on the ladder. "Don't worry, Dancing Girl. The rotten pieces of meat will not get in. We'll make sure they don't."

Only now did she recognize her converser, a prominent hunter belonging to her mother's clan, a good person, one of those who would always smile at her.

The ladder shook viciously, and she pressed it with her body to help secure it, intuitively ready to leap aside, to move out of the falling man's path. It didn't happen. A quick glance confirmed that their observer was still up there, unharmed. If anything, he was leaning out more openly now, oblivious to the fact that he was presenting a target.

"Careful with your bows," shouted someone from above.

And then, it dawned on her. Not a single arrow had landed on the ground since it all had begun, neither burning and oil-dripping, nor simply flint-tipped. Their side of the fence remained unharmed, unassaulted, with only the frantic running around and shouts of too many people serving to disturb the peacefulness.

The other side of the densely packed poles was drowning in deadly chaos, terribly familiar after the last day, and especially the last night, but not their side. And it only meant one thing. The enemy was fighting against other forces. It was not attacking the village. It was too busy for that.

The vastness of her relief made her body go limp, and if not for more hands securing the ladder now, her companion might have a difficult time holding it all alone. Oh, Mighty Glooskap! Their warriors were successful. They made the enemy fight, and if they did that, then maybe they'd manage to harm it as badly as through the night. Oh, but for that chance!

More people were pressing, crowding all around, making the air hot and difficult to breathe. Hurriedly, she slipped behind the ladder, feeling safer in the small getaway it provided, not liking the pressure of the crowds—a highly unusual occurrence in a village of their size.

"Let me up there!" Waving a bow he had managed to acquire by now, her neighbor shook the rickety construction lightly, attracting the attention of the man up there. He was one of the best shooters, she remembered, his arrows never missing.

The man from above whooped with excitement before jumping neatly, not bothering to climb down. "The War Chief is back, and about time, I say," he cried out, beaming. "Oh, but they will teach the enemy a lesson!"

Father? Kentika stifled a gasp. But how was it possible?

"How?" cried out several voices. "It can't be."

"It is, it is!" The man turned back to watch their shooter, dancing with impatience. "They'll show the dirty rats. Not a single one of the disgusting pieces of rotten meat will see our Father Sun going back to sleep today!"

The War Chief's face was sealed, expressionless as always, but the spark was there. She could see it most clearly. Father was pleased.

Studying him from a respectable distance, safe in doing so, forgotten with everyone besieging the returning leader with words of excitement and congratulations, Kentika shivered, her thoughts on the slaughtered enemy, killed to the last warrior.

Or so the returning men said. The villagers fought like mountain lions, like a pack of cornered wolves, and they were victorious, with the War Chief and his small reinforcements coming with perfect timing, like a reward for their bravery. Mighty Glooskap did not leave his people alone and unprotected. He fortified the defenders' spirits, and he sent them help when it was most needed.

A cornered pack of wolves...

She frowned, not liking the direction her thoughts were taking. The youth with the wolf tattoo. Was he dead now too, impaled by an arrow or crushed by a club?

Somehow, the thought made her feel strange, as though she was regretting it. He deserved to die, of course, like the rest of his terrible countryfolk, but maybe not right away. He had his wounded friend down there by the river, and he did let Schikan and her live, while anyone else, even her people, would have killed them both on the spot. And maybe even earlier, in the woods by the river, when she tried to shoot him with her bow. He should have killed her, but he did not. He punched her unconscious, yes, and he did break her bow. Oh, how angry that had made her back then! But now, upon a reflection, his actions didn't seem that bad, even logical. She did try to kill him, after all, and he did need to keep his presence there a secret. He had his wounded friend to take care of, the youth with a wrecked leg.

The thought hit her like a punch in her stomach. The wounded must have been still there, not in the best of shapes, probably, unable to walk, maybe dying by now from hunger or thirst. No, it was too early for that, and he surely could have hobbled down the shore. And yet...

She bit her lower lip, afraid of this line of thought. To check on the wounded enemy would be a silly thing to do. And what would she do if she did find him? Give him news of his people's defeat? Give him more water? He was so very grateful when she brought him that hollow bark before leaving. Just a boy, really, *a person*, like her playmates from the village, youths like Schikan and her brother. But how could it be? How could the lowlife enemy from the lands of the setting sun be a person like anyone else?

The bushes behind the ceremonial grounds rustled with a light breeze, inviting, encouraging. She sneaked a glance there, then another. Her semi-secret getaway was left alone again after the frantic night. Everyone who could walk was crowding the other side of the open space, congregating around the victorious men and the War Chief, listening avidly, speaking, or talking between themselves. Father wanted to know everything that happened since the invaders arrived here, every tiny detail. She knew the man well. He would want to hear about her discovering the enemy in the first place too, not pleased with her continued wandering about, but leaving the reprimands and the punishments for later. The matters of their people came before any private affairs, always. He was the War Chief for a reason, admired by most, even though his immediate family feared him.

Well, it wasn't fear, she corrected herself, negotiating her way out, anxious to attract no attention. They respected and admired the man as much as the rest of the village. It's just that he was not as reserved with his family, not as restrained as with the outside world or the people of other settlements. He had so much responsibility to carry, their entire village's well-being and protection. Of course it was easy to anger him, even though she never meant for it to happen.

Passing by the partly covered storage pit, she knelt beside it for a moment, scanning its contents quickly, afraid to be detected. One was not to pick anything one wanted from the storage places, but to allay one's hunger at people's dwellings, hoping to find enough remnants of the meals if it wasn't a mealtime. But to pass by her home would have taken more of her precious time, and Mother or any one of the other women might be there, asking questions. Hunger was not an excuse to stuff one's hands with portable food, such as slices of dried meat and rolls of cornbread, and she had no good explanation for her attempt to carry away some of it.

Her heart beating fast, she peered into the semidarkness, enjoying the smell of fresh earth mixed with the slight odor of bark that was lining the pit's sides, old but still distinct. A quick grab of some dried meat and a few cobs of maize, and she was back on her feet, facing Namaas and two other girls, all of them staring, wide-eyed.

Kentika's heart missed a beat.

"What do you want?" she blurted, hating the wave of heat that rushed over her face, making it burn.

Namaas' eyebrows climbed high, and her laughter made a piercing sound. "Are you that hungry, sister?"

She followed their gazes as their eyes slid down to her awkwardly folded arms, clutching the hastily-picked treasure.

"Yes, I am." Tossing her head high, she stood their stares. "I'm going home to eat, and if you follow me, I'll make all three of you regret it."

Their narrowing eyes and arching eyebrows, not to mention the disdainful glitter of their eyes, made her yet angrier, so she whirled around, heading toward her house, indeed—it was on the way, in any case—hating them and their laughter. They were such silly, useless rodents, all of them.

The gap in the fence was wider now, with another pole missing, and it still stank of blood and other revolting odors that came along with fighters, as she had discovered, the muddy ground all around it soaked and slippery. Breaking into a run, she dived into the delightfully fresh aroma of the woods, afraid to stumble over remnants of the night battle, a cut body, or maybe a limb, and yet feeling better by the moment. It was so good to be out there.

She let the breeze wash over her sweaty face. Oh, but she needed a good wash-up, come to think of it. She must have been stinking as badly as the ground back near the fence. After all that she had been through, how could she not?

The thought made her smile. Oh, yes, she needed to wash up, and this was as good an excuse as any. Even though women were supposed to go out in groups, to the nearest brook that was good enough to serve the purpose of washing one's body. There was no need to go all the way down to the river.

She shrugged. There was nothing wrong with bathing in the river. It was as good as the local stream, maybe even better, and if one was not too tired and willing to go all the way… She felt her tiredness welling, and pushed it away. She'd sleep and rest later. They wouldn't be required to go to the fields today, surely, and maybe not even tomorrow.

The river greeted her warmly, sparkling in the early afternoon heat, in an inviting manner. She shielded her eyes, the peacefulness of it disturbing, setting her nerves on edge. After the turmoil and agitation up there, it seemed unnatural, out of place. It was as though she had dreamed it all, the enemy and both battles, the burning houses and the dying wounded, all the running around and fighting and taking the boats. And the enemy youths, one wounded and unreasonable, the other annoying, frustrated and at a loss, issuing threats he could not follow through with.

You will be spared; when we take your village, no harm will come to you.

She stifled a chuckle. Wonder what he would say about it now that she was the one doing the sparing, she thought. By taking responsibility for his friend's life, deciding whether to take it or to leave it to him, as one word up there in the village…

Wandering down the shore, she remembered how it had been at night, where she tried to get away from him and slipped and got her leg stuck between the stones. Oh, but he had to enter the cold water in order to pull her out, and he could not talk straight for quite a long time after that, because of how cold it made him.

Frowning, she tried to push the sadness away. He was dead, and it was for the best. He was an enemy, even if he turned out to be a surprisingly decent person. The other youth would not survive either, not alone and wounded and so far from home, but at least she would return his friend's kindness by feeding him and making him feel a little better.

Scanning the muddy sand under the cliffs revealed nothing. No sight indicated that only last evening they had all squatted there, watching the wolf youth trying to make a fire. He would have managed too, as he was determined and his strokes of the flat stones generated many sparks. But the wind was against him, breathing more vigorously every time he had managed to have his meager pile of dry grass catch a spark. The angered spirits gave him no chance. But then, of course, they were right in doing so.

When she saw a faint blotch of what looked like old blood, her heart lurched. At last! The trail led into the woods, but it made sense, of course. No person in his right mind would stay in the open, not in such a situation.

The food piled in the hem of her dress that she had pulled up in order to carry it easier hindered her progress, but she climbed the narrow path, determined. No more suspicious-looking marks stained the ground, and it was discouraging. No footsteps, no trampled bushes. Did she go in the wrong direction?

"Are you there?" she called out carefully, forcing her mind to seek the words of their foul-sounding tongue once again. It came out weakly, barely reaching her own ears. "Shi-kon. You there, out?"

There seemed to be a rustling somewhere ahead, so she resumed her walk, careful not to slip on the slick moss. It was so quiet in here; again, too peaceful.

"Are you there?"

He materialized out of the thick foliage so suddenly, her heart tossed itself wildly against her ribs, then went nearly still. Fluttering in her chest, it sent waves of nausea up her throat, the trembling frustrating, making her wish to run away and disappear. She fought not to let the tanned leather of her skirt slip from her sweaty palms, but one of the cobs slid down nevertheless, rolling over the marshy earth after bouncing off the tip of her moccasin.

"You came back," he said, not asking but stating a fact, openly puzzled, the suspicion darkening his strong, muddied features.

She was still busy fighting with her dress, welcoming the distraction, postponing the need to face him with nothing to fiddle with. She must have looked so stupid, walking up that trail, calling out, then getting so scared.

A quick glance at him confirmed the worst. He was staring at her pulled-up skirt and the food in the improvised pocket it created with one eyebrow raised high, the creases of his forehead making an intricate pattern, clearly questioning her sanity.

"I did it... I not..." She cleared her throat. "Yes, I come back, back to see, to see if your friend, alive or not. That's why come back. No other reason!"

Why was it important to state her reasons? His gaze reflected the same question her mind was shooting at her in frustration. His other eyebrow joined the first, both arching in a suggestive way, as though puzzled but prepared to break down in amusement. If he laughed, she would try to kill him, she decided.

"Stop look, look at me like that!" Had she not known that doing so would just cause more food to fall from her skirt, she would have stomped her foot in frustration. "I come to your friend. Not you. He is bad, wound, feel bad. He needs eat, drink. I bring him food." She considered letting it all go for the sake of picking a cob to throw at him. "You not supposed, not alive even. How you not dead? They say you dead!"

That wiped the smug expression off his face at once. "Who said I was dead?"

The air again became thicker, like before the storm. She felt the danger spreading in waves, turning tangible, something she might have tried to touch if she dared. It was there, floating in the air, as though his moods influenced their surroundings. Did the last gust of wind have something to do with his tension? There had not even been a light breeze before.

"Who said I was dead?" he repeated, coming closer. "Whom did you overhear?"

There was an anxiety in his eyes now, the need to know. Somehow it reassured her, made him look less threatening than he might have.

Nevertheless, she took a step back.

"People said, father, warriors, hunters, they all said that." His growing puzzlement made him look silly, like a young boy. She tried to stifle a chuckle, but it sneaked out, quite a hysterical sound. "Not you in particular. They did not talk about you." Catching herself talking back in her people's tongue, she felt the blood rushing into her face again. "Not you. But all, all warriors. When say all, I think all, with you too, include, included."

"You don't make much sense." His frown was back, banishing

the youthful expression. "You must have overheard Kayeri. That dirty piece of rotten meat would say something like that, the greasy bastard that he is. He is so stupid, and he will lose more men, you just—"

Suddenly, his eyes widened, grew out of proportion to the rest of his features, turning almost round, becoming dazed. His mouth opened, gaping at her for some time before the words came out.

"There was a battle, wasn't there? When the sun was high?"

She just nodded, bewildered.

"They all died?" The intensity of his gaze was frightening.

She nodded again.

"All of them?"

It was unsettling, to watch the dismay, the baffled apprehension. He was so sure of himself before. Pale and disheveled, and bruised all over, not the vision of the dauntless, invincible warrior who had frightened her only a few dawns earlier, while spying on the enemy for the first time, but still tough and dangerous and full of decision. Well, now the self-assured determination was gone, and the person who stared at her was nothing but a youth, bewildered and lost.

Her apprehension disappeared all at once.

"Help me with the food," she said resolutely, indicating the fallen maize. "Your friend, is alive?"

He nodded numbly, still staring.

"Well, then we go, go to him." The dullness of his stare was annoying. "Pick those cobs and go. Friend, he need food, maybe water. Eh?"

"You brought us food?" he asked, blinking.

"Umm, yes." The uneasiness returned with redoubled strength. "He wounded, feel bad. I promised..."

His face came to life with a slightly amused, if a puzzled smile. "You are quite a girl, aren't you?" Back to his brisk, forceful self, he picked up the fallen maize, then proceeded to take hold of the rest of her burden. "Akweks is there, in the woods. He is not feeling too good, not yet. Had a rough night." His side glance and lifted eyebrows made her remember the night with uncomfortable clarity. "How is *your* friend? Still alive?"

The thought of Schikan twisted her stomach in a violent way. He was asking for her earlier, or so Namaas said. But then the battle began, and they were too busy, and then…

"Yes, he better, I think. I go see him when back." She swallowed. "You did good, good thing. I should thank…"

His grin was one-sided and lacking in mirth. "I wonder about that." Then the grimness returned. "Are you sure they are all dead?"

Without the need to balance her skirt, she fell into his step easily, climbing up the invisible trail.

"Yes. Father say so."

"Who is your father?"

"Father? Father is War Chief, our War Chief."

That startled him into nearly stumbling. "You have war chiefs?"

It was becoming familiar, this expression of puzzled surprise. She returned his gaze. "Of course. Why would we no, no have war chief?"

"I don't know." Shrugging, he resumed his walk. "I thought you were just a village."

That statement hurt.

"We are village, yes. And there, there are bigger, places, towns. Yes. But," she fought the urge to grab his arm in order to stop him and make him listen, "we are not small; we have many families, many clans. And warriors, yes. We are not afraid. We fight. Your people, they know now."

"Oh, yes, they do." His grunt resonated between the towering cliffs. "And if the stupid wooden-head Kayeri had listened to me, they wouldn't have had to pay…" A slippery, moss-covered stone went flying, kicked savagely, with much venom. Then a familiar shrug replaced it. "Your people are full of surprises, yes. And you, too." He motioned with his head. "Well, here we are."

The space between the cliffs was tiny, separated from the view of the river by a cluster of trees, shielded from the wind and the light, intimate. Like a very shallow cave, it gave one the sense of shelter. She blinked in the semidarkness. Not a satisfactory shelter, yes, but better than their previous refuge by the shore.

The wounded was curled on the unpadded earth, motionless, sprawling there, just a dark heap of limbs. Was he alive? Curious, she knelt beside him, acutely aware of his companion, who busied himself with arranging their treasures in a wide piece of bark he seemed to have made use of before.

"I need something better to bring him water in. Pity you didn't bring a flask or something."

"He is no good." She studied the thinned, drawn face, the eyes closed but moving under their lids, restless. Limbs jerking, chest rising and falling unevenly, not rapidly but not as calmly as that of a sleeping person, the wounded gave an impression of a sick man.

"He is asleep now, and it's good. He needs to rest." The wolf youth still fiddled with the bark, his back on them.

"He is not. Not just sleep. Think he get sick." She reached for the wide forehead carefully, afraid to startle the man. His skin was clammy but not burning, just mildly warm, unpleasantly so. It must have been good that his blood wasn't boiling, and yet somehow, she didn't feel reassured, not while looking into the sallow features. "Maybe no sick. But he is no good. No healthy."

"He isn't sick!"

The exclamation rang sharply, bouncing off the towering rocks. She looked up, surprised. His challenging glare met hers.

"His wounds aren't rotting," he went on, when she said nothing, just stared back. "So there is no reason for him to get sick." The defiance in his eyes grew. "His wounds are healing, both of them. One faster than the other, that's all."

"I don't know what you talk." She let out an exasperated breath, then turned back to the wounded. "He is no look good, look sick. That is it." Again, she touched the clammy forehead, taking the hand away when he stirred. "I don't know why you argue. It change not, nothing."

He grunted something, then knelt beside them.

"Akweks, wake up." Leaning closer, he put his palm on his friend's laboring chest, his scowl deepening. "Wake up." His nostrils widened, as he sniffed the air. "See, no smell? His wounds aren't rotting."

As though she had said something like that. She exhaled loudly, then got to her feet, the neatly arranged pile of food catching her eye, inviting. She hadn't eaten properly since the day before, either. They were not the only hungry people around, and she hadn't brought it all only for them.

"Wake up, brother."

The wounded groaned lightly, and she stopped her nibbling on a slice of dried meat, trying to see better.

"Wake up. You need to eat something." The wolf youth was shaking his friend's shoulder now, not especially gently, his voice ringing with urgency. Or maybe with a flicker of panic.

She came closer.

"What? What is happening?" The wounded groaned and tried to sit up, not making a good job out of it until his friend grabbed his shoulder, pulling him up firmly, helping to lean his back against the uneven surface of the rock. Even with help, the youth's broad face broke out with a sheen of sweat.

"We have things to eat." His companion was talking rapidly, no more successful at his attempt to sound light than his friend in the effort to sit up unaided. "What do you want, meat or corn?"

"Water," croaked the wounded, closing his eyes. "Just water. I'm not, not hungry; sorry…"

The wolf youth said nothing for a heartbeat. He didn't even move. Yet, she could feel his desperation welling, filling the closed space, making it look darker, although the light barely reached it as it was. She held her breath.

"I'll bring you water."

He got up slowly, as though hindered by a pain or a wound too. She watched his wide back, rigid like the surrounding cliffs, the cut under his shoulder blade long and clean, a neat crimson line, not caked with dried blood even. It looked like war paint, a part of a pattern, but for the bluish swelling at its edges.

"Will you watch him until I'm back?" he asked, snatching the arched bark without looking at her.

"Yes."

He was gone before she knew it, disappearing into the greenish foliage, leaving more tension in his wake. She let her breath out.

The wounded was peering at her painfully. "Local girl? You came back?"

She licked her lips. "Yes."

A hint of a smile brought some life into the sallow features. "You are full of surprises."

"I'm not." Kneeling beside him, she hesitated. "I bring food. You want?"

He shook his head vigorously, but the movement made him flinch, and his face lost the little liveliness it had gained, breaking out in a new bout of sweat.

"The damn thing," he muttered, when able to talk. "It hurts even if I don't move."

"I see, want to see."

He shrugged lightly, clearly afraid to move, his lips colorless, caught between his teeth. Carefully, she leaned closer, repulsed by the odor of stale blood. The gash wasn't too large, the size of a smaller pinecone maybe, brownish, swollen, dark, glittering with wetness. It looked painful, unhealthy. It made her think of the ointments the old healer was putting on wounds this very morning, and of his bag of sharp needles and lines of sinew.

"You need healer. He would close it, put ointment."

His groan bordered with a snort. She sighed. Yes, there was no use making that comment.

"Our men will know what to do." His lips twisted into the hint of a crooked grin. "Once they bother to come back."

"What?" Caught unprepared, she looked up, to stare into his face from too close a proximity. It was as though they were about to touch, or do something silly like kissing. The thought had her backing away in a hurry.

He stared at her, as embarrassed. "What?"

"You say, your people. But..." She hesitated, trying to gather her wits. "But they are dead. They are not—"

His eyes turned as round as his friend's had a very short time ago, gaping at her, enormously large. "What do you mean 'dead'?"

She just shrugged, then turned away to watch the bushes and the invisible path the wolf youth must have followed while heading down to the river bank.

"Tell me!"

Her heart twisted at the open dismay in his voice. Just like his friend's oh so very short time ago. It was easy to shatter their confidence, but she didn't find the experience pleasing, not as she might have expected it would be.

"There battle, there was a battle." She took a deep breath. "Your people, they dead."

"No, they are not! I know about the battle. Okwaho told me. He fought with them. He came back just before dawn and told me all about it." He shook his head vigorously, forgetting about his wound as it seemed, or too preoccupied to pay attention to the pain it brought. "Some died, yes. Your people too, more than mine! They... they didn't lose that battle, and they didn't die." A spasm twisted his face, and the heated tirade died away. "You think you know it all, but you don't," he muttered in the end, his eyes avoiding hers.

"Yes, I know. I do know." It should have been pleasing to prove him wrong, but it wasn't. She wished she hadn't started this conversation at all. "It's not, not the same battle. It's different. This morning—"

His clenched fist hit the ground. "You are lying!"

She ground her teeth, frustrated, her compassion trickling away. Why would she lie about something like that?

"You are lying to make us do something stupid, so your people will get us easier," he was almost shouting now, his face glowing with red as opposed to its previous paleness, eyes wild, about to faint, maybe. "You came to trick us. You told them up there in your ugly, stupid, worthless village... You told them all about us, and they sent you to scare us out. But it won't... it won't work... You will never... "

The flow of words was interrupted more and more often, his chest laboring, fighting for breath, both hands pressed against the ground as though he were about to try to get up. Not much chance of him succeeding in that. Still, she jumped to her feet, afraid.

"You are lying!" The shrillness of his voice was jarring, echoing between the towering walls of their small hideaway.

"What in the name of the Great Spirits?"

The sound of rapidly cracking branches brought the owner of the wolf tattoo back, breaking through the bushes, wide-eyed. The improvised water vessel balanced carefully in his hands held a barely adequate amount—the rest must have spilled as he hurried. He scrutinized them anxiously, eyes jumping from one face to the other.

Reassured that no one was harmed, he dropped next to his friend, his eyes narrowing into slits. "What?"

The wounded, by now half-sitting half-lying, slumped rather than propped against the rock, drew shallow breaths one after another.

"She said... she said our people... they were all dead," he murmured, coughing.

The contents of the bark disappeared, gulped all at once, trickling down the bruised chin.

"Lie back. Rest now." The wolf youth tossed his improvised vessel away. "I'll think about what to do."

"But she said..." Resisting the attempt to make him lie back down, the wounded gripped his friend's arm. "She said there was a battle, this morning. She is lying, isn't she?"

The wolf youth said nothing for a moment, again going still, lost in thought. "I don't know, brother," he said finally, getting up. "I'll think about what to do."

"But how? It's impossible. You said they didn't manage to surprise you at night. You said—"

A violent spasm went over the broad face all of sudden, transforming it, making the image of a wolf shudder, as though about to come to life. Watching the smoldering fire pouring out of his eyes, Kentika felt the old fear coming back, trickling down her stomach, making it twist.

"They didn't manage to surprise us at night, but that was not the case in the morning," he growled, and she knew that if it wasn't for his fear of being detected, he would be thundering now in the scariest of voices. "The stinking rat Kayeri! He didn't listen to me at night, when I came to tell him about you, but he did pay attention when I talked about the shadows sneaking out of the village. But in the morning, his ears were again full of moss, and he didn't listen any more. He chose to accuse me of cowardice, instead. He sent me away and ordered me to never come back!"

The vein pulsated on his forehead, and his protruding cheekbones turned dangerously sharp, enhancing the glow of his eyes, as dark as the river at night.

"He didn't," whispered the wounded, openly aghast.

The air hissed, drawn forcefully through the clenched teeth. "He did worse than that. And if he paid for his stupidity, I will not mourn for him, but I do for the others, those who didn't deserve to start seeking their Sky Path ahead of their time."

A silence prevailed, a heavy, suffocating silence. It was as though they had been cast under water, at the bottom of the river, able to see but not to hear, let alone breathe. So much impotent anger, so much frustration!

Like in a dream, she watched him unclenching his fists, turning around, glancing at her briefly, with no recognition.

"So it's true. They *are* dead!" The wounded sagged against the wall listlessly, fighting for breath, once again a heap of limbs. "I... I can't believe it."

Another bout of silence. Then the wolf youth shrugged. "I'll find a way out of it," he muttered, turning around and disappearing back in the direction he came from, his eyes blank, empty, not seeing either of them.

Still outside herself and not completely aware, Kentika stepped into the light of the late afternoon, letting the warmth wash over her, envelope her, encourage her spirit. It was all too confusing, too strange. It was time to go back. Before they noticed her disappearance up there in the village. Before she did something stupid, like helping these two to ... to do what? To escape? There was no way of escape for them. But why would she be concerned with it?

The wall of brilliant green stood in her way, urging her to take a different direction. It warned her, the rustling of the wind and the murmuring of the river so very close but still out of sight. Resolutely, she pushed the branches away.

He was sitting on the overturned boat, the smaller sort of canoe, a narrow dugout with two benches inside. The sound of her footsteps did not make him turn his head. His eyes were glued to the glimpse of the water the curving line of the shore provided, she discovered, coming closer, afraid but somehow needing to be near him. Squatting on a nearby stone, she watched the flying drops, the current strong even here, so near the shore, carrying broken branches.

"They are truly gone, aren't they?" he said after a long, strangely comfortable silence. "You weren't lying to us?"

She shook her head, then ran her palm over the smooth, pleasantly warm surface of her seat. "Father say, and he no lie. He is our War Chief. He always tells the truth."

"So not all of your people were out there, trying to surprise us at night." He phrased it as a statement, shaking his head, grimly amused. "He must be a good leader, your father, to plan all this."

"He didn't plan it." The wish to speak normal people's tongue welled. It was so tiring to talk in this stupid, simple way, seeking words every time she needed to say something. "Father, he was not, not here, not in the village. He was away."

"Then how?" He glanced at her, puzzled, the dangerous look gone, smoothed by the peacefulness of the woods and the river.

"I don't know, don't know who plan, or how. But my brother, he was not in the village. He was away, too. And then, then they came back, first Migisso, at night, then Father, in the morning." She shrugged. "Glooskap, maybe sent them, made them come and help."

"Who is Glooskap?" His frown deepened but did not turn direful, not ruining the peacefulness. "Another war leader?"

Against her will, she laughed. "Glooskap? War leader?"

His lips trembled as though he was about to join her in her laughter. "He isn't?"

"No! Glooskap is the greatest, the greatest spirit. He always good, always keep us, us people, safe. He, he protect." The curiosity of his gaze seemed genuine, not marred by hostility or contempt. "He has a brother, twin brother, Malsum. Malsum is bad, truly bad. He tried to kill, many times, to kill Glooskap, his brother. He didn't manage. So now he is in the Underworld, the wicked wolf-spirit. Still dangerous, but not, not in daylight."

His eyebrows climbed high. "Wolves are good. They are smart and loyal and strong. They are leaders, and they take care of their own. Wolf spirit can't be bad."

"Yes, he can," she insisted, the old annoyance with him creeping back. "Of course, he can. Malsum is a wolf and he *is* bad." His tattoo caught her eye, so wonderfully detailed, almost alive in the deepening shadows. "But yes, there are good wolves too, many of them good. We don't think all wolves bad. But this one is."

He shrugged. "My name, Okwaho, means wolf in Flint People's tongue, and my father chose it carefully, consulting the wisest of elders and the medicine men from both our nations. He knew from the very beginning, as soon as I was born. He knew, because he is the wisest man alive. He said wolves are the most beautiful creatures, the wisest. He said their loyalty is to be praised, and their sense of responsibility. He said this name honored me and that I should never let it down. He said he knew I wouldn't."

"He right? He was right?" It was difficult to follow his rapidly flowing speech, but the way his face lit and his eyes shone made her wish to keep him talking.

"I hope so. I hope he'll prove right over the course of summers. He is always right. He is a great man." His smile turned self-conscious. "And I didn't even need to change it when my time to pick a more appropriate name came. On my quest for the guiding spirit, who did you think was there, on the very first day of my fasting?" The excitement was spilling out of his eyes as he peered at her, pausing, as though savoring his own story. "The silvery wolf! Large, sleek, noble, the most beautiful creature you have ever seen. And the wisest, I could see that. I wanted to go down that tree, to come near him, to talk to him, to ask for his strength. One is not supposed to climb down, you see? One is to converse with his guardian only in spirit, but this wolf, you understand, he was real. He was there for me, and I knew he wouldn't harm me."

"And then?" she asked, mesmerized, imagining it too well,

despite the lack of some words—the woods, and the clearing, probably near dusk, some distant forest full of strange creatures, like this wolf; and this youth, just a boy back then, both belonging to the world of the spirits.

His chuckle shook the air, soft and mischievous, breaking the spell.

"By the time I managed to come down, he was gone. It took me time to do that, you see? I'm usually not a bad climber, but this time, I was so clumsy. I made so much noise." The widest of smiles revealed a bright row of teeth, with the gap of a missing one. "I'll never admit it, but my legs were trembling too badly. And my hands, too. But it wasn't fear. Well, not all of it. Some of it was excitement." Another chuckle, this time as provocative as the smile. "It was dark already, so when I saw he was gone, I rushed back up as fast as I could. I was not about to test him and his patience on the first time of our bonding."

She fought her own smile no longer. "How old, how many summers you see back then?"

"Close to fifteen."

"So old!"

He peered at her, surprised. "Why old?"

"Our boys, men, they do early, go and seek the spirit. Not fifteen."

"When then?"

"Maybe thirteen, or younger. My brother, he see, saw thirteen summers. And it was old too. But Father said no before. He wanted him to turn more... more prepared, more old."

"More matured?"

She appreciated his helpfulness. "What matured?"

"Experienced, grown, advanced, a person who did things already."

"Oh, well, yes, yes, matured. Most boys go out, seek spirit earlier."

He shrugged, unimpressed. "Well, our people are not in such a hurry. We have no enemies worth mentioning, no serious wars, not since the Great Peacemaker, so there is no need to hurry boys to turn into men. Your people should be more patient."

That sounded outright patronizing. She pursed her lips. "No enemies? But here you are, here make war."

"That is barely a war. Those are just raids, meaningless but for the people who are involved in them. The town of Cohoes Falls would benefit, yes, but for the League of the Five Nations, it's nothing." His wink held a sort of mischievous apology. "Raids keep young men from getting bored, from doing stupid things. It's nothing."

"Nothing?"

Speechless, she stared at him, too enraged to find anything to say. To keep men from getting bored? They came here, disrupting her village's life, killing people, wounding others, shooting fire arrows and burning houses, out of boredom?

"Well, you know." He shifted uneasily, dropping his gaze. "That's what warriors do. Your men are doing the same, I'm sure. Don't they raid neighboring villages or something?"

"No, they don't! Why... why would they?" A fly was buzzing next to her ear, and she waved it away impatiently, needing to say too much, not finding enough words to communicate what she wanted to express. "You evil, evil as Malsum if you come here, come here to harm because you are bored. It is evil, and wrong, and... " She stomped her foot in frustration at his audacity and her lack of words. "It is bad!"

His puzzled frown might have been a funny sight, had she not been so angry.

"Just don't start yelling, would you?" He shrugged, raising both hands, palms up. "Look, it is how it is. Warriors go out and raid other people's settlements. You said your father is a war chief. So you must have warriors, then. And they must go out and raid someone's towns and villages, don't they? Why would you have a war chief if you had no warriors?"

She almost groaned aloud. "We warriors, we have warriors to protect. To defend against people like you!"

"And they never go out to attack some of your neighbors' villages?" he asked, openly derisive now. "I don't believe you!"

"No, they do no raids. Our warrior only protect."

But she hesitated, for, of course, there were warriors, in their village and the neighboring ones, who would join the war parties organized at Skootuck, or some other large towns along the Great River Whose Waters Are Never Still. The talk of the alliance that Father was eager to promote, the reason he went to Skootuck this time, related to exactly that, the need of sending large, concentrated raids into the land of these same western savages. But it was different, it was!

His laughter made her wish to hit him. "You are lying now," he said, his voice trembling with genuine mirth. "So obvious. You are a lousy liar."

Bereft of words, she just glared at him.

"Of course your people do raid others," he went on, unconcerned. "Or they would not have put up a decent fight, or built that funny fence of yours."

"Our fence is not funny," she grunted through her clenched teeth.

"No, it's not. But it's not the most sophisticated palisade, either." His eyes lit again. "Our towns are protected by a double row of palisade, with a corridor in between, to make it truly difficult to fight your way in. Easier for the defenders, you see?" He made a face. "And our longhouses aren't built too close to it, so no one has much chance to put it ablaze with fire arrows. See? This is how you keep your people safe."

"People safe, but not warriors. Your warriors die, die when raid funny village with funny fence. All of them!"

His derisive amusement was gone, disappearing all at once, replaced by a tightened jaw and hardened eyes. The sight of it pleased her, despite the small twinge of fear, well familiar by now. He was dangerous when angered, even if he turned out to be surprisingly nice otherwise, interesting, even chatty.

"We are not done yet," he growled out, getting to his feet. "We may be full of surprises, too."

Following his example, she rose, trying to do it slowly, as though indifferent to his movements. She needed to hurry back home, anyway. They would be truly incensed with her now.

He was watching the river, eyes blank, seeing nothing, face again haggard and empty, the wolf on his jaw lacking in life.

The unwelcome ripple of compassion crept in, uninvited. Why should she pity him and his situation? He was an annoying, self-assured enemy, an arrogant beast with no respect and no mind to listen to anyone but himself.

"What do? What will you do?" The words came out before she was able to stop herself, surprising them both.

He looked at her for a long moment, then shrugged. "Take Akweks and sail away, I suppose."

"You can't now. He is sick, too sick. He won't, won't manage to stay living…"

His face closed again. "He will be better by the next dawn," he said sharply. "His wounds are not rotting."

"He sick." Now it was her turn to shrug. "Rotting, no rotting, he is sick. Can't sail. Need to see healer. Need ointment, need drink medicine."

The air hissed, escaping through his clenched teeth. "He will have to manage with no healer. He'll be all right."

"I come back, with dawn," she said, surprising herself more than she surprised him as it seemed.

She fought the urge to press her palms to her mouth, to push the words back, but his smile caused her forget the embarrassment, that same open smile that made his face look boyish, like before, when he was talking about his wolf.

"You are kind." His eyes glimmered softly, relaying his gratitude, and yet there was something in there, something else, something amused and mischievous. Something measuring. As though he was wondering if she was up to a challenge.

Embarrassed for no reason, she dropped her gaze.

"It's nothing," she murmured. "No kind. Just, just want help. You saved Schikan. Didn't kill when you can." Relieved, she looked up in time to see his eyes turning serious, attentive, losing that disturbing spark. "And your friend, I want to help." Shrugging, she looked away again. "I bring things. Food. Maybe medicine, eh? To put on his wound."

"If you do that," he swallowed, then drew a deep breath, his gaze grave, reflecting no amusement anymore, "I will repay you. I will find a way to repay you your kindness. You'll see."

CHAPTER 14

She was missing again, nowhere to be found. Migisso sighed.

His sister was incurable, such a restless spirit, made worse by the recent upheavals. The last two days should have calmed her down, made her understand the fragility of life, the fleetingness of it, made her respect the dangers and the customs that were created to minimize it. They should have made her more reasonable, less prone to her impulses and whims.

However, they seemed to do just the opposite. Instead of keeping low, like her other fellow women and many of the men did, she went about her life in a more independent manner than before, going in and out as she pleased, as though no enemy was prowling out there, shooting and killing, and setting houses on fire.

"Did you look around the ceremonial grounds, or just outside that opening in the fence?" Schikan had asked him earlier, when he came to check on his wounded friend for the tenth time through this daunting, exhausting day.

Schikan's broken arm worried him. It had not been fixed properly through the night, even though the protruding bone was returned to its place, and the wound cleaned most thoroughly. Still, the special splint he had carved out at night was nowhere to be found, with nothing but a hastily obtained stick securing his friend's broken limb.

Kentika!

He had grunted through his teeth, wishing to find her and shake her hard. Why couldn't she be trusted to stick around for at least one single morning in order to take care of his friend? She cared about Schikan, obviously enough to risk her life while saving him—an adventure he, Migisso, had yet to hear all about—but not enough to stay around and do something as boring as caring for the wounded. *Where was she?*

"Or maybe near the storage pits. Women might have decided to sort our supplies if stuck in the town for another day," Schikan went on, leaning heavily against a chest padded with a generous layer of blankets, not daring to move a limb. He should have been lying down, Migisso knew, but neither he nor the old healer were able to convince the stubborn man to do that. The wounded insisted on sitting up, and he would have been walking or crawling but for the unbearable pain any attempt of movement had caused.

Broken ribs must be a terrible thing to cope with, he thought, shivering. May mighty Glooskap keep him from such a trial.

He shook his head grimly, getting rid of irrelevant thoughts. "I looked everywhere. She is not in the village."

"Then where can she possibly—" The heated exclamation stopped in midair, as Schikan's face twisted, turning yet paler, breaking out with sweat.

His heart twisting with compassion, Migisso watched his friend's features contorting into an unrecognizable pattern, eyes closing, teeth making a mess out of the thin lower lip. How terribly painful it must be!

"You should lie down and rest, try to sleep a little," he said, when the new outburst of agony evidently receded, leaving the wounded's face empty, just a colorless mask.

"Don't want to," groaned Schikan, careful to move his lips only. "Want out, want to sit out there." The glittering eyes opened, dominating the lifeless face once again, a bit too glossy. Was his blood beginning to boil? Migisso suppressed his welling anxiety.

"Not now, not today. But maybe with dawn, eh? I'll come and take you out. I'll bring someone to help me."

"Bring your sister." Schikan's grin held a measure of grim amusement. "She is strong, strong enough to carry me all the way here."

"If I find the wild thing by then, and if she doesn't disappear again." Migisso grinned back, then shrugged, not amused. "She is getting worse as she grows. It is as though the forest is ruling her spirit, more so with each passing summer." He hesitated, uncomfortable with sharing such inner thoughts. "I fear it will claim her for good one day."

Schikan's eyes darkened. "I pray it won't."

For some time, they kept silent, each deep in his own unhappy thoughts. Did his friend care for her? he asked himself, suddenly perturbed. Did anyone?

She was such an outcast, a strange little thing, not pretty in a womanly way, not belonging. And yet she had seen close to sixteen summers. She was a woman. At her age many girls began casting glances and gathering admiration; many mothers began to think of proper arrangements. Did Mother? Or Father?

He suppressed a shiver, hoping he did not. She wasn't a woman, no matter what her age said, and she wasn't ready. She wouldn't agree to anything like that, and then it would be another war, another struggle to darken the insides of their family hut. More punishments for her, and maybe for him too, because he would have to stand by her side in this.

"What was she doing out there at the night of the battle with you?" he asked, mainly to channel his thoughts in a different direction.

A fleeting smile lit Schikan's sallow features. "I don't know. I wish I did." He shook his head lightly, almost imperceptibly; still, it made his face twist and the teeth attack his lips again, savagely. "She jumped out of nowhere, collided with me, you see? I didn't recognize her at all. It was so dark, and they kept popping up everywhere, like mushrooms, like the evil spirits that they are." Carefully, he drew a short breath, obviously afraid to do more than that. "It's a wonder I didn't hit her with my club. How were we to tell one from another in the darkness? But you see, something stopped me, made me hesitate. But then that warrior, he managed to surprise me. Oh, Benevolent Spirits, did it hurt, that blow!"

The anguished eyes closed again, as though desperate to hide.

Another heartbeat of heavy silence passed.

"She helped. In her very special way, you know. By messing this particular fight up. That man, I bet he didn't know what happened." The bloodied lips quivered into a thin smile. "I don't remember it all, but she seemed to hang onto him, and then somehow, they were on the ground, and while he struggled against her, it was easier..."

A shrug, even if light, proved to be of disastrous consequences, and while supporting the wounded in his agony, Migisso fought the familiar uneasiness. For whatever reason, she was there, in the middle of the battle, fighting, *actually fighting*, helping his friend, carrying him back to safety, saving his life. She, a woman, a young girl! While all he did was drag after warriors, not even expected to participate but to help, to guide when needed, to treat the wounded. To be of use, yes, not a coward, but not a warrior either. Not like Schikan. Or her, his little sister.

"You need to rest," he said when the agony receded and Schikan's panted breath began to have a semblance of normality. "I'll bring you water, then make you another medicine."

The young man just nodded, drained of strength. With practiced efficiency, Migisso brushed his palm against the damp forehead, feeling it out. It wasn't burning. He breathed with relief.

Inside the house, the water bin was still mostly full. His mind only partly on what he was doing, he fished a cup from the pile of utensils.

"There was another strange thing." Schikan actually seemed to look better. Half-lying against his padded prop, he drank thirstily, careful not to move a muscle other than those necessary for drinking. "I don't remember that clearly. My mind might have been wandering already when she brought me back. But..." A painful frown crossed the ashen features. "But I think I remember ... remember a warrior, an enemy. He was going to kill us both. You see, I could not fight, not by this time. But then..." The disoriented gaze clung to Migisso, agonizing. "Kentika talked to him. In their foul-sounding tongue, she talked to him and he, he listened. That warrior listened to her! He seemed surprised, puzzled. But maybe I wasn't there anymore. Maybe my spirit had already been wandering." Another harassed frown. "Yet, I remember reaching the opening of the fence, and the way we were struggling through it, and the healer. I remember us reaching the healer, and other wounded there on the ground. I remember that as clearly as that warrior, and her talking to him. And him staring at us. He was surprised, but he stared at her. And when he talked, he sounded almost amused. But only for a heartbeat. Because there was noise, people coming, and he said something in a hurry, and then he was gone. But it can't be, it can't! No enemy would... And her, how could she know what to say, all those strange words? I must have been crossing into the dream world by then."

"Yes, I think you must have, brother," said Migisso, his thoughts only partly on the frantically spoken words, the main part of his mind occupied with the question of where to find the necessary plants and how to make his brewing of them not very noticeable, not by the War Chief in any case. Had he been an accepted assistant of the old healer, he would have many roots and plants in his bag now, and a place to work with them in the bargain.

He stifled a sigh. "Rest now, old friend. I will be back with the medicine shortly."

Nodding at the women who lingered nearby, stirring bowls of maize dough, members of Schikan's immediate family, most of them, he hurried off, trying to pay no attention to the throbbing behind his temples.

These had been terrible two days, no sleep, no rest, no satisfaction in the victory even. The enemy was held off, then killed, yes, but the village had still paid the price. So many wounded, so many mourning ceremonies to conduct. Death in every other clan, wounded in almost each cluster of houses. Not to mention the repairs and rebuilding. These would take time and effort, and just as the entire village was so busy in the fields and the woods. Not to mention Father, and his ideas of this strange alliance with the neighbors that the prominent man had been busy pushing with his usual forcefulness and no consideration for the feelings of others.

Father!

He felt the knot in his stomach tightening, pressing his insides, reminding him that he needed to relieve himself. Father had been as efficient, as always, first finishing the enemy off, then coming inside to organize everything and everyone, without so much as a pause to take a breath. The man was truly a great leader.

He had found no time to see his family yet, too busy with attempting to return everything back to normal, but he had interviewed Migisso while speaking to the rest of the warriors, those who came back from Skootuck on the day before.

There was a glint of satisfaction in the man's deeply set eyes, as he nodded gravely, acknowledging his son's active involvement, not displeased with it, not like always. It should have made him, Migisso, feel good, but it didn't. He had been too busy thinking of his wounded friend and his missing sister at that time. Father would wish to see her too at some point, to interview her as he had the warriors and the others. Not as a daughter, but as a person who had been involved. It was she who had spotted the enemy in the first place; she who had been out there when no one was; it was she who had saved Schikan.

Oh, the War Chief would wish to hear it all, displeased with her, of course, no matter the helpfulness of her information or the mostly positive outcome of her actions this time. And when he summoned her, she had better be near and available, not missing again.

His legs took him toward the ceremonial grounds. Paying no attention to the hubbub and the people rushing all around, he nodded absently at their greetings. The things they said did not enter his mind; neither did their wondering stares register.

Around the maple tree there was not much activity, thank all the great and small spirits for that. Trying to act disinterested, he looked around. Some women were sweeping the ground, and a group of men hurried off, carrying axes and a half-shattered pole.

Lips pressed tight, Migisso strolled toward the giant tree, still ready to be detained, asked questions. He had every right to walk around, hadn't he? It wasn't like he was doing something bad.

Behind the wide trunk, it was dimmer and warmer, the soft afternoon light and the breeze not easily reaching through the thick foliage and the mass of the fence. His heart beating fast, he rushed on, not looking around, not anymore.

The gap between the poles greeted him reservedly, not friendly or hostile, but indifferent, the woods behind it darker, preparing for the night. He hesitated, but the gust of fresh wind beckoned, cooling his burning face. It was calmer out there.

The treetops above his head rustled reassuringly. It was good to be outside, he decided, his taut nerves calming. It was a welcome break from all the pressure.

Strolling in a leisurely way now, he headed down the hill, not sure of his destination. She was most probably wandering the river's shores, as she usually did, all her favorite places and little hideaways. She had been such a forest animal, this little sister of his. Annoying in her strange ways, yes, difficult to handle, but still such a good person, a pleasant reality of his life. To try to shield her from Father's disapproval and punishments as much as he could was his choice, not her demand. She deserved this, and he hadn't even thanked her for saving his friend's life last night. Instead, he flared at her for the same crime she had been scolded for all her life. As though Father's punishments and Mother's reprimands were not enough.

He rolled his eyes, then hesitated again. He could not possibly go all the way down to the river. It would take too much time, and he wouldn't even reach it before the dusk. The last part of the daylight should be spent in a better, more efficient way. He was not supposed to wander out there with no aim any more than she was. What was she doing, the annoying little thing?

A branch cracked in the distance, causing him to tense. An enemy? But the enemies were killed, to the last man. Or were they? Frantically, he reached for his knife, clumsy, cutting one of his fingers in the process.

The silence was natural, serene, rustling with the breeze. Undecided, he strolled along the hill's incline, toward the trail, remembering the night, the thrill, the expectation, the shame of the fear. Frightened and excited at the same time, what a strange combination. Ready to fight, undoubtedly this time, and yet relieved when they kept sending him back and forth, to bring things, to communicate messages, even when the fight erupted. Their mistrust hurt, but not enough to cause him to argue, or better yet, to make independent decisions, like most of them did. Communicating messages was a waste of time. No one listened to the other.

He shrugged, then caught his breath as a shadow fell across the trail.

"Oh, it's you!"

There was laughter in her voice, laced with an obvious thread of relief. Pale, dirty, and disheveled, she stood before him, beaming, her smile wide, her eyes sparkling with guilt. He tried to will his heart into a more reasonable beating.

"What are you doing here?"

Her smile widened. "Nothing."

"Nothing?" He took a deep breath, remembering his decision not to get angry with her—a difficult resolution to keep. "Listen, I came here looking for you. Come back and stay. Father will want to talk to you. Maybe he got around to sending for you already. Do you want to make him angry at such a time?"

The smile died away, replaced with tightening lips. "He was looking for me?"

"No, he wasn't. Not to my knowledge. But he might have by now."

She tossed her head impatiently. "I needed to wash up. It was a terrible day and an equally terrible night, and I needed to wash up, and I went to do it in the river." Her eyes sparkled with well-familiar stubbornness, set on fighting for her version of events, however unreasonable it might sound. She was always like that, impossible to be budged, especially when caught in a web of the silliest of lies.

He measured her with an openly questioning glance. "Did you enjoy your leisurely swim?" She said nothing, so he laughed outright. "You are caked with mud and what not, and you stink worse than a skunk after it got scared most thoroughly. Find a better excuse, not one that only a blind creature with no sense of smell would accept."

Her eyes narrowed into slits. "You think you are so very clever,

Brother!"

"One doesn't need to be clever, not in this case."

She stomped her foot. "Will you tell on me?"

He shrugged. "What can I tell? I don't know where you were and what dubious things you did, neither now nor on the day before. Or at night, for that matter. All I know is that right now, you lie about it, and in a ridiculous manner. That is all I know."

The frown made her look plain, almost unappealing. She was never held to be beautiful, or pretty even. She was too tall and angular, too awkward, too strong and swift when it came to doing men's things, running and climbing and finding one's way in the forest, but useless in anything the women did, clumsy to the point of ridiculousness. Careless with her appearance, she never bothered with a comb, let alone a needle to make her clothes better fitting. And yet she could sparkle like a lake on a sunny day. It was something about her eyes, or her smile maybe, the way she had usually spoken or moved, with a cheerful passion and unstoppable enthusiasm that he had yet to see anyone else displaying. She was rare and precious, and no one had seen it, but him.

"Well, I'm not lying." She was watching him from under her eyebrows, the way a petulant child would. "I went to wash up, but then something happened. So I didn't. But I did go out for that reason and nothing else. You must believe me on that."

"What happened? What prevented you from taking that swim?"

"Nothing." She dropped her gaze at once, staring angrily at the damp, messy ground. "I can't tell you now."

His suspicion was sudden but overwhelming. "Have you been going around with someone?" She stared at him blankly, but it did not serve to calm his agitation. "Have you been seeing a man?"

Her laughter brought the familiar spark back. "What? Don't talk in a foolish way." Bringing both hands up, she smoothed her hair, a surprisingly self-conscious gesture. "Me? Strolling around the woods with a man? How silly. Have you eaten something bad, Brother?" Her giggle trilled, free of guilt. "Or were you hit on your head by the enemy club?"

He tried to suppress an unwelcome urge to join her in her laughter. "I hadn't eaten for too long, and I saw less fighting than you did, you wild thing. So no, my head is in the best of shapes, all things considered. But you," he peered at her, still annoyed but amused now too, "you have much explaining to do, Sister. Whatever you will tell the others, you will not lie to me. Promise!"

Her teeth flashed, showing in the wideness of her smile, large, even, and very white. "I will tell you. Maybe. But later, not now. If you promise not to get angry. Or preachy." The guilt was back, sparkling out of her eyes, in no apologetic manner. "It is something strange, wild, and unacceptable. Still, well, it is something I want to do. I'm trying to understand something, you see." Now it was her turn to peer at him, with much intensity. "The enemy, they are vicious and alien and bad, yes, but you see, they... they are not all bad. Not always. Sometimes they are quite like us. I just found that out..." Her voice trailed off as her eyes strayed away, immersed in the study of the tree he was standing next to.

He stared at her incredulously. "How did you find out that nonsense?"

She wrinkled her nose and peered back at him from under her brow. "I can't tell you, not now."

"They are all dead, Kentika."

She just shrugged, her eyes blank, too blank. He tried to push the suspicion back where it came from, but it returned with a redoubled force, worse than before. If she was... But that was impossible, plain impossible!

"Tell me!"

She shifted from one foot to another, then shrugged again, resolutely.

"Later; I'll tell you later, Brother." The frown was back. "But now, I need to reach the spring before Father Sun goes back to sleep. Can't go to the village looking like that. I must be looking worse that one of the bad spirits residing in sick animals."

Again, the radiance of her smile proved impossible to resist. He pushed his suspicion away. For the time being.

"You look like a squirrel after a particularly bad winter. Like Msaijo the Squirrel, the one who served Malsum the Wolf and made him do bad things."

All of a sudden, she looked slightly dismayed. "That bad?"

"Worse."

"Oh, please!" Then she beamed again. "Wolves are not all bad, you know. Only Malsum. But other wolves are loyal and strong. And good, sometimes."

"I know that." He studied the pattern of dried mud that covered her face like war paint, splattered all over, yet not enough to conceal the darker glow her cheeks suddenly colored with. "Since when are you interested in wolves? We are not Wolf Clan people."

"I know." Another shrug, another thorough inspection of the ground. "I'm just curious about things. That's all." The guilty smile flashed again. "I better be going. If Mother asks about me, tell her I'm around and on my way."

"And Father?"

Her face lost its previous glow. "He won't ask for me. He is too busy."

"They say you were the one to spot the enemy in the first place. Schikan says you went with them, to show them the place where the enemy hid their boats. He said you helped to remove them, to carry them to another shore."

"Oh, yes." She nodded vigorously, eyes sparkling. "They didn't want to believe me. Many of them. They went out to see if there was truth to what I said, but they were angry with me." She made a face. "Paqua was particularly mean, more than usual. But Schikan diverted his attention as much as he could, and when we found the boats, he was so proud of me." The shine of her eyes dimmed. "He is not wounded badly, is he? The old healer said he might live, if he won't vomit blood or turn hot, or—"

"If you stayed in the village instead of running out there, on these mysterious missions of yours, you would have known the answer to that already." Her gasp and the open fear in her eyes made him feel bad for implying the worst. "He is alive, and he won't die. Not probably. But he is wounded badly enough, and he was asking for you, but you were not around. You were busy elsewhere." He shook his head. "He was worried about you as much as I was, Sister. He wanted to talk to you, to thank you, I suppose. He seemed to be able to think of nothing else. And also..." Hesitating, he remembered the last thing his friend had whispered, suffering and in pain, but still unable to forget, needing to talk about it. "He said you were speaking with the enemy."

Her face drained of color at once. No more healthy glow or blushing. "I did not," she muttered, frowning painfully, again immersed in observing the ground. "Why would he say something like that?"

"I don't know." He studied her carefully, not liking what her body language was saying. "Why do you think?"

Her shrug held a familiar amount of defiance. "I can't possibly know that!" Mouth pressed stubbornly, she faced him. "He is wounded badly enough, you said. Maybe his mind was wandering, so he thought he saw me talking to the enemy."

"Yes, he said that, that he wasn't sure. It was dark, and he was in great pain. He remembered a warrior, and you talking to him. He said this man should have killed him, and you maybe, but he didn't. Because of something you said."

Her open relief puzzled him. It was as though a sun peeked from behind the gathering storm clouds. Not only her face but her entire body seemed to relax, with her eyes turning brighter and the pressed lips stretching into a shy smile.

"Oh, yes, it happened, it did happen. I was so tired and scared, and Schikan was so heavy, and bleeding on me. I feared he would die. And this man, he seemed reasonable." Again the caginess, the quick averting of the eyes. "I told him that Schikan is wounded. I didn't think he'd listen, but he did."

He tried to make sense of her rapidly spoken words.

"How... how did you know what to say?"

And then it hit him. But of course! She used to be close with the captive woman. What was her name? He didn't remember, but she had been tall and light-hearted, outrageously out-spoken. That is when she had learned how to speak. For the few summers that the woman had lived in their village, Kentika had followed her, just a small girl back then, a wild-eyed thing playing with boys. Until the foreigner appeared. Then the running around and shooting at rabbits was temporarily forgotten. She was wandering all over, bragging about her newfound friendship and whole phrases of strange-sounding words that she had learned. When the foreign woman died, Kentika had been the only one to mourn for real.

"You still remember how to speak their tongue?" he asked her now, perturbed. Too many aspects of her story did not make sense, but her uneasiness, her caginess were the things that made him doubt what she said. Although, what was there to suspect her of?

"Oh, yes, I do," she said proudly. "And not badly at all. You wouldn't believe how easily..." Again, she stumbled over her words and fell silent.

He listened to the chirping of the late birds, chattering in the treetops, fluttering their wings, preparing for the night. The dusk was not far away now.

"Well, you better hurry up, before it turns dark. Or before Father sends for you." He looked at her sternly. "Whatever is happening, whatever trouble you have gotten yourself involved in, try to sound more reasonable when you talk to him. He will see through you most easily anyway, but at least try." He shrugged. "I don't know what trouble you are involved in, but it doesn't sound good, Sister. Not good at all."

"I'm not—" she began hotly, then shrugged in her turn, her eyes, large and too widely spaced, filling with mischievous mirth. "You know me too well, but believe me, it's not really something bad. I promise to tell you all about it, but not now. When it's over for good, or if I'm in too deep of a trouble on account of it." The playfulness was spreading, spilling out of her eyes. "If you could save me from Father's interrogation, it would be helpful. Can you?"

"Why should I?" he asked, curiously annoyed. Yet, his inner self was calculating, thinking of the way of helping her to avoid Father's questioning. The War Chief would be busy, most surely.

But for how long? "Maybe he won't find time to question you tonight," he said. "And even if he does, he won't have much of it to do it in a leisurely way. So just be ready to mostly listen and not to talk. Answer shortly, and don't brag. He won't know that bit about talking to the enemy. That's something only Schikan and I know. So you don't need to worry about that."

"I'm not worried." The sudden wideness of her smile made him forget some of their troubles. "It seems that a whole span of seasons passed since it all began. Don't you think?"

Yes, he thought. *It does. But what did you do this long span of seasons between Father Sun's previous appearance and the next one?*

"Come back in a hurry. Don't wander about again."

A wave of her torn, muddied skirt was his answer, as she whirled around and was gone, running away with her usual speed, having no patience for simple walking.

He shook his head. Oh, but she better have a good explanation for all this. What trouble had she gotten herself into this time?

Back on the head of the trail, a group of men burst upon him, coming from behind the main opening, speaking loudly, their clubs out and ready. Achtohu, his arm in a sling and one side of his face swollen badly, raised his good hand in a careless greeting.

"Come along."

"Where are you going?" He fell in step with them, curiously comfortable, enjoying the sense of comradeship he had never experienced before.

"The boats. The lowlifes' vessels should be picked up and stored and put to great use. Stupid to let them rot out there."

CHAPTER 15

Squinting in an attempt to see better, Okwaho studied the shadowy grove, desperate to find something, anything, a clue.

What to do? he asked himself for the thousandth time, his head pounding, exhaustion overwhelming. But for Akweks' sickness, they would have sailed already, leaving the accursed shore once and for all. What possessed him to go and look for the watching local, or his footprints, on the day of their landing? But for his insistence, there would have been no change of plans, no splitting of forces, no disasters that followed.

Were they truly all dead up there?

The girl insisted that they were, but Akweks did not believe her, and now, away from her overpoweringly intense, curiously appealing presence, he began doubting her words as well. She was something else, this wild local thing, a confusing creature, one moment all aggressive, trying to kill him with that silly child's bow; the other, surprisingly helpful, bringing food, speaking their tongue but keeping quiet when needed, making him wish to talk to her, to tell her things he hadn't shared with anyone, neither family nor the closest of friends. About the silvery wolf only Father knew, because to talk to Father was always safe. But now, the wild local girl, all scratches and messy hair, knew more than anyone about his guiding spirit. How bizarre.

Refocusing his mind on more important things, he eyed the pair of oblique cliffs, inspecting them critically, looking for clues. From where he stood, it looked solid, a wall of stone, with no hidden entrances in between the towering rocks. Good, he decided. This will do.

Tiredly, he shifted his shoulders; his back hurt, muscles aching, crying for rest. In a regular condition, he would have found no trouble in carrying a boat of even greater size than a narrow canoe for a few people to sail. Not a small dugout, neither was it a huge vessel to carry warriors and goods. Still, with all the bruises and cuts his back sported now, it wasn't an easy task at all.

However now, at least one canoe was safe from the locals, who should have been coming for the rest of their vessels, lousy warriors that they were. Why didn't they? If the battle had happened in the morning and they were as victorious as the girl had claimed, then they should have been coming to pick up the boats long ago. In the first place, they should not have been storing them in such a way, hiding most of their loot on the very next shore. How stupid it was to move the boats from one shore to another. Couldn't the enemy be bothered to carry their findings up the hill and into the town? Lazy rats.

Leaning against a tree, he fought the urge to slip along its trunk, to close his eyes, to curl among the protruding roots and fall asleep. But for such luxury!

He took a deep breath. In a short while, the moment he returned, he promised himself. In the relative safety of Akweks' hideaway, after it grew dark, he would sleep a little. At least that. After the darkness, after he was sure no victorious locals would come to retrieve the last of their boats.

Earlier, the moment the girl was gone, he had rushed to the shore, almost kicking himself for not thinking about that possibility right away. If the locals came to claim their rightful spoils, he and Akweks would be left with not even a remote chance of survival, no means to sail away. The renewed vigor the idea and the necessity to implement it brought gave him power to carry the small boat away, to seek a good place and hide it anew, but now he felt as though he could not move a limb anymore.

The pangs of hunger were not that bad—the girl's food offering was truly helpful—but the thirst kept haunting him, no matter how many times he stopped to drink, crouching near the low river's banks, revolted by the tepid, muddied water it offered. Nothing to rival the fresh coolness of a forest spring. Yet, even had he dared to venture inland, he had no vessel to carry the beverage back with, so all the danger of running into bloodthirsty locals, surely confident with the unexpected victory, would not be worth the trouble, while Akweks needed to drink fresh water more than he did.

The voices reached him as he neared his destination, barely giving him an opportunity to freeze, let alone seek cover. Someone was climbing up the riverbank, a group of people.

Not daring to breathe, he slipped toward the nearest tree and the generous foliage behind his back. If worse came to worst, he would dive into the thickest of the forest, he decided, where it would be easier to fight back, facing one or two rivals each time, not the whole pack at once. Judging by the voices, there were more than a few people coming up.

Five, he discovered, pressing against the rough trunk, the knife slick in his sweaty palm. But for the club he had lost, or a good bow! He held his breath.

The men were armed with clubs, in high spirits, talking rapidly. All but one, a tall, stringy-looking man, trailing behind, quiet and observing. An easy prey, decided Okwaho. This one would be swiftest to get rid of. But what about the rest?

He could handle them, he decided. Not much chances of coming out alive from such an encounter, but he wouldn't go down without putting up a good fight. They wouldn't have cause to remember him with contempt. They would—

More voices and the sounds of breaking branches made his heart sink. This time, his eyes counted about ten more people. Oh, Mighty Spirits!

Fighting the urge to crawl away, into the beckoning safety of the woods, he watched them conversing loudly, gesturing, so very sure of themselves. The boats. In such numbers, they surely came to fetch the boats. But to do that, they would have to...

The ice in his stomach kept growing, making it difficult to take in breaths. In order to reach the boats, they would have to go past Akweks and his shelter, the cozy hideaway the rocks and the huge tree trunks created, hidden well in the generous foliage yes, but not well enough. What if his friend was awake now, groaning with pain, maybe. One murmur would be enough to catch the prowling enemy's attention, to help them discover the survivor.

The men upon the shore strolled in a leisurely manner, in no hurry. Which was a wonder. Did they plan to make their way back in the darkness? It was already near dusk, and there were seven vessels there to find and carry.

No, six. One small canoe was missing. Would they notice? Were they the same men who had discovered and hidden the boats on the different shore in the first place?

His eyes scanned his surroundings, satisfied with a pile of stones they spotted, some large and moss covered, some perfectly round, hand-sized. He made his way there carefully, eyes still on the enemy. To have a hurling weapon close at hand felt good.

To his surprise and sudden surge of relief, he saw them heading for the woods not anywhere near the place he had entered earlier with the hobbling Akweks. Was there another trail, a better one? He held his breath, hoping they all would disappear behind the thick greenery.

A futile hope. The first five stayed where they were, conversing idly, not in a hurry or concerned. But for the thin bastard. Not about to mingle with his peers, that one wandered off, scanning the ground, deep in thought. Was he a scout?

Okwaho strained his eyes, trying to see better. A nosy type, the invader was heading toward Akweks' hideaway, not purposely but steadily, as though sensing something, facing the woods in what he was sure would appear as a peering gaze, then it was back to the study of the mud under his feet.

Okwaho's grip on his knife tightened, his muscles going rigid with tension. To throw it from such a distance would do no good, even had he been able to aim properly and hit his target. Yet, a stone… His hand caressed the pile without looking, his fingers picking the most rounded missile. It fit perfectly in his palm.

One of the enemies called out, yelling something in that foul-sounding tongue of theirs, clearly addressing the scouting man. He wished the girl was still by his side, translating. The thought made him smile. She had been fairly helpful. Then why not in this way, too? She clearly didn't feel threatened, especially now, when her people won the day. A little beast. Why did she come back? Because he didn't kill her and her friend, or lover, back on the hill? Did she feel grateful? Not likely, but with those strange people, one never knew.

The thin man looked back, then shook his head. Not a reassuring gesture, as after a brief moment of hesitation, he resumed walking toward the darkening trees. Okwaho tucked his knife back into his loincloth, or what remained of it, the sash tying it on torn and hanging in places. Hurriedly, he picked up another stone, having one for each hand now, before starting his careful slip toward the more open ground.

The congregating people were looking up again, waving in the direction where their peers had disappeared moments before. One left the group, but his steps took him toward the scouting man, who was gesturing, demanding a company, unmistakably this time. Okwaho hesitated no more.

His feet feeling light, welcoming the motion as opposed to the frustration of crouching, he rushed into the last of the light, aiming as he ran. The first stone hit the walking man square on the back of his head, shoving him forward, to hit the ground and sprawl there in a heap of limbs. The others turned swiftly, their clubs out, surprised but ready to fight. Two of the three rushed forward with no delay, but their lack of bows gave him another heartbeat of respite.

The second stone swished, flying in a beautiful arc. If not for the distance, it would have been a better hit. Still, before he bolted toward the river, he saw the scouting man disappearing from his view, falling down most probably. Good!

There was no time to rejoice in his victory. Akweks might have been safe for the time being, but three clubmen were quickly closing the distance, very determined, every advantage on their side. Having a club, he might have played with the idea of facing them. As it was, he sprinted toward the river, eyes upon the steep bank, scanning it frantically.

To jump in might have been an easy way out. If he broke no limbs or didn't bash his head open by the rocks lining its bottom, he might have a fair chance of getting away. And yet, that would

leave Akweks here alone, facing these people, and just as they had
been lifted from the illusion of killing all enemies in the morning.
They must have been thinking that, judging by their behavior, if
not by what the girl had said.

He calculated fast. Having no bows or other shooting devices,
these men could do nothing more than run after him. As they did.
He heard their shouts, the heaviness of their breathing.

*Make them put as much distance between themselves and this place
as possible,* his mind kept repeating, pounding in a perfect accord
with the thumping of his heart. If only he had been at his best
now, not as tired or bruised, not as alien to these woods.

In a desperate leap, he gained the upper ground of the nearest
cliff, miraculously not slipping upon its slimy surface. A quick
glance back showed him that only two men were still in hot
pursuit. Another one, a youth with a sling and a badly swollen
face, had a hard time keeping up, his good arm clutching a club
that did nothing but hinder his progress. The people with the
boats were nowhere to be seen. Busy with their precious cargo?
He hoped they were.

A quick scan revealing no proper objects to hurl at his chasers,
Okwaho looked down, at the current rushing below. Not an
inviting dive. He hesitated, then saw a small tier, not wide enough
for even one man to stand on, unless he was careful.

Another glance at the indifferent river. He calculated again.
The less people left up there to investigate the matter, the better.
The dusk was upon them, and those who went to gather the boats
would be in a hurry to go back.

Struggling upon the slimy surface, he didn't care for the noise
he made while sliding down and into the uneven terrain, almost
falling for real, clinging to the ragged stones with his entire body,
balancing desperately, hearing the splash of small rocks in the
water gushing below. The footsteps of his pursuers echoed above
his head. He held his breath, sure that the wild hammering of his
heart would give his presence away. It would be impossible to
miss him, but all he needed was a brief moment or two, a surprise.

The rasping voice reached him as the man's upper body
shadowed the last of the light, his shoulders wide, chin scratched

and on full display. He was kneeling most probably, or maybe crouching, peering into the water, noticing nothing untoward at first. The other one was talking above, not joining his peer, not yet. It was time.

Sacrificing his painfully gained balance, Okwaho reached out, grabbing the first man's shoulder, pulling with the remnants of his strength. If only his other hand could have found something to clutch onto, something steady, something that would give him even a faint semblance of support. As it was, he was hanging onto the man he was trying to make fall, a ridiculous situation.

His victim was tottering but holding on, receiving no help as it seemed, with his companion probably stunned momentarily to react in a proper way. Okwaho felt his grip slipping. In desperation, he hurled his body upward, giving up on the possibility of staying where he was, his other hand catching something. A tuft of hair? He didn't care. The fall was inevitable, but his rival would go down as well. With only one unharmed man left up there, Akweks might be relatively safe.

Another heartbeat saw them still tottering, with Okwaho's instincts acting against his judgment and will, his legs struggling to locate the tier again, to gain a bit of steadiness. It was ridiculous. He knew his grip was slipping, but when a moccasin smashed into his face, and he felt himself pushed into nothingness, stunned but still lucid, he was still clutching his prey.

The fall turned out to be not as long, made faster by the weight of his rival's body. In no time, the agitated water hit them, then hurried to swirl and whirl and hurl Okwaho away from his victim, but by this time, he didn't care. The need to breathe became the first priority, and he kicked toward the last of the light frantically, near panic, as always when under the water and unprepared.

Slick rocks and drifting logs were everywhere, eager to hurt, but he paid them no attention, catching one unsteady surface after another, until managing to hold on.

Blinking, he scanned the rushing water, trying to see through the deepening dusk. The yells from behind him were muffled, but only because his ears were full of water. Still, he didn't hurry to dive back and let the current take him farther away. The unfamiliar river might prove dangerous to swim in, especially in the gathering darkness, and he still needed to make sure they had left this place and Akweks alone, with or without the boats. Not to mention the possible danger from the man he had dragged along while falling.

Wiping his eyes against his upper arm, he scanned the river again, not daring to release his grip of the untrustworthy, slippery surface he now clutched with both hands.

Nothing.

As far as he could see, only the water seemed to be alive in this place. That, and the cliff he had fallen from. Adorned with more than one head, it looked very much alive, disturbingly so.

The temptation to dive back into the current and put as much distance between himself and these people welled. Knowing every bend of this river, and having so many men and plenty of boats, the enemy would be fools not to attempt to hunt him down. And fools they were not. That much he had learned so far. Not fools, nor cowards, despite what his countryfolk used to say about these Eastern River's dwellers.

What to do?

He watched the cliff, finding it difficult to see in the rapidly disappearing light. The night would force them to go back. Unless they decided to pitch a camp here, to wait for the morning. *Oh, Mighty Spirits; oh, Benevolent Right-Handed Twin, don't let them do that.* The night should give him enough time to come back and remove Akweks from the accursed shore. If his friend felt better, then all was well, as then they would sail, to try to locate the rest of their forces. It was the best of solutions, even if a risky one. The enemy countryside was an enigma, and yet they were strong and tough, and now bloodied in battle at long last. They could make it.

Unless Akweks was not feeling better, but worse.

He narrowed his eyes against the constant drizzle, eyeing the darkening silhouette of the cliff, the heads upon it gone, the shouts subdued. Or were those his vision and hearing playing tricks on him?

Oh, let them take the boats and go away! Because if Akweks was not feeling better, he would load the wounded into that small canoe he had hidden and then he would sail for home. A long journey, and not a promising one, but what better solution was there? If Akweks' wounds truly began to rot, the young man had no chance whatsoever, not without a good healer, good care, and the benevolence of the Great Spirits. None of which he could provide now unless they reached Cohoes Falls fast.

The abrupt splash behind his back tore him from the intensity of his observations, in time to see the man he had dragged along down the cliff struggling not far away, beating the water with his arms, not doing a good job of keeping afloat.

Catching his breath, Okwaho let his rickety support go, his hands seeking frantically, terrified that the rough fall or the wild current might have torn his knife out of its sheath.

The water enveloped him once again, muddy and alien, hostile. He tried to see through the obscure haze. A blurry form was hovering not far away, fluttering with its limbs, raising clouds of mud. As though the waters were not marshy enough.

Desperate not to get his limbs caught between multitude of protruding obstacles, ready to pounce, Okwaho tore at his sash, his fingers locating the knife, its touch familiar, reassuring. Losing sight of his enemy, he kicked for the surface once again.

This time, the marshy sand greeted him, dotted with logs and prickly vegetation aplenty. Pleased to have a stretch of somewhat steady ground under his feet, he clung to a long branch, desperate to stabilize himself, ready to fight.

Another quick check of the river did not reassure him. The man was gone. Where to?

More scanning. Ah, there, by that cluster of rocks. An inanimate form was flapping with the ripples, beating against the surrounding stones. Okwaho hesitated, his head buzzing from his own struggle with the current, too disoriented to analyze properly. The man was swimming strangely before, yes, more struggling than progressing. Did he break something vital while falling down the cliff? Maybe. Which would be the most perfect of solutions. He, Okwaho, could do with no additional fighting for now.

Groping his way up the shore, the semidarkness making it impossible not to trip, he fought the urge to lie down and close his eyes. But for the enemy being too near, in a questionable condition or not, he would have done just that, crashed down and waited for the darkness to come. Or better yet, slept through the entire night, to wake up to none of this trouble. As it was, he pushed on, following yet another bend of the shore, aiming to reach the cluster of rocks with no additional swimming.

The man was dying, that much was obvious. Lying awkwardly, with one half of his body supported by the stony surface—the wrong half, as his upper part was not only tilted downwards, washed by the water, but also pushed by it again and again, to bump gently against the neighboring rocks—he looked as broken as a person still alive might be, one leg turned at an impossible angle, the other bent strangely, blood trickling down his forehead and out of the corner of his mouth, his eyes opened but blurry, reflecting no understanding. Still, he was alive enough to pull his face away from the water each time the next ripple covered it.

Sighing, Okwaho knelt beside him.

"It'll hurt for only a heartbeat," he said, trying to sound calming.

His hands trembling from the effort, he caught the wounded's shoulders, pulling him up, struggling to maintain his own balance. The man groaned, but didn't cry out, biting his lips instead, drawing more blood.

The newly achieved position was barely satisfactory, but no water covered the drawn face now, and after the agony receded, the man's features relaxed, his eyes turning calmer, reflecting an understanding.

Okwaho squatted beside him, as uncomfortable.

"Now prepare for your journey," he said, remembering what faith keepers would say on such an occasion. "Go calmly. Not with anger or fear. Your Sky Path will be easy to find if you seek it with your heart open and your spirit calm. Think of good things."

He listened to the serenity of his own voice, and it surprised him, but calmed him too. There was no need to thrash about, seeking perfect solutions. They would come once one thought lucidly, once one was prepared to accept that not everything would work out exactly as one wanted. He could almost hear Father saying that, in those very words as well as in different ones.

If only Father were here now! His fingers found the small leather pouch, still attached to the remnants of his girdle. It didn't surprise him at all. As long as Father's necklace was there, everything would be well.

Glancing at the darkening sky, he concentrated on the broken man in front of him. "The Sky World awaits you. See how clear it is now? No clouds, no mist, no wind. You'll find your Sky Path easily."

The man's eyes followed his gaze, then came back, expectant, washed with pain, concentrating then blurring again. He did not understand a word of the foreign tongue, of course, but the general meaning must have been clear to him, must have been calming and reassuring. Okwaho went on.

"Think of your guiding spirit. Ask for his help. He might be willing to accompany you. Wish you could tell me what it is."

The inappropriate comment shamed him. The man might not understand a word of what he said, but the spirits did. Foreign or local, it didn't matter. Great Spirits were Great Spirits.

He forced himself to concentrate, to think of the Sky World, of the Grandmother Moon that was already glowing in the darkening sky, ready to collect this departing spirit, to weave this man's hair into her mantle.

The shivers took his charge, his limbs jerking now and then, but his eyes clinging to Okwaho, pleading. He swallowed, wishing to pause, to get up and drink, to run away from here.

"The Grandmother Moon is here, you see?" He pointed at the sky. "She is smiling, happy to take your hair and weave it into her beautiful mantle. And Gadowaas, he is waiting for you up there, to admit you into the Sky World when your journey is over."

Did they know about all this, he wondered. About the Sky World and Gadowaas, and the importance of one's calm, tranquil departure? He would have to make sure to ask the girl. With her strange tales of that Glooskap and another one, the bad wolf spirit.

He suppressed a grin, his mind-eyes seeing her and not the broken man in front of him. Such an outlandish thing, restless and vital, with the funniest way of talking, as though in a rush to say it all, not pausing for breath, not caring for proper sentencing, eyes large and so widely spaced, strange but appealing, somehow. He would ask her about all that. If she came as she had promised.

CHAPTER 16

She stared at her brother, unable to take her eyes off the crusted cut above his ear. Swollen and ugly looking, it glared at her, distracting her from what he said, impossible things in themselves.

"Why did you split in the first place?" demanded Father, curt and matter-of-fact.

He had squatted near the fire, their only illumination in such a late part of the evening, motionless, his face a mask carved out of wood, hands folded, holding no pipe or cup or bowl with forest nuts like many men would have done. No, not Father, she knew, shivering, worrying for her brother. There was no accusation in these words, not yet, but the question sounded accusing.

"We thought it was the best to scan the shore. Just in case. In case the enemy left any signs." Migisso swallowed, visibly unsettled. "You see, there were prints on the shore. Fresh prints. From the time the enemy was supposed to be defeated, gone. I followed them, the footprints, just as. . ." The young man's voice trailed off.

"Just as the enemy bothered to give clearer signs of them not being dead or gone." Father's words rang icily, cutting.

A brief silence prevailed, while Kentika's thoughts rushed about. So the wolf youth had been discovered, she realized, her stomach turning uneasily. Discovered and chased, but not caught. Not according to her brother. The stones he threw wounded people, some severely, some relatively lightly. One cut Migisso's ear, but didn't do much damage.

She had thanked mighty Glooskap and all the rest of the sky

spirits for that, promising a beautiful offering the moment she could find something worthwhile to offer. Because had the wolf youth managed to harm her brother, she would have turned into his enemy, and she didn't want it to come to this, not yet. Maybe later. But not now. She still needed to bring him more food, and some medicine to his friend, like she promised. The wounded was not in good shape, and she even played with the idea of asking for her brother's advice on the matter. After running into him earlier, on her way back, she debated that thought with herself over and over while bathing in the spring, and later, while rushing through the alleys of the agitated village or brushing off Mother's admonishments. Migisso might have been willing to help. And why not? The wolf youth and his friend weren't bad. But now...

She studied his face once again, set and dark with what looked like genuine anger. Migisso was usually placid and good-natured, reserved, closemouthed, difficult to see through. An enigma. But not to her. She was able to read him as clearly as drawings on stones. When he was angry, or pleased, or upset, no one knew, not even Father. No one but her.

"So the enemy is still out there, wandering about as they please." Father's voice dripped with an open disdain.

Migisso winced visibly. "There was only one warrior up there. Only one."

"Which our brave men, those who stayed to 'scan the shore,' you included, didn't manage to catch or kill, or even just injure." Not a muscle moved in the renowned leader's face, but the tone of his voice said it all.

Kentika frowned. Her brother did not deserve such a rebuke. And neither did the others. They did everything they could, she was sure of that. They were not as useless as Father's words implied.

Migisso's face seemed to reflect the same sentiment. "He was injured, most surely he was," he said in a firmer voice. "Achtohu pushed him down the cliff, and saw him being swirled with the current like a broken log."

"Along with Amuau." The War Chief's nostrils widened as the air hissed, drawn in with too much force. "Achtohu was stupid to do what he did."

"He didn't..." Migisso's face fell. "He tried to hold on to Amuau, but his arm, it was in a sling, broken, you see? He couldn't hold on. And we still hope to find Amuau alive and well. He might have been carried away by the current." His fighting spirit gone again, Migisso stared at the earthen floor, his shoulders sagging. "It was too dark to look for him, and we needed to bring the boats back. But tomorrow with dawn—"

"Tomorrow with dawn you all will be out there, looking for the dirty enemy!" The cutting edge in Father's voice made Kentika wince in her turn. Heart pounding, she stared into the suddenly contorted face, not a mask but a thundercloud now, about to burst with the deadliest of storms. "If you think that Amuau just swam while the enemy went down like a rotten log, you do not deserve to be called a man, a warrior, a proud hunter. Your place should be with women, tending plots and grinding maize." The venom was there, dripping out of the dark eyes. "I dared to hope you were finally beginning to turn into a man. People talked positively of you, your involvement in the previous day and night's battles. But they evidently had lower expectations than mine."

Mesmerized, she watched the glowing eyes, boring into her brother, making him shrink, or maybe melt like a snowball under the strong sun. As always, it angered her, the unfairness of it. Migisso was not like everyone else, true, but he was good and courageous, even if in his own different way.

Still, she held her tongue, huddling in the far corner, glad to be out of their sight and their possible attention. She needed to think things through, and she needed to get some medicine, anything, an ointment preferably, but maybe a bunch of dried herbs and roots would do.

It was bad enough that Mother had caught her poring through her brother's possessions, his precious bag of herbs and strange assortment of tools. She had tried to explain it as best as she could, pleading numerous scratches and bruises her own body displayed, but it only made Mother angrier.

"Go and ask the Honorable Healer to help you with those, you disobedient child. I don't want to know how you came by all your injuries. I simply refuse to know. After I told you—"

"There was an attack on our village, Mother, in case you didn't notice," she had said, not caring about her tone or her words, so inappropriate, so lacking in respect. But the accusations were just too unwarranted this time! "I helped, yesterday, when they were shooting fire arrows, and this morning, when we all were there, expecting another attack. Everyone was out and helping, girls too. Even Namaas, that whiny example of perfection and the most appropriate behavior, even she was out there by the fence, useless as always, but trying to help."

"And why is she, or any other girl or woman of our attacked village not scratched and bruised like you are, not as disheveled, with their clothes still intact, not torn into a near lack of them?" her mother retorted, hands on her hips. She was a quiet woman, reserved, not outspoken, but sometimes, she could be pushed into anger.

Kentika ground her teeth. "They are! They were as tousled and disheveled, I'm sure they were. But they bathed in the spring once the enemy was chased away and killed, and they put on other dresses."

"And you?" Mother's voice had a victorious ring to it.

"I hadn't had time to do it properly yet."

"Of course, you wild thing. You were busy out there, doing forest spirits know what." Picking up a large bowl and her grinding stick, the older woman turned away. "You are testing my patience, Daughter. And as for your father, you better hope no one has enough time to inform him about your last escapades." An impatient shake of her head relating her bitterness, her mother was gone, heading for the neighboring cluster of houses, their clan women's favorite place of gathering.

Oh, please! she had thought back then, but her confidence disappeared as quickly when Father, with Migisso in tow, had burst through their cabin's opening shortly thereafter, before she had time to decide which ones of the tied bunches of plants looked more promising, or at least a little familiar. Just as her brother's fascination with herbs and their magical qualities was bottomless, hers was next to non-existent, no matter how the basics of this priceless knowledge was tried to be drummed into her, along with the other girls of her age.

And here she was now, watching her brother's humiliation, afraid to think Father would find time to question her as well.

"The expedition to bring the boats was meaningless, just a simple task," Father was saying, eyes narrowed into slits, glowering dangerously. "And yet, you could have proven yourself. The enemy provided you with a perfect opportunity, which you let go in that typical way of yours. All of you did. Useless!"

The air stood still, frozen, like it sometimes did after the lightning struck when the thunder had yet to roar. Kentika pressed her hands together, sensing the violence. Would Father... He hadn't struck any of them for quite a long time, but this time, he was truly angered.

Her eyes darted between their faces, one broad, wrinkled, strong, a face one would not forget in a hurry, a pleasant sight but for the rage that contorted its features now; the other also broad and handsome, but lacking in vitality, closed, muffled, subdued, eyes facing the floor, shoulders sagging. As tall, as strong physically, maybe, but she knew if it came to violence, it would be no contest, as it always was.

Oh, Benevolent Sky Spirits, please give him strength, please fortify his spirit.

She took a step forward, then another. Their eyes leaped at her.

"Go away, Daughter." Father's eyes focused, but the growl of his voice made her shiver. "Now."

"I will not." She swallowed hard, but it did not help. Her mouth was as dry as the neglected field in summer. "I will—"

The footsteps burst into the hovering silence, and the voices. People were coming up the alley, looking for the War Chief, undoubtedly. The next heartbeat confirmed this conclusion.

"Honorable Leader?"

Father pulled himself up with an admirable swiftness, one moment a thundercloud about to burst, the next a respectable elder, composed and in perfect control. A curt motion of a head gestured both of them out while the visitors, a large group of elders and other prominent men, began pouring in.

Barely aware of her movements, Kentika dared to breathe only when the soft night air washed over her burning face, cooling it, or attempting to do so, as nothing seemed to be able to stop the flaming. She tried to concentrate, peering at the campfires that glimmered everywhere, people still crowding the alleys and open spaces outside their houses and cabins, congregating at the ceremonial grounds most probably. There seemed to be many voices coming from that direction.

Her brother's presence was nothing but a shadow walking by her side.

"He was so unreasonable, so wrong," she said, needing to break the silence. It hurt almost physically, to be enveloped by it. "I can't believe that he blamed it on you."

"He was right." His voice was empty, lacking in expression.

She halted abruptly, but he didn't stop.

"No, he was not! How could you say that?" Catching up, she tried to peer at him through the darkness. "You can't be blamed for the failure of an entire group of people, people you didn't lead but only went along with." He said nothing, hastening his step. "Also, you all went there to get the boats, and you did bring them back, didn't you? So it wasn't a failure."

"We lost two men while doing something as simple as fetching boats." This time, it was his turn to stop, to turn and stare at her through the faint moonlight. "One lowlife on the loose, some sneaky pest our warriors didn't manage to kill in the first place, disposed of two of our people and wounded one—me, that useless shadow of a person who calls himself your brother." He drew a deep breath and the sound of it tore at her. "Achtohu was wounded anyway, so it left no one to try and hunt that lowlife down, to follow him in his swim, to not let him get away. You say it's not uselessness, not a shame? I say it is!"

"But he caught you unprepared." She grabbed his arm and fought when he tried to wrench it away. "You weren't prepared to run into anyone down there. So of course you didn't expect—"

"Well, we should have, shouldn't we? Only this morning, we fought them, and here we were, strolling our shores as though inside the safety of our village's fence." His silhouetted shoulders sagged anew. "He is right. I'm useless. Always was, always will be." A sigh. "We all were, but this was their first time, while mine..."

"No, it is not like that." She tried to recapture his hand, but he took a step back, and his gaze kept avoiding hers she knew, even though it was a mere guess, impossible to confirm in the darkness. "He took his anger out on you because you were close at hand. Because he could not have taken it out on anyone else. He is angry with more things than the stupid failure at the shore. This entire attack angers him, the burned houses, the neglected fields. The enemy surprised us and disrupted our life, and it angers him greatly. He takes it personally. He always does, doesn't he?" A stubborn silence was her answer. "He is angry with the filthy enemy sneaking up on us, catching us barely prepared. And maybe he is frustrated with more things. His mission at Skootuck, eh? They didn't listen to him, did they?"

His shoulders lifted lightly, but it made her feel better. *He was listening.*

"This mess at the shore is only a part of it all, a small part. And it would have made no difference, if he hadn't already been angry." She drew a deep breath, afraid but needing to say it aloud, at long last. "He took his anger out on you, like he always does. Or me, or Mother even. Don't tell me you never saw it as it is."

The silence enveloped them, broken only by voices carried by the wind. People were everywhere, and yet their small corner of the world was empty, abandoned, saved only for them. For a reason, she knew. Because some things needed to be said, at long last. Because Father was not the good man everyone assumed him to be, but only now did she realize it.

"He was angry with you for his failures, not yours!"

His arms came up abruptly, as though trying to push her words away.

"No, he was not." It rustled hoarsely, a mere whisper.

"Yes, he was," she insisted, her own anger rising, surprising her with the suddenness of it. "He never admits failures. But he must be responsible for some, mustn't he? He can't be without fault."

He shook his head tiredly. "Maybe. But you can't try to make him answerable for mine." A helpless shrug. "He may have his faults. Oh, yes, he does. I'm not blind, and not stupid, Sister. But what happened today at the river was not his fault, but mine."

She barely managed to restrain herself from stomping her foot. "Ten more men were there, and you weren't their leader!"

"I could have tried to take the leadership. That was what he said."

"How?" The darkness was less oppressive now, with her anger cooling and his despondency obviously lifting, if only a little.

"I don't know. Somehow." He shifted his weight from one foot to another. "There was something strange about this shore. Something wasn't right there. There were footsteps, fresh footsteps. Not prints from the day before. I wanted to see where they led." His shrug was clearly visible, this familiar apathetic movement of shoulders. "They argued, but Achtohu listened. He said we would stay until they fetched the boats. Since we came back from Skootuck, he has come to trust my instincts, for some reason. I wonder why he would trust me when no one else would."

Another spell of silence prevailed. She felt her stomach tightening uneasily. "Did you find something? Do you know where the footprints led?"

"I'm sure I would have, but then the dirty lowlife came out of nowhere, hurling stones. He killed Ponak right away, would you believe that? Broke the back of his head, made it cave in."

She shivered, remembering his cut. "He hit you, too."

"Yes, but by that time he was already on the run, as Achtohu and Amuau charged toward him."

"Thank all the great and small spirits for that," she said fervently. "My gratitude is limitless."

His sigh was quiet, full of acceptance. She brushed it aside, more interested in other aspects of his story now.

"What did the youth who threw the stones look like?"

He looked at her, puzzled. "What do you mean? What youth?"

"You know, the one who threw stones at you." Embarrassed, she looked away, forgetting that in the darkness he couldn't see what her eyes held any more than she could see his. "He... he must be a young warrior, no? I assumed that."

"I don't know," he said slowly. "Achtohu is the one who may give you an answer to that. He saw the traitorous rat up close. He fought him. Kicked him down the cliff, too. Right into the river." Another sigh stirred the darkness. "He didn't manage to hold on to Amuau. The filthy enemy clutched him too firmly. He was determined to take him down with him. He didn't even try to resist the fall, Achtohu says. He just hung there. Like an ugly flea."

"He wanted to lure you away. He didn't want you to find his friend," she muttered, her mind back there, near the rocky shore, in the cozy enclosure the cliffs and the trees provided, the makeshift shelter with some grass spread on the earth, to make it softer, and the leaking piece of bark, his improvised water vessel, the one that held barely any liquid in it. Did his wounded friend feel any better now? Or was he still limp and sleepy, breathing shallowly, tormented, but not with heat. He became so upset, so unreasonable at her suggestion that his wounded friend was sick, from rotting wounds maybe.

The heavy silence enveloped her, not comfortable or welcome anymore. She felt her brother go rigid, turned to stone, staring at her. Even in the darkness, she could see his widening eyes.

"What?" She tried to find something to say. "I just asked questions. Why do you get so upset?"

"What do you know about all this, Kentika?"

She said nothing for a moment, desperate to gather her thoughts.

"What do you know about the 'youth that threw stones'?" he repeated, his voice rising. "And 'his friend'? What friend? I don't understand. What do you know about any of this?"

"Nothing!" As always when pressed, she felt nothing but anger. He had no right to yell at her. "What do you want? I asked questions, that's all."

He came closer. "What do you know about the enemy? Did

you meet him before? Do you know what he looks like? Are there more of them out there?"

She tossed her head high. "I don't have to tell you anything!"

The incredulousness of his stare turned so intense it pierced the darkness. She could feel it, boring into her. His gaping mouth made her wish to laugh, but not in a merry way.

"Don't stare at me like that. I did nothing wrong. And it has nothing to do with your fighting on that shore."

"Tell me," he breathed, still frozen in that ridiculous pose.

"There is nothing to tell." Suddenly perturbed, she shifted her weight from one foot to the other. What if he insisted? What if he told the others about it? "I was just curious. Also," she glanced at the flickering lights of the ceremonial grounds, "we better go there now, hear what they say. I want to go to sleep. Wish they weren't always gathering in our house to discuss things."

Not waiting for his answer, she hurried off, her heart beating fast, thoughts racing. Could her trip back to the shore wait for the morning, as planned? Now, with that youth on the run, about to be hunted by every man that could wield a weapon with the coming of dawn, she might be required to rethink her plans.

And it was not even certain that he was still alive and well. Maybe he was dead down there in the river, drowned, bleeding and broken-limbed. Or maybe he was wounded, dying on this or that low shore. And then, there was his friend, still undiscovered, but not for long.

She shook her head, determined. There was not enough moonlight to travel all the way, but there would be, probably, later on. If the wind held and the clouds dispersed.

CHAPTER 17

The quiet and the darkness were getting the better of him. Crouching in the far corner, sheltered from the wind and its coolness by the low row of bushes, Migisso tried not to let the relative comfort of his hideaway lull him into sleep, despite the all-encompassing tiredness.

Just a few more heartbeats, he promised himself. He would count to one hundred, then another round, maybe. If she doesn't come out by then, then he was wrong, plain wrong, and she must have been fast asleep now, enveloped in the coziness and the friendly warmth of their cabin.

Rubbing his eyes, he shifted, then tensed. The rustling inside the house was unmistakable. Someone was moving there, careful to disturb nothing, neither an object nor a light sleeper.

So she hadn't gone to sleep upon her return. He clasped his lips together. Of course she didn't. He didn't expect her to. Clearly, she was up to something, hiding vital things, involved despite her claims that her secret had nothing to do with any of it.

Of course it did, but in what way? He didn't know. She had rushed off too abruptly, avoiding his company with real determination ever since. But he wasn't about to let her get away with it, not this time.

The new wave of anger helped to banish the sleepiness. Leaning forward, he peered into the darkness, made better by the reappearing moon. Soon his vigil was rewarded with her sneaking out, a faintly outlined silhouette, unmistakably hers.

Peering ahead, she hesitated, then, adjusting the bag more comfortably behind her shoulder, she charged into the night, her pace swift and determined, sure of itself.

He forced his limbs into stillness, the effort to stay motionless not coming easily, not this time. To guess her direction was not a difficult task, but to follow her undiscovered would prove more challenging, he knew. Her senses were sharp, her hearing exceptional, long summers of wandering about the woods giving her a clear advantage over even some experienced men. And yet, if she headed where he thought she was heading, there was no need to follow her closely. They would arrive at the same destination anyway. Silently, he slipped into the house, glad that his bow was always within easy reach.

What was she up to? he asked himself, as the night enveloped him, unpleasantly cold. What did she know about the enemy? What did she do with them?

A new wave of anger threatened to take him, but he fought it down, determined not to let it spoil his chance. If she brought him all the way to where the enemy might be hiding, it would give him a perfect opportunity to redeem himself, at least in Father's eyes.

He shuddered, then concentrated. To think about Father, or what he had said, hurt. But she was mistaken. The War Chief was correct, as always. He had been the leader of their village for many summers, and even people of Skootuck listened to him from time to time. No, such a man could not be guilty of the pettiness and false pride she had accused him of. She was definitely mistaken, obviously guilty of crimes of her own, as it turned out.

The opening in the fence showed clear signs of someone heading through it a very short time ago: the warmth of the parts of the wooden poles, the trampled plant that was striving to return to its normal position. He studied those, satisfied, blessing the moon for besting the clouds in order to show him the way. Had it been truly dark, he would have never been able to follow her without the aid of a torch that would have given his presence away in a matter of heartbeats.

The familiar trail twisted, taking him on a path he could have walked with his eyes shut. Down, all the way to the river. Oh, mighty Glooskap, was she truly guilty of aiding the enemy? His stomach twisted painfully. Kentika, his little sister, his only friend. A wild thing, yes, unruly, impossible to understand or to make behave properly, but still a good girl.

No, it could not be. She would not do anything like that. He was wasting his time following her, and yet, where could she possibly be going in the dead of the night, sneaking away, carrying a bag?

Wriggling out of his soaked loincloth, Okwaho sighed with relief, spreading it before the flickering flame, glad to be free of its cold, sticky touch. It needed to be dried, somehow, if not washed thoroughly. The tanned material, usually soft and decorated, was now stiff with all the sweat, blood, and mud it had accumulated during the past few days. The last forced swim in the river didn't help to wash it out at all. It only made him terribly wet and cold.

Fire, he thought. What a blissful thing it is. Warm and friendly, it helped to banish the chill, to disperse the worst of the darkness. To lift his spirits as well. Only a little, as much as anything could have in their troublesome situation. Still, it was better this way. It gave him the opportunity to relax and to think.

When he had managed to make his way back, well after the darkness fell, he had found Akweks undisturbed, curled awkwardly at the same corner he had remembered leaving him at before dusk, drifting between their world and that of the spirits and dreams, in pain. There was no improvement in the youth's condition. His strength did not seem as though about to return, the gash on his thigh still wet, still oozing liquids, spreading a light odor, now unmistakable. He didn't need to lean closer to smell it. The peculiar scent filled the closed-up space, noticeable now, especially when one came from the outside. Akweks was in bad shape, and there was no point in deluding himself, convincing them both that all was well.

He eyed a half-eaten cob of maize rolling in the dust. Had he had any energy left, he would have gotten up and picked it from the ground, dirt or not. The violent twisting in his stomach must have been the result of hunger, not fear. Or so he hoped.

Would he manage to take Akweks away? He didn't want to face this particular question, not yet. When the time came, he would manage, somehow.

When? he asked himself, staring into the darkness, desperate to sense the danger if it was near. How long did they dare to stay here?

Not until dawn break, surely. The enemy would be certain to start combing this shore with the coming of the first light. He should not have attracted their attention in the first place. The girl said they were thought to be dead. She was surprised to run into him here, alive and strolling about. So the rest of her countryfolk must have assumed the same. But not anymore. Now they knew he was out there, on the loose. To hope they assumed him dead now would be naive. He could have died like that other man, yes, but he didn't. They would be fools not to scan every tree and bush around here. And fools they were not. Now he knew it for certain.

He stifled a curse. But for the nosy bastard who, instead of helping his companions to carry the accursed boats, had to start sniffing around, none of it would have happened. He would have waited patiently, and they would have taken the boats and gone back to their stupid village, leaving him and Akweks alone, in charge of the shore, to decide what to do. However, now he was left with nothing to decide but to stumble his way in the darkness, carrying his wounded friend to the boat he had had enough sense to hide—at least that!—to try to sail home, hoping he would be able to make that journey in time for Akweks not to die.

Bracing himself against the cold, the wind sneaking in, threatening the small flame, he stared at the fire. Was it wise to make it at all? What if the enemy was wandering out there in these very moments?

"It's still, still night... yes?" Akweks' voice was barely a whisper, but it made him jump all the same.

"Yes, it's near midnight." He took a deep breath, trying to calm the wild pounding of his heart. "I made some fire. They won't be looking for us before dawn."

"Do you think... you think we have any water... left? Just a little..."

Okwaho stifled a groan. "I'll... yes, I'll bring water." The loathsome piece of bark that leaked more than it held in stared at him from the floor, thrown carelessly where he had left it earlier, before the last trouble began. "May the Left-Handed Twin take them into his realm and make them suffer for all time to come!"

"They will be looking for us, won't they?"

"Yes, they will." He rubbed his eyes, bracing himself for groping his way back to the shore. "But we can stay here for a little while, until the second part of the night. To get some rest, gather our strength."

"Why did they—" A sudden outburst of coughing left the wounded gasping. Okwaho shot to his feet. "Why did they chase you?"

He held the sweat-soaked shoulders, helpless to contain their trembling. "I... They were looking for our boats. They might have found you."

Another bout of coughing. "If I can't make, make it to the boat ... don't stay. Sail."

The lump in his throat was forming fast. He swallowed it.

"We'll sail together. Before the next dawn, we'll be away from here, moving against the current. Four, five dawns and we are back in Cohoes Falls, with that roaring of your stupid cascades forcing us to yell at each other. Why did they have to build your stupid town right under that thing?"

The smile was faint yet unmistakable. "Your Little Falls is not any better, I hear. They say ... they say your falls are nasty ... not little. They lie with that name."

"Those are not my falls. Little Falls is not my town. I've never been there but for a short stay when I traveled to your place. Where I came from, all is quiet and pretty. You can sail our streams without listening to their every murmur."

The longing for home swept him with a breathtaking suddenness, gripping his insides, twisting them viciously. The cozy town sprawling upon a hill, longhouses spreading up and down, in cheerful disarray. Everything hilly, uneven, full of small rivers and springs, plenty of ponds to swim and fool around in, barely enough flat land to have decent ballgames that were usually organized in the neighboring Onondaga Town, that haughty capital of the entire nation, where the annual meetings of the Great Council were held. Many wondered why Father, the War Chief of the Onondagas and one of the most prominent leaders of the entire Great League, did not live in the capital itself. It would have been more fitting. Yet Father claimed that High Springs was his home, even though he had no extended family there, no roots, nothing to tie him to a relatively unimportant settlement. Still, he preferred to travel every time the meetings of the Great Council needed to be organized, or some pressing matters of the Five Nations taken care of.

"Father came from Little Falls, yes," he said, wishing to have this great man here now, and not only his necklace. Oh, Father would have taken care of it all, solved this terrible mess. He would have made it all work, with no failure, no loss of men, no defeat, even though the Onondaga War Chief dealt with the matters of peace more often than with the matters of war. There were no wars in the heart of the Great League.

"Little Falls, yes. The Great Peacemaker performed his first miracle there." Akweks' pale lips stretched into a broader smile. "He should have come to our Cohoes Falls, tried to jump those. They would have demanded no other proof if he survived our falls."

"They demanded nothing more, anyway," said Okwaho, remembering the tale.

Like everyone else, he had heard plenty of stories about the wondrous prophet, the Messenger of the Great Spirits, the Great Peacemaker. But one day, Mother laughed and told him to ask Father about that miracle. She said there was more to this particular tale, and if he managed to make Father tell him the truth about it, she'd make a whole bunch of his, Okwaho's, favorite sweet maple cakes only for him. Her eyes glimmered with mirth, like those of a young girl, teasing, but no matter how many times he tried, Father would shrug and refuse to tell him more than everyone else knew. So Okwaho had no favorite cookies all for himself, although Father admitted that he had been there with the Peacemaker. Well, of course he was. He had been the man the Peacemaker trusted the most.

He shrugged. "If the Great Peacemaker died in Little Falls but came back with the rise of Father Sun, then he would have done that in your Cohoes Falls as well. It didn't matter where he would have been required to perform the miracle. He was a divine messenger. He didn't care about the height of the cascades or the amount of water in it."

Closing his eyes, Akweks sighed, but the smile still played on his colorless lips. "If he came there in fall, he would have to climb down a few stones and save himself all this miracle-making. The falls dry up dreadfully during the summer."

Okwaho tried to remember. "Yes, I think they came before the Cold Moons. My father was with him. He was the one who brought the Messenger to our people." It came out too proudly. He moderated his tone, embarrassed. "Or so they say. It must have been strange back in their days."

But Akweks' face lost the trace of a smile, covered again with a sheen of perspiration. Clenching his teeth, as though bracing himself for a difficult trial, the youth shifted, then tried to sit up. Despite Okwaho's supporting hands, it was a difficult feat that left him breathless, unable to suppress his groans.

"I'll bring you water."

Snatching up his knife along with the accursed piece of bark, he dived back into the cutting wind, glad to escape the suffocating closeness. It was colder now, but the wind made the clouds disperse, with Grandmother Moon shining stronger, lighting his way. No need to grope and stumble in the darkness, spilling most of the water on his way back. A quick trip back and forth, a bit of a rest, and then they would be gone, never to return. Akweks would manage to stay alive until they reached home. Somehow. Somehow he, Okwaho, wouldn't let him die.

The rustling in the woods uphill made him dive into the thickest of the bushes, his heart lurching in fright. It might have been the wind, he told himself, or maybe an animal, this or that forest creature.

He clutched the knife tighter, regretting not having brought his newly acquired club along. One good thing had come out of the evening disaster. The club of the man whom he had dragged along into the river was washed ashore along with its dying owner, so now he possessed a prettily carved, decorated spoil of war, to make up for his old weapon that he had lost. Yet, it wasn't at hand now.

He cursed, then listened. The suspicious sounds continued. Sporadically, with no pattern to them. Once silence, then resumed rustling, then an occasional stone rolling down. Not an animal. A person. Someone sure-footed, and in a hurry. Once again, he cursed himself for leaving the club behind.

Trying not to stumble in the surrounding darkness, the prickly vegetation thick, not letting the moonlight through, he moved as silently as he could, the constant hum of the river distracting, not allowing him to listen properly. A stone rolled out into the open patch of ground. Why would someone—

The figure that followed it didn't seem in a hurry to dive back into the protective darkness of the tree. Instead, she stopped and looked around, one hand clutching something that looked like a bag, the other darting up, pushing the hair off her face in a familiar gesture.

He watched her for another heartbeat.

"What are you doing here?"

The question didn't seem to startle her, as though she knew she was being watched. But when he stumbled on a root and almost fell out of his hiding place, flopping his hands to stabilize himself, instead of stepping out gracefully and in control, she covered her mouth and jumped back hastily, almost stumbling on something herself. Her eyes were enormous, wide open and gaping, traveling up and down, her mouth ajar. In the brightness of the moonlight, it was easy to see her lips moving, yet no sound came out.

"Don't," he whispered. "Don't get frightened. It's me. I was on my way there." Hurriedly, he pointed at the direction of the river, as though it explained it all. "Did you come back here looking for us?"

She just nodded, still pressing her hand to her mouth. Her eyes slid downwards, then flew back up hastily. Suddenly, he became aware of his nakedness.

"I-I was on my way. To get water. I made a fire. Back there, where Akweks is."

He heard his own stammer, and it made him angry. There was nothing wrong with going down to the river to bring his wounded friend water, or with doing so bared of clothing when one's loincloth needed to be dried. What was wrong with him, or with her?

"Wait for me up there, with Akweks," he said firmly, his voice low but not whispering anymore. "I'll be back shortly."

His returned briskness seemed to have a calming effect. "I brought things," she said hurriedly. "Medicine, a little. Food."

"Oh, good!" He moderated his voice, still uncomfortable, not attempting to come closer. It seemed inappropriate, somehow. "Thank you. I'm grateful. Without you—"

A rustling like that of a rolling stone came from the direction of the river this time, a distant murmuring. He saw her turning as well, tensing visibly. A silence prevailed.

"Did you come alone?" he whispered.

She nodded readily.

More silence. His senses honed, tuned to the humming of the river and what it might be hiding, he let his eyes roam toward her bag, wondering as to its contents. A little medicine, she said. Oh, but it might be a perfect timing.

He found his gaze lingering, studying her face, safe in doing so as she was looking away, in the direction of the suspicious sounds. Outlined clearly against the dark sky, her profile presented an enjoyable sight, with the tip of her nose tilted teasingly and her forehead pleasantly high, free of hair that was now pulled backwards, collected in a braid, not sticking out everywhere like before. He didn't remember her being pretty or attractive on either of their previous encounters, but it was different now, somehow.

"I don't think someone follow," she whispered, turning back, her frown deep, taking away the magic. "I was careful. I move quiet, no sound. Can do that better. Better than men!"

The challenge in her voice made him wish to laugh loudly.

"Better, eh?"

"Yes." Her smile flashed suddenly, catching him unprepared. It brought the magic back, this time in force. She was not a pretty thing, but the attraction was there, in her wild, unusual sort of a way.

He turned away abruptly, wishing to conceal certain sights. He should have tied his loincloth on before going out, whether it was dry already or not.

"Thank you for bringing things. The medicine, it's good. He needs it. You see, he doesn't get better." He waved his bark in the air, glad to have something to fiddle with. "I'm going to bring water. You wait here. Or maybe there, with him. You remember the way?"

She nodded again, averting her eyes in too obvious of a way. Damn it.

"Well, then go there now. Tell Akweks I'll be back shortly."

She lifted her bag, undecided. "You go bring water?"

It was his turn to nod, his thoughts on the way back. Just a short run, to reassure Akweks that the girl meant nothing but good. And to put his loincloth back on, disgustingly wet as it was.

She was still fiddling with her bag, obviously embarrassed.

"Here." Her fidgeting produced a round, fairly large vessel. "Your bark is no good."

"Oh!" Excited, he snatched the flask, feeling it hollow and solid, made of light pottery, not a gourd bowl. "That is wonderful. Exactly what I need!" He eyed her in wonder. "You thought of everything."

"Just things." She shrugged, but her smile spread again, even more charming than before. "I remember you running, running with silly bark. All water spilling. Bring just drops."

He tossed the annoying bark away, then regretted it. Useless and leaking, it provided some sort of a cover.

"I come with, with you," she was saying. "The wounded, he get scare if see me alone. He doesn't like me. He think I'm bad."

"No, he doesn't. It's just…" Now it was his turn to shrug. "He felt very bad, scared. You brought us bad news. But he doesn't hate you or anything. He appreciates what you did for us as much as I do." Arriving at the decision, he turned resolutely. "Stay here. I'll tell him to wait for us, to be ready. Be back in a few heartbeats."

It was a relief to walk in the cover of the merciful darkness, away from her gaze. She didn't hesitate to face him before, not even when he had captured her at first, sniffing around their stolen boats. She had looked back at him angrily, fearless, telling him her mind and not what he wanted to know, frustrating and yet strangely comfortable, easy to communicate with, even as enemies. And then, later, after the exhausting night battle and the disconcerting morning, when she brought them the terrible news, but some food too, and some encouragement, not an enemy anymore, but a friend. There was not a moment when either of them felt uncomfortable around each other, he was sure of that. But now they just didn't know where to look or what to say. Why? His silly lack of clothing could not be the reason. People strolled naked everywhere when needing to wash or change their clothing. There was nothing wrong with it. Her people could not be that different.

Akweks was again drifting, his breathing jerky, uneven, muttering and in pain. Okwaho brushed his palm against the clammy forehead before snatching his loincloth, despite the fact that it was still revoltingly wet. To tie it quickly was a challenge; still, in no time he was back, rushing into the night.

"The medicine, is it ready to use?"

She was standing in the same pose, as though ready to run, but at the sight of him, she relaxed visibly. "What?"

"What sort of medicine did you bring?" Pleased with the way she fell into his step, easily, with no need for any sort of inviting gesture, he glanced at her bag. "Is it something we can put on his wound? An ointment?"

"Well, no, I don't, don't think ointment." Her voice rang hesitantly, pausing between each word, as though tasting them. "I don't know what there, in the bag."

"You don't know what's in there?" Halting abruptly, he stared at her bag rather than at her. "But how? What did you put in there that you don't know?"

Her eyebrows created an almost a solid line beneath her creased forehead. "Oh, I didn't put. It's not mine. This bag, it's not mine."

"Whose then?" Pushing the shrubs away, he motioned her to pass first, registering her surprise but with no real interest. The medicine matter was more important. "Whom does this bag belong to?"

"My brother," she said simply. "I needed hurry, you see. Could not go through it. So took the entire bag." Turning to face him, as they emerged into the wind of the shore, she peered at him. "I have to bring it back. No damage, no missing things. Except what we use, need to use."

"But what?" he exclaimed, dropping back to the whispering with an effort. "What do we use and how? Neither of us knows a thing about healing. Do we?" A hopeful glance at her confirmed the worst. Of course she knew nothing about plants or the way to prepare them. How useless! She must have grabbed that stupid bag, and run here, feeling oh so very helpful. Indeed, a medicine. "This entire bag is of no use to us. No more than your silly child's bow was to you out here."

Even in the darkness, he could feel the intensity of her gaze, and the rage in it. "I do what can! I don't have to, to do things. You say thank. No accuse of stupid things."

For a heartbeat, they glared at each other, but again, the annoying sense of helplessness and frustration, so familiar since landing on this shore, mixed with strange warmth, with an urge to laugh at her and tease rather than say something angry.

"Stupid things, eh? You'll make a good Clan Mother when you are old. All bossy, busy telling people what to do. I pity the man who will come to live in your longhouse."

She was studying him with an open suspicion. "What mother?"

"Clan mother. You know, the women who run the longhouses. The Clan Council."

Her blank gaze made him remember the ridiculously short dwellings he had witnessed while watching her village. Didn't they have proper longhouses at all?

"I don't know what you talk," she was saying, her frown as deep as before. "What woman? What mother? What clan?"

Resuming his walking, he shrugged. "Don't you have clans?"

"Yes, we have, have clans."

"Then you must have Clan Mothers as well. Women who run your longhouses." The river was upon them, murmuring loudly, not especially friendly, protected by slippery stones. "Whom do you live with?"

"My family." She walked beside him briskly, not concerned with the possibility of slipping, obviously at home in these surroundings, darkness or not.

"Like, father-mother family? Or aunts, uncles, cousins and all that?"

He slowed his step and listened, the drone of the river bringing back unpleasant memories. What if some of the enemy stayed to pass the night here?

"Yes, father, mother, my brother. Aunt and her daughters." She was speaking more loudly, trying to overcome the hum of the water. "But people are there, there in our house, all the time. Father is the war leader, you see, so the gatherings, every time they need to meet and talk..." Suddenly, she caught his arm. "Not there. Come, I know, know place better, better to get down there."

"Our War Council meets outside, always." Relieved by her taking charge, he followed, still careful, but now more sure of himself. No more spontaneous swimming in that river. "They don't get together anywhere near the longhouses, or inside the town's fence even. Their meetings are to be kept private, for the leading warriors' ears alone."

He remembered Cohoes Falls and the days that preceded the War Dance that signified the preparations for their current expedition. The Mothers of the Clans did not hurry to give their consent, and so many meetings outside the town were called, many arguments ran back and forth between the War and the Clans' Councils. Being those who supplied the provisions for the raid, Clans Mothers had a final say, to the bitter resentment of many young warriors and their leaders.

"Do your father and other leading warriors have to ask for the Clan Mothers' permission?"

Halting upon the last of the stones, she turned back, obviously puzzled. "Ask for mother's permission?" Her laughter overcame the noise of the river easily.

"Not *your* mother." Annoyed, he stared at her, but her unreserved hilarity proved difficult to resist. "You are impossible!"

"You said… you said ask mother. I didn't say that! You say…" By now she was doubled over with laughter, hugging her stomach with both hands, not falling into the river raging behind her back by a miracle as it seemed.

"I said 'clan mothers.' The heads of the Clan Council. Not every mother that is wandering around the town." He took a deep breath, trying to overcome his own outburst of mirth. "Stop laughing. You'll bring every two-legged creature roaming these woods tonight here."

"No one is … roaming." Her stutter mixed with the murmuring of the water, not as loud as before, her panted breath making him think that if she fainted, he would have to fish her out of the river again, like on their first encounter. "I just try to imagine … to imagine Mother say no go to Father…"

"You are insane." Pushing his way past her, he bettered his grip on the flask, then reached out, trying to fill it without getting wet. He was too cold for that, his loincloth still revoltingly clingy and his moccasins in the worst of shapes. "Think about him asking *you* if he can go on a raid. That will make you faint from too much laughter." Her renewed guffawing made him feel better than he had felt in days. "I can just imagine it, you know? 'Oh, no, Honorable War Chief, you can't go. It is not advisable. Not so soon after the Harvest Moon.'" He lifted the flask, pleased with its solidness. No more half of the water lost while he raced back as fast as he could. "But I know who can, eh, who can replace the warriors on the raid."

"Who?" she breathed, leaning on one of the stones, still hugging herself, still trembling, gulping the air.

"Don't you guess?"

"No." Her eyes sparkled as she leaned forward, lips partly opened, expectant. Again, a very pleasant sight in the more generous illumination of the shore.

He got to his feet, trying to pay no attention to the wild thought of pulling her closer. "The girl with the toy bow. If they sent her on the raid, that would make the fiercest of enemies shudder."

"Starting with you!" The glow of her eyes deepened, reverted back to the old daring spark, but this time there was something else there, a different sort of a challenge. It made his struggle to control himself more difficult. "You be scared, you shudder, fierce enemy. Yes?"

He forced a light grin. "We'll see about that."

Luckily, she moved along as he turned to go, avoiding the necessity to push his way past her again. Relieved but somehow disappointed, he followed.

"So your mother tell your father what to do?"

He hastened his step, not wishing to lose sight of her as she skipped between the glittering stones, too briskly for his general state of exhaustion.

"No, she doesn't. Well, not very often, unless it's something to do with our clan or our longhouse. She is a member of our Clans Council, you see? She is listened to by the people of our longhouse and the others around the town. She has a lot of influence." Concentrating on his step, he hid his smile, thinking about Mother and her lively, determined way of talking, with this slightly wrong way of pronouncing some words. "She came from the lands of the Crooked Tongues, you see. She wasn't born among our people. Still, no one ever mistrusted her, or belittled her words or opinions. She was elected to be one of our Clan Mothers, and no one thought it to be a bad choice."

She paused to let him catch up with her. "So clan mothers, what they do?"

"Everything." He shrugged. "They make it all work, the longhouse and the clan. And the town, if you ask them, although, of course, it's not true as we have a Town Council to deal with important matters." Halting beside her, he grinned. "They tell everyone what to do. That is their main duty. To order everyone about. That's why I said you'll make a good Clan Mother."

She answered his grin with a face, wrinkling her nose in the funniest of manners, one of her eyebrows climbing so high it almost met the fluttering fringes of her ruffled hair. "We don't have this, this sort of mothers. Our people do good without them."

"Who manages your clans' affairs, then?" He looked around as the darkness thickened, the gathering clouds concealing the moonlight, letting it pour down more faintly, not as generous as before.

"The chief, the head of the clan." She looked around too, clearly perturbed. "We better go."

"Yes."

This time, he led the way, hurrying to cross the open space, wishing to be in the safety of the foliage again. It was still too bright to feel safe on the open ground.

"What you do?" she asked, catching up with him. "What will do now? About your friend."

Suspiciously, he eyed the bushes ahead of them. Something wasn't right there. What?

"I don't know," he muttered. "We'll see in a little while."

"He no better?"

He pressed his lips. "No."

"It's bad. He weak? Hot? Dreaming?" She halted as he did, not about to give up.

"He will be well soon."

"But what if not? What you do, will do?" He could feel her searching gaze, sliding over him, expectant. "If wounds rot—"

"They are not rotting!"

The sharp exclamation shook the darkness, and he clenched his fists, angry with himself as much as he was angry with her.

"He will be well," he repeated quietly, suddenly aware that with no constant humming of the river, it was back to whispering for them.

Again, his attention drifted to the darkness under the trees. He could feel it watching him, hostile and afraid, just like the first time when they landed here.

"You don't yell, stop yell at me!" she was saying, not bothering to keep her voice low. "I say what is reasonable. I say good sense. Even if you afraid, don't want to hear—"

"Quiet!"

Grabbing her shoulder, he pressed it urgently, signaling her to keep still, but, of course, she did not comply. Instead, she fought to break free, a wild thing. Even amidst his mounting worry, he felt the familiar tickle of amusement. This girl was an untamed creature, the fierce spirit of the east.

"Stop it, you wild fox. We need to keep quiet."

The darkness broke with an urgent rustling. Before the familiar hiss followed, he pushed her away from the possible range of an arrow.

Her cry of surprise barely registered in his mind as he threw himself down, hearing her stumbling and falling as well. The arrow swished above, harmless.

As he pushed himself up, to half-run half-crawl toward the source of the shooting, his fingers tore at his sash, reassured by the touch of the knife, locking around its smooth handle.

Another arrow sliced the air, too far to his left to make him worried. Whoever it was, he must have been a lousy shooter.

The darkness of the trees enveloped him before the third arrow came. Feeling safer under its concealing protection, he let his senses guide him toward the foreign presence. Oh, yes, the frantic rustling and some breaking branches told him that the enemy was on the move. Also, that he might have been there unaccompanied, a lone shooter.

Oblivious of the bushes and trees that stuck out everywhere, trying to prevent his progress—the local woods proved to be hostile time after time—he put everything he had into the effort to reach the source of the noise, to get to the enemy before the dirty piece of rotten meat caused any more trouble.

Eyes strained, ears pricked, he spotted a silhouette darting behind the low cluster of shrubs. Throwing his body toward it, he caught a glimpse of a gaping face, as his shoulder smashed into the wide chest, using his own body's accumulated drive to push the enemy off his feet.

It wasn't a difficult goal to achieve. In another heartbeat, they were both on the ground, with Okwaho's fist crashing into his rival's face, his body bettering its position on top of the sagging form, pressing with all its weight, his other hand jumping up frantically, fastening its grip on the knife.

The man didn't even squirm. Seemingly stunned, he just lay there, face gaunt and thin, one cheek swollen, eyes round, enormous, reflecting no understanding. Okwaho brought his knife up.

"No!"

The cry tore the darkness. Like in a dream, he felt the body underneath him jerking back to life, his own lurching as well, trembling with the surprise and the accumulated tension. His hand holding the knife shook, struggling against a force he did not comprehend for a moment, with something hindering its progress. Attempting to shake it off, he felt her familiar presence. She was crouching next to them, her hands fastened around his arm, clinging to it with desperation.

"What in the name of the …" He tried to shake her off without removing his other hand from his rival's throat. A difficult feat as she clung to his arm with both hands, her entire weight upon it. "Get off me!"

"No, no, don't!" she was moaning. "Stop. No kill, don't kill…"

The man underneath was squirming with more spirit now, gurgling, trying to wriggle free from the strangling hand.

"Stop, please!" Her eyes were very close, pleading.

He let her pull his arm away. "Let go!"

Rolling off his rival was easy, a relief. He watched the man closely, ready for his next move, but the stupid would-be-attacker was helpless, sprawling on his side, coughing and drawing such loud breaths, Okwaho fought the urge to smash him into unconsciousness, just to make him shut up.

The girl was kneeling by his side, whispering urgently, her foreign-sounding words muffled, interrupted by hiccups.

"What is happening? Who is it?" The feel of the rough bark behind his back was welcome, offering support. Still, he left it for a heartbeat, picking the fallen bow, this time a good, impressively large weapon, something worthy of keeping. First the club, and now this. Since the enemy came to collect their boats, his arsenal of weaponry had grown considerably. He pulled it closer, not amused.

"That brother, my brother," she said, straightening up, her hair askew, fresh mud staining her face. "He didn't want to harm. He didn't know."

Okwaho rolled his eyes. "He was shooting. At both of us! That first arrow might have been stuck in you."

"It's not..." Frowning, she dropped her gaze, hunching above the coughing man again, supporting his head. "He is not, not the best. No shoot good." This came out quietly, in a hesitant manner, atypical for the forceful fox.

Okwaho leaned back against the tree. "What was he doing here?"

Her shrug was barely perceptible. "Maybe he follow, follow me."

"Probably!" He watched the man struggling to sit up, suddenly too tired to think. "What do we do with him now?"

"I... well... I talk, talk to him."

He wanted to shut his eyes, to let his exhaustion lull him into oblivion, at least for a little while. It was all too much, too many things to worry about, to take care of. Akweks and the hidden boat, and the enemies that would be scanning these shores first thing in the morning, looking for him. Not to mention their people who were killed, all of them, to the last man, and the rest of their forces somewhere down there at the mouth of another great river, raiding some other settlement, killing more of her countryfolk. Was it right to do that?

He shook his head, to get rid of unwelcome questions. Would they understand what had happened when they came back? Would they blame him for this failure, like Kayeri had?

And most importantly, would he manage to bring Akweks back home alive? His friend's wounds were rotting. Or maybe only one of them, but one was more than enough to kill a person, to put him on his Sky Journey, and in the most agonizing of ways.

She was right about that. He was a coward to refuse to face this reality, but his reluctance changed nothing. Father said it many times: never succumb to the temptation of lying, not to yourself, surely.

So Akweks would die, and probably he, Okwaho, would too. And it would all end here, in this strange, foreign forest, on the windy shore, with no one to mourn their passing, no one to dance and pray and help their spirits find their Sky Paths, to avoid getting stuck wandering about. A true danger, a true possibility without the help of the mourning family and friends.

He watched her talking to the man, gesturing, her face alive with emotion, again a very pleasant sight. Maybe she would do that for him. Pray if not dance, with her funny way of using the words of his tongue, so fierce and strong but vulnerable too, needing protection. Protection from whom? Him or her people? Why was she helping him, anyway?

The man was saying something, talking angrily, with an open resentment. She overrode him quickly. Was this the same nosy bastard who had sniffed around earlier this evening, forcing him, Okwaho, into desperate means to take them away from his wounded friend? Somehow, he was certain it was. Her brother, of all things.

He watched her frowning, talking again, in a rush. Why was he spending his time here? Akweks needed his water, and if he had heard the noise, he would need reassurance as well.

Water! The thought hit him, the memory of the flask rolling away. He cursed loudly, forcing his way back onto his feet.

"What? What happened?" They both were staring at him, the girl startled, the man aghast.

"The stupid water got spilled," he hissed through his clenched teeth. "I have to find the flask. Fill it again, if it didn't get broken, curse all this into the underworld of the Evil Twin!"

"Wait." She jumped to her feet too, all flushed and breathless. "Listen, Migisso, he loves healing, good with herbs. He'll help, help your friend. Make medicine, eh? My brother no useless with herbs. Not like us. He help."

He watched her, taken aback. "He can make medicine?"

"Yes, yes, he can. I told you. I took his bag, remember? His medicine."

"Why would he agree?"

Her eyes sparkled. "I'll make agree. I'll talk, make agree."

"How?"

"I have ways, my ways." Again, her excitement was an irresistible sight to see. He fought the urge to touch her face, to run his fingers along the sharp curve of her cheek, to find out what it would feel like. "Also, he is to blame, no? Make mess, shoot at us. He owes, eh? Have to make it right."

Her eyes shone brighter than the stars, now that the clouds came to hide some of the sky again.

"I... I will..." He swallowed, finding it difficult to articulate his thoughts. "If you make him help us, help Akweks, I will never forget. I will do anything for you."

The glow of her eyes changed. As did the color of her cheeks. Licking her lips, she stared at him for a heartbeat, then dropped her gaze.

Embarrassed, he clutched the bow, wondering where the quiver of arrows might be. "You talk to him. I'll bring water."

Reassured by her nod, he headed off, not bothering to look at the man. This one presented no danger now, of that he was sure. She would be able to handle him. There could be no doubt about her ability to do so.

CHAPTER 18

"You must do that, you must!"

In the meager light of the small fire, the wounded's face looked grotesque, shadowed and pinched, with black, round holes for eyes.

Along with the wolf youth, Kentika held her breath. She could feel him by her side, as tense as a stretched bowstring. He had been all activity and vigor before, bringing water, talking, directing everyone, shooting direful glances at Migisso, but now he quieted down, succumbing to the solemnity of the moment, or frightened by it.

She glanced at him again, taking in his prominent features, his face pale and muddied, bruised all over, but still decidedly handsome, pleasing the eye, the sharp cheekbones protruding, inviting one to touch.

What would he say if she did? she wondered briefly, then forced her attention back to the present and the sagging figure of her brother, leaning against one of the cliffs, hugging his elbows in a protective manner.

"You must try, Migisso," she repeated. "Please. They have nothing to lose. The wounded will die anyway if you won't try. Why won't you?"

He gave her a dark look. "Plenty of reasons, Sister. Too many to sound them all."

"You must!"

Pressed lips were her answer, but quickly, his gaze returned to her companion, turning wary, defensive again.

"What does he say?" The wolf youth's voice rang eerily,

lacking in expression.

Dropping her gaze, she shrugged.

"He won't help," he said quietly, making it a statement.

His words held finality, a surprisingly calm acceptance. She shuddered. "I will convince him. He will help."

Drawing a deep breath, he seemed to be pondering his words for a moment. "Tell him I ask for his help not as an enemy or a friend, but as a person, just another person. Healers are helping people with no regard to their loyalties or belonging. Healers are above this. If he refuses to help because of us being enemies, then he is no healer, whatever his aspirations are, however he may like playing with herbs." She watched him bringing his hands up, palms pressed together, fingers interlocked. The gaze that shifted to her held nothing but affection. "Tell him I will not kill him, because he is the brother of the bravest and kindest girl, a truly good, worthy person. But," the eyes hardened, turned to stone, "he will stay here until we are gone, and he better keep very quiet and out of my way."

She wanted to dwell on 'the bravest and kindest,' but the sternness of his gaze made her concentrate, storing these words for later thinking. Did he just say…?

"And here you have it," she said, giving her brother a stern look of her own. "The enemy behaves in the noblest of ways, when you, out of all our people, coming out as prejudiced, as petty and narrow-minded as you can."

"What did he say?" Migisso's face lost the last of its coloring, and his voice rang faintly, barely heard, holding that familiar old despondency she remembered well from his infrequent confrontations with Father. Back home, it would make her indignant, to hear the old leader harping on her brother's worthlessness. Now it did just the opposite.

"He said you are not worthy to be a healer, because you do not help people in need. He said this is not the way of the healers." She let her own gaze relay the depth of her contempt. "But he won't harm you, he said. You'll stay here until they are gone, then you can go home."

"And you?" he asked hoarsely, eyes haunted like those of a

cornered animal.

"I can do whatever I want. I don't need his mercy, nor his help. I'm not a prisoner of theirs." His falling face made her compassion return, but she pushed it away, too angry and disappointed to let it interfere. "But you are, Brother. You tried to kill him, and he took you as a captive. And he should have killed you, or he should take you away. But he won't. He is not that kind of a person. He is good and worthy."

She felt *his* eyes, darting from face to face, as though listening to their exchange. It made her stomach tighten. He believed in her ability to convince Migisso. And he thought her to be brave and kind.

"Healers help people. They ease pain and suffering. They treat people, all people, and not just the ones they like or expect a returned favor from." That was an undeserved slur, but she didn't care. He was not being fair. He didn't want to help her, and just as she needed it desperately. "You don't want to help someone wounded and in pain. What does that make you? A healer? I think not."

The wounded shifted lightly, his groan no more than a murmur, smothered behind the clasped lips. Their eyes went to him.

"It's not that simple," Migisso's voice was strained, his cough a short, dry sound. "I could have tried to treat him, but for his wound. It looks bad. It's rotting. My treatment won't save him. No medicine will help him now."

"But you can..." Helplessly, she looked back at him, desperate to hide her budding hope. "Surely there is something you can try to do. Anything."

He shook his head, his gaze avoiding hers.

"What does he say?" The question in the foreign tongue bounced off the cliff's walls, not really an inquiry. He knew the answer as well as her brother did. That's why he was so angered when she had mentioned the rotting wounds for the first time.

"He says there is nothing, medicine no help." To talk helped. The silence between their phrases was too heavy, pressing against her chest.

"No medicine, but…" The wolf youth took a deep breath, and she watched his jaw tightening, his eyes turning dark, as black as the night, and as unreadable. "It's very early yet. Not much rotten flesh. A healer can cut, cut the rotten flesh away." His throat convulsed as he swallowed. "I saw it happening once. The healer cuts, makes wound worse, but the rotten flesh goes away and the wounded gets better. Eventually." Straightening his gaze resolutely, he faced her. "Ask him about this."

Now it was Migisso's turn to lean forward, following their words with his gaze as though hoping to understand. "What?"

"He says…" She swallowed hard. "He says healer can cut, you see, cut the bad parts away, the rotting parts. Do you know something about it? Can you try to do that?"

He backed as though she had struck him. "I can't. It's terrible, and it won't help." His arms shot up, palms forward, pushing her words away. "No, no, it's a terrible thing. The wounded suffers so! And it doesn't help. He dies anyway." His head shook violently. "No, no, I won't do that. It's of no use."

"You have to!"

"I can't. I'm not good enough. Even our medicine man didn't manage."

"Tell him I'll find a way to repay him." The wolf youth said eagerly, needing no translation anymore. "Tell him it will be worth his time. I promise to keep my word. I'll find a way to make it worthwhile for him."

"It's not, not about make worth." But her eyes went back to her brother, boring at him, willing him to agree. "You have to, you have to try. We'll help, both of us. The wounded, he has nothing to lose, has he? He'll die either way. Won't he?" His pursed lips were her answer. "You have to try. I promise, I will be so grateful. I'll make it all worth it, somehow. I'll find a way." She nodded at their host without looking at him. "He said he'll make it worth, too. He will repay you."

But Migisso shook his head angrily. "It's not about that, Sister, and you know it! I can't believe we are having this conversation…" The fire in his eyes died as suddenly as it lit. "You want me to cut this man? Well, I'll do it. Maybe this way I'll have one killed enemy on my count of achievements." Abruptly, he straightened up, suddenly tall and resolute, more sure of himself than she had ever seen him. "You will help. And him, too. Tell him to bring more firewood, make a bigger fire. Also water. We need to boil much of it. And cloths." His gaze encircled them, narrow and concentrated, deep in his inner thoughts. "We need something, anything. Tell him to think how to get pieces of cloth."

"What for?" she began, but his glare made her stop babbling. "He says we need, need things. You know, material. Like from your clothes…"

The wolf youth nodded, understanding better than her, apparently. "I'll cut a piece from my loincloth, and from his, where there are no decorations…"

His knife flashed readily, as his eyes assessed his scant clothing, seeking the parts that could be cut away. For a wild moment, she wondered if he'd have to take it off, to sacrifice all the available material for the healing process. Earlier in the night, she had been embarrassed greatly, encountering him walking the woods naked. As though she had never seen people bare of clothing before. How silly! There was nothing wrong with men strolling about with no loincloth, especially when heading for the shore as he did. And yet she had to fight the urge to avert her eyes, if not to turn away and run. Even now, the mere memory of it brought a wave of heat to wash over her face.

"I need more than one piece of cloth. Tell him. There will be much blood and… and other things. The cut will need to be cleaned over and over." As always when treatment was involved, Migisso assumed control naturally, distributing orders in a calm, matter-of-fact voice, lacking its usual indecisiveness. Proudly, she watched him for another heartbeat. "Tell him to take care of the fire for now. It needs to be large enough to make the water boil."

The wolf youth was still busy with his loincloth.

"He want you, he wants you make fire, big fire. And also," she eyed the pitiful remnants of his garb, "stop ruin this. It will not help. Not enough. I take care. Have a lot to cut. See?" Lifting the torn rims of her dress, she grinned. "I cut, enough for all. My brother says we need many, many pieces. I have enough. You don't."

As he was staring at her, his eyes narrowed, but his lips quivered with a hint of a smile. "That you have. Well," he jumped to his feet readily, "I'll collect firewood, before the moon hides again." A mirthless grin flashed for a heartbeat. "Or before that brother of yours changes his mind."

The flames soared, filling their small hideaway with a wave of heat, suffocating, not welcomed in the least. Aghast, Kentika watched them licking the razor-sharp edges of the knife. They did so hungrily, as though trying to consume it.

"Now the other side." Migisso was watching the knife too, having checked with the boiling pot for the tenth time, stirring the pieces of torn material floating in there with a stick from the pile of branches the wolf youth had arranged. "Tell him to turn it over and hold in the fire for the same amount of time."

The young man looked up sharply. "What now?"

"Now other, the other side." She could barely recognize her own voice, the way it rasped, low and gruff. "Same time. Count to few times ten, yes?"

He just nodded, turning the knife obediently, saying nothing for a change, clearly uneasy crouching so close to the fire, with his hands practically stuck in it. The knife's handle was not long enough to burn the blade comfortably. Luckily, it was made out of stone and not wood, she reflected, still wondering as to why they were roasting it like that over the flames.

"Now tell him to give me the knife, then get a good hold of his friend." Her brother's eyes indicated the wounded, who was half-lying and half-sitting now, staring at the fire too, wild-eyed. "Tell them it'll hurt, so the wounded has to be held very tightly. I can't treat him if he fights and struggles."

Not waiting for the translation, the wolf youth got to his feet. For a heartbeat, he scanned his knife with a troubled gaze, then offered it to Migisso, as though understanding with no more need of her translating services.

"Now what?"

"You catch him. Hold him. Tight. No move." She demonstrated with her hands. "Brother says it hurt, so he'll move. But you can't, can't let him move."

The last of the color washed out of his face, but again, he just nodded. "Should he be laid down?"

More translated questions back and forth. She watched the wounded biting his lips, his fear spilling, open, unconcealed, eyes so wide they turned round, the only feature to dominate the lifelessness of his face.

"It is going to be well, good, no trouble," she said, coming closer. "Not so long, I'm sure. I help." Crouching beside them, she looked up, facing her brother, who inspected his newly acquired knife calmly, if a bit dubiously. "Should he lie down? Or sit? What do I do to help?"

"Lay," Migisso frowned absently. "Yes, lay him down, and you two hold him, because he will be struggling. Well, in the beginning, at least. Let us hope his mind will go off wandering fast. For his sake."

She shuddered, unwilling to hear more. "We hold, together," she said, addressing the wolf youth. "Both, me and you. It won't, won't be long, I'm sure. He be well again. You'll see."

His gaze clung to her, troubled, tormented, but expectant, as though wishing to hear more, as though needing her to keep talking. Was he reassured by her heedless promises? The thought made her stomach constrict violently, as though she had eaten something bad.

"He will be well again. You see ... will see."

His throat moved visibly as he swallowed. A slight nod and he was leaning toward his friend, talking rapidly.

Migisso came closer. "He'll hold his upper body. You, his legs, especially the wounded one." Another deep frown. She watched her brother's eyes wandering, scanning the ground. "He needs something to bite onto. Something firm but soft, or he will break his teeth."

"What?"

His gaze brushed past her. "For the pain. It helps. To keep the screams in." He shrugged indifferently. "But we don't have anything fitting, so he'll have to manage. Tell him to keep as quiet as he can. Unless they want our entire village around and helping."

Where was her timid mouse of a brother? She peered at him, puzzled as he fished one of the floating cloths out of the pot, then knelt beside the wounded, the knife ready, held expertly, just an extension of his hand. Was it someone else and not the man she had known her entire life?

"Be ready with more pieces. When I give you the ones I used, throw those back into the pot. Let them boil for a while." Another frowning scan. "Make sure to keep the fire as large as it is now."

The wolf youth was listening too, avidly, as though trying to understand.

"You just hold, hold him, don't let him move," she said, too frightened to add something reassuring. "I keep fire … when need. You just, just keep him quiet."

She heard her voice trailing off, her eyes glued to the knife as it neared the swollen mess of the wounded's thigh, assessing, hesitating, yielding its turn to the wet cloth at first, not in a hurry. A mere touch of the soaked material made the patient's body arch, and she strangled her own cry, horrified, watching his companion fighting not to let the flailing limbs escape.

"Stop his screams!" Migisso's voice rang with urgency, but his hands didn't tremble, didn't stop, wiping the revolting mess away, cleaning the wound. Then the knife began its work.

The wolf youth's entire body was busy making sure his friend didn't move, still, he managed to free his hand in order to cover the twitching mouth, strangling the screams back. He was practically lying on top of the struggling body, but she was as busy, investing all her power into holding the leg she was responsible for from flailing about in its wild fight against its tormenters.

"Give me another cloth."

She arched, trying to reach the pot without letting her charge go. Her fingertip burned, but she didn't care, wishing nothing else but to get this nightmare over with. Anything but to witness the inhumane treatment.

"Put the other one back in there."

"What?"

Migisso tossed the reeking, revoltingly sticky cloth at her without looking, his eyes on the wounded, whose body went limp all of a sudden. As she struggled with the repulsive mess, trying to bring it back to the pot without touching its worst parts, her brother and the wolf youth bent simultaneously, examining the lifeless form. Petrified, she followed their example, staring at the glaring white where the eyes of the man should have been. It made her wish to vomit.

Migisso put his head to the sweaty chest and listened. Then, unperturbed, he went back to work, more relaxed now, swabbing and cutting, then wiping some more.

"I need more light. Tell him."

She fought her growing nausea, desperate to dart outside, away from the stench that filled their small hideaway, rising like tide, or pressing from above, like a thick blanket.

"He needs… he wants, he ask me to tell you…"

The wolf youth looked as though about to vomit too, his lips just a colorless line, eyes wild. "What?"

"He light, needs light."

He whirled back toward the fire, as though welcoming the chance to get away, even if for a short while. His improvised torch, just a burning stick, did not look promising, but it did increase the illumination around the wounded.

"More cloths."

The short order brought her to the fire, too, fighting the urge to dive into the nearby bushes. But for a small gulp of fresh air; just for a brief moment with no stench that assaulted her nostrils viciously, filling her lungs, suffocating, unbearable. How did they stand it? She found herself envying the wounded his unconsciousness, the yellowish, putrid liquid soaked into the used cloth she held clinging to her skin, promising to stay there forever. Oh, Mighty Glooskap!

"Wash the knife thoroughly."

From the corner of her eye, she saw the wolf youth tensing, following the progress of his weapon with his gaze. The water in the pot was not bubbling anymore.

Unaware of her movements, acting as though outside herself, she added another log to the fire, then washed the jagged blade hurriedly, before the water warmed to unbearable again.

Migisso straightened up, eyeing his work with the critical eye of an artist admiring a carving he had just made.

"It should be closed up," he commented, then shrugged. "But I have nothing to sew it with. And maybe it's for the best. More of the bad things will come out, and dry." He eased his shoulders, then glanced up for the first time since the beginning of the treatment. "Are you well, Sister?"

She tried to nod as calmly as she could. "Is it over?" The trembling of her lips made it difficult to form words.

He just nodded.

"Will he live?"

Shrugging, he glanced at the wolf man, instead. "Tell him I did all I could. Tell him he may live, but he needs to be watched closely for some time. If he didn't go to the worlds of the spirits by now, maybe he'll manage to stay. I'll make something for him to drink, something that might help to make his body stronger. Since you stole my bag, we have all we need here with us, haven't we?"

"Oh, I—"

"What did he say? Is it over?" The wolf youth cut into her speech, his voice trembling, face ashen.

"Yes, he say, he say he did everything. Maybe live. But need care. Drink brews. Take care."

She watched his mouth twitching, his throat moving jerkily with each swallow. He would do better moving away from his wounded friend when he vomits, she reflected randomly.

"He looks dead." His voice was also difficult to recognize, such a low, throaty sound.

As though understanding the comment, Migisso leaned forward, putting his ear to the lifeless chest. They held their breaths.

"He is breathing." Straightening up, her brother eased his

shoulders once again, then reached for the bag, forgotten under the nearest stone. "His heart is beating. Not strongly, but steadily. If he wakes to drink the medicine, he might live."

The wolf youth's expression made her aware that there was no need to spend her energy on translation, not this time. His face lost some of its haunted look.

"Tell him I'm grateful. Grateful that he tried. I won't forget."

"He says—"

"We have no time for the idle talk." Migisso cut her off unceremoniously, with such unfamiliar decisiveness, she found herself gaping. His gaze held hers, firm, determined, a man in charge. "Empty this pot and tell him to bring more water and more firewood. And he better hurry." The cold flicker in his eyes was unmistakable. "They don't want to be here by the dawn break. Or all my work here will be in vain."

"Oh!" The pang of fear was painful, resonating in her chest.

"Tell him to bring water first. And quickly."

The wolf youth was staring at her, openly perturbed. "What does he say?"

"We need water. Clean water. For medicine. And more," she gestured at the branches, suddenly forgetting the appropriate words of the foreign tongue. "More this."

"Yes, of course." On his feet, he eyed her briefly. "He'll make medicine?"

"Yes."

"Tell him I will repay. Tell him—"

"No time, you need hurry." Now it was her turn to cut him off, the urgency dawning on her at long last. By daybreak, every man who could carry a weapon would be here, looking for him. "I come with you. Bring branches."

He nodded curtly, but his eyes flickered in a manner that made her knees weak. He did appreciate her help, oh yes, he knew how good she was to them, and he was grateful. And also...

Her heart fluttering strangely, she followed him as he dived into the bushes, wondering what was in this gaze of his that made her so unsettled. A simple gratitude should not have done this. She knew he was grateful. He told her so quite a few times.

The night enveloped them with its blissful freshness, with a crisp wind, cold but oh so very welcome. Busy going through the contents of his bag, Migisso paid their exit no attention.

"I will not take the freshness of the night for granted, never again." Looking up, her companion inhaled loudly, drawing in as much air as he could, she suspected. She was doing the same, but in a quieter manner. "The lack of stench, that's what was missing."

Against her nervousness and foreboding, she giggled. "I will not, too. I thought I will, will take it all out there, everything from my inside." For the life of her, she could not remember the word for 'vomit.'

"Yes, it was not easy not to retch all over." His voice lost some of its previous lightness. "How did he do this? I mean, he was so … so sure of himself. Is he a great healer? He looks too young to be so good. He must be highly sought after."

She glanced at him briefly, seeking signs of him teasing her. "Migisso? He is no healer, no sought after. He… he loves healing, loves herbs, but he can't, can't be healer. He is to be warrior, you see? Like Father. Warrior, leader."

"Warrior?" This time, she felt his gaze brushing over her, his voice trembling with a hint of mischief. "Your brother is no warrior."

"He, yes, he can be." The open contempt of his words hurt. "He just … he needs learn, practice. He be warrior, one day he will be…" Enraged, she halted, staring at him, hating the crookedness of his grin, one side of the mouth up, one eyebrow arched, the picture of open doubt. "You don't know, you just meet."

"Just met, yes. In an ambush. He was shooting at me from the bushes, obviously having watched us for some time." His laughter was the most annoying sound, rolling softly, laced with unbearable superiority. "He should have succeeded, you know. The most mediocre warrior would have. Also, he should have been ready for the chance of missing, ready with his knife, or a club." A good-natured wink and he resumed his walk, not bothering to make sure if she followed or not. So much arrogance!

"You are the better warrior than he is. You gave me a hard time upon our first meeting, and if you bothered to hide in the bushes instead of just running and shooting, I would have been impaled right away." Another soft chuckle reached her as she followed, too enraged to just turn around and go back. "Your family has a strange way of introducing themselves to people, local girl. What is your name, anyway?"

"Kentika," she grunted out through her clenched teeth. "And you, you have strange way of coming, coming visiting. You come with warriors, and fire arrows. And you complain, complain your welcome. You ..." Frantically, she searched her limited vocabulary, frustrated that she could not say all she thought about him in a normal tongue. "You don't dare complain."

The river was again upon them, not lit as strongly as before. His chuckle wafted in the air as faintly.

"Yes, you may be right about that." Bettering his grip on the cumbersome pottery, he hesitated before taking the familiar rocky trail. "Your brother is a good man. I owe him much, whether Akweks lives or not. I wish I could repay him, somehow. He is a good man, and an accomplished healer. Even if he wants to be a warrior, instead."

"He doesn't, doesn't want." Watching his wide back disappearing between the rocks, she hesitated in her turn, then followed, as though tied to his girdle by invisible rope. "He wants to heal, yes, to heal people, to treat. He loves doing this. He is good, yes. He took care of Schikan. Schikan was hurt badly, and his arm, it was broken. But Migisso made... he made..." Another attempt to find a missing word. Oh, but it was frustrating to talk to him for longer than a little while. "He tied, tied two sticks, you see? To hold it..."

"A splint?" His voice reached her from quite far. Obviously, he needed no more guidance while following the already-familiar trail.

She hastened her step. "Yes, splint. Migisso made splint, good splint. And he made brew for Schikan to drink. You see? He took care. The medicine man, he trusts, let Migisso help, take care. He knows my brother do good."

"Then why? Why is your brother not taking his real path, if he loves it and is good at it?" He was kneeling on the last rock, one hand holding onto a protruding edge, the other dealing with his vessel; quick, efficient, matter-of-fact. Wasn't he as tired, as spent and exhausted as she was? Lacking in sleep, lacking in food, didn't he need to rest from time to time? Or was he sent here by Malsum or some other spirit after all, evil or good, or maybe both, but not entirely human?

Fascinated, she studied him, as he jumped back to his feet, balancing his cumbersome cargo with no visible effort, swift and agile, in an obvious hurry, a spectacular vision, even in the meager night illumination, showing no signs of exhaustion. How did he do it, when all she wanted was to crawl somewhere, to curl around herself and sleep for a whole span of seasons, forgetting the terrible treatment she had just witnessed most of all.

"What?" He peered at her, puzzled.

"I think you Malsum. Not as evil as they say, maybe, but yes, Malsum the Wolf. Not human. Not just warrior."

One of his eyebrows arched. "Didn't we talk about it before?" A light half-grin playing in the corner of his mouth, he pushed himself past her, beckoning her to follow. "I have nothing to do with your local spirits. But my guiding spirit is a wolf, a wonderful silvery vision I told you about. And he is good. Nothing evil about him."

"Did you ask, ask for his help?" She shielded her face against a new gust of wind. "Did you try talk, call him?"

He said nothing, and she regretted asking a question as intimate as this. One didn't prompt people to talk about such private matters. It was beyond good manners.

"I did." His voice drifted quietly, floating with the wind. "Just as I came back to our world, having been washed to this accursed shore with Akweks. I called on my guiding spirit, and I thanked him for giving me my life back. And yes, I may have asked for a little help." There was a smile in his voice, a good smile, full of kindness, lacking in amusement. "I know one is not supposed to do that, and I didn't really. I just asked for advice, for a little guidance." Another brief pause filled the strangely comfortable silence. "Little did I know in what way my prayer might have been answered. Such a tortuous way! And it took me time to understand. Do you think the spirits are having a good laugh at my expense?"

With the trees back upon them, he slowed his step, turning to face her, nothing but a dark form, yet somehow, she knew what his eyes held, and the knowledge of it made her shiver with a strange mix of fear and expectation.

"What? In what way?" It felt safer to talk. She swallowed hard. "What do you mean …" Her voice trailed off, but she didn't take a step back, suddenly wanting him to do something, something wonderfully dangerous, deliciously wrong. Would he …

From so close up, his eyes glimmered. "I mean that I never expected them to send me help in such an untamed, forceful, wildly attractive form."

With the round bowl getting in his way—he was still balancing it in both hands, careful not to spill its contents—his face was the only thing to near hers, leaning forward, beaming at her. Not grave or foreboding, but happily animated, mischievously expectant.

She hadn't spent time pondering the matters of love, but on the rare occasions she did, she had imagined it to be a solemn affair, full of gravity and celebrative foreboding. Not a laughable matter. And yet, there was none of it here, on this wind-stricken shore, with his eyes holding nothing but playful expectation, so very close now, glittering with mirth, and his lips dry and cracked but somehow welcome, warm upon her mouth.

The time stopped. The night, the wind, the sky, even the stupid bowl, disappeared, melting away in oblivion. Only the overpowering sense of his presence remained, his smell, the warmth of his breath.

Dazed, she felt her own lips reacting, welcoming his, her mind in a jumble, a small part of it worrying that she might fall as her legs were weak, while the rest of it went blank, giving in to a dazzling sensation. No ritual solemnity, no dancing spirits; nothing but the all-pervading warmth, and the fluttering in her stomach, and the soaring of her spirit, like when jumping from a high cliff headfirst, this wonderful sensation of letting go. That, and the annoying trembling in her knees.

Forcefully, his lips parted hers, and it made her shiver. The pleasant warmth disappeared, giving way to a splash of near-panic. Frightened, she jerked away, sensing him shivering too, struggling not to let the bowl slip from his grip.

"We better bring it back quickly," he murmured, still fiddling with his burden.

She tried to contain the trembling.

"Are you all right?" Now his eyes were upon her, hesitant, not amused anymore.

Pushing her hair out of her face, she nodded, shamed by the way her hands shook. Her teeth would have clattered, had she not been clenching them tight.

He made no attempt to move. "I shouldn't have … I …" Shifting his cargo to one hand, he rubbed his face with the other. "I… I don't know what happened to me. I'm sorry." Resolutely, he straightened up. "Come, we need to hurry."

CHAPTER 19

The wounded's breathing was light, imperceptible, his chest barely moving under Migisso's ear. Listening to the faint heartbeat, he held his own breath, trying to hear better.

Was the man dying? He didn't know. A faint heartbeat was not a good thing, but it was better than none.

"His heart is still beating," he said, straightening up. "He hasn't left our world yet."

They both stared at him, frozen in their dread. Was he to check on their breathing, too?

He motioned with his head. "Take the pot off the fire for now."

The man was the one to react, doing as he had been told, understanding with surprising ease. One didn't always need to talk in order to communicate, reflected Migisso, reaching for his bag.

"Now tell him this."

Glancing at his sister, he again found himself puzzling over the change. Since coming back from fetching the water, with no firewood loading her arms—did she just follow the foreigner back and forth?—she had been like that, quiet, absorbed, deep in thought, moving slowly, with a measure of uncertainty. His sister? The restless, lively Kentika?

Pushing his puzzled observations aside, he fished out a slim bunch of dried leaves.

"Take these and crush them into the smallest of pieces. They should be ground, but we have no vessels and no tools to do that. So just crush them into as many pieces as you can. And tell him to bring more firewood. We'll need to make it boil in a short while."

"I..." She hesitated, as though about to argue, then her gaze concentrated. "Well, yes, of course."

A short address in the foreign tongue, and the man nodded stiffly, avoiding her gaze. Not that her eyes dared to rise higher than her converser's chin. Where did the cozy atmosphere of the earlier part of the night go? All the affectionate smiles and friendly laughter that made him so angry when he had watched them from behind the bushes. Well, now these two were as wary as two male coyotes on the same clearing.

He sensed the wounded's pattern of breathing changing, and it made him forget his musings. Enemy or not, this man was his responsibility, entrusted into his care, a difficult problem, a challenge to any healer, even the most experienced one. He had done something not every medicine man would agree to try, and he had managed so far. The youth didn't bleed to death, which could have happened several times throughout the operation, the upper leg having many dangerous areas where the blood could have burst all of a sudden, in an unrestrained flow. He had to cut very carefully, and he wasn't always certain the lethal gush would not erupt anyway. But he had managed, he had! And if the wounded lived, oh, mighty Glooskap, if this youth lived, he, Migisso, would have proven once and for all...

"When will he be waking up?" Kentika's voice broke into his thoughts, interrupting him in the process of counting the wounded's heartbeats. He motioned her to shut up.

"He may stay like that for a long time." Having finished the counting, he watched the stark, lifeless face, fearing the worst. Some people may stay like that for dawns, their chances of returning to the world of the living not good, but not impossible either. With proper care, appropriate brews and foods, one might tempt such spirits to return.

With proper care.

Something this youth would not receive. He would either wake up, drink a hastily composed medicine, smear a sloppily prepared ointment over his half-severed leg and hobble away, carried by his fierce companion, before the break of dawn, or he would die. To stay in such a state would bring him nothing but a quick dispatching by his, Migisso's, fellow villagers. And even if he managed to wake up before dawn, his chances were slim at best, nonexistent at worst.

"This will do." He watched her long, muddied fingers squashing the leaves, jerking nervously, letting the precious crumbles fall to the ground. "Now drop it into the pot, all of it. Or what is left."

A pointed glance at her, then at the foreigner who had just come back carrying another armload of branches, and he busied himself tugging at the wounded's eyelids, not sure what he was looking for. He had seen the old medicine man doing this when some of the sick were wandering the world of the dreams in such a manner.

"He is ... he is still wandering." The whites of the man's eyes stared at him, frightening with their lack of pupils. "I don't know if he'll wake up."

He felt the silence almost physically, enveloping him, pressing against his back. It was as though he had been left alone here, he and the dying warrior, alone in the entire forest, or maybe the entire world. He straightened up.

"Keep stirring this thing," he said curtly, wishing her gaping gaze to be anywhere but on him. "It will be no good if it boils."

Would it be any good if it didn't? he wondered. With no right quantity of sap compared to the amount of water, with the fire changing constantly from too small to too large and back into fading away, would proper stirring save the ointment?

He felt the questioning gaze of the foreigner upon him. Avoiding it, he just shrugged.

"Give me that stick."

She yielded her improvised spoon, moving back to the warrior's side readily, as though belonging there. It angered him even further.

"What do we do?" she asked after a quick exchange of whispers. Why were they whispering as though he could understand what they said if they yelled it at the top of their voices? The wish to throw something at them welled.

"I don't know. It's his decision. I did all I could. Now it's his time to think." The contents of the pot were beginning to boil again, so he moved it away from the fire, maneuvering in the way that didn't let him stop the stirring. It was most important to let the ingredients mix thoroughly. "Is your glorious hero capable of some thinking?"

Her eyes flashed at him, not frightened or lost anymore. "He is capable of many things, Brother!"

More ardent murmuring. What a foul ring their strange-sounding words had!

"He will take him away, sleeping or not."

"Where to?"

A flicker of wariness passed through her eyes, too obvious to miss. "I don't know."

"Of course you don't." He tried to choke the venom back. Why was he so angry with her? "He can't go before the ointment is ready. Conscious or not, this man's wound needs to be dressed. He can't be dragged around the way it is gaping now. If not cared for properly and covered, it'll rot even faster than before, whether my treatment helped or not."

She sucked in her breath before turning to her companion, whose gaze was boring at him, as though understanding the exchange. More urgent whispering followed. He stood the intensity of the dark eyes, their glow unsettling, the silhouette of the wolf upon the sharp cheek threatening.

"How long before the ointment is ready?" Her voice broke the staring contest, welcome this time.

"Not long." A shrug helped to banish the fluttering sensation in his stomach. "But they can't wait even that long." He motioned toward the gap between the cliffs, indicating the thickening darkness. The moon was fading. The night was going away.

She drew another convulsive breath. "Then what..."

The foreigner was talking again. They both turned to listen.

"He asks if we can't use it, the ointment, as it is now."

"No, we can't."

He could feel their frustration coming out in waves. There was no need to see it in their faces. The dying fire did not give enough light, not anymore. Reaching for one of the longer branches, he sighed. Compassion was a good thing, everyone said it, but sometimes it came in the worst of timings.

"Stir it." He pushed the pot into her hands, refusing to meet her gaze, feeding the fire instead. "Maybe we'll have enough time. Our people might not be heading straightaway here. Maybe he'll be able to drag his friend into the woods. If he crosses the river, he might be able to hide there in the hills for some time."

"He can't. He needs to reach the river. The canoe..." The way she choked on her own words was almost funny.

He wanted to laugh but in no merry way. "Oh, so he does have a canoe hidden somewhere around, eh? That's why he was throwing stones!"

Kentika's eyes refused to leave the ground, but as the foreigner began talking sharply, a question in his voice, her lips pressed tight.

"What did he say?" Again, it was difficult to stand the piercing gaze of the man that bore at him instead of her.

She answered with a petulant shrug, but her eyes jumped up when they both burst out talking, overriding each other. The foreigner's eyes blazed.

"Stop it, both of you!"

They paused for a heartbeat, but their eyes did not leave each other's face, trying to read, to predict one another's reaction.

"Stop yelling," she repeated, adding a phrase in the foreign tongue, repeating the same, probably. "It's not, not the place to argue." He felt her eyes resting on him. "He wants to know why you are so angry with me. He says this entire happening has nothing to do with me. What happened is not my fault, he says."

The warrior's glare was burning holes in his skin.

"I'm not angry with you. I'm angry with him and his people, dead or alive. I'm angry with this entire situation. I'm angry with the burned houses of our village, and the arrows that pierced our people or made them burn. I'm angry with Schikan's broken ribs. I'm angry with the fact that I'm stuck here, on this shore, forced to help the despicable enemy." Running out of breath, he stopped momentarily. "These are the things that make me furious. The fact that my little sister is helping the enemy behind our people's back is not the most prominent among any of these. A despicable deed in itself, yes, but for now, more important things make me angry." He watched her face darkening with defiance. "Tell him what I said. He asked a question, and he deserves the answer."

For a heartbeat, it looked as though she was going to argue. Then she turned away and began speaking slowly, in a halting manner. What she said made the foreigner's face close up in a way that promised no good.

"He says it's not that simple," she answered, chewing her lower lip in a familiar way. She always did it when not sure of herself.

"Tell him it looks simple enough from where I stand." The bowl was cooling rapidly in his hands, but he didn't notice, not frightened for the first time in his life but enjoying the sensation of saying whatever he wanted with no consideration for the consequences. He was always thinking too much. But not anymore. "Tell him there is nothing complicated about it. Tell him his people came to rob and kill. It is that simple."

"Our people raid their villages too. Sometimes."

"No, they do not! When did you see our hunters, people of our village, going up their Great River, eh? Can you remember it happening, ever? No, you can't. Because it didn't."

"But other settlements... Skootuck!" Her eyes flashed triumphantly. "They send war parties against the other river's current. They do. Neewe was a captive."

"We are not responsible for what they do in Skootuck."

Forgetting about the warrior, he almost jumped as the man moved all of a sudden, crossing the cramped-up space in this long, forceful stride of his.

His heart leaping up into his throat, Migisso just watched, knowing that he was done for, now for certain. The treacherous enemy was going to kill him. He was of no more use anyway, and he did awaken the beast by arguing. Oh, Benevolent Glooskap!

Unable to move, to try to get up in order to defend himself, maybe, he watched the wide shoulders bearing down on him, the rough palms snatching the bowl out of his hands, cooling and forgotten.

He didn't dare to breathe a few more heartbeats after the man backed away, striding toward his wounded friend, squatting beside him, the bowl pressed between his knees, the hand with the stick moving monotonously, in dull circles.

Their voices rang as dully, as though coming through a light mist. He shook his head to make it work.

"For how long will he have to stir it?" she asked after they finished. "Do we put it back on the fire?"

Migisso tried to get a grip of his senses. Did they notice his fright? With every fiber of his being, he hoped they did not.

"You stir it for some time. Then yes, we put it back on fire, but not to let it boil, just to warm it." He cleared his throat. "It has to be perfectly smooth when it's time to put it back on fire." Unable yet to meet the foreigner's glare, he pursed his lips. "Tell him to stir it less vigorously. He doesn't need to turn the entire thing into a mass of bubbles."

She gave him a reproachful look, before talking to the warrior again. What she said caused the tightly pressed lips to twist into the hint of a grin. The man's voice rang dimly, barely penetrating the gathering darkness, and the fire was dying along with the moon.

"He asked me to say that he is grateful for what you did." Kentika's voice also lacked her previous agitation. "Whatever you think of him and his people, he says that what you did for his friend is true kindness, whether he lives or dies now. He says he will never forget. Not even when in the World of the Spirits."

He tried to suppress the welling in his chest, that unwelcome wave of compassion again. "Do they know about the World of the Spirits?"

"He used different words, but I think he meant Glooskap's world of the spirits, yes." She shook her head resolutely. "I'll be going now."

"Where to?"

The warrior looked up as well, as though understanding what she said. Paying them both no attention, she smoothed her dress, frowning at the fluttering fringes, where it was cut carelessly earlier through the night. "Mother will kill me for this," she muttered.

"Where are you going?"

"Home." Another vigorous brush against the stiff, mud-covered material. It was difficult to imagine that this dress might have looked pretty once upon a time.

"Won't you wait for me?"

"No." More fiddling with the fringes. Her gaze kept avoiding his. "Please stay. You promised."

"He won't need me after the ointment is ready." Helplessly, he looked at the wounded, still an inanimate form, his inner being there but faded, unclear, undecided whether to stay or not. "Why don't you wait?"

"It won't be ready in time." Now her gaze met his, determined, unafraid.

What do you mean? he wanted to ask, but her eyes did not let him escape into evasiveness.

"No, it won't."

She nodded, then gestured the warrior to wait as he was talking again, addressing her, an urgency to his voice.

"I'll try to prevent our people from coming here. You will have enough time. I'll make them look elsewhere." The creases that crossed her forehead stretched deep. "Promise to stay as long as they need you."

The lump in the pit of his stomach became heavier. Against his will, he held her gaze, wishing to look anywhere but into the defiant glow of her eyes. His little sister, the sweet, wild thing that he had loved since the first moment he had seen her, a squirming little bundle his mother brought from the birthing lodge when he had seen but four or five cold seasons. Now almost as tall as he was, inappropriately strong for a woman, inappropriately opinionated, inappropriately everything, with her spirit so unruly it could not be tolerated even in men, she was still just a girl to him, a little sister. But not anymore.

Suddenly, he knew why he had been angry with her. Not because she had helped the enemy, the ferocious warrior with the terrifying temper and an evil tattoo upon his face. That might be understandable, somehow. She wanted to help. She was always the kindest of persons.

No, that was not what made him wish to break something, to scream at her and accuse her of all sorts of crimes. Her way of looking at the foreigner, her way of taking his side in every argument, the obvious trust she put in the terrible man did this. Her heart had made her act, and not her mind. She had made her choice, at long last. Even if she herself might not realize that as yet.

"You will try to mislead our people," he said tiredly, making it a statement, anticipating a wave of rage, feeling nothing. There was only sadness, the all-encompassing exhaustion. Nothing else. "How will you do this?"

"I'll think of something." Eagerly, she turned back to her warrior, her eyes taking on an additional glow. What she said made the man argue, but not overly so. His gaze was glued to her, his smile shining, a knowing, surprisingly soft, comfortable smile that she answered with a shy half-twisted grin. It made Migisso's anger soar, an odd person in the coziness of *their* night. It made him wish to turn around and leave. They wouldn't have noticed if he did, he knew.

"I'll be going now," she said after a long while and much talking in a foreign tongue, her eyes brushing past him again, not seeing him, not for real. Her mind was already away, examining the problem, preparing her explanations, concocting lies.

He wanted to tell her that he wouldn't stay, that he wouldn't take care of her lover in trouble, but she was already gone, her briskly moving silhouette disappearing behind the bushes.

He turned away, avoiding the warrior's gaze.

CHAPTER 20

The dense mist filled the enclosure, flowing in slowly, hesitantly, giving no hope. Shivering with cold, Okwaho hugged his knees, tired beyond measure.

The fire was dying, but he didn't try to bring it back to life, not this time. It was of no use to them anymore. The brew had boiled and was cooling off now, but there was no one to consume it, with Akweks still lying lifeless, still wandering other worlds.

Even when the healer spread a generous amount of ointment upon the frighteningly gaping wound, their patient didn't even stir, no matter how thoroughly it was rubbed into every corner of the bloodied mess. Which was a bad sign, of course. His friend's spirit was determined to stay where it was, about to remain there indefinitely, the bleak gaze of the annoying healer told him, with no need to utter a word of their foul-sounding tongue.

How frustrating! He could not even kill the irritating skunk for his brassiness and bad manners. Her brother, of all things. He owed them both too much not to try to hang on to his temper, no matter how provoking the hate-filled gazes of the man were.

What do you do? he asked himself, forcing his hands to unlock their grip on his folded legs, wishing nothing more than to curl up right where he sat and sleep for all eternity. To leave the troublesome place, even if by the way Akweks did, and the rest of their people, aside from those who had sailed on.

The thought of the other warriors' force helped. They would be back. Sometime, they would have to return, victorious probably, up to this or that measure of success, passing through these shores, seeking them, the remaining warriors. All dead. Everyone!

Would they wonder?

"I'll try to wake him up again. Can't wait here for an entire span of seasons." Getting up to his feet helped. His body might have been exhausted beyond its limits, but his mind needed to do something, anything. Even the short walk toward Akweks and the healer helped.

The wariness of his unwanted companion increased. As he squatted beside them, he could see a wave of fear washing across the broad features. What a forest mouse! He didn't even look like her, aside from the broadness of his face. His eyes were not large and not widely spaced in a curious manner, and they held nothing but resentment and fear. How such a timid creature could claim family ties to her he didn't understand. But maybe it was just a figure of speech. Maybe she called the young healer by this title as a respectable address. Why didn't she stay instead of this one?

"Try to wake him up. Make him drink." He reinforced his words with appropriate gesturing. "No time. Have to go."

The man's hands flew up in a helpless manner.

"Eyes. You looked into his eyes before. What did you see? Can you look into his eyes again?" More vigorous gesturing.

This time, the man frowned, but nodded and complied. Leaning alongside, his stomach twisting with fright, Okwaho peeked into the frightening whiteness as his friend's eyelids were forced open, the dark orbs peeking from their edges blankly, with no life in them. He backed away before able to control himself. Oh, but it was hopeless! He wanted to break something.

The healer was still immersed in his study of Akweks' eyes, his posture more confident, somehow. When he pulled at the other closed eyelid, Okwaho had to fight the urge to push the man away. It was as though the nosy healer were trying to peek into his dying friend's dreams.

He listened to the flow of unfamiliar words.

"What?"

The man motioned toward the bark that contained the excess of their water, or what was left of it, pulling the dried-up piece of cloth off the wounded's forehead. Dipping it in the last of the murky liquid, he sprinkled Akweks' face, then tried to moisten the cracked lips.

Okwaho held his breath, sick with expectation. The man had done this before, several times, but now something was different, something about the healer's reactions, if not his patient or the surroundings.

Excited muttering of unfamiliar words preceded the shuddering of Akweks' body, the slight movement of a palm, only a finger really, but it was a movement.

"He is waking up!"

The healer held his hand up, demanding silence. Okwaho clenched his teeth tight. Desperate to contain his impatience, he listened to the vigorous chirping of early birds, trying to read their message. Was it all quiet out there? No wandering people?

She promised to make them look elsewhere. She was confident she could do it, especially when he told her about the body of the man who had drowned in the river, and its whereabouts. She grew all excited with his suggestion of luring them out there and away from here using this pretext. It should give him and Akweks enough time.

The wave of warmth was back, this time accompanied by regret instead of fear. If they managed to get away, he wouldn't be able to see her again, tell her of his gratitude, and maybe talk some more. She was so easy to talk to, so strangely comfortable to be with, to laugh and tell intimate things. It was still difficult to believe he had told her about the silvery wolf.

Was she all right out there? What if she got in trouble on account of her involvement? Her brother was angry in too obvious of a way. The cheeky rat! He glanced at the man sprinkling more water on Akweks' lips, trying to prompt a reaction.

A curt nod had Okwaho dashing to fetch the pot.

"Is he still hot?" he asked, mainly in order to break the silence, reaching for his friend's glittering forehead. It felt clammy against this touch. Maybe cooler, yes, but unpleasantly damp. Was it a good sign?

The healer was dousing the wounded's pasty face with the last of their water. Okwaho swallowed to make his thirst go away. He would have to go out and bring more water soon. As soon as they used the brew in the pot, he decided. He wouldn't run all the way to the river, risking certain exposure in the brightening daylight, to bring back a few gulps he would manage not to spill out of the accursed bark. That would be too much to ask from him. But for the girl still being around.

The warmth in his chest grew again. What was it about her that made him feel this way? She wasn't pretty, or womanly, or even sweet in the way some girls could be without sporting beautiful features or alluring curves. She didn't make his blood boil. Or maybe she did, but only this last time. What had possessed him to kiss her, and in such a demanding manner? He didn't plan for it, didn't want to do anything of the sort. That kiss surprised him as much as it surprised her. As though he had been a silly boy of little summers, he who had lain with girls, and even women. Hadn't that woman in Cohoes Falls, a widow, a person who had seen more than thirty summers, taken a fancy to him for the entire time he had spent in this town, luring him into the woods every now and then, giving him so much pleasure he was left speechless and breathless every time anew? She made the memory of the girls, those whom he fooled around with at home, look artless and meaningless. What did they know about giving pleasure or demanding the same? But even they would do better than that local girl. Or maybe not.

Akweks stirred again. And then there was another sound. He heard it clearly, and it made his heart stop. The distant hum was coming from the river, a steady noise that belonged to a large body of vessels progressing along its current. Or maybe against it. Unmistakable!

Snatching the bow, he darted back toward the bushes.

"Watch him! If something happens to him ..."

His gaze must have reflected the last of the phrase well enough as the healer positively froze, staring at Okwaho as though facing a poisonous snake about to pounce.

"I'll be back shortly." Paying the frightened man no more attention, he reinforced his words with more gesturing, before diving into the entanglement of branches.

Heedless of his step, but still careful not to make any noise, he didn't rush toward the shore, but made his way upward, in the direction of the cliff he was forced to jump on the previous evening, while luring the enemy away from Akweks.

Could it be? He didn't dare to let the hope enter his mind. If only...

Crossing the open ground in a zigzagged run, just in case, he clawed his way up the nearest rock, his breath coming in gasps, heart threatening to explode in his chest. No, these could not be their men. It was too early for them to return.

The river sped ahead, far below his feet, as unfriendly, as treacherously tortuous as before. Indifferent, empty. And yet, the familiar hum of the rushing water was interrupted more clearly here. Somewhere beyond its numerous bends, a group of vessels was progressing. *Against the current.*

Oh, Mighty Spirits, please let it be them!

Still careful, ready to duck should his gaze spot any other hint of movement, he shielded his eyes, not allowing his hope to surface, not yet. All sorts of fleets may be coming from the enemy's heartland. And yet, the main part of their warriors was there now too, hopefully victorious, full of high spirits. Was it too soon for them to return?

His mind was calculating frantically. How many dawns had passed since they separated? Five, six? It was too soon. And where were the locals? The peacefulness of the awakening woods all around frayed his nerves. It wasn't right. Weren't these shores supposed to swarm with villagers, eager for his blood? Was the girl that successful at taking their attention away? With all her fierceness and incredible determination, he didn't believe she would manage. But maybe she had.

When he finally saw the first canoe appearing behind the distant curve, his nerves were as tight as an overstretched bowstring, about to snap. Biting his lips into a raw mess, he strained his eyes, seeing one long canoe cutting the glittering surface, then another. His heart made its way up, to flutter in his throat, the elation impossible to push down, not anymore.

The warriors were returning!

CHAPTER 21

"What were you doing out there, wandering these shores at night?"

Swaying, Kentika tried to catch her balance, caught completely unprepared by the fierceness of the grabbing hand.

It had been so hectic since she had left in the middle of the night, so frantic, and turbulent, so unreal. What had happened there on the shore still hadn't settled in her mind, the treatment of the rotten wound too terrible to even think about it, with Migisso cutting revoltingly glaring tissue, widening the wound instead of closing it, swapping foul-looking, foul-smelling fluids that didn't even look like blood, the smell terrible, silence unbearable, her own fear impossible to deal with. She would have run away but for the wolf youth, but for his reassuring presence. He needed her there. Somehow, she had been sure of that, and also of the reality that he would not abandon her if she fainted, would not laugh or ridicule. He trusted her, and so far, she hadn't disappointed him. Well, maybe once, on their way back from bringing water for the last time, when it all became too confusing. Another thing she didn't dare to think about.

"I…" Startled, she looked up, her mind refusing to accept what her eyes were telling her, Father's fiercely glowing eyes boring at her, his face contorted, not an impenetrable mask as before, when she had burst into the meeting with the elders uninvited, against every possible custom and rule. "Like I told… told the elders, I was looking for, looking for… helping. I wanted to help…"

Desperately, she tried to find something plausible to say. Back at the meeting, they hadn't dwelled on this particular question.

Once over their indignity and shock with her rude, unheard-of interruption, they turned to the practical side of this unexpected development. No one had asked what she has been doing out there at night and alone, not once they heard her news.

Oh, how smart he was in suggesting that she tell them about Amaue's body and its whereabouts. That caught their attention! And yet, she was smarter, smarter than that. The smile that had threatened to sneak out back then was easy to suppress under the sternness of their suspicious gazes, but she still couldn't wait to tell him of her improvisation. Why limit her discovery to one body? Why couldn't she claim she had found two bodies there, that of Amaue and of his rival as well? Why couldn't they both get killed down there in the river?

He had explained where it was, describing the inlet until she believed she would recognize the place, even though, of course, they could not be sure the body was still there, and not washed away or dragged by some hungry forest dwellers. They all knew that such a possibility existed, so if there was no body, no one would hold it against her. They would be angry as always, yes, but they would not be able to accuse her of anything. And if so, then who could blame her for one missing body if she claimed that originally there were two corpses there? Why couldn't they both be washed onto the same shore?

Oh, but it was disheartening to stand their piercing glares, to handle their probing questioning. Still, she had stuck to her story, and in the end, when they told her to wait outside, but not to go anywhere, she knew she had been successful. She would be leading them out and away from the *right* shore. Unless Father insisted on coming.

She had addressed all the spirits she dared, asking for their help in keeping him inside the village, and yet her plea didn't help.

"Don't lie to me, Daughter!" His eyes didn't let hers sneak away, glowing in too close a proximity, taking away the relative protection of the people rushing about. "Why were you out there, tonight or on the day before, or at the time of the enemy's arrival?"

"I-I was just..." She swallowed, but it didn't help. Her throat was like a corn husk left at the mercy of the sun. "I wanted to help." Stubbornly, she kept studying the ground under her feet.

The grip on her arm tightened painfully. "You will tell it all to me later, when we are back. Don't think you will be able to get away with your lies."

Relieved beyond measure, she watched him turning away, talking to people who were supposed to come along. Quite a few men, all renowned hunters and warriors. Her eyes counted more than ten. *Oh, Benevolent Spirits, oh, Mighty Glooskap*, she prayed. *Please let me keep them away for as long as I can.*

She tried to pay no attention to the glances shot at her from all over. They all stared, the members of their searching party, and the rest of the villagers, their curiosity great. What was her part in all this? What had the wild girl who did not know her place done wrong this time?

It was a relief to leave the fence behind. Yet, the woods outside did not greet her with their usual warmth. Instead, they towered all around, foreboding and solemn, relaying their displeasure. The spirits did not favor her pathetic attempt to deceive her people, that much was obvious.

"Here." Clearing her throat helped, but only a little. "We need to go down here."

"Why?" asked one of the warriors.

"This will bring us to that shore faster." Wondering why her voice still sounded firm, she met their stony gazes. "That inlet, it's some walk toward the rising sun."

Father and the others exchanged glances.

"We'll split in two," said Father finally. "Eight of you will go to the shore with the boats. Scan it most thoroughly. If you find nothing, follow the river from the point where the lowlife jumped." His gaze rested on the youth with a sling, relaying a message, not a friendly one. "Achtohu, you'll lead. Make sure there are no failures, not this time."

The youth nodded, his lips pressed tight, eyes glittering.

"The rest of us will follow my daughter to the shore where she found the bodies."

A curt nod invited them to proceed.

"But Father—" His gaze cut her words off before they were born, but still she went on, desperate. "Why go to that other shore? There are no people and no boats there anymore. It'd be—"

Their glares made the words die away. As did the dark cloud that shadowed Father's face as he turned abruptly, stomping on through the rustling greenery.

The awakening forest enveloped them in its freshness, but there was no familiar ease, no comfortable friendliness she used to enjoy while wandering out in this awakening part of the day. The trees rustled above, distant, aloof, not approving. She was to fail, and it was only expected. They didn't approve of her treachery. They were not about to help.

Her legs as heavy as drifting logs, mind numb, she followed the familiar trail, oblivious of their following footsteps. Eight men. Would he be able to deal with eight furious, battle-hungry, highly alert men? Would he manage to trick them away like he did on the day before, to allow Migisso to take the wounded somewhere else? It didn't seem like a possibility. But then, he was so quick, so resourceful. He might find the way, if only she could warn him, somehow. He trusted her to succeed, and she was failing him, failing miserably.

The foliage all around her glittered brilliantly, still wet with dew. What if she tried to run? Just dived into the thickness of the nearby bushes and ran all the way. Would she manage to reach him in time? Or would they catch her? Was she their prisoner?

She shook her head angrily, trying to get rid of stupid thoughts. These were her people, not her enemies. *He* was the enemy. But not anymore. What was he to her? And did Migisso stay? What would her brother do when Achtohu and his men started combing that shore? Would he try to help, or would he abandon the wounded, the person he worked hard to save from a certain death this night? But he had been forced to help, she remembered. He didn't come to help voluntarily, not like she did. And yet, Migisso was a decent person, courageous when pressed. He would not disappoint her. He always did what she wanted.

Another turn.

The trails became steeper, and the smell of the river grew along with the fresh wind. It pounced on them from behind the protection of the woods, as though trying to warn them, to make them slow their step.

Shivering, she listened, but it was someone's warning grip on her hand that made her halt. It made her heart stop too, but her senses told her not to move, or protest for that matter, to do as her companions did, their frozen forms surrounding her, eyes on the foliage.

The hum of the river was strong, but even the strengthening wind did not camouflage the sounds of a large body of vessels progressing up the stream, the splashing of paddles and the occasional voices distinct enough, reaching their ears despite the wind.

All eyes went to her father, who gestured silently, singling out some men, indicating the others to stay behind, his face a wooden mask, calming in its determination and lack of fear. As the green foliage closed behind them, Kentika let out a held breath. Father would not let this new danger harm them.

What was it? she asked herself frantically, staying near the swaying branches, the presence of the others not reassuring, not like Father's was. They were peering in the direction of the river too, tense and ill-at-ease, six more men and she, a useless girl. If attacked, they had no chance. She thought about the way the wolf youth moved, so swift and deadly. Were those his people rowing out there? But it could not be. His people were dead.

More sounds of splashing paddles came from behind the trees, more distinct now. Were those people from one of the neighboring villages, or maybe Skootuck itself? The enemy could not be coming from the direction of the rising sun. His people would be coming from the opposite side.

Barely aware of her movements, she went closer to the now-calm foliage, her senses probing and not her eyes. Father must be near the shore now, crawling along one of the lower cliffs, scanning the river. What did he see there?

The branches blocked her way stubbornly as she pushed through them, relieved to notice that no one paid her any attention. They were too busy trying to listen. Oh, but why did they have to split with the rest of their people? Regardless of her original plan, if it was the enemy down there, making their way against the current, then close to twenty people were better than barely ten men trying to do something. And if she dwelled on that, then surely Father might have been getting angry over exactly the same thought.

The sun was shining strongly now, reflecting off the furiously spitting water with a glow that hurt the eye. Crouching behind the nearest rock, she blinked again and again, eyes desperate to adjust, mind refusing to comprehend.

The canoes were many, of various sizes, made of bark, larger and smaller, but with no tiny one-man dugouts among them. Progressing in a strikingly organized manner, they made their way against the current, determined like an army of ants, unstoppable, impossible to delay. Not even people of Skootuck would move in such numbers.

As though in a dream, she stared at the approaching boats, not surprised when one of the larger vessels turned toward the shore, nearing the cliff where Father and his warriors crouched, where she clung to the rocky surface transfixed, not daring to breathe, or even to blink for that matter. *The enemy was coming again.* Against all odds and from the wrong direction, they were coming all the same, to harm their village despite it all.

Trying to make her mind work, she watched Father gesturing to his men, moving as though through a fog, slowly and deliberately, with no sounds accompanying his motions. One of the hunters slipped back into the foliage she had emerged from before, coming back in a short while, followed by the rest of their people, while the boats kept nearing, now disappearing under their cliff, impossible to see from her vantage point.

Mesmerized, she peered at the sparkling surface behind the curve, hoping against hope that it would stay calm and undisturbed, with the enemy swallowed by the angry current down their cliff, every one of them, to the last boat. Behind her back, she could hear Father's warriors spreading along the rocks. Preparing to do what?

Pressing against protruding stones, she didn't dare even to blink, desperate to catch a glimpse of the boats, when the first arrow swished, tearing the crispness of the morning air, shattering its peacefulness. Many more followed, pouncing downwards, like birds of prey.

Crawling closer, she watched the people in the canoes reacting swiftly, diving to take cover behind their vessels, those closer to the rocks of the shore paddling vigorously, in a hurry to land. To hope that the enemy would panic was to wish for the impossible, she realized, swallowing a bitter taste in her mouth.

Fists clenched until she could not feel them anymore, she watched one of the canoes swishing right beneath her hideaway, in a tempting proximity. Oh, but for her old bow at hand. She could have shot the warrior at the boat easily, maybe not kill him but wound him badly enough, making it more difficult for him to join the fight. Her bow was not useless as the wolf youth claimed, even if it was not a warrior's bow. How dared he break it as though it were just a stick!

The thought of him made her head clear. He was still out there, vulnerable and in danger despite her attempts to take their people away; still sought after, he and his wounded friend. Did the other youth come back to life? Or did he stop breathing for good? And what about her brother?

Her heart came to a halt at the thought of Migisso out there too, stuck with the enemy. No, not the enemy. The wolf youth would not harm him, never, not after everything he had done for his friend. And yet, with more enemies out there now, oh, mighty Glooskap! Was Migisso in danger now too; and because of her?

Crawling closer, she tried to see better, to decipher what the enemy was doing, and where her father's people were now. A volley of arrows coming from below let her know that the enemy was not about to hide, nor try to avoid the fighting. Prepared and battle-hungry, coming from the heartlands of the Great River Whose Waters are Never Still, they must have raided some people or settlements already. Surprised or caught off guard they were not, something Father must have been counting on, she realized all of a sudden, ice piling in her stomach, making it flutter in an unsettling way. Otherwise, why would he try to attack a force much bigger than his, with no planning and no preparation? Why shoot at the passing fleet? He must have been counting on confusing the enemy, on disrupting its confidence, but all he got was the invaders stopping their progress back toward their homeland, turning to row vigorously toward their shore, instead.

A hand catching her shoulder made her jump, and her heart went still, but it was only one of the men, peering at the river, his eyes narrow.

"Run back to the village, girl. Bring help."

He was gone before she had a chance to answer, or even just nod.

The roaring of the river mixed with the shouts of people, and the clamor of vessels increased as he struggled down the bank and along the protruding rocks, swaying under Akweks' weight. His friend's limp body was heavy enough, but the need to carry him carefully, without letting his wounded leg brush against the sticking out obstacles and flogging branches was truly a challenge that made Okwaho stumble with every other step, as though he were a bear that had eaten a wrong plant.

Desperate for a heartbeat of respite, he halted next to a steep cliff, remembering passing by it at the dusk of the previous evening, returning from his forced swim, having helped the dying enemy start his Sky Journey in a proper way. Had he only known that the help was on its way already, sailing here, battling against the current!

Shutting his eyes for a heartbeat, he inhaled deeply, trying to draw a bit of additional strength out of the thin air. A vain hope. His strength had vanished long since, but he needed to reach their people nevertheless. It was that or die, both he and Akweks, captured by the enemy or eaten by the forest creatures, a fate he had struggled too desperately to avoid through the past two dawns.

And then, there was the girl. Wasn't she wandering out there, trying to take her people away from his shore, now in danger herself, in a possible reach of his own people? While devising a plan to lure the search party to the other shore, they didn't take the possibility of his people's return into consideration. All they wanted was to give him some time, to allow Akweks to come back to his senses and him, Okwaho, to take his friend away, into the hills of the opposite bank, having crossed the gushing river, somehow. It was not a good plan, but they had no better one.

He remembered her bruised, dust-covered face, glowing with that wonderful smile of hers, eyes glittering brightly, promising him to take them away, for sure, nothing to worry about. So cheerful and unafraid! And the healer, her brother, glowering from his corner beside Akweks, arguing with not a single familiar word; helpful too, yes, but in no cheerful way. No, they could not be real siblings, he had decided back then. The gloomy thing would have nothing to do with a rare, exquisite creature like her.

The thought of her gave him the strength to straighten up, to move his legs on, but Akweks groaned and jerked with his limbs, shattering the painfully gained balance. Clutching the nearest trunk with his entire body, trying to stabilize it using his free shoulder, Okwaho stopped breathing at the attempt not to fall. If he did, he knew, he wouldn't be able to pick his friend up again. He would give up.

The panting breath of the wounded warmed his ear in the most unpleasant of ways.

"Are you good?" he groaned, not expecting an answer, not for real.

Since coming back from the world of the dreams, with the best possible timing, just as Okwaho returned on the run, his news encouraging, Akweks' mind had been wandering on and off, unable to concentrate, disoriented and in great pain. The improvised brew the healer had made him drink helped, but mainly against the pain. It did not return lucid thinking to the young man. If anything, it seemed to do the opposite, sending his spirit to float somewhere there, between the worlds. An inconvenience, as by then, they had heard the enemy roaming around as well.

Shivering, he remembered his desperation welling, the sense of doom invading in force. It was hopeless—hopeless!—and with the help so near.

"You go, go away," he had told the healer earlier, after coming back, reinforcing his words with appropriate gesturing. Reassured by Akweks' improving condition, he was busy calculating how long it would take his people to reach this shore. It was important to be out there, to signal them and make them find the correct landing. "My people coming. You don't want to be caught out here. Go back to your village."

The healer's face lost some coloring, showing that he understood well enough, probably the vigorous gesturing.

"I'm grateful, very much," repeated Okwaho. "I'll find the way to repay, you and her. But now go."

Akweks' murmuring, cut off by a dry cough, caught their attention, and the healer's face cleared of fear. He needed to drink, his gesturing told Okwaho, while his hands snatched the bowl. At least that one was ready! He remembered all the precious heartbeats spent at bringing the fire back to life earlier, making the water boil, then cool, then boil again. A tedious process. The plants that were tossed into it refused to mar the water's clearness, causing the healer to frown and mutter, whether words of prayer or resentment, it was difficult to tell. Akweks was groaning with pain, so Okwaho was glad to busy himself with tending his friend's frighteningly gaping wound, applying more ointment to it, supporting and reassuring as much as he could.

The young healer was glad to be left to his own devices, he suspected, deciding that he could do nothing but trust the man. She would be furious if her brother betrayed them, of that he was sure. The thought of her making this man's life misery if he failed made him smile, but the sense of brief amusement disappeared as he heard the unmistakable noise of people roaming the nearby woods, coming from the hills, most surely. His people? No, it was too soon for that.

The healer stopped stirring and was listening too, intently. When their gazes met, he knew he had been right. Those were the people of the village. So she didn't manage to lure them away.

Another heartbeat of staring. He felt his palm tightening around his knife's hilt, not taking it out, but ready to do so. Then he shrugged and motioned toward the pot.

"Is that thing ready?"

The open relief in the healer's face told him he understood it all. Picking the pottery off the fire, he motioned Okwaho to bring up his bowled bark, pouring some of the bubbling brew with an utmost care, eyes narrow and measuring, calm, although his hands were trembling. From the effort of holding the heavy pot? Okwaho doubted that. Still, the man was no coward, he decided, respecting his unwanted company against his will. This one was no mountain lion, yet a forest mouse he wasn't either.

"Here, drink this." Receiving the cumbersome bark with a nod that he hoped relayed his appreciation, he crouched beside Akweks, shaking his friend's shoulder urgently, trying to will the clouded eyes into semblance of concentration. "This will make you feel better."

Yet, the painful effort of drinking resulted in violent retching that left the wounded gasping in agony, on the brink of leaving their world again, while the noise outside grew, the voices of the villagers carrying clearer, reaching their hideaway. It was hopeless! Okwaho took a deep breath, then reached for the healer's bow.

"No!" The man's hand was light on his upper arm, resting there rather than grabbing it, the meaning of the exclamation clear.

Wait, the penetrating gaze told him, both palms up now, asking for patience, not imploring or begging.

Reassured, the man knelt beside Akweks. Whatever he said, it seemed to have a calming effect on his patient, the words pouring out, incomprehensible but giving hope. This time, the wounded managed to keep the drink down, choking a little, his upper body leaning on the supporting hands heavily, yet his eyes clearing, filling with life. They clung to his savior, unblinking.

Okwaho held his breath, but the voices from outside kept reaching his ears, not drawing closer, but not going away, either.

They were scanning the hillside, he knew, soon to come upon the clearing and the shoreline covered with marks. It wouldn't be long before they found their way here.

The pot the healer tucked into his hands burned his palms, still scorching hot.

Go, gestured the man's free hand. *Take the wounded and go. Do it now.*

He stared at the pale, taut face, trying to slam his mind into working.

"Where to?"

Anywhere, suggested the wave of the hand. *Out there, away from the voices.*

Another heartbeat of staring. The narrowed eyes held his, unblinking. Now he saw the similarity. She had the same gaze, honest and revealing. It was easy to read their expressions.

He drew a deep breath. "Thank you," he said, his voice ringing gruffly, constricted somehow. "I will never forget."

The hint of an easy smile transformed the man's face, made him look more prominent, less insignificant. Why did he dismiss him as a forest mouse before? The words that followed were still impossible to understand, but the expression and the urgent nod sealed the promise. He would take their attention away, would hold it as long as he could. Just like her, even if she didn't manage. Why were they both so kind to him?

"Thank you," he said again, struggling to help Akweks up, but once upright making sure to look back, to let the man see the depth of his gratitude. Oh, but he would repay them, somehow!

And now, away from the accursed shore, and not chased and hunted down, not yet, he gathered the rest of his strength, determined to reach their people whatever the cost. They had made it so far, he and Akweks, they had managed to survive, not to die when all the others did. Due to the circumstances and not to dishonorable deeds, they were still alive, and the help was near. To lose his spirit, to succumb to his overwhelming exhaustion, would be an act unworthy of a warrior, of his father's son. Father would never give up or give in. He would fight on, and he would make it all work. The entire union of five powerful nations depended on Father's good judgment and skill, but what was required of him, Okwaho, now if not a bit of resilience and determination, some confidence and strength, and yes, the ability to talk and make himself be listened to.

He clenched his teeth tight, forcing his feet to move on, one after another, his stomach heavy, constricting with waves of uneasiness. For he knew what was to be done in order to repay her and her brother's kindness, what was the right thing to do. Her village. It should not come to any more harm. Not a single fire arrow, not one shattered pole of the fence. Her village should not come under another attack, as it would come for certain now but for his ability to convince Tsitenha, their warriors' leader, to sail on, not to pursue the feat of revenge on the easy target. But how was one to do that?

"Let me down," groaned Akweks when Okwaho stopped again, this time not because of exhaustion. The hum of the river grew louder, interrupted by the unmistakable sounds of people fighting, shooting and running for cover, yelling out blood-freezing war cries. "I can… can manage."

He hesitated, then let his friend slip off his back, ready to catch him, not trusting his ability to stay upright. Indeed, the young man faltered instantly, groping for a nearby branch, clutching it unsuccessfully, his hands having not enough strength to hold on. But for Okwaho's supportive hand, he would have fallen heavily; as it was, he just slipped onto the moss-covered stones, both of them hitting their limbs in an attempt to protect the wound.

"I'm good, I can … can manage." The wounded shut his eyes, his voice vibrating with pain, or maybe a hint of panic. "Just a heartbeat, or two … just a little bit. I'll be good."

"I better carry you on," muttered Okwaho, himself half lying on the jutting stones, welcoming the respite. He had no strength to pick himself up, let alone the limp body of his friend. "We are almost there."

"Our people, they came back?" A sheen of perspiration covered the youth's face like a coat of paint, and his eyes, partly opened now, were clouded, reflecting the effort to stay, and the impossibility of it.

"Yes, they did." Blinking away the sweat that rolled into his eyes, Okwaho forced himself up, swaying, catching a branch in his turn to stabilize himself. His other hand traced his sash, slipping past the knife and the bow tied to it, seeking the reassurance of the small leather pouch. Father's necklace. It was still there. He breathed with relief.

"We'll reach our people now, and then all will be well." It came out surprisingly confident. He was tempted to believe it himself.

"They ... they are fighting. Aren't they?" The cracked lips twisted into a hint of a grin, the taunt in it obvious, bringing the old Akweks back. "All will be well, eh?"

"Yes, it will." He didn't fight his own smile from showing, elated. Oh, yes, Akweks was getting better. "We reach them, help them beat the enemy, *then* all will be well."

The smile disappeared in the desperate bout of coughing. He wished he had carried the pot with the brew, or at least that stupid piece of bark to bring Akweks water. "Let's get you to the river first. You need to drink."

"She lied..." The words were hardly understandable, but they hit him like a punch in his stomach.

"What?"

"The ugly fox, she lied." Akweks was swallowing desperately, determined to say his piece. "She said our people were dead. But here they are, not dead. They're fighting, killing her stupid people."

He readied himself for the feat of pulling his friend up. "It's not them."

"What?" The wild gaze bored at him, imploring, the color leaving the handsomely broad face again. "Not them? Then who?"

"The rest of our people, those who sailed on." He pressed his lips tight. "Come."

"No." With a surprising strength, Akweks resisted the pull. "Wait. Listen, you can't, can't carry. Go on. I'll wait here. I will be well." The eyes peering at him narrowed painfully. "I can take care ... I'll manage, until you come back. Like before. Like when she came. I went through the night. I didn't die." The wounded's dried tongue had no chance of moistening the cracked lips. "And it won't take you so long this time. I know it won't. Our people … they won't die. Not this time. Will they?"

"No, they won't. Not this time." The memory of the mission ahead of him made him wish to stay. "They can't. They are many, and prepared. And led by a wise person and not that dung-eater Kayeri." If he had any moisture left in his own mouth, he would have spat. "They won't die, and they won't lose. And yes, I have to reach them in time." He narrowed his eyes, his tiredness back, making him wish to drop down and die in peace. "Are you sure you will manage until I get back?"

"Yes." The frown of the young man deepened, banishing the painful expression. "You will try to stop them … from harming the village."

"Yes."

"Because of the girl?"

Okwaho just shrugged.

"They won't listen. Our people deserve to be avenged."

"We attacked them first. And …" He saw the resentment, the flicker of anger crossing the tormented features. There was no point in spending his energy on arguing here in the woods. "It doesn't matter. But that girl and the healer saved your life. And, well, we do owe them something."

"You can make sure they are not harmed. The girl, the healer. But not the filthy village." Another bout of coughing. "Forget … go. I'll be all right."

Helpless, he watch the anguished eyes closing, the colorless lips pressed, forming an invisible line. There was nothing he could do for his friend now but to rush on, to reach their people and get help. And then, yes, join them in the fighting. That village was doomed, wasn't it?

"I'll be back before you know it." He forced a grin. "With help, real help this time. Our people. No helpful locals."

A faint grin was his answer.

"Take cover!"

The sharp call made Migisso shudder, but he didn't take his eyes off the sparkling snake of the river and the far inlet where the shoreline turned decisively, brushing against the protruding cliffs.

His heart beating fast, he watched the small figures rushing to and fro, some dragging their boats up the rocky shore, disappearing out of sight, others shooting or waving clubs. Arrows must have been descending on them from the towering cliffs, not densely but steadily, enough to prevent the invaders from climbing the rocks right away, forcing them to seek cover, instead. He wished he could have been standing on the opposite bank in order to have a good view.

"Why don't you jump up and down and wave your hands?" grunted Achtohu, grabbing his arm and pulling him down their cliff where the others congregated, seven more men, mostly young hunters, with not much experience. Their gazes followed their progress, expectant.

"What do we do now?"

The man who had asked clutched his bow tightly in one hand, with the other ready to dart for the quiver of arrows behind his back. The rest of them stood in a ridiculously similar pose. They were all armed with bows and a decent supply of arrows, all but him. He fought the familiar heaviness in his stomach.

"We follow the shoreline," said Achtohu, tossing his head in a decisive manner, leader-like. "Try to surprise them. If it works, good. If not, we'll still be of use to the War Chief." Kicking at the rotten log that blocked the trail, he turned away, beginning to pick his way between the rocks. "We have nothing to do here, anyway. The lowlife we are hunting is either dead or with them. Isn't he?" The glance shot at Migisso was pointed, as cutting as a sharpened flint. "You've been wandering around for only-spirits-know-how-long. You should be able to tell us."

Trying to gain time, Migisso just shrugged, but this time, they were not about to let him get away with pretended indifference. Their gazes bored into him, openly hostile.

"How long have you been out there?"

"Since before dawn." It came out well. He was surprised by the steadiness of his voice. The pangs of fear were gripping his stomach again, and his heart was racing in no reasonable manner.

"Why?" Achtohu didn't stop, but his tone made it clear that he might, if not answered.

"I wanted to scan this place again. Those footsteps, they didn't let me sleep." Still firm words. He marveled at the fact briefly, watching his step as the stones they tread upon turned slippery, awash with the nearness of the river.

"Why alone?"

This time, it felt proper just to shrug. Their hostility seemed to lessen with the need to watch their step, and Achtohu was busy scanning the river ahead, motioning them to slow down.

Migisso struggled not to let out a sigh of relief. Turning his eyes on the gushing water in his turn, its noise drowning everything out, the sounds of the battle as well, he tried not to think about the night, and the following dawn, and the unreality of it all.

Did he really help the enemy, the very man his people were desperate to catch, the despicable foe, the lowlife who had killed Amaue, while wounding him, Migisso, and the other man?

It didn't seem possible, not in the clear daylight, even without another battle developing farther down the river. Where had more enemy come from, the underworld spirits sent by evil Malsum as they were? Nothing made sense anymore, his own actions and those of Kentika coming like a natural part of the world that was turned upside down.

The thought of her made him shudder again. She might be out there now, caught in the middle of the fighting, surely being with the group she had knowingly lured away from their rightful prey. How enraged her intention to do so had made him back during the night. Oh, but for the warrior with the wolf tattoo, he would have tried to stop her, physically maybe. Fierce and passionate as she was, he was still older and stronger. He might have managed to restrain her. But then what? She did what she did for her own reasons. If she wished to help the enemy, then that was that. Convention never ruled her, never interfered with her ways. She couldn't be stopped from helping that warrior.

So he had been left with her fearsome companion and his dying friend, doing what he always did best, brewing medicine, making sure the wounded did not embark on his journey to the other worlds before his time. There was nothing better to do for him, anyway.

He shook his head angrily, suddenly incensed. Why lie? Whom was he cheating by lying to himself? He wasn't forced to help. Yes, he was, in the beginning. The bloodthirsty warrior would have killed him instantly, but for her. Even when he said he wouldn't, whether he, Migisso, treated the wounded or not, he still did not believe the filthy enemy. Not like she did. And yet, he didn't agree to operate out of fear. Of that he was certain. The challenge of doing something as complicated as cutting a rotten wound was what drew him by then, what made him agree.

A young man of his age, with nothing but summers of study on his own, sprinkled by only a little bit of guidance from the kind medicine man, would barely be allowed to boil a brew against simple aches. He would never be let anywhere near the attempt to actively treat a person in order to make the sick heal. Not even to stitch a wound, let alone to cut a rotting one, when the person's mind was already beginning to wander. It was too late by that time, and the only time he had seen a healer attempting to do that, it did nothing but send the person who suffered onwards in more agony than without the operation.

Oh, it was a hopeless attempt. Yet, they both, his sister and her foreigner, begged, and he knew he could not let such an opportunity pass. Back home, even if allowed to take that path, to learn from the medicine man openly, he would not be entrusted with such responsibility until he himself was old.

Following his peers, he proceeded along the slippery path, trying to curb his welling excitement. He had done the impossible, hadn't he? By cutting the rotting flesh off the warrior's wound in that certain manner that had enlarged the wound but not to a lethal extent, he had brought the dying man back into the world of the living, doing something even the revered old healer, the most trusted medicine man of the village, didn't manage.

Stealthily, he glanced at the sky, squinting against the fierce glow of Father Sun. Was there an answer up there, behind the puffy clouds, where Revered Glooskap might have been living among other Sky Deities? Was he correct in insisting on following his heart, even against Father's wishes? Did his true path lie in healing people and not in warring and hunting? The spirits may have been showing him the way, and if so, they would not be angry with him for lying to his peers, for misleading them the way she did. Or would they?

Recalling the dawn in the cramped, suffocating, smothering hideaway made him shiver again. Why did he help that warrior escape? When the man came back running, motioning vigorously, obviously trying to make him, Migisso, go, he did not understand the real meaning of ardent gesturing. Responsible for his charge, who was by then showing clear signs of coming back to life, he had stayed and made the wounded drink the necessary broth, assuming that maybe the warrior had seen their village's searching party. An assumption that was proved true when they heard voices later on. So she didn't manage to lure their people away, apparently.

What happened next was still the most puzzling. The warrior should have killed him, Migisso, and been gone. He had seen the man going for the knife, most clearly at that. Speechless, they stared at each other, but then something made the enemy change his mind.

Shrugging with acceptance, he had motioned toward the medicine, and then they went on making the wounded drink as though nothing happened, until Migisso had made his suggestion, for a reason he himself couldn't fathom. Instead of letting his countryfolk catch their prey, he had helped the enemy against everything he believed in and against any better judgment. He even went to such lengths as going out there and deceiving— actually deceiving!—Achtohu and his followers the way she had done, by concocting some story and making them look elsewhere. Not that it was a difficult feat, as by that time, the distant yelling and shouting had reached them, and it was not long before they could catch a glimpse of the developing battle, standing rock-still and aghast on the edge of the same cliff where the warrior with the wolf tattoo had battled Amaue and Achtohu on the evening before and won.

From his companions' urgent talk he had gathered that, yes, the main part of their people was out there, searching for the bodies, led by his sister. So she had been successful, even if partly.

And then, suddenly, he knew, chill filling his stomach, what the warrior was trying to tell him, why he insisted on his, Migisso's, departure. He was trying to make him leave before his own people came. *He was being decent.*

The realization that should have helped, but it didn't. Instead, he felt something close to disappointment. The enemy was proving honorable time after time. How so?

"Wait."

Achtohu's urgent whispering tore Migisso from his reverie in time to halt along with the others. The clamor was more distinct now, mainly of people shouting and arrows hissing, and boats being dragged hastily, bumping against rocks and splashing water. People were talking in a foreign tongue, so familiar by now. Had Kentika been here, he thought suddenly, she would have been able to understand what they said.

He scanned the towering cliffs, seeking the source of the flying arrows. Was she huddling up there, watching the battle, or had she snatched up some fallen man's bow the way they said she had back in the village and was shooting alongside the men now, forgetting her affection for the handsome enemy with the spectacular tattoo? And where was this young man and his wounded friend? Did he manage to reach his people?

"We wait for our warriors up there to resume the attack, then we join," whispered Achtohu, motioning with both hands, reinforcing his words. "You," his eyes rested on Migisso, "go up there. Find our people. Tell them of our plan."

"Why him?" asked one of the youths. "I'm a better scout."

"Not an outstanding achievement," someone said as he chuckled.

"Quiet," hissed Achtohu, his eyes flashing dangerously. "He is a better messenger than you are. Stop arguing and keep quiet!" His head motioned Migisso to proceed, inviting no argument, had he had anything in a way of an argument to offer. Which he didn't, of course. This was a sensible mission. With his lack of appropriate weaponry, even more so.

"He has no weapons, nothing to shoot with." This reached his ears as he worked his way up the cliff, about to disappear out of their view. "He is good for running messages. He proved himself over the past few dawns."

"At least something he is good at." The chuckles that followed this phrase drowned in the general noise of the river and the enemy, but this he didn't regret.

CHAPTER 22

"Gather the boats under that rock, together with the wounded."

Tsitenha wiped his face impatiently, squirming against the constant drizzle, his wide forehead creased in what looked like a web of direful strips.

"How many dung-eaters do you assume might be out there?" he asked, turning back to Okwaho, his hand waving in the direction he came from.

There was no accusation in the man's voice and no hostility. At least that! He didn't expect an ardent welcome, not after his earlier experience with Kayeri. Bearers of bad news were rarely received well, getting the blame for the unfavorable information they delivered.

Well, it didn't happen this time. Not yet. If anything, he had been received most warmly, as he stumbled into the frenzied activity in the shallow, angrily rushing water, under the relative protection of the towering rocks. The warriors were busy dragging their canoes into the tiny inlet, no more than just a curve of a shoreline, where the arrows could not reach them, carrying the wounded along. Quite a few men sported fluttering feathers and shafts, protruding out of their limbs or clothing. The locals knew how to shoot.

Luckily, many were unharmed and in high spirits, not about to panic or act recklessly, trusting their leader, listening to his words. Tsitenha was no Kayeri; and it was thanks to his quick reaction and even quicker directions that not many had been hurt. The local lowlifes were good, everyone agreed, their ambush timed and executed well.

Little did they know, reflected Okwaho, fighting the urge to lean against the inviting slickness of the nearby cliff. The locals were here for another reason.

"I assume there were no more than ten men. Maybe even less." He forced his back into straightening, not about to show his exhaustion. Or his uneasiness. His reception was warm and cordial, but it would change in a heartbeat the moment he started arguing, he knew. Yet, what choice did he have? "They wouldn't send a large party to hunt one man."

"And the warriors up there?" Tsitenha's eyes narrowed, as his head motioned toward the source of shooting.

"Also not a large party. Probably of the same size." Even a shrug proved like a chore, his shoulders heavy, too heavy to lift. "Yesterday, when they came to collect the boats, there were about fifteen men. I would assume the same party came back, but split for some reason."

Some reason! His stomach churned as though haunted by hunger. The reason they split must be up there now, among the shooters, about to get attacked. How to prevent that? How to keep her from harm?

Tsitenha nodded curtly, his eyes darting from place to place, assessing, making sure his men did what he wanted. Not all their boats could be secured in the small hideaway. Some had to be piled atop the others.

"Ten men will stay here, to keep the canoes and the wounded safe." A vigorous gesturing brought forth the men that were singled out. "Keep an eye on the cliff. When Kanadera and Oware come back with his wounded," a curt nod indicated Okwaho, "tell them to stay here with you. You," the flinty eyes brushed past him, lingering for a heartbeat, assessing again, "come with us. We'll need your knowledge of this land."

Some knowledge, thought Okwaho, preferring to stay, knowing better than to argue. It would have been, of course, more logical to remain with the men guarding the boats, to catch even a few heartbeats of rest, to make sure Akweks was brought here with no trouble. What if Kanadera and Oware didn't find him? Or what if they ran into the lowlifes that were most probably now hot on his heels?

And yet, he was needed up there more urgently. And not because his people wished him to guide them up the cliff, or anywhere around these woods. He was needed up there, to do whatever was necessary, whatever it took.

The path he had climbed last night, after seeing the dying local off, beckoned. It might give them cover for at least a part of the way. He scanned the river, trying to track the direction of the arrows.

"They are on the top of that cliff, spread evenly," said the leader calmly, as though reading his thoughts. "Which way will bring us up faster?"

"This trail leads up there and into the woods." He tried to remember his climb that was blurring somewhere there, in the depths of his memory. It was already dark back then, and he had been in a terrible hurry. "I think it may provide a bit of a cover. There were thick trees on both sides of the trail. Not all the way, but most."

"I see." Tsitenha's grin held no mirth. "So this is where they expect us to appear? Good." Another mirthless chuckle, the wave of the weathered hand. "Follow me." The man's decisive footsteps echoed between the towering rocks, heading in the opposite direction.

Okwaho tried to slam his mind into working. As though in a fog, he followed, finding nothing better to do. To concentrate on his steps while trying not to slip into the gushing current seemed like a worthwhile cause. The remnants of his dwindling strength would not extend to do much more than that. All he wanted was to crawl somewhere into the quietness of the woods, to curl around himself and sleep for all eternity; to wake up back to the reality of a simple warrior, with no difficult questions or dilemmas, with no nagging thoughts about the enemy and their plight. Or his debt to these people.

The climb was precarious, uncomfortably steep, with no trail and not always footholds, forcing one to hang on the strength of one's arms only, unless wishing to plummet back into the raging stream. Not necessarily a lethal dive, as his adventures yesterday could have attested, but for the demand to keep absolutely quiet. Tsitenha was not the leader to be incensed by disobedience. For the thousandth time, he wondered how such a man could have made the mistake of leaving a nonentity like Kayeri in charge of twenty warriors and an unknown target. What did he think of the following disaster?

The man had shown none of what he might have felt upon hearing Okwaho's terrible news. His lips tightening, eyes closed and unreadable, he just nodded stiffly, then turned to deal with the more pressing problems. Under the shower of arrows, there was no time to rage or fume, or to ask too many questions. These could wait until after they dealt with the ambush, or the people who shot at them, or the accursed village. Against his will, he shuddered.

Upon the widening shelves near the top of the cliff, they paused, listening intently. The whispering of the woods related no visible danger. Were the ambushers gone? It was eerily quiet up there, with even the regular sounds of the high noon turning silent.

Spread out, motioned the leader's hand. *Get the clubs ready. Not the bows.*

By the time all twenty men reached the top, the first wave was off, scouting. Forgetting his tiredness and his original misgivings, Okwaho slid into the quietness of the grove, giving in to the familiar pleasure of scanning the earth, of reading her messages.

Oh, yes, people had been all over this place, and a very, very short time ago. Many people. He counted more than five different prints. One of them smaller than the rest, familiar. *Hers?*

He fought the tightening in his stomach. So it was her footsteps he had followed in the first place, the footsteps that had brought nothing but disaster upon them all. Was it the Left-Handed Twin's, the most evil spirit of the underworld, doing? Or some game the local spirits were playing? What did it all mean?

"They sneaked away." The warriors' voices jerked him back from the darkness of his thoughts.

"They didn't go far yet."

"Less than ten people," said Tsitenha. "We follow. Catch them before they reach their village."

"We won't manage. They know these woods, we don't." Again, he wished to bite his tongue off for saying things without thinking. Would he never learn? Their disapproving stares burned his skin.

"Would you presume to advise without being asked to do so?" asked the leader coldly, but his eyes weren't blank or furious. Instead, they measured Okwaho in a somewhat taunting way, as though daring him to speak, as though approving.

"No." He knew he should drop his gaze before muttering his apologies, the safest behavior under such circumstances. "I would not presume to advise a leader of your knowledge and experience, but ..." he hesitated again, the goading gaze daring him to proceed.

"But?"

"This village, it's well defended. It is not as small or as insignificant as it looks. Their fence is high, and many warriors are in there. We made the mistake of underestimating its people. The man you left in charge of our group insisted on attacking it, even when all hope was lost." His mouth felt as dry as an abandoned field in summer. He tried to swallow, failed. "We should not repeat this mistake, should not let more of our warriors die for nothing."

The silence lasted for less than a heartbeat. Interrupted by the thundering crack of a breaking branch, it brought the warriors back to life all at once, sent them darting into the shadowy grove. Shouts followed, and the muffled sounds of a struggle. In a few more heartbeats, two of the men were back, dragging a crumbled form, bloodied and stunned, bumping against protruding roots.

This time he held his tongue, even though his heart jumped all the way to his throat, for he didn't need to come closer to recognize the healer who had saved Akweks, the man's long limbs dangling listlessly, offering no worthwhile resistance. The warriors dropped their cargo, disdainful, not hurrying to finish their captive off or make sure their charge wasn't about to do something harmful.

"Useless piece of meat couldn't even move quietly, let alone fight."

One look at the barely animated form made Tsitenha shrug with indifference. "Must be a stupid dung-eater who fell behind. Finish him off."

"Wait!" Again, the dark stares. Okwaho rushed forward, paying them enough attention to make sure no one brought his club up yet. "Don't kill him." The two warriors stared as though he had just sprouted another head. "This man can tell us things. About the ambushers. Or anything else. No need to kill him before we make him talk."

Eyeing the bushes that separated them from the edge of the cliff, the leader snorted. "And how do you propose to ask, or understand his replies?" The tip of his moccasin, smeared with mud and still dripping with water, jolted the groaning man with enough force to make him roll over, revealing the terrified face, bruised and plastered with fresh earth. "Unless the few days in their woods made you learn how to speak their tongue."

"I can ask him with signs." He tried to catch the healer's gaze, to reassure him somehow, but under the coat of the mud, it was difficult to do that. "He must have..."

The memory of this man's ashen face, tired and sweaty, concentrated, determined to help Akweks, and later on, to allow him, Okwaho, to take his wounded friend away before this man's people found them, brought another, making him gasp. The people who were looking for him back upon the first shore. They must have been here by now. Otherwise, why would the healer run all over this place?

"They are here, the people who were after me, they are here now, too." More faces turned to stare at him. He tried to concentrate on his hearing, to listen to the woods.

"Those who were shooting at us?" Tsitenha spent no time on demanding explanations. His entire pose screaming the highest of alerts, he was obviously probing with his senses, as tense as an overstretched bowstring.

"No, other people. Those who were chasing me here."

"Are they here now?"

"Yes."

Again, no questions as to how he came by this knowledge. His appreciation of the man grew.

"Spread out. Check this part of the cliff again." These words addressed no one in particular, yet the warriors reacted all at once, wondrously coordinated, like many parts of one body.

Okwaho stayed near the prisoner, just in case, wishing he had her command of foreign tongues, to question the man, or to reassure him, or both. He had a fair guess why the other party had stopped shooting, leaving its position the moment his people began climbing that cliff. Clearly, they did not have enough men to invite a face-to-face battle. Yet, where were the healer's companions, those who combed the first shore? Why was he wandering here all alone?

The commotion coming from the river answered the last question, even if partially. There was an obvious fighting there, but if the leader didn't worry about it, he decided not to pay too much attention to it either. They had enough warriors left to deal with the ill-organized locals. And yet, he owed her much, her brother's life being only one of the ways to repay them both.

The man groaned again, this time actually squirming, trying to sit up. Okwaho knelt beside him. But for the ability to use at least a few words of their tongue!

"I'll make sure you are not killed," he whispered, trying to relay confidence he didn't feel. Had the man been in better condition and maybe only tied, he would have cut the ropes, helping the captive slip into the safety of his native woods, setting him free, repaying the debt. As it was, he needed to do more, to reassure that one, somehow, until able to do something. "Can you walk?" Even the gesturing was impossible as by doing so he would attract his fellow warriors' attention.

The sanity flowed into the gaping eyes all at once, as though the man actually understood. Frowning painfully, he whispered back, a long, hectic phrase. Okwaho shrugged, then patted the wide shoulder and got up.

In time, as it turned out, just as the air exploded with war cries and branches cracking under many running feet, with the familiar hissing of arrows adorning the bedlam. Ready, his fellow warriors did not need to coordinate their actions, spreading in the direction of the noise while diving for the plenty of cover the trees and bushes provided.

Thanking the spirits for making him drag the healer's bow along, although back upon the accursed shore, it had been tempting to leave it behind, to carry nothing but his wounded friend, Okwaho darted toward the group next to Tsitenha, adjusting one of the arrows as he did.

Diving into the safety of their bushes, he listened rather than looked, trying to determine the direction the danger was coming from. From behind, his senses told him, but as he turned carefully, pressing close to the damp earth, another volley of arrows came from his left, unexpected. Were they surrounded?

"The five of you, go there. Circumvent the shooters from the direction of the rising sun. Signal the moment your first arrow is about to fly out." Tsitenha's whisper rasped by his ear, welcome in its unperturbed confidence, calming. "You stay." Another curt whisper made Okwaho stop in mid-turn. "Those are more of your pursuers, to our left, aren't there?"

"Yes, I think so." He forced his mind off the healer he had left behind, hoping that by now, the man had enough sense to pick himself up and scamper away into the woods. "And the ambushers who returned for some reason."

"You seem to understand the enemy surprisingly well." The thread of animosity in the leader's voice was unmistakable. And unsettling. Until now, the man was unperturbed, no matter the news, in perfect control. Okwaho swallowed the bitter taste in his mouth. Would he be accused of treason, cowardice, or suspect loyalties by this man as well? "Why did they return?"

"I suppose … I suppose they managed to communicate with their people down there by the river, those who were chasing me." He swallowed again. "I suppose they think they are now a large enough group to stand up to us." He licked his lips, staring into the momentarily calm clusters of trees, with no one shooting, or moving for that matter. It was safer to study the lay of the land instead of standing the intensity of the questioning gaze. "But I think they are wrong. We are still more numerous and much better organized."

He felt more than saw the man nodding curtly.

"The moment our men start shooting, we'll run out and close the distance between the enemy ahead of us. Go and tell this to the rest of our men."

Crawling the length of their bushes and then running low, zigzagging between the trees, refreshed him a little, the solitude of this errand welcome, helping to organize his thoughts. Tsitenha might have grown angry with him, as they all would, but he was attentive to his words, not about to toss them aside without due consideration. The man was wise and experienced, not above listening to younger people if what they said made sense. But had his words, indeed, made sense? And what to do about the village? How could he prevent his people from harming it, while not coming to harm themselves? Was there a way to do that? No, of course there wasn't. They came here to raid, to punish the enemy for similar raids, to go back carrying valuables and supplies of food. There was no other way of dealing with the enemy. And yet, it was up to him to make sure her village wasn't harmed.

On the other side, their men were split equally, in pairs and trios, crouching behind their various covers, watching intently.

"Tsitenha says to run in the direction of the shooters when our men give the signal."

He was about to crawl on when a hand grabbed his shoulder. "No need to rub your stomach more than necessary. I'll signal the rest of our men." The warrior who said that grinned good-naturedly. "See this grove up there? There are some dung-eaters that sneaked in a short while ago. We are keeping them in sight. Go back and tell our leader we will be taking care of those upon a signal."

Okwaho shielded his eyes against the midday glow, trying to see the pointed hill. "Where did they come from?"

"From up there, opposite to our location." This time, the squinting gaze looked at him with a measure of seriousness. "To the right of the rising sun."

"Did you see them?"

"No, but had they come from any other direction we would

have."

"They came from the village." He heard himself muttering the words, still not sure how this conclusion was to help them. "They must have been sent for, the reinforcements."

"By the dung-eaters who tried to ambush us?" All eyes were upon him now, narrow and thoughtful.

"Yes. And if so…"

He shut his eyes to make his mind clear of irrelevant thoughts. The ambushers had sent for more people when they saw their canoes nearing. Then they started shooting, disrupting the progress of the fleet, forcing the invaders to get out and fight away from the village and not on the ground of their choosing. But why did they leave, if they expected reinforcements? Unless…

"They didn't sneak away," he breathed. "They tried to deceive us into chasing them!"

The warriors around him just stared, with no disapproval marring their gazes, not this time. "Where is that village?" asked the man who detained him.

"Up there, behind the hill."

Several heads nodded. "It makes sense."

"You better go back and tell the leader of our observations and your conclusions. He would know what to do with it."

The sincerity of their gazes made him feel better. So not everyone thought him to be nothing but an argumentative nuisance, or worse. There were those who were prepared to listen, despite his young age and the dubious circumstances of his survival.

Yet, it would not last, he knew, crawling away, cursing the rocks and branches and pinecones that covered this ground, making it their business to get in his way, to tear at his bruises and scratches. His solution would not be acceptable, not by even the most open-minded of the warriors.

"Our people are ready. They'll wait for the signal." Back next to Tsitenha, he felt his tension welling, threatening to get the better of him. He would have to bring the matter up soon now. "But there are enemy warriors lurking up there, in that grove. Our people saw them."

The leader's lips pressed tighter. "Who saw them?"

"Ahsen and his people. He said they'll take care of them upon the signal."

"Good." The man nodded stiffly. "You two," he said, addressing a pair of warriors, "go there, but return and join our attack if they can take care of them by themselves. The rest of you, be ready to attack the dung-eaters who were shooting from the woods."

"And the enemy at the riverside?" asked someone.

"We'll take care of them after we have finished the main group. Attacked from both sides, they'll be surprised, thrown out of balance, easier to deal with." A brief glance in the direction Okwaho returned from. "Especially if Ahsen takes care of his grove quickly and joins us from yet another direction."

"So they are surrounding us, and we are surrounding them," muttered Okwaho, knowing that it was time now, struggling against the temptation to keep quiet. It was different back with Kayeri, whose decisions were plain stupid. He didn't need to summon special courage to argue, the words of protest coming up all by themselves, plain logic pushing him into suggesting all sorts of better solutions. But now, oh, now it was an entirely different situation. Tsitenha was a good leader, wise, experienced, enterprising. He was making all the right choices, taking all the correct steps, doing what needed to be done, and but for the obligation to save the village, *her village*, he, Okwaho, would never have dreamed of arguing or making trouble.

"Surrounding us won't help them," said someone. "We are stronger and more numerous than they are. Not to mention our fighting skills and our spirit. They are nothing but rats who have gathered enough courage to shoot from a great distance, scampering away as soon as we left our boats. Filthy rats!"

"They didn't scatter. They tried to ambush us again."

This time, even Tsitenha turned to watch him. "What are you trying to say?"

"The people who are facing Ahsen came from the village. They must have coordinated their actions, or maybe sent for reinforcements while preparing the first ambush." Using his elbow, he shoved away a pinecone that was jutting against his side. "By pretending to run away, their War Chief tried to lure us into following them, exposing ourselves, making an easy target."

This time, the measuring gaze was accompanied by one arching eyebrow.

"They have a war chief?"

Before he could mumble something to explain how he came by this knowledge, a loud cry that sounded like a giant bird from the underworld of the Evil Twin made them all nearly jump, although they had expected it, of course.

"Follow me!" Not making sure if his words were obeyed or not, Tsitenha burst out in a low run, as the sounds of yet another developing battle reached them.

Okwaho jumped to his feet together with the rest of them, forgetting his qualms for a moment. The foreigner's club was lighter, not as sturdy or as long as his original one, but he didn't feel like complaining, glad to have a good fighting weapon, something to rely upon. No bow or knife could rival this; or the pure satisfaction of the attack. No more defensive maneuvering, or running away. He had had enough of these.

The small clearing greeted them with a volley of arrows, forcing those who had yet to cross to duck for cover. Panting behind a cluster of bushes, Okwaho scanned the shadowy trees. A man beside him was struggling with a feathered shaft in his side, trying to get up, making much noise. Glancing at the fallen bow, its arrow still pointed, Okwaho crawled next to the wounded.

"Stay where you are, brother," he gasped, taking hold of the twitching shoulders. "Let me see."

The arrow was buried deep in the man's lower torso, in a most unpromising way.

"We'll make you comfortable here for now." Wrestling to pull the fallen warrior into a sitting position without hurting him more than necessary, he heard the others running past them, some pausing, but only for a heartbeat. "Sit here. We'll be back shortly."

A blood-smeared palm clasped his arm in a surprisingly crushing grip. "Don't forget to come back." The colorless lips moved with an effort, cracked and fading already. "Don't forget."

"I won't."

More arrows flew, in every direction now, theirs and the enemies', difficult to tell apart. Trying to spot their prey among shadows darting between the trees, Okwaho straightened up, only to halt as abruptly. His club leaping high, in a perfect accord with his lurching heart, he peered at the man who pressed against the nearby trunk, staring back, aghast. It was easy to recognize the haunted form, yet not as easy to make his hands stop their progress. His club jerked aside at the last moment, to strike the nearest cluster of bushes, instead.

"Why are you still here?" he cried out, then drew a deep breath, trying to calm the frantic pounding of his heart. The healer seemed to be in a passable shape, beaten yes, yet not hurt. But for his fright, he might have already made it back to his people.

"Go away. Go to your people." Reinforcing his words with appropriate gesturing, he readied at the sound of more footsteps, but these belonged to his fellow warriors, as he was quick to discover, with Tsitenha in their lead. A quick glance that clearly took in the entire picture, the wounded, the captive, and Okwaho, did not interfere with the leader's vigorous gesturing, as he sent some of the men to circumvent the clearing ahead, their bows pointed and ready.

Another wave of a hand with a club indicated Okwaho. *Finish that one off and follow*. The message was unmistakable.

With the renewed outburst of arrows forcing them to duck, or to press against the nearest trees, the gasps and groans of those who were hit while running around the clearing reached their ears. The enemy was clearly able to guess their intentions, not about to give up.

Tsitenha cursed softly. Kneeling between the branches, he shot arrow after arrow, as did some of his followers, drawing the cries of the hit enemy in their turn. Okwaho wished he had picked up the bow of the wounded man. Wondering if he might make it if darting between the thick trunks, he saw that the owner of the desired weapon was already listless, dead without being seen into his Sky Journey, all alone, with no one to calm him and help him into his new beginning.

His chest tightened. Was this the fate that awaited all of them? No, not with so many warriors and an able leader, but still, many would be on their way to the Sky World tonight. Too many. Them and the enemy. But for what purpose? Was this village that important to sacrifice so many lives in order to take some of its goods?

"The damn locals!" muttered Tsitenha. "We must finish this quickly. Can't stay in these accursed woods for the entire day."

The accursed woods, indeed, reflected Okwaho, clutching his club tightly. But for the girl…

The thought hit him again, made him curse his own stupidity. She must be somewhere around, having led her people here in the first place in order to save him. No, she was not the type to leave once the fighting had begun. She would be in the thickest of it, judging by the night of the battle with the villagers. She would be around, trusting him still, most likely, able to speak both of their tongues …

Forgetting his safety and the need to run low, he darted toward their prisoner, grabbing the man's shoulders, making them both sway.

"Your sister," he cried out, disregarding the terrified flash reflecting in the wide-opened eyes. "Kentika, your sister. We need to find her. She must be here. Call for her, somehow." Gesturing frantically, he repeated her name again and again, peering into the glazed pools, trying to will them back into understanding. "Kentika. Need to talk to her. Now!"

Suddenly, the terrified blankness gave way to a flash of comprehension. He saw the calm flowing back, making the bruised face fill with resolution. Just like during the previous night, when the man decided to help Akweks, taking control with untoward briskness, changing in too dramatic of a way, one moment a forest mouse, worse than the least of the frightened women; the other, determined to the point of presuming to lead, about to do what was right no matter what.

The curt nod and a long phrase in the foreign tongue, invited Okwaho to follow.

"What is this all about?" Tsitenha's palm was as hard as a rock on his elbow, and as unwavering.

"I know someone who can talk both our tongues. She'll be able to help us."

"Help us how?"

He stood the stony gaze. "Help us talk to them. Stop this fight."

The silence was so heavy, he felt it in his chest, pressing his insides, hurting them. It was back to the pre-dawn mist, after the night fighting and before the one that had resulted in the death of them all.

He swallowed hard. "We need to stop the fight. It is fruitless. Our people die for no reason here."

"This is what happens in fights, warrior." The leader's voice didn't rise, but it was cutting like the sharpest of flint. "Are you afraid to die?"

He shook his head, unable to move his lips in order to answer.

"Because if it so, maybe you should go back and never come along again, son of the Onondaga War Chief."

The mention of Father helped.

"I'm not afraid to die, nor to fight," he said, marveling at the fact that his voice rang firmly, loud and clear. His mind was a whirlpool of fragmented thoughts, spinning around, with no hope to grasp or channel them into reasonable thinking. "I fought in two battles over this accursed village, and I proved myself worthy of my father. No one will have a cause to accuse me of stepping away from danger or death. My father will not be shamed by my actions!" He listened to his words, feeling as though it were someone else talking, in this hard, cutting voice, inviting no argument. The club now clasped firmly in one hand, the fingers of the other found the pouch with Father's necklace, wrapping around it, feeding on its strength. "I will not be accused of cowardice!"

The stony gaze didn't waver, but there was something in the leader's eyes now, something different, changed. A flicker of interest?

Losing his line of thought, Okwaho clenched his teeth, feeling the reaction, desperate to control the trembling of his limbs. What if they saw it? What if they thought it was proof of him being afraid, and not just enraged beyond measure?

"So you propose to talk to the enemy?" The voice disclosed no concession, ringing rigidly, ice-cold.

"Yes." Okwaho swallowed again, mainly to try to make his heart slip back into his chest, as it was fluttering in his throat, threatening to jump out and be gone. "This village, it's fortified and well defended. It stands on an elevated ground, surrounded by a high palisade." He licked his lips, not daring to lie more than this. "The locals are ready to defend it to the last of their men and women. Kayeri was shooting fire arrows and regular ones for half a day, and they just doused the fires and shot back until someone managed to hit his oil jar. They are high-spirited and not afraid to fight." Another attempt to draw a deep breath. Why was it so difficult to let the air in? Was his heart, still fluttering up there, blocking its way? "If we could stop it here and now, stop fighting, negotiate a temporary agreement, we could leave this accursed place with no more warriors killed. We reached our goals." He remembered the longboats some of their people were left to guard, the boats and the treasures they held. Clearly, Tsitenha's venturing into the heartlands of the eastern people was more successful. "We filled our canoes already. Why fight for something we can't even take away with us?"

He paused, blinking the sweat away, not daring to wipe his brow. His whole body was awash with perspiration, but he hoped that here, in the relative semidarkness, it didn't show too clearly. With the sound of resumed hostilities deeper in the woods, their eyes left him, if only for a heartbeat, and he was grateful for the respite.

"What makes you think the enemy will listen to you?" The leader's eyes were now mere slits in the broadness of his face, but his words were still dispassionate, still stony and cold.

"I know someone who can speak both tongues." He glanced at the healer, all ears like the rest of them, as though he understood. "The War Chief's daughter, she can speak our way, and she won't be afraid to do so."

"I daresay I don't want to know how you came by *this* knowledge," grunted Tsitenha, turning away, measuring the trees with his gaze, the fighting again not heard or hopelessly muffled. "Well, go and find your interpreter. You have a few hundred heartbeats to make them stop shooting. If you are not back by then, we will resume our attack, and this village will be burned to the ground, no matter what it takes." A curt nod. "Go, take you prisoner and go. Bring back that war chief, if you can. To talk, to converse. Convince them of that."

With the wide back upon him, the man's voice still reached him, quieter and holding a brief but obvious lightness.

"Try not to get yourself killed. You made me curious, young warrior. I should wish to talk to you some more later on. To hear of your adventures upon these shores."

CHAPTER 23

"This man, he wants to talk." Again, licking her lips didn't help. Her mouth lacked any moisture, her tongue as dry as the earth of an abandoned field in the hottest of summer moons. "He asks you to open your ears to what he says."

Peering at the stony impassiveness of Father's face, she held her breath, hoping against hope that the man would listen. He never had, never before, but maybe now, at such a crucial time and when so much was at stake, maybe this time …

In the surrounding silence, she tried to read his expression, or the lack of it. Was he angry? Furious? The wave of latent fear was back. Of course he was.

Since coming back to nothing but disaster piling upon disaster, the man was like a thundercloud, about to burst. Others may not have been able to read him clearly, to see what the usual stone mask held, but she had known the man all her life. Like her mother and brother, she had learned diligently to try and predict his reactions, mainly in order to avoid the outbursts, and now her danger signals were up, screaming a warning, whispering that this time they all had been treading on the thinnest ice. One careless, hurried step, and it would break, dragging everyone into the frozen depths; her, her brother, their people, and ahead of them all, him, the wolf youth, the man who had enough courage to try to do something.

Afraid to take her eyes off Father's face, she still felt *his* presence, physically, as though he had stood next to her, which he did not. Still, she knew that he would, if need be, with his palms resting on her shoulders, maybe, or even encircling them. But for this to happen! Still, even at the distance of quite a few paces, he was here, pale, tense, smeared with mud and new bruises and scratches, but as forceful and sure of himself as before. He wouldn't let Father hurt her, if worse came to worst. He was on her side.

"To talk?" Father's lips twisted into an inverted grin, the edges of his mouth climbing downwards, threatening to spill down his chin. His eyes were very dark, and they didn't linger on any of them, but traveled on, encircling his audience, his entourage of ten men, standing rigid and tense, clutching their weapons, with more hunters spread between the trees, watching for the enemy's possible approach. "Surrounded and defeated, the enemy suddenly wishes to talk!"

Another spell of silence prevailed. No one dared to say a word, not even grunt or nod. Their eyes glued to their War Chief reflected nothing but bewildered expectation. They waited to be worked up, she realized, the ice in her stomach shifting, making her wish to go away and relieve herself.

"This is the quality of the foe we are fighting against!" Father's voice picked up in tempo, turning louder, surer of itself. "They are brave against barely defended villages, but as soon as they encounter our warriors, they ask for mercy, beg for their lives."

"They are not asking for mercy!" Their eyes leaped at her, Father's too, and what his gaze held made her choke and lose her line of thought. "This man says they want to talk. He says..." But this time, her voice broke, and it came out weakly.

"Keep your mouth closed, girl!" Again, his nape turned to her. "Your advice is not asked for, and it is not welcomed. Take her away."

"But she is the only one who can tell us what the enemy says," muttered someone, glancing around, before returning his frantic eyes to their uninvited guest.

"We don't need to hear the enemy. All we need to do is kill the invader and clean our shores of their filthy, contaminating presence once and for all. That is all we will do now that they came crawling, begging for mercy."

"What is he saying?" The wolf youth's voice burst upon her

through the growing veil of their words, ringing with urgency.

Unsuccessfully, she tried to clear her throat. "He would not... he doesn't..." It was difficult enough to force her mind into thinking, let alone form phrases in his foreign way of talking. Why were they all speaking at once? "He would not ..."

"Tell him—"

"They are not begging for mercy, and they are not defeated!"

Startled, she whirled around, unable to place the familiar voice with unfamiliar firmness in it.

"I came from their side of the fighting. There are many of them, up here in the woods, and down the river by the boats. They are more numerous than we are, and they are determined."

Satisfactorily tall and broadly built, Migisso was, nevertheless, never an imposing figure, never a person people bothered to listen to, probably because his shoulders would usually sag and his eyes would study the ground, refusing to meet those of the people who addressed him, unless asked to help with herbs and medicine. Yet now, he stood there, straight-backed and dignified, reserved but not indecisive, meeting their gazes, his own calm and unblinking, not hesitant, not afraid.

"The situation back there by the cliff and down the shore is not good for us. But it is not that good for the enemy, either. And this is why I urge you to hear what this man wants to tell us." The hastily drawn breath was the only sign that disclosed his nervousness, and Kentika held her own, so proud of him, desperately wishing that he would not lose his spirit, not yet. Oh, her brother was not the weakling that they all thought he was. He was a man, and a worthy, admirable man at that!

"While trying to reach you here, sent by Achtohu and his men, to let our leader know about our whereabouts, I fell into the enemy's hands, and this man did not let me die. He argued with his leaders instead, and he made them listen. This is why I brought him here. What he says is worth hearing. I implore you to hear with your ears open and your minds unclouded by prejudice. I implore you to *listen!*"

Oh, but he was an orator, too. She felt her heart squeezing with pride. Shooting a quick glance at the wolf youth, she tried to relate her encouragement, but his eyes were glued to her brother's face too, and she knew he understood.

"How dare you interrupt the speech of your elders?" The thundering of Father's voice jerked her back from the temporary cloud of cheerfulness. "You, who have never fought as bravely as any of these men; you, who unashamedly admitted falling into the enemy's hands; you, who is considered good enough for nothing but running messages even by leaders younger than yourself— how dare you?" This time, the War Chief's face twisted with terrible rage. "You will go back to the village at once, and you will await your judgment there." Another dismissive wave. "Go away!"

She watched the familiar face crumbling, fading before her eyes, the broad shoulders sagging in their typical way, the eyes already dropping to the ground, to stay there forever, she knew.

"No, he is not any of that!" she cried out. Clenching her fists, she rushed forward, oblivious of reason, too enraged to think clearly. "My brother is brave, and he is a good warrior. He is right in what he says. The enemy is not helpless, not begging for life. This youth, he is also brave, brave enough to come here and offer to talk about what is happening. He is not afraid to endanger his life, and neither is my brother. They are both brave, and they see beyond their anger or hatred, or yes, the prejudice."

His voice penetrated her ears as she paused for breath, afraid to lose her thoughts, to stumble over her words again. He was talking in a breathless rush, telling her what to tell them, but she didn't listen. The sound of his words and his presence were enough to give her all the support she needed.

"There will be much killing, and many people will die. For nothing. On both sides." Oh, yes, maybe she was repeating his words, but she didn't care, trusting him to talk nothing but good sense. "The villagers, our people, they will die, everyone who is here now. Even if it will stop them, the enemy, from storming the village, would it be worth the price of so many good men dead? If we stop now, we go back, and they go their way, and it will end, instead of turning into the death of everyone. The fighting here is fruitless. If we can stop it, why won't we do it?"

So, he was not as good an orator as her brother turned out to be. Pausing for breath, just as he did, she felt like chuckling, in a hysterical way, yes, but chuckling. He was talking in such a simple way. And yet, what he said was worth listening to. She saw it in their faces, peering at her from everywhere, grave and full of suspicion, but attentive, wishing to hear more.

"It's not the time to think of what has been done." By now, he was standing next to her, and his nearness gave her spirit more power. "Our leaders can meet and talk about it. I can't promise my people will never sail these waters again. But what we should not do is keep on fighting on this hill today. Enough lives were sacrificed, enough blood was shed."

Loving his last phrase—some oratory at long last—she tried to translate it to its fullest, but a scornful voice overrode hers this time.

"His people's lives mainly. Not ours." The man who said that pressed his lips tight and fell silent, but in his eyes, she could see more than just hatred and resentment. There was a need to hear there too, the wish to be convinced.

"All our lives are in danger now. We have both lost enough people," she said loudly, heartened by his resumed speech.

"If there was a reason for the continued fighting, yes, but there is none, not today," he was saying.

Contemplating how to translate these words, she heard one of the watchers calling frantically, "The enemy, they are nearing!", and even though her heart missed a beat, she didn't move, didn't gasp or dart away among the growing commotion, with the people around bringing their bows up, groping for their clubs.

Instead, she looked at him, and then moved closer, and went on translating because he paused for no more than a heartbeat, his voice peaking, drawing attention despite their tension and fear.

"They are not coming to fight you," he cried out. "They are coming to talk!"

She heard him clearing his throat, and her heart went out to him. He must be dead tired, hungry, thirsty, exhausted, with his various wounds still fresh, and yet he didn't give up, didn't sit back and let the others fight it all out. His people were still many, too many, battle-hungry, used to victories, not about to wait, not even until he finished. They were coming, and it would be either the talk they wanted, the talk he was trying to force everyone into, or the resumed attack, and the fight in front of the village's fence again. Migisso must have been right about that.

The urge to sneak a glance at her brother, to see if he had regained his spirit, welled, but she didn't dare to turn her head, afraid to draw attention to her and away from his words. He needed her help, her translating abilities, but also her support, her readiness to fight alongside him if necessary. She hoped he counted on that just as she had counted on his loyalty to the end, should the worst happen. He wouldn't let his people harm her village, and she wouldn't let her people harm him. But for how long would he have to repeat the same thing? Why wouldn't they listen already?

"Do not fight now. Let our leaders speak to each other. Let them meet and talk, and solve this…"

Somehow, they still held people's attention, or at least a part of it. She paused for a heartbeat, to marvel at that fact.

"Take positions! Don't let the enemy near." Father's voice overrode hers easily, accustomed to directing people, in his element. "Do not let this treacherous man deceive us with his lies and half-truths." Eyes blazing, face glowing a dark, unhealthy red, fists clenched, the War Chief stepped forward, his arms coming up, shaking above his head. "What are we reduced to? Are we helpless children, guileless creatures of the forest, to let an enterprising foreigner, a bloodthirsty invader, calm us with a few artlessly put together phrases, translated by a stupid girl? Are we not people with minds of our own?"

And still, people stood undecided, their gazes darting between their leader and the intruder, their bows or clubs clutched tightly, ready to be used, and yet hesitating, lacking in confidence.

"Let us do what is right this time. Let us…" She paused when he paused, out of breath, the noise all around them growing, taking both their attention away. His people were near now, she could hear it most clearly. They did not try to conceal their advance. Why?

The question that didn't have a chance to articulate itself, as her father's rock-hard palm locked around her upper arm, pulling her hard, making her fight to stay on her feet.

"Go away now," he hissed, pushing her in the direction opposite to the gathering warriors. "If you stay, or say one more word, you will regret it dearly."

Startled and ready to panic, she yanked her arm away, only to be jerked off her feet with the force of his pull. But for the firmness of his grip, she would have gone sprawling. As it was, she found herself dangling by his side, struggling to break free, to no avail. He was so strong!

The commotion grew, and many voices were talking now, her brother's among them, she could hear that. The foreigners were shouting, too, somewhere there among the trees. Father was talking rapidly, addressing no one in particular, or everyone at once.

When she felt the wolf youth's palm catching her shoulder, she threw herself at him with the last of her strength, doing the unspeakable by kicking at her father's leg.

That took the renowned leader by surprise, and for a heartbeat, he stumbled over his words, and his grip relaxed, enough for her rescuer to wrench her out and away.

Not really away, she realized, clinging to the safety of his chest as he turned, all sweat and mud, smeared with fresh and old blood, reeking, but solid, familiar, *safe*!

"You all right?" he breathed, pressing her tightly, but looking above her head, at the commotion. Still hoping to solve it, somehow, she knew, to bring the calm back. Which would be difficult without her translating. She made an effort to gather her courage.

"Yes, I-I-I'm—"

Determined to complete at least one silly phrase, shamed by the annoying stuttering and the trembling of her voice, she felt more than saw the sudden movement, and her instincts told her to lurch away, to avoid the danger.

Clutched safely in his arms, she pulled him along, but he resisted, too strong for her, not moving at all, his attention on the commotion behind her back, shouting to his people.

"Okwaho!" Somehow, his name came to her now, although he had told her that only once, a lifetime ago, when they first talked like people, with no anger and hatred, even though she never thought of him using this name.

He looked back fleetingly, eyes wild, but the sunlight flashing off the polished flint blade already dimmed, sliding up his side, burying itself somewhere in his lower back, and her elbow colliding with the hand holding the knife didn't help. Or maybe it did, but the ragged flint was still in there, in the depths of his body, and she felt him tensing, twisting away, just a heartbeat too late. For a moment, the world went still. The sounds disappeared, all the shouting and yelling, and there was only the weight of his body, leaning on her all of a sudden, heavy, still on the move, still trying to do something.

It was happening too fast. Feeling as though if she did the right thing it would all reverse back to normal, she peered at him, trying to see his face without letting him go. He would know what to do, he always had.

"You ... you all right?"

His eyes glowed, the only living feature in the paleness of his face, too widely open, their pupils enlarged. The rest of it was just a pasty mask, a wooden carving with no colors applied to it.

"Yes, yes. Listen!" His grip was hurting as he clutched her with both hands now, with an obvious desperation. "Go there. Go to our warriors ... my people ... go there now... Find Tsitenha. Ask them to take you to him. Talk to him." A spasm made his face twist, and he pressed his lips and fell silent, drawing one convulsive breath, then another. "Go now, talk to them ... tell them ... tell them what I said before. Make them talk to your people ..." Again, the loud gulp, his hands hurting from the force with which they clutched her. "Go now..."

"No!" Wavering, as he leaned on her with all his weight, she swallowed to make her voice work, but the tears were choking it, not letting any air in. "I will not ... not leave..."

"You have to!" Gathering himself together with an effort she felt physically, seeping through his strained limbs, he grabbed the branch of a nearby tree, pulling himself away, as fiercely determined as always. "Go! They will start fighting if you don't. And then, then it all was for nothing." Stumbling, he let his grip of her go, but as she rushed to catch him, his colorless lips twisted in a hint of a smile. "After you are done … come … come back. I … I'll need it. You always came back, didn't you? And then, then it will be all right." The fear flashed out, peeked out of his eyes, gone as quickly, dominated by his will. Oh, but he was a great man! "Go now, before they start fighting. Don't let them …"

People surrounded them now, their people and the enemies, talking, in both tongues, too rapidly for her to understand any of them. How could she talk to them? They would never listen, not to her, or anyone. It was only him that they had listened to for a short while, before Father … before he …

She pushed the thought of her father away, unable to deal with it, not now. Because now, she needed to find the way to make someone, anyone, listen without his forceful presence by her side. He trusted her to do that. He said that otherwise it would all be in vain, everything that they had been through. She had to do it for him!

"Migisso!" she shrieked, and when her brother's badly bruised face sprang into her view, she knew it would be all right. "Please!"

He was staring at her, aghast. "What happened?" His hands enveloped her, supporting. "The blood! Are you hurt?"

"No, no!" The hysterical pitch of her voice was the ugliest, most annoying sound. She drew a violent breath. "Go to him, please, go now. Back there, by that tree. Please, help him. Please!"

He narrowed his eyes. "What happened? Who got hurt?"

"The wolf youth. He got stabbed. *Father stabbed him!*" The wild sobbing was back, impossible to dominate, not anymore. "He is dying! Please!"

"Take me to him quickly!" The familiar decisiveness in his voice reassured her, helped to gather her senses back. "Where are you going?"

"I have to go, go there. I promised him I would talk, help his people understand ours. I promised him that there will be no fighting."

CHAPTER 24

The trail twisted, then turned steeper, but Migisso did not pause, did not slow his step, rushing along the forested hill, paying his surroundings no attention. The sun was against him, challenging, hurrying toward its resting place, but he needed its light, every little bit of it. Although, of course, one could act under the illumination of a fire, if one was desperate and had no choice. He had proven that last night, hadn't he?

He frowned, for the first time through this mad, terrible, bizarre day remembering the youth whose leg was rotting away. Was he still alive, this one? Back in the pre-dawn mists, he hadn't thought much of this warrior's chances to survive, but who knew? If he wasn't dead by now, he was probably getting better.

The path forked, and he hesitated, wishing Kentika was around, to tell him which way would bring him back to the shore he needed to reach faster. She was as good as a scout, better than some. Not many knew these woods that well, not even the hunters.

The thought of her made his insides shrink anew. Poor thing! But did she really mean what she said? That she would never, ever step inside their family home; would never address their father or even look at him? How did she propose to live if abiding by such a resolution? Where and how?

No, she must be just distraught and at a loss after the ordeal. Even for her, such a day must have been proving too much, and she was just a girl who had barely seen sixteen, seventeen summers, despite all the courage, all the determination. He still didn't know how she had made them all listen, when the anger and hatred threatened to explode in more violence, in another deadly combat in the face of a treachery.

And treachery it was, indeed. How could Father do that?

The man claimed confusion. With everyone running around and shouting, about to resume the fight, Father had said he thought the foreigner was attacking his daughter. So he acted accordingly. There were many people around, many witnesses to confirm that, indeed, it was all very confusing, and the man who talked peace leaped toward the girl when the War Chief tried to push her away at the face of the arriving enemy. So maybe it was just that, the confusion. But for her refusal to come back to the village when it all was over for good, everything might have returned back to normal. Or partly normal. Oh, all the great and small spirits!

The smell of the river grew, and he hastened his step, measuring the sun once again. Was the wolf man still alive? He found himself praying that he was.

Because of his sister? He wasn't sure.

The man was truly an outstanding person, enemy or not. Violent and impulsive, too young to display such strength of spirit, such extraordinary thinking, he did save them all, with exceptional fortitude and resolve, with much confidence and belief in what was right to do, despite the convention. Benevolent Glooskap should not let such a man die, even though he was an enemy. But who was he to offer the Great Spirit advice?

Pausing to catch his breath, he clutched his bag tighter, thinking of its contents. The medicine man's supplies of ready-made ointment and his private collection of tools for patching wounds, various-sized needles, rolls of sinew and other smaller accessories, were most welcome, giving Migisso much confidence. Although, of course, no sewing was likely to take place, not so long after the event.

Frowning, he recalled the wound, the narrow gap where the knife had slid in, not going straight into the depths of the man's torso, but gliding downwards, along the ribs and around them, to bury itself in the muscle of the lower back. A dangerous blow that seemed to be deflected, somehow, probably by the man himself.

After all, the foreigner was a fierce warrior. Of course he reacted and tried to save himself.

Still, even if not immediately lethal, the wound was bad enough, and it took Migisso much deliberation before deciding how to pull the knife out in a way that would not cause any more damage. Too many people were crowding all around, glaring or urging or giving advice, his fellow villagers raising their eyebrows with an open contempt. No one believed in him, as always, but it was the wounded's gaze that made him disregard all the hubbub, all the threatening gazes and mistrust. The glittering eyes, though clouded with pain, held his, willing him to proceed, to do whatever he felt was right, forceful, *trusting*. The warrior knew how good he, Migisso, was, no one better.

The camp of the enemy was easy to locate, and although the watchers were spread all around—clearly no one trusted the most unordinary cessation of hostilities—they let him pass unchallenged, their nods motioning him on, their gazes following him, cordial, reserved. The wounded must still be alive, he decided, his stomach constricting painfully, heart fluttering, wishing he hadn't come.

Protected from the wind, the small enclosure was bordered with canoes piled upon the shore, creating a sort of a wall, an embankment. The glimmer of several fires, with smells of freshly roasted meat spreading over some of them, gave the place an air of friendliness, the feel of a home. Like a hunters' camp after a successful foray. Migisso felt his taut nerves relaxing.

Following a curt nod by one of the warriors, he bypassed the fires, diving into the shadow of a sharply tilted cliff, another smaller enclosure, a cozy one. The hides spread upon the ground added to the homelike sensation, padded with grass and more hides, with people lying upon them, either asleep or curled around themselves, suffering stoically, hiding their pain. Oh, but the noon battle left enough wounded, on both sides. Against his will, his eyes went to the nearest man, assessing his situation.

"Migisso!"

She was upon him before he knew it, almost pushing him off his feet, pale but clean, with no mud or blood smeared upon her.

At least that! Eyes glittering wildly, she clutched his hand between both of hers, peering at him, excited, so obvious in her delight at seeing him.

"How is he?" he asked curtly, aware of the eyes all around them, hiding his affection, and his relief at seeing her unharmed. Following the wounded into the enemy camp had been her choice—wild bears would not be able to stop her from doing this—still, without the wolf man's active protection, he wasn't sure she might not be harmed.

"He is sleeping now. And it's a good thing, isn't it?" Her gaze lost its vividness, fixed on him, pleading for confirmation.

"I don't know," he said, pushing her away gently. "Take me to him and we'll see."

Treading his way between the wounded and those who sat beside them, treating or succoring, he felt his uneasiness returning. They were at the heart of the enemy's camp. Oh, Benevolent Spirits!

Another familiar face beamed at him as they neared the hide spread behind the cliff's corner. It took him a heartbeat to recognize the wide, prominent features, now clean and relatively lively, unlike back at the improvised cave at night, the wideness of the man's grin.

"Yes, he is much better now," said Kentika proudly, smiling at the youth, who was partly sitting, leaning against the wall, his leg propped comfortably, the wound gaping, uncovered, glaringly red but not smelling, not rotting away.

Migisso grinned back, at ease again. "Tell him I'll check his wound when I'm through with his friend."

She burst into the long tirade, and again, he wondered how one masters such a strange-sounding foreign tongue.

The wolf man was, indeed, asleep, lying on his good side, his wounded back open to the touch of the fresh air. Good!

Not sleeping peacefully, as she had made it sound, the young man breathed fast, his limbs jerking every now and then, murmuring, restless and hot. Pursing his lips, Migisso knelt, studying the wound, the swollen edges of the cut, the wet, glaring crust. No odor surrounded it, other than the familiarly unpleasant smell of the fresh blood. At least that! However, it was too early to tell, and the main thing was to determine if the man's insides were not damaged. If only a muscle was cut, and no other tissue, then this one might be able to survive. A lucky man. Such a blow should have gone straight into him, killing him in an instant, delivered by a warrior of Father's caliber. He pushed the troublesome thoughts aside.

"How is he?" she asked, kneeling across, taking the wounded's hand in hers with an easy familiarity of a person who had done it before.

"The cut is still fresh. It needs to be treated with ointments." Annoyed with her again for no reason, he shrugged. "I brought a salve and another medicine the Honorable Healer gave me. It should do good."

"Oh, yes, yes!" She squinted, and her grip on the wounded's hand tightened. "Will you close it?"

"No, of course not. It's too late for that." He sighed. "He may live, if that's what you worry about, Sister. He doesn't look too good right now, but with proper care, he may live."

"Oh, please, please!" Leaning forward, she caught his hand in her free one, almost squashing their patient in the process. "Will you care for him? Properly?"

"Yes, I will. That's why I'm here, am I not?"

The man stirred. Groaning, he tried to turn over, looking up, still disoriented and wild-eyed. In a heartbeat, she was back in her previous position, pressing his palm, whispering reassuringly. The youth's face smoothed, and he closed his eyes, exhausted.

Migisso drew a deep breath. "Don't let him fall asleep again. I want him to drink the medicine first."

She resumed her whispering, and more helpful hands came to prop the wounded up, to help him drink the bitter brew out of Migisso's jar. As the man coughed and choked, doubled over with pain, trying not to retch the medicine out, there was much fuss and attempts to help, but all the while, her hand was clutched tightly in the sweaty palm, not released even after the man was laid back, spent, groaning, drifting back into an uneasy sleep.

Eyeing her pale, twisted face, with its sharp cheekbones and prominent nose, and those strange too-widely-spaced eyes of hers, no feminine gentleness about her, no refinement, he felt his compassion welling. If that warrior died, something in her would die, too. Maybe all of her, even. What a puzzle. His boyish, unfeminine sister giving her heart to an enemy warrior, a fierce foreigner with unusual ways. How odd.

"He will be well," he said, catching her eye, having finished smearing a generous amount of ointment upon the wound. "He won't die. We'll make sure of it."

Her eyes clung to him, full of hope. "Thank you, Brother. I will never forget!"

"Nothing to feel grateful about. I let myself into this mess some time ago, haven't I?"

Her smile was a fleeting affair. "It all got out of hand."

"Yes, it did." He sighed. "But he prevented the bloodshed. Your hero, he did this, and no one else. He made sure our village was not invaded for the second time."

She just nodded, her lips quivering, pressed tightly, unable to move.

"Because of you?"

Her shrug was light, hardly perceptible, her hand careful not to move out of the wounded's grip.

"He asked you not to leave him now." He made it a statement, not needing to see her confirming nod. "I saw it in people who were afraid to die. They cling to all sorts of beliefs. Sometimes, yes, they insist the person close to them not leave. If that person leaves, they actually die, sometimes."

"He isn't afraid of anything!" Cut by a sob, her protest sounded weak, unconvincing, but her grip on his hand turned so tight, he wondered how it didn't crush the man's bones.

"It's nothing to be ashamed of. Sick or wounded people do need these things to recover. It's good that he knows what he needs." Again, some of the old resentment surfaced. "Schikan wanted you by his side, too. He kept asking. He needed you badly, but you weren't there."

Her eyes leaped at him, frightened. "How is he? Is he … is he alive?"

"Yes, he is. He is getting better. I saw him briefly. He is recovering. When you come back, make sure you spend some time with him. He needs all the encouragement he can get. Broken ribs are a nasty thing."

She nodded listlessly. "I will." But her eyes dropped to the ground and stayed there, refusing to meet his. He watched the tears falling down, huge, silent, wetting the earth.

"It all will be well," he muttered helplessly, not knowing what to say. It wouldn't be, of course it wouldn't. There was no solution to this.

The wounded stirred again. Raising his head, he tensed, murmured, but her soothing touch made him relax, her free hand caressing, running alongside his body in the gentlest of manners, avoiding the long, twisted cut and the swelling around it, easing him back to sleep.

She could have made a good healer, thought Migisso randomly, feeling out of place, an odd person, an intruder, having never suspected her of having so much patience and tenderness.

Frowning, he got to his feet.

"You are not leaving, are you?" she asked, looking up, eyes pleading. "Please don't leave. Not until it gets dark. Please!"

"I won't leave," he said curtly, not meeting her gaze. "I'll stay as long as it takes. Until we see if the medicine helps." Easing his shoulders, he sighed. "Then I will go, but I'll return to see him one more time, before they leave. They'll wait for the dawn, won't they?"

She nodded eagerly.

"I'll see his friend, in the meanwhile. We promised him that, remember? And then maybe the other wounded, if they ask me. I don't have to sit here beside your hero the way you do. He is not groping for my hands."

That made her smile. "I should hope he wouldn't do that." Then the smile was gone, replaced with the deeper glow, shining out of her eyes, making her again irresistibly beautiful. "You are an outstanding man, Brother. I will never forget, never!"

Abruptly, she opened her eyes, frightened. Had she fallen asleep? The roaring of the river and the wailing of the wind outside the protective cover of the cliff were disturbing, telling of danger. Where was she?

The soft hum of people's voices carried in the crispness of the night, not raising or threatening. Still, they made her insides freeze, their foreign-sounding words a reminder. So many terrible things happened through the past few days.

Heart pounding, she straightened up, then relaxed all at once, sensing his presence. He was watching her, half-sitting, leaning against the wall, eyes glimmering in the semidarkness, not feverish and not clouded. Calm, tranquil, holding a smile.

"I think I sleep, a little," she muttered, feeling incredibly silly, heart still fluttering.

"Yes, you did. You have a nice sleeping face." His smile intensified. "Lovely, peaceful. Pretty."

"I'm not..." Nervously, she pushed her hair away, wishing to look anywhere but into the unsettling glow of his eyes, yet unable not to. "I... I'm sorry. Didn't want to fall, to fall asleep..." Then the memories flooded in. "You are better! You not hot or dreaming. You are awake!" Involuntarily, her eyes strayed toward the sticky mess of his side, the ointment covering it thickly, concealing the wound. Evidently, Migisso didn't spare on the healing substance, spending not a half of that amount on all the other wounded put together.

"Yes, I am." His nod was careful, barely perceptible, not moving the rest of his body at all. "I'm better now, much better. Thanks to you."

She felt the blazing wave of heat washing over her face, making it burn.

"No, not me. It was you. You did, did so wonderful. Saved. Saved us all, the village, and the people, and your people. You did this. Not me." Uncomfortable under the strange glimmer of his gaze, she rushed on, breathless. "It was incredible, incredible how you faced them, my people, with no fear. I didn't believe, didn't think possible, but it was. And then, oh, Mighty Glooskap, when I saw the knife, oh, it was… I tried to warn… but it was fast, too fast! And I failed, and he stabbed, and then…" Her voice broke, but his palm reached for hers, and it made her feel stronger, like it always did. Oh, but she had already grown accustomed to relying on his strength. "I afraid, afraid so!"

His smile didn't waver. "Nothing to be afraid of, not anymore. We managed, didn't we? We stopped that fight, and neither of us died, and our people didn't kill each other. And all will be well now." He hesitated, and his smile faded, as his eyes concentrated, studying her, darkening. "This leader, he was your father, wasn't he? The War Chief."

"Yes," she whispered, dropping her gaze.

The silence lingered, uncomfortably heavy.

"I'm glad you came down here with us after what happened." His voice rang stonily, the fury in it well hidden, but she knew it was there, bubbling not far from the surface. "He wouldn't have let you leave the village if you hadn't."

"I will never speak to him again." Her anger came back as forcefully, as intense. "I will never look at him, nor address him by name or title. I will not step inside his house, and I will not remain in his vicinity. Never again will I mar my sight with his treacherous image."

Was she speaking her own tongue instead of his? She didn't care, as long as his hand tightened around hers once again, encouraging, full of understanding.

"Not see, or speak, or look at this man," she repeated in his tongue, grateful that he didn't ask how she'd do all that. Because, of course, she didn't see the clear way. "Never!"

"So, it seems you have nothing to come back to."

The stony expression was gone, and the warmth that flooded his voice made her look up. There was a strange tickling in her hands and feet, and a wave of breathless expectation that splashed through her stomach. Did he have a solution to all this? And if so, why was he amused?

"Maybe you shouldn't return to your village at all."

The mysterious smile that made her blush so badly before lightened his tired features. She stared at him, at a loss, aware of the way her face began burning again, hoping he would not see it in the semidarkness.

"Where go then?" she asked, stumbling over the words, her voice tiny and thin, like that of a child. She tried to collect her thoughts.

"Come with me," he said quietly, his amusement gone, replaced by calm sincerity. With an effort, he leaned forward, disregarding the pain in too obvious of a way, pressing his lips, his skin glittering with perspiration. "I know we happened upon each other in the strangest of ways, and I know we are not supposed to, but..." His eyes bored into her, questioning, or maybe expecting her to say something right. "But if you come with me, I will make sure you will not regret it."

She stared at him, speechless, frozen in surprise, her disappointment so vast it threatened to choke her. He wanted her to come along, to follow him into the distant lands of the sunset, leaving behind everything she ever knew, her village, her woods, her family and clan. He wished her to follow him into the lands of her people's sworn enemy, the fierce foreigners she always feared and abhorred. But for what? To what end, what purpose? He was ready to take her along because she had nowhere to go, no other reason. Oh, but he was so annoying, so unfair!

The tears were near again, and she turned away quickly, ashamed. Oh, Benevolent Spirits, let him not see this!

"What?"

His hand tried to reach her, but she backed away, not ready for his touch, not anymore.

"What happened? Was it something I said?" There was an anxiety in his voice now, an open worry. "Wait!"

On her feet already, she turned to run but hesitated, unable to see through the tears, afraid to tread on the sleeping figures of the other wounded, unwilling to face all the warriors out there, sleeping or not.

"Kentika, wait!" He was leaning forward, as though about to get up, wavering but holding on, his teeth gritting with pain.

"Don't run away." It came out more like a grunt, but now that he gave up on the effort, leaning on both hands instead, relatively steady, he was glaring at her, his gaze holding hers, willing her to obey. "Come back, and tell me what's wrong."

Drawing one convulsive breath after another, she tried to make her head work.

"I don't, don't want come back." It came out sounding childish. She clenched her teeth in frustration. "You don't need, don't need anymore. You get better now. Don't need I come."

"Yes, I do," he said firmly. "Come back now!"

Next to him again but refusing to sit down—a compromise; he couldn't tell her what to do—she peeked at him from under her eyebrows.

"Tell me what's wrong. Why did you try to run away?" Clearly, it came to him with an effort, this need to look up, but he didn't complain, although his face again lost its vividness, turned frighteningly pale. In the corner of her mind, she wondered if Migisso was on his way back, bringing more medicine. The brew in the flask he had left was to be used again not before dawn, according to his firm instructions.

"I did not, did not run away." Still refusing to meet his gaze, she linked her arms across her chest, not knowing what else to do with them. "I just think you better, got better. So no need to have me now."

"Yes, yes need. Sit down!" It came out like an order, but his voice rang stridently, not managing to gain its usual firmness.

"You have rest, need rest." She knelt but refused to squat comfortably, expressing the temporary state of her position.

He regarded her with pointedly narrowed eyes. "I'll rest after you tell me what's wrong; what made you run away?"

"Nothing!" Oh, why did she kept sounding like an angry child?

"You don't have to come with me. It was just a suggestion."

"I don't want to!"

His eyes narrowed into two slits. "I see."

"You want me come, come for what? So far away, no family, no people, my people, and to do what?" The tears were spilling again, ruining her ability to talk coherently. *What was wrong with her?* "You don't want me, you just say that, to help, to solve. You think you put, put me in trouble. So you say come. But I don't, don't want it. I won't come—"

His hand locked around her wrist as she tried to jump to her feet again, rock-hard, although it made him struggle to maintain his balance.

"Stop yelling. Calm down, just calm down!"

"I'm not, not yelling," Her feeble attempt to break free didn't help. Wounded and exhausted, he was still stronger; now that she had made him angry even more so.

"Listen, Kentika, just listen." With an effort, he pulled her closer, bringing the memory of the shore back in force, how he leaned forward back then and how his lips felt upon hers. "You got it all wrong, you wild thing. I do want you, I do! Don't you remember what happened on the previous night? But for all the trouble, we would have done more than kissing, wouldn't we?" With the tension and anger gone, the unsettling glow was back, causing her heart to slide up her throat, to stay there and flutter weakly, her thoughts scattering helplessly, in spectacular disarray. "I want you, and I need you, and I think we'll make a good family. It is something about you ..." His eyes strayed, sliding over her face, studying it in wonder. "Maybe all your women are like that, or maybe it's just you, but in my lands, I have never met anyone like you, no girl of that kind. And I love it about you, your untamed spirit, your strength, your loyalty. Those eyes of yours that reflect your every thought. The smile." His gaze deepened as the mischievous spark left it, and now it was her who had to lean on him and not the other way around, because her limbs lacked the strength to support her. "When you are excited, you smile, and then you are as beautiful as the Rainbow Goddess."

"Who is this goddess?" she murmured, but his lips were already pressing hers, parting them forcefully, like back on the shore. Dry and cracked, with the bitter taste of the medicine upon them, they still felt breathtakingly enticing, a thrill she had never experienced before, no matter how exciting it was to hunt a rabbit or beat someone in a climbing contest. No excitement could compare to this, the wild pounding of her heart confirmed, while her lips explored his, enchanted by this newfound delight.

Breathing heavily, they stared at each other, and then the twinkle was back, and his laughter held all the mischief.

"See?" he whispered, leaning back heavily, exhausted but still in high spirits, still trembling with laughter. "Will you go back to your village and miss this?"

Giggling, she made herself more comfortable, reaching out, touching his face, running her fingers alongside the firm line of his jaw, something she had wanted to do for a long time, she realized.

"So you want, yes, you prove. You no lie." Taking in his pallor, and the way his eyes were sunken, she straitened up resolutely. "But now you rest, until time drink medicine. No more kisses, not now." Unable to fight the temptation, not knowing herself if she wished to kiss some more or just to tease, she brushed her lips against his, escaping his groping hand. "No, not now. Now healing. Be good. Behave. And then, then later, yes, more kiss."

Letting her words hang, she beamed at him, suddenly so happy she was afraid it would come out in a shrieking whoop or some other inappropriately loud expression. Oh, but it was good to be free with him, free to laugh and tease and touch whenever she wanted. It was better than scouting or gorging on the deliciously sweet first maize, ten times better and more!

She let her fingers play with his warrior's braid, now a stiff thing that needed to be washed and redone, most of its decorations gone.

"You sleep now. Until the medicine. Until my brother comes back."

He barely nodded, his exhaustion and pain taking over, his smile flickering weakly, but still there, still glimmering, washing her with its warmth. Caressing his shoulder, she curbed the temptation to let her fingers wander on. Later, when he felt better, she promised herself; there would be plenty of time for that.

"Rest now. No worry. I will not leave, never! You can trust. Sleep until I wake you up."

As he closed his eyes obediently, she let her smile blossom, her happiness soaring. Oh, but she'd take good care of him, and he'd never regret bringing her along.

In the graying mist spreading everywhere, heralding yet another victory of Father Sun, she could see the bare outline of her brother's face, the sharp angle of his cheekbones, the dark circles of the eyes. Huddling under the towering rock, hugging her elbows against the coldness of the pre-dawn wind, she wished she could see what his eyes held. His voice was tranquil and his words kind, but she needed more reassurance than that.

"You haven't gotten much sleep, have you?" she asked, trying to lighten the atmosphere with at least a little small talk.

"No. I haven't slept for two nights, if you recall." Again, no malice, no accusation, just the atypical, unperturbed calmness that seemed to warm the night, to make it less realistic.

"Yes, I recall. Akweks, he is getting well, now for certain. He can't walk, not yet, but he will. He feels good. He eats and drinks and he doesn't need medicine to make him cool anymore. I talked to him not long ago. He asked me to tell you how grateful he is. He said you are a great healer. Every warrior in this force is aware of what you have done, and they all agreed that only a true medicine man, the one who has the full blessing of the Great Spirits, can do what you did without causing the warrior's death. They are awed by your skill, Brother, and these people are all hardened warriors, not easily impressed. Oh, it makes me so proud to tell them that you are my brother!"

She could feel his smile. Starting with the depths of his eyes, it spread, smoothing the frown, enlivening his face, straightening his shoulders, as it never did before. Unable to see any of it, she still knew it for certain, and it warmed her insides as well.

"They said all that?"

Grinning at the pretended indifference—he could try to fool anyone but her—she shook her head. "What do you think?"

"I don't know what to think, not since you made me question

everything I knew for a truth."

Her happiness fled. "Yes, I know."

The silence prevailed once again, not heavy or pressing, but not as comfortable as before.

"I talked to him."

The calmness of his words misled her into keeping her peace for another heartbeat, before the meaning of what he said reached her.

Her heart lurched. "You did? What did you tell him?"

He kept peering at the river and the figures moving about, dragging their boats into the shallow water.

"I told him who I am and what I intend to do."

"You did?" Unable to keep still, she caught his arm, feeling it cold but firm, not listless or limp as before. "How did he take it?"

His chuckle held no mirth. "What do you think?"

"Badly."

Another long pause.

"I will be living with the old healer now. He agreed to take me in, to teach me the ways of the spirits. He is the kindest man I know."

"He always loved you. He knew what your true purpose was. Hasn't he been teaching you, or letting you learn, against Father's clearly expressed wishes? For moons and summers he did this. He believes in you, just like I do. But he didn't see the proof, while I did." She wished he could see what his eyes held. Oh, but she would miss him! "You will be the greatest medicine man, the greatest spiritual leader that people of our village could ever have. I know that much!"

"Since when do you deal in prophesies, little sister?" But again, she knew that his lightness was not real.

Their attention caught by the voices of the warriors shouting to each other, coordinating their actions, they let the silence hang.

"You won't be here to see it, will you?" he said, and this time, his voice held no pretended indifference.

She shook her head, unable to talk for a moment, choked with grief. Oh, but what would she do without him, the man she had known all her life, such a huge part of it? What if she didn't see him again, ever?

"He asked you to come with him?"

"Yes."

More silence.

"He will make you his woman, yes?" This time it was an older brother speaking, worried, suspicious. "He promised?"

"Yes, Brother. He wants me to be his woman, and I want to be his woman, too. You needn't worry." His silly questions made her grief disperse. "I know what I'm doing."

"Didn't you always?" His shrug was something she couldn't miss, even in the last of the darkness. "I never expected something like this to happen. I knew you might do something wonderfully different, maybe turn into some kind of a warrior-woman. You know, like in some of the wintertime tales. But this ..." He shook his head, then sighed. "How will I know that you are well, not harmed, not hurt? How will I know what will become of you?"

As he tried to pull his hand away, she pressed it tighter, winning the contest easily, as always.

"You will, Brother. You will. Your spirit will find the way. It always did."

Pushing her fears away, she tried to be brave, for his sake. The doubts, oh, but she would not let them harm her. They had sneaked upon her only once during the night, when she had to leave his side in order to wash and to relieve herself. The warriors' looks made her uneasy, the strangeness of their gazes. They clearly did not see her worth, did not understand his insistence on taking her along, a clumsy, dirty, foreign thing, not pretty, not womanly and seductive, not anything that made it worth the trouble of taking a woman back home. Just a little savage out of the east. The realization made her shudder in fear. What if he tired of her after some time? What if he didn't want her anymore?

She pushed the troublesome thoughts away, squeezing her brother's hand instead, for after getting back to the wolf youth's side, the doubts had vanished. For the remnants of the night, watching his sleeping face, holding his hand and caressing, making sure he was not turning hot or beginning to feel worse otherwise, she had felt the confidence flooding back, a happy, trustful reassurance. She was right in her choice. To give up on him, and because of silly fears, was not an option. Whatever was going to happen would happen, but he would make sure she did not regret it. He promised.

"Just make sure not to forget me," she said, smiling at her brother through the fading darkness. "Glooskap and the Sky Spirits will guide me and keep me safe, just like they'll be watching over you now that you stepped on your true path. They will not keep us apart and in the darkness, not for our entire lives. They will ensure we'll know about each other, somehow." She tried to smile reassuringly. "You know their ways, better than me. You know they will not let us lose each other."

He was squeezing her hand in his turn, clutching it desperately, his face pale in the grayish mist, jaw tight, lips nothing but an invisible line.

"I will never forget you, Sister. I will pray and offer every day of my life. The fragrant tobacco smoke and many other valuable gifts. I will make certain the Great Spirits will not forgo you, or leave you behind. Just as I never will."

And that was that. There was nothing more to say, or to wish for, but she knew she would be safe now, and looked after. Her brother would make sure no harm would come to her. He was always the man she relied upon the most, always.

Side by side and in a lighter mood, they watched the sky turning brighter, with Father Sun rising as he always did, winning his night battle, to spread his light and warmth, and his wonderful benevolence.

The new day was born, and she peered at the pinkish glow spreading behind the treetops of the opposite bank, her excitement welling, threatening to spill. She was stepping on a new path, and the Sky Deities were blessing her, happy, smiling upon her. Oh, but this path would take her to wonderful places. Now she knew it for certain.

AUTHOR'S AFTERWORD

While having a fairly large amount of evidence as to the time of the Great Iroquois League formation, we cannot tell for certain when the Mu-hee-can (Mohican) People came to occupy the valley of Hudson River. It might have happened not many decades after the Great Peace of the Iroquois was established, or maybe a century or so later.

According to some of the legends, the Mu-hee-can People's ancestors came to the Hudson River valley after much wandering, seeking the lost homeland of "great waters," finding it in this mighty river that "flowed and ebbed like no other." They came to call it Muheconneok, which roughly means "The Waters That Are Never Still." Here they settled, to became known to their neighbors as River People, or Mu-hee-can, Mohican as we know these people today.

But the Great League of the Iroquois (Haudenosaunee, People of the Longhouse) had spread to the west, a strong alliance of five nations, an amazing democracy and a regional power that no one could overlook or dismiss lightly. Wary of strangers, this powerful league did not hesitate when it came to waging war, in defending their towns and villages, or, like in many cases, taking the warfare into the enemy territory.

Out of the Five Nations, the members of the Great League, the People of the Flint (Mohawks) were the ones responsible for the eastern neighbors of the confederacy and their behavior. Carrying the title of Keepers of the Eastern Door in the metaphorical Longhouse of the Great League, these people took their responsibilities seriously. The wars between the Mohawk and the

Mohican People were reported to last for centuries, relentless and uncompromising.

In this novel, I explore the possible beginning of this turbulent history, when around the thirteenth century, these people might have begun coming into more and more contact. The Great League was certainly already flourishing back then, but the presence of the Mohican People might have been pure assumption. Maybe they had been around by that time already, or maybe they had arrived a century or two later. What we do know for certain is that by the seventeenth century, the conflict between these two nations was an established fact, carrying much history in it, going back centuries as reported.

At some point, the Mohicans were reported to form an association of four or five nations as well, not a confederacy but an alliance, for defensive purposes probably, and to maintain trading ties. Unlike the Great League, there was no mutual government and no sense of political body with strict sets of laws proscribing everyone's conduct.

And yet, these people continued to be a force to be reckoned with, even though, at the time setting featured in this novel, the idea of such cooperation might have only been beginning to form, promoted by some farsighted leaders, probably, not yet to bear fruit.

What happened next is presented in the second book of the **"People of the Longhouse"** Series, **"The Foreigner."**

ABOUT THE AUTHOR

Zoe Saadia is the author of several novels on pre-Columbian Americas. From the architects of the Aztec Empire to the founders of the Iroquois Great League, from the towering pyramids of Tenochtitlan to the longhouses of the Great Lakes, her novels bring long-forgotten history, cultures and people to life, tracing pivotal events that brought about the greatness of North and Mesoamerica.

To learn more about Zoe Saadia and her work, please visit
www.zoesaadia.com

Made in the USA
Middletown, DE
29 December 2018